THE LEGEND OF HARRY DOWNS

Nancy Veldman

Nancy Veldman

ISBN: **1979473323**
ISBN 13: **9781979473323**

PROLOGUE

The road to success is paved with blood and guts. Scars that show great effort no matter what. That is what Harry Downs was told when he joined the Marines. He'd seen movies, he'd heard stories. But this time, in one frozen second in time, he would experience what the words *blood and guts* meant.

On a cloudy day in Afghanistan, several men in a Humvee were tackling counterintelligence, computer screen lighting up their faces as they tried to connect with the almost nonexistent GPS signal. The terrain was rugged and difficult to maneuver the vehicle. Harry was good at what he did. One of the best. His concentration was beyond human understanding even though he was surrounded by the enemy and his comrades were yelling above the gunfire in the near distance.

The noise was deafening, but not near as deafening as the sound of the IED that blew up underneath their vehicle. Harry didn't remember anything but a loud explosion, and then dead silence. No words were spoken at all. No screaming from the pain. Just a huge explosion in the dark and the sound of metal crashing to the ground. Bodies were on the ground.

Harry was knocked unconscious and lay as still as the two dead soldiers lying on the ground near him. But he stirred eventually when he was being placed on a stretcher and airlifted by a Medivac to an ambulance that rushed him to a base hospital and into the O.R. It all took place quickly as he floated in and out of consciousness. He felt no pain until they moved him onto a cold steel table in surgery. He was given pain meds but before they kicked in, he felt a searing pain that shot down what once was his leg. He reached for it, but it was no longer there. He closed his eyes and gave in to the drugs they were putting into his veins. His world had changed forever.

CHAPTER ONE

As Harry drove his old blue and white Chevy pickup down a dirt road that led to his house, the wind stirred up the dust and swirled it behind him like a small tornado. The radio was blaring on a country station, the window on his side was rolled down, and he wore his favorite baseball cap on backwards.

It was a hot and sweaty day in August. Even the birds were hiding in the massive trees along the sides of the road, gaining shade from the hot blaring sun. He wiped his brow on his shirt sleeve, smiling. His mother would have killed him for that move that all boys did when they were sweating. But nothing mattered to Harry since Afghanistan. He wasn't the same man and his mind was on other things now. Like rehab, like learning to walk without a limp, and deciding what in the world he would do with the rest of his life. What life he had, that is.

He absolutely ate, drank, and slept military. He loved being in the Marines and loved responsibility. He had taken his job seriously, and so did the other men who fought alongside him. It was a dirty, filthy war and he was frustrated most of the time. But he

1

loved the feeling it gave him whenever he had hacked into a system that had previously been unhackable.

When he got out of the hospital and was stuck in rehab for months and months, he decided he would move out of his parents' home and build a house of his own. He didn't want sympathy or help from his parents. They fought him at first, and his father wanted him to work at Glassco in Memphis, a large pharmaceutical company his dad had built from scratch. Harry tinkered around with the computers there but he wasn't interested in ever owning the company. He knew it hurt his father, and maybe years from now his mind would change on that matter. At this point in time he wasn't sure what he wanted to do with himself or what he could physically manage. But he was determined to find out.

Harry had always had a love for horses, and when he found some acreage outside of town, he knew it was large enough for him to raise up a barn and have a few horses feeding in the pastures around the small lake. He suspected he would never ride again, but they were glorious to watch. He'd hired Joe Rand to work on the barn, and Joe brought a few of his friends with him. He could tell that the construction was moving along nicely and he waved at Joe as he drove up to the barn.

"Lookin' mighty good, Joe. Looks like your men know what they're doing."

Joe wiped his face with his shirt. "Been doing this a long time, Mr. Downs."

"You're not that much older than me, Joe." Harry chuckled.

Joe didn't crack a smile. "Started when I was just a kid, handing tools to my dad."

"Well, it paid off. You do a great job."

"Thanks, Mr. Downs. Always like to hear a compliment now and then to keep me going."

"If you need me, I'll be in the house working out. Just open the door and holler. I'll hear you."

"Yes, Sir. But I don't think we'll need a thing. You been mighty nice to us."

"I do my best, Joe. I do my best."

⊰┼⊱

Harry parked the truck under his favorite oak tree and walked inside the house. It still smelled new to him. His stump was sore but he wanted to sit on the back porch a moment and drink a cold glass of iced tea. Sweet tea. It tasted so good in the summer. He grew up drinking gallons of it on hot summer days.

He walked into the kitchen and poured a tall glass and walked out on the screened porch overlooking one of the small lakes and barn. He could hear the men working in the distance. He sat down on one of the rockers and took off his hat. He was hot and was thankful for the fans on the porch. Sitting there looking at property he owned, he thought back on how desperate he had felt after he lost his leg. Things were definitely looking up, but he still had no idea what direction his life would go. He had no plans, no thoughts on what to do with his life. It was not a good feeling as young as he was. He'd not had a real chance to live his life, but he wasn't going to allow pity to take over. His father was pushing him pretty hard about Glassco, but he knew in his gut that he would never give in to that choice. He really wanted back in the military in some form or fashion. Not behind a desk, but something else. He didn't know what just yet.

He finished up the tea and walked inside, setting the glass on the counter. It was time to work out so he headed to the upstairs room where he had set up a gym to strengthen his body at home. He still had to go to therapy twice a week, but he was a very determined individual. He went beyond what the doctors said, and he was recovering at the speed of light.

At six feet two inches, Harry stood tall and strong. His arms had plenty of muscle, although his right arm was a bit weaker from the explosion. His left leg had taken a brutal amount of weight and stress after the injury, but now he could put plenty of weight on the prosthesis without hurting the stump. People stared at him, but he had learned to ignore it. They were just curious and his mind was so set on making a good life that he didn't have time to worry about what they were thinking.

There were no women in his life just yet. He hadn't had the time or the inclination to date since the injury. It would take a special lady to want to date an amputee. He was certain of that. He had a fear inside that the loss of his leg would turn most women off.

Brushing those thoughts aside, he fixed a healthy dinner and sat down to watch the news. It was an election year. All hell was going to break loose. He turned the channel to the World Series and dozed off watching the Cubs and the Indians. When he woke Joe and the other carpenters had gone, and the Cubs had won the World Series. He was upset that he'd missed the whole game, but proud of the team for pulling such a win after so many years.

Harry's older brother David was a real estate broker in Cordova, just outside of the Memphis area. He might be accused of coddling his younger brother, but Harry loved the attention. They were only three years apart, which was a big gap when they were younger but not so much anymore. David was married to a knock-dead gorgeous girl named Taylor, and they had two small children, Jack and Sara Jane. The kids loved Uncle Harry and were only a little squeamish about his mangled leg when he came out of rehab. But now they loved seeing him walk with the prosthesis and things were back to normal with them.

When the phone rang and he saw it was David, he answered quickly with a big grin on his face. "Hey, brother. How's it going?"

"I'm doing fine. But a little concerned about you, little brother. You keep yourself pretty well hidden these days. The family would love to see you more often."

Harry tucked his head. "I know, Dave. Just got things to do. You know how it is."

"Yeah, I know, all right. Ever since your injury you've pretty much been a hermit. That isn't good for your mind, Harry. We are all worried about you."

"I'll make it just fine. You have to give me time to rebuild myself. I took a pretty good hit over there. Do you realize how tough it is to lose a leg?"

"No, I don't. But make sure that is all this is. Because I don't want your mind wandering off to some dark place where I can't pull you back."

"No way that will happen."

"You getting things done at your place? Need any help?"

"Nope. I hired Joe Rand to do some work for me. He brought a couple guys with him and they are working their butts off getting the job done. I'm impressed."

"Okay. Well, be sure and let me know if I can do anything. And we'd love for you to come by for dinner one of these nights. The kids miss you."

"I'll be over soon. Just keep Dad off my back. He wants me to take over—"

David interrupted. "I know. I'll see what I can do."

"Thanks, Dave. I'll see you soon. Appreciate the call."

Harry hung up the phone and shook his head. It was going to be a long time before he was "back to his old self," as the family put it. If that would ever even happen. His head was still messed up over losing some of the best guys under his command. He had been told this could happen and that his mind might not want to let it go. But he was going to get past it. If people would just let it be.

CHAPTER TWO

The bedroom filled with light as the sun came bursting through his bare window, leaving streaks across his covers. He threw them back and sat up, brushing his thick brown hair out of his eyes. The eyes that had seen war. Blood. Destruction.

This morning he was thinking about a dog. For some reason, he really didn't know why, he felt like a dog would help him recover and also keep his mind off himself. He dressed, grabbed some hot coffee and a stale piece of bacon that was left over from yesterday, and headed to his truck. There was a cooler breeze blowing, perhaps a sign summer was nearly over. He wiped the seat off and hopped in, started the engine, and pulled out of the driveway.

Suddenly he saw Joe and his men working. It was just sunrise. These guys were crazy dedicated. He waved and pulled out on to the main highway and headed towards town. He would stop and get a breakfast sandwich at McDonalds and kill some time until the Humane Society was open. He was hoping it was before ten.

There was a long line at McDonalds, but he had nothing else to do so he pulled in to take his turn at the order screen. He turned on the radio to a country station and leaned his head back against the headrest, smiling. It felt good to be alive, but he couldn't go any farther than that today. So he left it alone. Soon he was at the window and ordered a sausage biscuit with egg and a large Coke. He couldn't wait to feel that burn on his throat. His order was ready at the next window and he paid and pulled out on the highway. He drove into Memphis, found the Center on Farm Road, and pulled into the first parking space near the front door. It was just about time to open, so he walked up to the door and waited for someone to unlock the door. He didn't have to wait long.

"Good morning, Sir. You're up bright and early this morning. I'm Mary Jones."

"Yeah, wanted to look at your dogs."

"We would love for you to. Please come in. The dogs are in the back."

"Thank you, Mary. You must love animals to work here."

She smiled but there was a tad of sadness in her smile. "I do love them. But they don't stay here too long."

Harry didn't want to ask where they went. He pretty much could figure that out. He walked to the back and saw the line of cages that were clean and full of dogs of all sizes and breeds. He didn't really know what kind of dog he wanted, but he knew he wanted a large dog.

It was painful to look at their faces as he passed the cages. He petted them all and their eyes were screaming for him to take them home. He forgot how it felt to see caged animals that needed someone to love them. It was devastating and he hoped he could find one quickly and get out fast.

In the corner was a huge German shepherd. He sat back in the cage just staring at Harry. He bent down and spoke quietly to the dog. His name was Hack. The dog sat there looking at him without moving towards the door of the cage.

Harry opened the door, even though Mary was warning him not to reach inside the cage. For some reason, he felt good about Hack. He called his name softly and the dog took one step towards him. Harry sat down and started talking to the dog and soon Hack crept towards the open door of the cage. He was very close to Harry's hand, so Harry moved in closer to the dog. Suddenly he was touching his paw and he left it there to see what Hack would do. Slowly, so slowly Harry could barely see him moving, Hack bent down and licked his hand. Harry was so surprised that he nearly pulled his hand back. But instead, he began to stroke the dog's head and talk to him in a low voice.

"Looks like you found your guy." Mary was standing there smiling.

"I kinda think so. He is a beautiful dog. Do you know anything about him?"

"We think he was a military dog. What we heard was that his owner was killed and the family didn't want to keep the dog, but since I am new here, don't take that as fact."

Mary had no more spoken the words when Harry stood up and pulled out his wallet.

"How much do you want for this dog?"

"We would normally get about a hundred dollars for a dog that has been here for two weeks. To cover neutering and shots that we have given to him. Heartworm and fleas. And he has a microchip. So he is ready to go, if you want him."

Harry wiped a tear out of his eyes and leaned down and patted Hack on the head. The dog sat down right beside his prosthesis. He was almost certain that the dog knew he was wounded.

"I'll take him home. I think this is my dog."

"He'll make a good pet. But he's been pretty quiet in here and if anyone tried to stick their hand in the cage he would growl. We didn't push it. He obviously was pretty upset. But with you, he must have sensed something."

"I'll give him plenty of space. He can take his time getting to know me."

"That sounds perfect. He's a beautiful dog. I just think he's heartbroken."

"Well, that will work out just fine with me, because I'm pretty broken, too."

Mary looked alarmed, but Harry had already handed her the money and took the leash out of her hand.

"Thanks for your help, Mary. One less dog without a home. Hope you have a great day."

Harry couldn't get out of the shelter fast enough. It was a sad place for most of the animals would never have a home. But this one dog was lucky. He put Hack in the front seat next to him and pulled out of the parking lot. Hack just sat there looking proud and strong. Harry could tell he was trained well, but they had a lot to learn about each other. He was excited about having an animal in the house with him, and he was pretty sure that Hack would be good company. As he pulled up in the driveway, Joe came running towards him.

"I thought I saw a dog in the front seat. So you got you a dog?"

"Yeah, just picked him up a few minutes ago. A military dog, if they have their facts straight. I think we'll fit together just fine, what do you think, Joe?"

"I think it's a perfect match."

"Everything going okay with the barn?"

"She's going up fast. I think you'll be pleased when you see the headway we've made."

"I'll get him inside and settled, and then I'll check out your progress."

Inside the house, Harry took the leash off and Hack began nosing around, checking out the rooms. Harry let him go wherever he wanted to go, and set out a food and water bowl in the kitchen. Soon Hack came looking for him and he sat down on the floor and petted the dog and talked to him. He gave him a few commands and the dog responded immediately. It was amazing to see how well Hack reacted to any command. Harry was certain that he had only touched on the tip of how intelligent this dog was. He stood up and walked towards the back door, looking back at Hack.

"I'll be right back, boy. Don't you worry."

Hack sat still and watched. He didn't move a muscle. Harry opened the door and walked towards the barn, waving at the boys working on the roof.

"Joe, this is amazing." He patted Joe on the back.

"It's what we do, Mr. Downs. Great to be able to work at something I can take pride in. I think you're gonna love this barn."

"It's plenty big for what I'll use it for. It will store hay and give the horses a place to bed down when it storms or is too cold. That's all I need."

"We got a couple months before it gets too cold for those beautiful animals out there in the pasture. You're a lucky man, Harry. I mean, I know you lost your leg and all, but look what you do have. You can make a good life here."

Harry smiled. "That's just what I plan to do, Joe."

"Still need to get the doors on the stalls, but it's shaping up inside. I can't give you a time frame just yet, but it won't be that long before we're done."

"No race to be run, Joe. You're doing just fine. Thanks for all the hard work."

Harry turned to go back to the house and he saw Hack sitting by the door looking out. He was still as stone, but his tail was wagging.

"Hey, Hack! You're such a good dog." Harry knelt down and wrapped his arm around the dog's thick neck.

"I've got some reading to do on my computer, Buddy, so let's go sit for a while."

Hack followed him into the small office and lay on the floor beside Harry's chair. It was like he was home at last. Harry was taken by how quickly the dog adjusted to the house and to him. He opened the computer and worked for an hour on a few issues his father was having at Glassco. When he was finished he leaned back in his chair and dug into his back pocket and pulled out his wallet, folded the receipt from the Humane Society, and tucked it into an unused slot in the wallet.

A photo caught his eye and he pulled it out. He took a deep breath. It was a faded photograph of Anna Shaw, his first love. He'd dated her in high school but when they graduated she went on to college and he joined the Marines and later went into counterintelligence with a close friend of his, Josh Lane. He and Anna had tried hard to stay in touch, but the distance was too difficult for her to deal with and he was overseas so long that he told her to find someone else. It wasn't fair to keep her hanging. And the work he did was dangerous, so he wasn't even sure he'd make it home.

He looked down at his damaged leg. His eyes scanned over her face. He wondered if she would even remember him now. She was probably married and had a family of her own. But he sure loved her.

His hand touched her hair and straightened the bent corner of the photo. He took another deep breath and put the photo back in the hidden slot and stuck the wallet in his back pocket. Memories for another day. But the pang in his heart didn't go unnoticed. He had learned to compartmentalize things that hurt too badly. And this was one of them. Major pain.

CHAPTER THREE

Glassco Pharmaceutical was massive. It had competitors but no one really touched the amount of drugs manufactured in such a short amount of time. There was always an ungodly wait period for the FDA to approve them, but the whole world knew about that delay. The FDA was a mothership of confusion, delay, and miscommunication. But there was no way around it, so Joseph Downs taught himself to be patient. And it paid off. Harry was there to make sure no one hacked into their database and stole information pertaining to the formulas for certain new drugs. When a pharmaceutical company was researching a new drug to treat a major disease, there were antennae out everywhere, unseen demons waiting to pounce on any bit of information about the new drug so that they could copy it close enough to be the first one to produce it and get it through the FDA. It was a ruthless fight, but Harry was good. Real good. He had fire walls that Samson himself couldn't break through. But Harry was always looking for that young kid with the slingshot. Sometimes the hole was so tiny it couldn't be seen, but there was always someone who could find it. He learned the hard way that there was never anything that was impenetrable. When you thought there was, you'd already been hacked.

This morning Joseph was in a snit because one of his best biochemists had informed him that he feared his computer had been hacked. He'd received some strange messages and his computer was not performing correctly. When he tried to open some data that he'd saved, he got an error message that was in a foreign language. Joseph picked up the phone immediately and dialed Harry's number.

"Son, I need you to come in this morning. I think we may have an issue with one of our computers. You got time?"

"Sure, Dad. I'll be right there. Can I bring my dog?"

Joseph hesitated. *What dog?* "You got a dog?"

"Just got him yesterday. He's well trained. You won't even know he's around."

"Sure, bring him in. But we cannot allow a dog into the research area."

"I'm aware of the restrictions. I'll keep him next to me."

"See you at ten o'clock then."

Joseph hung up the phone and went into his office and shut the door. The possibility that someone had gotten into their computer system always made him nervous because no matter how hard he tried to keep an eye on things and no matter how good his security was, there was always the huge fear of being hacked. And today just might be the day. Fred Mason was one of the best biochemist around and he was fortunate to have him working on the new drugs. He'd been with the company for eight years and was loyal to the bone. So if anything was going on with that computer, he could say without a doubt that Fred wasn't involved in anything subversive.

Harry came through the door with the largest German shepherd Joseph had ever seen.

"Good morning, Dad. This is Hack. Now what's the problem?"

Joseph walked over and patted Hack's large head. "I think we either have a mole or we've been hacked. I hope to God we don't have a leak in here. I know it's not Fred. So maybe lay that aside for now. You need to look at his computer. It's acting funny and some messages he gets when he tries to open certain files are in a foreign language."

Harry raised his eyebrows. "What kind of language?"

"That's for you to discern."

"Show me the computer and let's see what I can find."

Joseph led his son to the desk of Fred Mason and Harry sat down. "It'll take me a while, Dad. So you need to leave me be while I work on the computer. Hack will sit here by me, so don't worry. You'll be the first to know if I find something."

Harry watched as Joseph walked away smiling. He knew he was one of the best in the country and if anyone could find the mole, he would. All these years he had avoided anything happening. But hackers were growing throughout the world. It was almost an admirable trait among some of the college-age students. Overseas it was happening every minute of every day. He was certain there was no stopping it. He just had to create the toughest firewall he could and have it layered so that if they made it through one firewall, there was another one facing them that was tougher to get through.

As he began to dig around, a message came up in the center of the screen. "Your computer has been hacked and your files are corrupted." Harry started digging into the message to locate where it came from, and what he discovered was that it appeared to be coming from a Russian source.

He ran some scans and all the files were there. But there was something odd about how the computer was operating. Twice while he was looking at coded data about certain drugs that were in research, it appeared that another person took over the mouse. He could tell someone else was on the computer the same time he was. He shut the computer down and called his father on his cell.

"Dad, you need to come back to Fred's desk. It's obvious this computer has been hacked and while I was on it, someone else was using the mouse. That means they have remote access to this computer. They could be in this building or in another country."

"I'll be right there."

Joseph was panicked. He knew Harry could hear it in his voice.

"Son, what do we do? I need to protect the information in that computer at all costs."

"They already have what is in this computer, Dad. We need to keep them from getting any further into your hard drives and stored data. This is serious. The language was Russian, but all they said was that the computer was hacked. I shut the computer down, but I really need to transfer everything onto a separate hard drive not connected to this company. That way I can examine everything and not transfer any information into their hands. I hope it isn't too late. Has anyone else said anything about their computers acting funny?"

"No, Fred was the only person who was having any issues."

"I just wonder why they chose his computer."

"That was what I was thinking, too. Let's bring up his file on my IPad and refresh ourselves about his background. He was vetted before I hired him so I don't expect to dig up something new at this point."

"Nor do I. But something stinks. I don't like the fact that someone had control of my mouse. It happened twice. That computer needs to be emptied out."

"Why don't you do that now, and I will check into the employee file. We may have to do some detective work, which is what you are trained to do."

"If it's overseas, I doubt I will find out too much about who is doing it. But I need to control what damage they are doing here at Glassco. I have built some heavy duty firewalls that should protect you from this very thing, but they are not in place yet. Let me clean the computer and I want to be there the next time you talk with Fred."

Joseph looked at his son with a frown. He was beginning to get angry now. The fear was turning to anger. "I'll be right back. Clean that damn computer off and then we can talk after you've had time to look through the files.

Harry reached down and patted Hack, smiling as the dog licked his hand. The bonding period was a powerful time in the life of a military dog, and Harry loved every moment of it. He downloaded all the data off the computer, which took longer than he'd planned, and cleaned the computer completely. He then took the hard drive to another laptop that was used when employees wanted to search the Internet without exposing anything on their computers to viruses. It took a while to load, so he went to the lunchroom and picked up some snacks to munch on as he searched for something Hack could eat. He had to settle for a hot dog, which he detested. But Hack ate it like a bear and lay down and fell asleep at his feet.

Finally the transfer was complete and Harry opened the files. He shook his head. The hacked information was about a new drug for cholesterol that was going to change the landscape of lowering HDL levels. The Russians apparently were after this information, but Harry wondered how they knew it was on this particular computer.

That was why he was concerned about Old Freddy Boy. What did Fred know? Or rather, who did Fred know? He scanned for viruses and found a few, cleaned them up, and kept searching. Then he reloaded the information back on Fred's computer and changed all the passwords, added all the new firewalls, and closed it out. It had taken him most of the day to finish the job. It was time to talk to Fred.

CHAPTER FOUR

The tension in the room was thick as pea soup. And Fred Mason looked nervous, even though he wasn't aware yet of why he was being called in for questioning, other than the fact that he'd reported something was wrong with his computer. Harry was sitting at the other end of the table, quietly checking his messages on his cell. Hack was lying down beside his chair, but he growled once when Fred walked into the room. Harry took note.

Joseph spoke fear into the silence. "Fred, we've called you in this afternoon for a meeting about the security of your computer. You informed me yesterday that you were afraid your computer had been hacked. So I called in my son, Harry, to check it out."

Fred started to speak, but decided against it.

Joseph continued. "I know you shared that a message appeared on the screen in a foreign language and that you felt like the computer wasn't running like it normally does. Is that true?"

Fred swallowed and answered firmly. "That is correct. I noticed that I couldn't move about the same and that message box kept popping up saying my computer had been hacked."

"Any idea why this would happen to your computer, in particular?"

"I have no idea at all. That is why I contacted you immediately, because I know how secure this data is. In fact, all the data stored on all of our computers is highly classified."

"That is correct, Fred. I'm wondering why they chose your computer."

Harry was watching Fred like a sniper. What he saw was the tiniest bead of sweat about to drop from his brow down the side of his face, following the bulging blood vessels by his temple. It didn't mean he was guilty, but it did mean he was nervous.

"I was wondering that myself. How did they work their way through our firewall?"

"That's what Harry is trying to find out. I'm just hoping we don't have a mole, Fred. Someone who would sell information for money."

Harry leaned forward, watching Fred's reaction to that statement.

"Why would someone do that to you, Joseph? You have been so good to your team." Fred's left hand was shaking slightly. Ever so slightly. But Harry's eyes were on it like a laser beam.

"How you doing financially, Fred? You short on funds for any reason?" Harry interjected this question to watch how he reacted.

Fred swallowed. "No, I am fine. I get paid very well here and have always been a penny pincher of sorts. That's probably why I'm not married."

"I'm certain that whoever is after this information would pay plenty of money to get it. Surely it's not someone here hacking into our computers!" Joseph said quietly.

"I'm sure no one here would do that."

Harry stood up and glared at Fred. "Well, someone hacked into your computer and I'm going to find out why and how. That's what I am trained to do. If it's China we'll find out soon enough."

Fred spoke up quickly. "Oh, it's not China. I would know that. It looked more like Russian to me."

Harry looked at Joseph and shook his head. Fred saw the look. "Hey, guys. I'm nervous as a cat and had no idea why I was being called into this room. I'm a bachelor and I love my job. I would never sell data for money. I don't need money. I'm not a greedy person and I'm also not stupid. So if you see my hands shaking, or how nervous I am, it is because there is a giant of a dog eyeing me like a piece of meat, and you both are questioning me like you're FBI. Anyone would be nervous under these circumstances."

"We know that, Fred, and we totally understand. No one here is accusing you of anything. But we do need to ask questions because we are trying to find out why they chose your computer," Harry remarked, glancing at Joseph.

"That's correct, Fred. I told Harry that you've been a good employee and hard worker. I totally trust you. But you can understand the depth of my concern when it comes to the data that is on our computers here at Glassco. We are sitting ducks if someone has come through our fire walls."

All three men stood up and shook hands.

"I feel pretty good in knowing you had nothing to do with this, Fred, but there are still a ton of questions hanging in the air that I would like to have answered." Joseph smiled a thin smile and watched as Fred left the room.

"Dad, I don't think he had anything to do with it, but I am still going to look deeper into his computer. So far I see nothing that would incriminate him, but we don't know about his cell phone. Do you have his number?"

"I sure do. I have everyone's number. I will send it to you in text. We are not going to leave a paper trail in this office for anything, but I also will feel good knowing that you've layered the fire walls. What about encrypting the data on our computers?"

"I have standard software for that. I use Blowfish, strong pass-words, and with a little luck we will be impenetrable." Harry smiled and grabbed Hack's leash. "I guess I have more work cut out for me here. I'm going to run Hack home, feed him, and return to finish the job."

"Sounds good, Son. Thanks for all the hard work. And by the way, I heard your dog growl when Fred walked into the room. What does that mean?"

Harry grinned. "Well, we haven't had a discussion about it yet, but it's tough to fool a dog. Some dogs can sense things, and I believe this one has a strong sense about him. But I'm not going to overthink that right now. It could mean he just doesn't like the guy."

Joseph smiled. "Maybe I should have Hack in the office with me when I am hiring someone. What do you think about that?"

"Probably not a bad idea, Dad."

CHAPTER FIVE

Evenings on the farm were dead quiet except for the occasional coyote howling in the distance. Harry loved sitting on the porch listening to the crickets and that random howl. He had a habit of propping his feet on the railing and leaning back in his rocker, sipping his iced tea and thinking.

Tonight he was thinking of Anna. She had a nice way of sneaking into his mind but it was useless dreaming. He knew that. The chance of meeting up with her again after all these years was slim and none. Zilch. He allowed himself to look into her eyes again. He had to hold on to the chair or he would have slipped into them and disappeared for good. He glanced up at the stars and let his mind go. What if he could find her on Facebook? It was a bad idea for multiple reasons, but he was just curious enough that he got up and walked into the house and headed toward his office. Hack came along but didn't seem too enthusiastic.

Underneath the tough-as-nails exterior, Harry Downs admitted he was a rotten romantic at heart. He didn't let that news out to just anyone. Because it would be used against him. He'd learned in the military to keep most things to himself.

Harry sat down at this desk and turned on the light. The moon was coming in through the window, laying its soft light in streaks across his mahogany desk. He turned on the computer and waited for it to load. His stomach had butterflies, but he pushed them away mentally, because this was a useless exercise in futility. He was not going to obtain anything but pain from going through the motions of looking her up.

Finally, the home page was loaded and he clicked on Google. He first tried to just type in her name, Anna Shaw. Surprisingly, there were several in the world. But nothing on the one he wanted to see. He then went to Facebook and signed in. He hadn't been on Facebook for many years, but his homepage was still there. He put the cursor on the search bar and typed in her name again. This time there were about ten that showed up. He had to look closely because the photos were so tiny beside each of the names.

He sucked in a breath, which made Hack raise his head and look at him with a questioning look. Anna's face was looking at him. He clicked on her name and it opened up to her homepage. He nearly threw up his supper. He grabbed his tea and drank it down. He was nervous but wanted to see if he could tell where she lived now and what she was doing. In the personal informa-tion, she hadn't filled out very much detail about herself. But it did say that she lived in Collierville. That made him nervous. She was very close to him as the crow flies. She had not filled in the married-or-single status, and there was nothing about work writ-ten in. He clicked on photos and bingo—her lovely face filled his computer screen. It was a newer photo of her than what he had in his wallet. Her hair was shorter and she had blossomed. But her eyes were still the same. Blue. But with brown hair. Very unusual. He loved that about her. He sat back and allowed himself the joy of just staring at her. Why hadn't he thought of this before? He could make her face his screen saver, but then, that might be a little sick.

He clicked off the photo and looked at her timeline, what he could see of it. He scrolled down a ways, enjoying her posts and looking at the photos of friends and family. Then one post came up with Anna and a boy. A brown-haired kid that looked to be about ten years old. They were both laughing and it looked like they were at the Mid-South Fair. He smiled, remembering those days when he was a child. He was surprised to see that the fair was still around.

He leaned in to look at the boy and propped his head in his hands. His face was very close to the computer screen and it almost felt like the kid was staring at him. Anna was looking in the other direction. He leaned back, scratching his head. For some reason, he didn't know why, the boy looked vaguely familiar. He was a handsome fella, and looked so happy. So did Anna. Harry rested his head on the back of the chair and closed his eyes. *Wonder how our lives would have been if we'd gotten married when I signed up to serve in the military? That could have been my son.*

He laughed out loud at his meandering thoughts and clicked to minimize the Website. It was probably best he didn't spend too much time looking at her page, but it was nice to know she wasn't that far away. He was very curious to know if she was married. Well, she had a son, obviously. But there were no pictures of a man. A husband. He could hope, but hope had sort of been erased from his vocabulary while serving in the Marines. He worked on facts now. Pure and simple facts. They didn't allow you to surmise or give your opinion. Because lives were at stake, everything had to be based on facts, mathematical surveillance, or military intelligence. So for him to even entertain the thought of ever seeing her again and that she would be single, well, that just didn't fit into the equation. But it did cross his mind.

Harry dropped his left arm down and touched Hack's fur. He sat there in a daze rubbing the dog's head and scratching his back. His thoughts were rambling but directed at his future. He loved his house and the barn. The pastures. He knew the horses would be great company to him and he enjoyed taking care of them. But inside, deep inside past the wounded parts, Harry wanted to be back in the military again. That was a stupid thought, but he allowed it to rise to the surface now and then. For one thing, the military would see him as wounded and not able to serve. He would put others at risk. They wouldn't be willing to do that. But he was so good at what he did, that maybe, just maybe, there would be a time, a place, a mission that they really needed his expertise.

He wondered what had happened to Max McIntyre, who lost an arm and a leg during the explosion that took Harry's leg. Max was his favorite team member, and they had fought side by side against the enemy. He would love to see Max again. To talk about old times, but maybe also talk about the future.

On a wild hair thought, he picked up the phone, clicked on Max's number, and listened to it ring five times. He was about to click the red button to end the call when a familiar deep voice answered.

"So you've decided to call me from the grave, did you?"

Harry fell out laughing. "Yeah, my bones are calling out to you. How in the world are you doing?"

A sigh was heard. "I'm fighting back with all I have. How about you?"

"Doing the same thing. Building my body back. Determined for the enemy not to take my whole life away."

"You still got that same fire in your gut, don't you, Harry?"

"Eating me alive, brother."

"Same here. I would give anything to be out there now. I don't know what to do with myself now that I can walk again. I am feeling strong and want to sink my teeth into something, but what? What do I do with myself now?"

"We are on the same page, as I am sure all vets are. I'm really not ready to quit, Max. I don't want an office job. That would bore me to tears. There has to be a way they can use us, Max."

"You mean the military? They think we're done."

"I know they do. But you know yourself how good we are at counterintelligence. There is no one to match us. I was wondering if we really worked on our physical condition, if they would consider positioning us somewhere out there where we can do some good."

"That's a nice thought, Harry. You always were optimistic."

"So you're saying that no one will take us seriously?"

"I'm not sure they would return our call."

"Really."

"All I'm saying is that we got injured severely enough to get medical leave. They think we are done. We would put others at risk."

Harry paused. "What if it was just you and me? What if no one else was exposed to our pitiful weak bodies? We are willing to risk what we have left in us to help the war on ISIS. I have nothing to lose, frankly. Do you?"

"Zero. But will they see it that way?"

"It's worth asking about. We could call Mike Murdock. Remember him? He's a four star general now and maybe he could use us. What would it hurt?"

"We have no idea, Harry, what is going on at this point in the fight against ISIS. We have been out of it for a year. It has taken us that long to pull ourselves back up, and now we discover we want back in."

"They would be fortunate to have us back. We could work alone. Just the two of us. No one else would have to be put at risk. And truth be known, we would probably do better than a guy with both legs and arms who wasn't as intelligent or experienced as we are at what we do."

"I'll give it some thought, Harry. I love the idea. Almost scared to even hope that we could get back in. But can you imagine what we could accomplish together, because we are not worried about our lives anymore? We've been there, done that. Now we can run unafraid into the war."

Harry grinned. *Now we're talking.* "I'll give him a call. Or at least put a call in. There's no way that I will get straight through to him first try. Stay put. I'll keep in touch. And work your ass off getting ready. Just in case we get a 'yes.'"

CHAPTER SIX

The barn was almost finished. It was a cloudy day with the wind blowing ninety to nothing, but he was excited to see Joe's progress. The guy was a frigging genius when it came to construction. Nothing but an F4 tornado would take that barn down. He walked out to the first pasture and called the horses in to feed them. It was early morning but a threat of storms loomed in the sky. The clouds looked heavy and full of water. A good hard rain would grow grass and he needed that right now. Five horses and three of them were pregnant. It was going to be a good spring.

There was an older horse he called Belle who had a slight limp. He had called Sam Pendleton, the closest veterinarian in town, and he was coming out in an hour to look at her leg. He hoped it wouldn't be something that would take her down. She was a beautiful paint and stood sixteen hands high. Even tempered. Well-trained. He could ride her if he chose. But this limp had come up and he wanted to take care of it fast. He was in no mood to put a horse down.

After feeding the horses, he walked inside with Hack and went to his office to drink coffee and check Facebook. That was going to become a habit since he'd found Anna. He wasn't her friend on Facebook so he couldn't see all her posts. But he just wanted a chance to see her face again. He got lost in her photos and didn't watch the time. But he did hear the knock on the door. And Hack was already at the door barking.

"Hey, Sam. Really appreciate you coming out this morning. I'm worried about this mare."

"I could hear it in your voice when you called. Let's go see what's going on with her."

Harry walked outside with Hack and headed towards the barn. He'd pulled Belle up and put her in a stall. Sam wasn't far behind, looking at the other horses out in the pasture grazing.

"Gonna get some badly needed rain shortly. I was hoping to beat the downpour."

"It's her left front leg, Sam. Check it out and tell me some good news."

Sam smiled and bent down, running his hand over the leg gently. The horse seemed to know that Sam was there to help. She didn't move a muscle. He bent it and pushed on it, making her put her weight on it. She favored the leg as she walked around the stall, almost stumbling when she got near the door of the stall.

"I need to take her in, Harry. She's older and I don't want to make any diagnosis until I have spent some time on that leg. I know you're worried, so let me have her for a week and see what I can do."

"I'd feel better if you had her. She won't lie down and she still tries to keep up with the younger horses. I have three that are due this spring."

"I'm just glad you didn't wait any longer or we'd probably have to put her down. I'll pull my trailer up to the barn so we can load her up."

Harry walked Belle out of the stall and led her outside the barn. She was a little nervous but somehow must have known she was in good hands. She stepped into the trailer and never looked back.

Harry swallowed hard. He really liked that horse. She was so mild mannered and he'd hoped to ride her before too long. His leg was healed and he was building strength in his legs and body so that he could grip the horse. It would be part of his recovery to ride again. But it had been years since he'd sat on a horse, so he wasn't expecting miracles. He would wait for Belle.

He waved to Sam, who was pulling out of the driveway, and walked back into the house as he felt the first drop of rain hit his face. It was fixing to pour. Hack had run to the door and was waiting to get inside. As tough a dog as he was, he hated thunder. Harry made some coffee, got Hack a treat, and went to his study to make a phone call. He pulled up Facebook, which he'd minimized, and looked again at Anna's face.

"Anna, I'm going to make a risky call to Mike Murdock. I know him well. He believes in me, and in my buddy, Max. I have nothing to lose, right?" He smiled at the photo of the girl he always thought was going to be his wife one day. But her silence was palpable. He closed the computer and dialed the number of a man who could change the course of his life with one word.

⊶⊷

"Boy, are you trying to give me a heart attack?"

Harry smiled. "Hello, General. How you been?"

"Well, I never thought I'd hear from you again. How you doing, Son? And call me Mike."

"Son"? That sounded nice. "Considering my Humvee got blown to bits, I'm doing terrific."

"I seem to remember something like that happening to you. Damn, Harry. It's so good to hear your voice."

"Really, Mike, I'm doing great. I've been working out for a year, totally recovered from my injuries. I'm strong and feeling healthy."

Silence. "That's good to hear, Harry. What can I do for you?"

Harry's swallowed hard. "I know this sounds crazy, but I'd like to run something by you, Mike."

"Shoot, Son."

"You remember Max McIntyre? We served together in Iraq."

"How could I forget Max?"

"We both incurred severe injuries but we haven't allowed that to slow us down. We both worked hard and have totally recovered from our injuries. We feel strong and ready to serve again. I realize this is not the normal protocol for servicemen who have been honorably discharged, but we are not ready to just sit, Mike. Can you understand that?"

"Sure I can understand, Harry. But what exactly did you have in mind?"

Harry took a deep breath. He knew he was walking a thin line. "I don't have to discuss with you what our abilities are. You trained us. You know us to the bone. To be honest, we are ready to jump in again. We want to do something to stop ISIS."

"You've sacrificed enough Harry. You and Max both."

"That's just the point, Mike. We don't care what happens as long as we are a part of the fight. There is no way I can ever just sit here in a rocking chair. Or do a desk job. I spoke with Max and he is fit to be tied. Give us something to do, Mike. Send us into the battle. We have nothing to lose."

"I am touched by your passion to fight for your country. I know what kind of job you are capable of doing. But it is not protocol to send a wounded veteran back into battle. That just isn't done."

"I would agree with you if we were old and badly wounded. But we are both young. Thirty years old. We aren't married. We're two of your best. Let us prove to you that we're still capable."

"I won't say it's not tempting, because there are plenty of missions going on and we could use your help. I would have to give it some thought. I'm not saying I'll approve your request. But I'll think about it and walk it past someone I respect. I'll call you first part of next week and let you know what I've decided."

"You have no idea what this would mean to me, and to Max. I'll be waiting for your call, General. Thank you so much for considering my request."

"Good to know you're doing so well, Harry. You'll hear from me shortly, but don't get your hopes up too high."

Harry winced. "I am too optimistic to do otherwise."

Harry sat back and blew out a big sigh of relief. That was a difficult conversation, even though he really liked Mike Murdock. Totally respected him. Owed him everything. But all that emotion wouldn't hold a candle to the feeling he would have if he got a "yes" to go back to war.

He leaned against the back of the chair and closed his eyes. His mind was blank for a moment and then he saw Anna's face. He opened the computer and looked at her Facebook page again. He wanted to contact her. He was dying to know if she was single. The thought of it made him almost nauseous. He was shocked to find out how much he still cared for her. The effect she had on him was powerful. Just her face alone. He really had no way but Facebook to let her know he was alive. And then the thought hit him. She might even think he was dead. That he'd been killed in the line of duty. Well, he nearly had been killed. But the shock of hearing from him might be too much.

He laughed out loud. He was trying to talk himself out of sending her a message. Or just sending her a friend request. That would blow her mind. But was it the way he should let her know he was alive? They hadn't talked in nearly ten years.

He looked down and saw Hack looking at him. He touched the dog's head and looked back at the screen. He needed to think this through. He didn't want to do the wrong thing. Sending her a private message or sending a friend request seemed so shallow. He should look up her phone number and give her a call. But not today. He'd had enough emotions flowing through his head already. It had to happen soon, though. Because he was hoping he would be going to war again. And then he wondered if he should call her at all. The confusion was making his head hurt, so he got up and grabbed his coffee cup and went into the kitchen. He gave Hack some water and a treat, and headed into the workout room. He was going to work out until he couldn't think anymore or had a clear direction about Anna.

What was funny about the whole dang thing was that he was more nervous about calling Anna than going back to war. How pathetic could a man get?

CHAPTER SEVEN

The computers at Glassco were clean. Harry had layered the firewalls so well that even Satan himself could not get through them. At least for the moment. It seemed that each generation produced highly intelligent people who refused to spend their days at a desk but rather choose to spend all of their mental energy breaking through layers of firewalls all day long, so that the average human being could no longer do his job. They didn't mind tearing down what others had spent a lifetime building. The agenda was to steal information. Some just wanted the challenge of breaking through firewalls that claimed to be impenetrable. At any rate, it was one of the most difficult issues any corporation had to deal with. It was easy in some ways to develop a new drug, but it was nearly impossible to protect it. Someone was after it the moment the information on the drug entered cyberspace. Before it even became a pill, there were feelers out, like the fire from a dragon's tongue, trying to capture the data. Invisible people whispering in the darkness out there, peeling back layer after layer until they had what they were looking for.

Harry needed to have a talk with his father. It wasn't something he was looking forward to at all. But it had to happen. He walked into Joseph's office and pulled up a chair. He swallowed hard and touched the head of the faithful dog who followed him now everywhere he went. Without question.

"You need something, Son?" Joseph looked up from his desk where he'd obviously been studying formulas.

"I need to talk to you, Dad. You need to know what I've been thinking about for the last few months."

Joseph looked up from the folder he held in his hands and put his pen down. Harry knew he had his full attention.

"You remember Max McIntyre? A fellow Marine?"

"Of course I do, Son."

"I spoke to him the other day. It was so good to hear from him. He lost a leg and arm in the explosion. But it sounded like he and I have chosen the same path to recovery because he said he was back to normal. He no longer has a limp. He is ready to get back to what he was doing.

"That's wonderful to hear. There's a point to this conversation?" He raised his eyebrows.

"I'm sorry, Dad. I know you're busy. I just need to let you know what I've decided."

"I'm all ears, Son."

"Max and I want to return to the Marine Corps. We want to get back to doing what we are really good at. What we were trained to do. I have spoken with General Murdock, who trained me. And he's going to think about the possibility of using us in some type of mission. I don't know if it will happen. I am awaiting his call now. But I had to tell you what has transpired so you wouldn't be totally blown away."

Joseph stood up and walked to the window near his desk. His head was shaking slowly. Harry could tell he was upset. Harry got up and walked over to his father and put his arm around his broad shoulders.

"Dad, I know what you are thinking. I've already lost a leg. Why would I want to go back into war and maybe not come home this time? Well, you and I both know life is not that simple an equation. I loved being a Marine and I want to go back. Max feels the same way. We are not married, we have no children. We are perfect for going into a dangerous situation because we've already been injured. We know what that is like. I am not afraid of death anymore. That may be hard for you to understand."

Joseph turned and looked at his Son. "How can you say that? I fought in a war. But I don't understand your obsession with war. What is wrong with rebuilding your life? Getting married? Living a normal life?"

"I guess I don't want that right now. I love the military life. It's like I was born to do that. Just be prepared, because if the General calls me and says he will use Max and me, I am heading out. I don't need your permission, Dad, but I do want your blessing."

"Son, how can I give you my blessing when I know you won't come home? That's asking way too much of your father. I watched you suffering. It ripped out my guts. And now you are telling me that you want to go through that again? I question your sanity."

Harry moved away from his father and sat down, putting his head in his hands. He was not surprised at the direction of the conversation. But he had hoped it would be different.

"I am sorry to disappoint you, Dad. I guess I can't expect you to understand how I feel. But it is ironic that Max was feeling this same way before he even talked to me."

"You're a grown man, Harry. It isn't my choice how you live your life. But I don't have to like it, and neither will your mother. I hate to even think about how she will react to this."

"Don't tell her yet, Dad. Let's wait to see if I even get in. The General didn't promise me anything. It would be very rare for them to use us again. It was worth it to ask, though. I would never forgive myself if I didn't at least try."

Harry walked out of his father's office with a heavy heart. But he knew in his gut that he was about to do something that he felt compelled to do. That is, if he got the chance. That was all he needed, just a chance to do what he was put here to do.

CHAPTER EIGHT

Rain was beating against the window of his office as Harry sat staring at the computer screen. He was becoming obsessed with looking at Anna's photos. He had looked up her number; it was under her name so he assumed that meant she was no longer married. The number was written on a sticky pad right next to the phone.

He stared at it but couldn't bring himself to dial her number yet. Even though he would have walked through fire to see her again, there were a couple of things that kept him from making the call. One was the obvious thing—they hadn't talked in so long that she might be completely over him. She'd been married and had a child. Or he assumed as much. Secondly, his leg. Even though he'd adjusted to having one normal leg and a prosthesis on the other one, he wasn't sure how a woman would react to that. It might totally turn her off. Either way, he wasn't going to put himself through that span of emotional upset just to be turned down by his first love.

He sat back in the chair and rocked back and forth, thumbing the pad and humming. Hack lay beside him, looking up at him with sad eyes. He reached down and patted his head.

"You have no idea the dilemma I'm in, Hack. If I don't call her, she will never know I'm alive. If I do call her, she may not care anymore. And there's the issue of my leg, Hack. I'm not sure any woman will be able to deal with that."

He looked down and Hack was asleep. Or at least he had his eyes closed. No help at all. Time was ticking and he knew if he was going to contact her, it needed to be soon. He felt sick in his gut as he touched the pad and looked at her number. So many scenarios ran through his head of why he shouldn't be calling her. He stared at her face and tried to imagine what it would be like to actually see her face to face.

He swallowed hard and picked up his phone. He dialed her number and put the phone to his ear. He was sweating and words were racing through his head before she answered.

"Hello?" Her voice was a little lower than he remembered.

At first he couldn't speak. He almost chickened out. "Is this Anna?"

Hesitation. "Yes, yes it is. Who is this?"

"Anna, this is Harry. Harry Downs. We haven't talked in years, and I just wanted to see how you were."

There was complete silence on the other end of the phone.

"Anna? Are you still there?"

Her voice was weaker. "Harry. I was afraid you were dead. I . . . thought you were gone."

"I am so sorry, Anna. I knew this was going to be a difficult phone call for us both, but I knew if I kept waiting it would be worse. How are you, Anna?"

"Harry, where have you been? Are you okay? I have a million questions I'd like to ask you."

"I've been recovering from my time in Iraq, Anna. I'm much better, and growing stronger every day."

"Where are you living now?"

"Just outside of Memphis. I bought some acreage and have built a small farmhouse and barn for my horses."

"I see. Are you married?"

"No, I never married, Anna."

Silence. "You never married?"

"I really haven't had time since I was discharged. I have been recovering from my wounds. I was involved in an explosion which killed most of the men with me. My friend Max McIntyre was also injured. But at least we survived."

"How awful." Her voice was trembling.

"This is difficult for both of us, Anna. Is there any way we could possibly meet somewhere and talk?"

"I . . . I guess so. I'm in shock, Harry. I really thought you were dead."

"Can I see you tonight? I have a good reason for wanting to see you immediately, which I will share with you when we get together."

"I'll have to see about getting someone to stay with Zach, my son. But I think I can manage it. Where do you want to meet?"

"At the small deli on White Station Road. Simon's. Know where it is?" Harry smiled at the thought of her having a son.

"I think I can find it."

"The few times I've been there, it was never crowded. And we don't need a crowd right now."

"That sounds good. What time?"

"Seven. If that's okay for you. I won't keep you out late."

"See you at seven, then."

"Anna, it's so good to hear your voice after all these years. I look forward to catching up on your life."

"Thank you, Harry. I'm just thankful you're alive."

Harry was elated when he hung up the phone. He was nervous inside because all the feelings he had for her were trying to surface after so many years. But he knew it was wise to keep those hidden because life had a way of taking over and people change. Her voice sounded so different. But maybe she felt the same way. He was just grateful that she agreed to meet up with him. It could have gone the other direction and he would never see her again.

He patted Hack on the head and smiled. "I'm going on a date, tonight, Hack. With a beautiful woman I once loved. You would like her. She's one of a kind."

Harry got up and walked into his workout room and started lifting weights. His mind was running rampant about seeing Anna again. He had no expectations, of course. But his heart was cracking open; which was saying a ton for a Marine who'd experienced the nightmares of battle. He had closed his heart up a long time ago and he wasn't prepared to open it just yet. But there was a small crack, and if anyone could change Harry Downs it was Anna Shaw.

He was thinking about his leg. Or the lack of. He couldn't help but wonder how that would affect her. The old Anna wouldn't mind at all. She wouldn't even notice. But this was different. Their love had been put away for many years. And he was scarred now from battle. So many questions that he wanted answered but he also knew she would have her own list. It had to happen now, because what he really wanted was to head right back into war. He wanted to make a difference and he knew he and Max could do it if they were just given a chance. His mind drifted from Anna to General Murdock. He had not heard anything from the man yet; the odds were against the military even considering giving them another mission. But it would give his life meaning and purpose. Most vets wanted that; it was what drove them.

He worked out hard and took a shower. He still had some time before he left to meet Anna. His nerves were getting to him and his mouth was dry as cotton. But this was a chance in a lifetime that he had not counted on, so he was going to make the best of it. All those nights staring at her photo on Facebook were going to finally pay off. This was going to be the one time they both would have to see if anything still existed between them. To see if there was an "us" left after all the years apart. And maybe that was too much to expect in this first meeting.

He stared out the window at his barn and the horses that were gathering to be fed. He grabbed Hack and went outside to grab the feed and poured it in the troughs. It was windy and fortunately the rain had stopped. After checking the horses, he ran back to the house with Hack. He was ready to see Anna. But scared at the same time.

CHAPTER NINE

S ometimes life throws you a fairy tale. And today was one of them for Anna Shaw. She was so unnerved by the phone call that she didn't know what to do next. Hearing Harry's voice brought back so many memories and emotions that she really hadn't wanted to rehash. Her life had taken a turn and she had accepted it, alone. Harry was under the assumption that she'd been married and had a son. That maybe her husband had passed away or there was a divorce. She did have a son, but it was not from a marriage. She raised the boy alone, working as a school teacher to support herself and Zach. He was ten years old. She was nervous that Harry would figure things out after he found out she had not been married. Her life had been pretty mundane all these years, just teaching and raising Zach. She dated a little but really wasn't interested in men who were self-absorbed or couldn't deal with Zach being around. It was easier just to remain single and live a quiet albeit lonely life. The hardest thing she'd ever done was to make the decision not to tell Harry that he had a son.

Her nerves were shot. But she was excited about seeing him, regardless of the outcome. She picked out her favorite pair of jeans and red top, brushed her brown hair, and put on red lipstick. It had been forever that she'd been excited about going out to dinner. Tonight was very special. She wanted to look her best, but at the same time be relaxed so that she could enjoy being with Harry. He was her first love. She'd not fallen for anyone else since. But who knew where this night would go, after so many years apart? She put on her black heels, grabbed her purse, and checked the mirror one more time before she walked into the living room where Zach sat on the sofa playing a game on his IPad.

"You going to be okay while I'm gone?"

"Yes, Mother."

"I left you supper in the microwave. Just heat it about one minute. Got it?"

"It's not like I've never done that before, Mom."

"I won't be late. Jennifer is coming any second to sit with you."

"Okay. Have a good time."

She leaned over to kiss his cheek. He cringed. She pinched his arm.

"Ouch, Mom! Go already. I'll be fine."

"You used to let me kiss you. Now you pull away."

Zach glared at her. "I'm a guy, if you haven't noticed. We don't like it."

She laughed and walked towards the door. Jennifer opened it before she could leave and laughed her way into the house.

"Hey, Zach! What's up?"

The air had changed in the room. Anna was left out as the two young people totally ignored her. Jennifer plopped down on the sofa to see what game Zach was playing. Anne walked out and closed the door. Even though he was only ten years old, the separation was happening where he didn't need her as much. It hurt but she knew he was going to go through puberty and that it might not be fun.

On the short drive to the small restaurant, Anna's mind swirled with thoughts about Harry. She really wasn't sure if she would tell him about Zach. Zach thought his father was just "out there somewhere." She'd told him that she didn't have any idea where he lived. It was going to be really sticky when it all came out. But if she and Harry weren't going to get together again, and that was very iffy at best, then there would be no point in spilling the beans to either of them. Zach would go ballistic. It might ruin their relationship. Oh, how did she get into this dilemma? The odds of Harry reentering her life were so slim that it had never occurred to her that she would ever have to tell him about Zach.

She pulled up to the restaurant, checked her hair and lipstick, and walked inside. Harry was standing near the front, leaning against a wall. He was taller than she'd remembered. He was talking to the hostess, who was standing near a podium holding the menus. A thin smile came across her lips, but her words were caught in her throat. He was so handsome. Probably the best looking man she'd ever seen in her entire life. And here, after ten years apart, was a chance to see him again and catch up after all the years of wondering where he was, and if he was alive. And her words were stuck somewhere in her throat.

He turned and walked towards her with a smile that would have shaken even the most stoic of women. Her knees were weak as she walked towards him. But he took care of everything. He somehow sensed her faltering steps and understood what she needed. He took her hand and pulled her to him in a warm hug, laughing.

"How in the world are you, Anna? It is so good to see you again." He sounded so relaxed.

She took a breath. "It's so good to see you, Harry. How are you? You look wonderful." He smelled wonderful. So fresh. What was that cologne?

He smiled again. She lost her words. "Let's go sit down so that we can talk. I hate I decided to see you in a public place. I wanted to sweep you off your feet again."

She walked beside him to their table in the corner. The place wasn't very busy at the moment and she was thankful for that. She slid into her chair and he sat down beside her, grabbing her hand.

"Anna, I'm so nervous about seeing you. It's been so long. I don't even know where to start."

"I feel the same way, Harry." She put her hand on his and smiled, trying to gather herself. "Harry, you've been through so much. I know you've told me you bought some land and built a house and barn. But let's talk about the last few years. How was the war? Did it mess with your mind like it does so many of the men in the military?"

"Anna, you have no idea how difficult it was. War is ugly. It is everything and more that you see on television. Only it's real. It's happening right in front of your eyes. Your best friends are being shot down. Ruthless."

"I know it has to be the worst thing in the world to experience."

"Well, crazy thing is that I really love being in the military. Military intelligence. I'm good at what I do, and so is my friend, Max McIntyre. We served side by side and were both injured in the same explosion."

"So you were injured, Harry?"

The waiter came and took their orders and served them a glass of wine and warm bread and butter.

Harry paused. "Yes, I was injured, Anna. I lost a leg."

Anna sucked in air and put her hand over her mouth. "I had no idea. You didn't limp. I never saw anything! Harry, I am so sorry."

He patted her arm. "It's okay. I was dreading telling you, actually. I didn't want you to pity me. I've done very well with it. Spent a couple years rebuilding my body. I feel I am as strong today as I was when I entered the military."

She could hear the pride in his voice. And she could see his strength. It was in his eyes as he looked at her.

"I'm sure of that, Harry. It's just like you to turn your head away from the weakness and fight to build yourself stronger than you were before. So competitive."

"I am. That may not always be a good trait to have, but it has served me well while in the military."

The server brought their meals and poured fresh iced tea in their glasses. Anna chose to use that time to watch Harry, remembering all the years they had known each other. Thinking about how close they were in spite of their youth. He seemed like he had it together, that he knew what he wanted and he was going after it with all his strength. She had forgotten how handsome he was, and his slight aging had only increased his looks. He seemed unaware of her eyes on him as he concentrated on the plate of steaming food.

Her appetite was waning as she remembered the secret she'd carried all these years. Zach. How in the world would he react to know he had a son? Would he ever forgive her for not telling him? She reached for her fork but could barely eat. She was afraid he would notice, so she tried her best to enjoy the food. She felt his hand on hers and looked up to find that he was staring right through her.

For a second she thought he could read her thoughts. She shivered but hid it behind a weak smile. He raised an eyebrow and smiled back. She felt like Cinderella at the ball with the most handsome man in the room. There were no words that would fix what was going through her mind. Echoing inside her whole being. Love had fallen flat in front of her again and with the same man. But the secret she was keeping was bigger than the moon. And it just wouldn't fit into this moment in time.

CHAPTER TEN

Sometimes you hit a home run and sometimes you bunted. Harry knew he was at bat with the bases loaded. This beautiful woman had reentered his life at a time when he just might disappear again. There was no mathematical formula that would make it work out so that no one was hurt. He had pushed hard to get to meet her again. It was his idea, not hers. And now that they were sitting in the restaurant across from each other, he felt like he was floating. He felt like a goof ball. What had he been thinking when he dialed her number, knowing he wanted to leave the country on a mission that might not bring him back home! In his mind, and probably Max's, he'd resigned himself to the fact that if Murdock called and they got their mission, it might just be the last thing they did on the face of the earth. But he also felt the old love he'd carried for her for years creeping its way back into his heart. And he was pretty damn sure it was showing up on his face.

Anna was gorgeous. She was brilliant. There wasn't much he didn't like about her. She hadn't changed that much but he knew they had a lot to catch up on. Her eyes still bored a hole right through his skull and they hadn't spent even an hour together. He felt nervous, he felt stupid, yet he was still driven to know her again. What kind of reasoning was that? Was there even a name for it? He had no plan. He wasn't even thinking past tonight. He reached for her hand. She seemed like she was far away for a moment and he was wondering what was going through her mind. If she was regretting even seeing him again.

"Anna, a penny for your thoughts."

She hesitated. Her face was solemn for a moment. "Oh, just trying to catch up to the moment. It's hard to believe I'm sitting here with you again. Almost like no time has passed. But it has. Ten years have gone by."

"I feel the same way. It is surreal, to say the least. But I had to call you, Anna. I wanted to see how you were, at the very least. You look wonderful. You haven't told me what you've been doing all this time. Talk to me."

"Well, frankly, this whole thing is hard to wrap my mind around. I haven't seen you in ten years and suddenly we are talking over dinner. I'm not quite sure how to fill you in on the last ten years, Harry. So much has happened. I have Zach. My life's been busy, but lonely, at the same time."

Harry had forgotten about Zach for a moment. "I'd like to meet your son. I have seen his photos on your Facebook page."

"I'm not sure that's a good idea just yet, Harry. I don't let him meet anyone that I date unless they are going to be around for a while."

"I didn't think about that. Let's finish our meal. I want to take you to my farm so you can see how I have rebuilt my life. Would you like that, Anna?"

"Harry, that would be wonderful. I don't think I can eat another bite. Let's go now. We have too much to catch up on to waste our time eating a meal we really don't want."

Harry laughed. "You are so right. Come on, Anna. Follow me to the farm. It won't take us long. I know I promised you I wouldn't keep you out late."

Anna smiled. "I'll be right behind you, Harry."

⊷┼┼⊷

They both pulled up at the house and Harry got out of his truck and opened Anna's car door.

"Anna, I have a dog now. You'll love Hack. He's a military dog. But it's like I've owned him all my life."

"Look at your barn! And all the horses. Harry, you've really got yourself a wonderful place here. I know it has been good for you during your recovery time."

"It's pretty new. But I had to start somewhere. Horses have always been a love of mine. I am not sure if I'll ever ride again, but I do love having them around."

Anna walked up to the fence and a smaller horse came over to see her. She reached out a touched the horse's muzzle and smiled. "I have always loved the way horses smell."

Harry nodded. "Let's go in and see Hack. I know he hears us outside and is wondering when I'm coming inside."

They walked in and Hack came running to the door. When he saw Anna he sat down in front of her.

"What a gentleman he is! Did you teach him to do that?"

"I've never seen him do that, frankly. You can pet him. He won't bite."

Anna knelt down and patted Hack's head. He lay down and put his head on her lap. She looked up at Harry with a questioning look. He just shook his head and grinned.

"I told him he would love you if he ever got to meet you. And now look at him."

Anna grinned. "You haven't lost your touch, Harry Downs."

They both laughed. Harry walked to the sofa and patted the cushion beside him.

"Anna, will you sit beside me? I have something I want to share. I need to get it out of the way so I'll stop worrying about it."

Anna sat down beside him. "Harry, you don't have to prove anything to me."

"I know I don't. But I want you to see my leg." He raised his pants leg and showed her his prosthesis. He watched for any sign of her pulling back. Instead she reached over and touched his leg.

"Anna, you didn't have to do that. I just wanted you to see what I've had to overcome for the last couple of years."

She was quiet. He looked at her and smiled, but she wasn't smiling. Tears were streaming down her face. She leaned over and grabbed him and started crying.

"Oh, Harry. Why did you join the Marines in the first place? We were going to get married. Remember that?"

He held her close and touched her face. "Oh, Anna, I'm so sorry that I've hurt you. That wasn't my intention. I felt I had to do it. I really felt I had no choice. And I ended up loving the military life. But I missed you for a long time. And then I thought you had probably found someone else and married."

Anna wiped her eyes and looked at him.

"I am so sorry to have made you cry. This was supposed to be a special night for us to catch up with each other. I've ruined it. I probably shouldn't have brought you here to the farm."

Anna found her voice again. "No! I love this place and am so happy that you have made a new life for yourself. It just hurts to know that you suffered like this. I had no idea, Harry."

"Of course you didn't know. I spared you the details."

He pulled her up and held her in his arms, whispering in her ear. "I've missed you, Anna. I didn't mean to lose you for so long."

She spoke in a low voice. "It's so good to be near you again. We really don't know each other anymore, but I want you to know I have missed you and thought of you a million times."

"And I, you. Do you think we can see each other another time? I know you need to get back home to Zach."

"I do need to leave, but yes, we can do this again. We don't have to eat out. We can bring something here to the farm and eat. Or just go for a walk. The weather isn't too bad and I love being here."

"You remember how we used to laugh all the time? How carefree we were back then?" Harry searched her face.

"I do recall that. You were so funny then. I see a more serious side to you now."

"Well, life happens. The war happened."

"Yes, we both have had to face things that weren't all that easy to deal with. It would have been nice to have had you around to help me."

He pulled away and looked at her. "Help you? What were you going through?"

She almost spoke but stopped. "Oh, just life. You know what I mean. Ten years of life."

He was sure she was going to tell him something, but she changed her mind. He wondered what that was about.

"Anything you want to share with me?"

"No, not tonight. Maybe the next time I see you."

He walked her to her car. Hack followed beside Harry and sat down on the gravel driveway, wagging his tail. "I do want to see you again, Anna."

He tilted her face upwards and kissed her softly. She smiled a soft smile. He noticed the small freckle near her mouth. He'd forgotten about it but now it looked suddenly familiar.

"I hope that was okay for me to do that."

"I'm glad you did. Just brings back memories of other kisses."

"I'll call you. I really hate for you to leave tonight. It feels so good to hold you again."

"Just let me know when you want me around again. I loved our time tonight."

"It will be soon. May I kiss you one more time?"

She shook her head. He pulled her to him and kissed her harder. She moved away and laughed.

"Look, you've already taken my breath away. I better leave or we will be making out in the back of your truck, like we used to do."

Harry laughed. "Oh, how could I forget those nights?"

"I look forward to your call, Harry. Thank you for a wonderful night."

"You sure there isn't something you want to tell me? I thought you hesitated a moment ago."

"It can wait for the next time. We can go slow. We have plenty of time, Harry Downs."

He smiled as she drove away. "*We have plenty of time.*" The thought hit him in the gut that maybe they didn't have that kind of time. But he shoved it away and called out to Hack to follow him back to the house. He took a hot shower and slipped into the cold sheets on his bed. Hack lay at the foot of his bed, watching him closely.

"What? I told you she was special."

Hack wagged his tail. But the room was quiet except for the ticking of the clock in the hallway. He dozed off with wonderful thoughts of Anna running through his dreams. He was rebuilding his life, and he wanted her back in it. It felt so good, so natural to find her back again. To pull her up next to him and breathe her in. She belonged near him. He could feel it. Time would tell. He was so glad he got the nerve to call her up and ask her out. It went better than he thought it would. She didn't mind his leg. The fake one. It made her cry. He had no more tears, but he understood her feelings. The war had taken all the tears he had left. But he still had a heart. And as he fell asleep, he felt it aching for her. That girl. Anna Shaw.

CHAPTER ELEVEN

"You awake?" Max's voice was deep and raspy.

"Yep. What's up?" Harry yawned.

"Just wondering if you've heard anything from the general."

"Not yet. I didn't expect him to make something happen that fast."

"I can't stop thinking about it, Harry. I sure hope we get that chance."

"Me, too. But I have a little complication at the moment."

Silence. "What would that be?" Max cleared his throat.

"Um, you remember me talking to you about a girl I loved in high school?"

"Barely. What about her?"

"She's back into my life, and I want to see her again."

"Well, what's stopping you?"

"What if we get called out for a mission? I cannot do that to her again."

"Then why did you call the General?"

"'Cause I want to do it, but didn't realize we would connect so quickly. I'm going to have to tell her that I'm thinking about going back out on a mission."

"That's going to go over well."

"I don't need your sarcasm." Harry frowned.

"What can I say, Harry? Why did you reconnect with her if you knew you might be going out again?"

Silence. "I don't know. I just felt I had to see her again."

"Listen, Harry. Life is difficult without us making stupid decisions that complicate it more. You've made your first move, and now this next decision will set your life in a direction that you cannot pull back from."

"Oh, great. Help me out here, Max. I know I risk hurting her again, but how could I go the rest of my life and not see her again? You don't know this woman. She's extraordinary."

"I've thought that about tons of women, Harry."

"You don't know her. When I showed her my leg, she didn't pull away. She reached out and touched it."

"Well, that's something, all right. But what are you going to do about her? Were you planning on marrying her now? What was the point of seeing her again if you weren't going to keep her around?"

"Max, I don't have all the answers. I wasn't thinking straight. It was totally on impulse that I contacted her, not knowing we would move through a time warp and still feel the love. It was insane, really."

"I'm sorry, Harry. Really."

"Don't worry. I'll figure something it out. And I'll let you know if Murdock calls. It will be a snowball's chance in hell if we get to do anything. But if he says yes, you'll hear me shouting from here."

"I haven't wanted anything this much in my life. Never thought we'd get this opportunity. Glad you had the nerve to make the call. We'll see, Harry. But while I'm waiting, I'm getting ready for war."

CHAPTER TWELVE

Harry woke on Saturday feeling unsure about everything. He glanced at the window near his bed and saw a partly blue sky with the sun bursting through the clouds. At least it wasn't going to rain.

He yawned. Hack was waiting to go outside, so he slid his legs over the side of the bed, put on his prosthesis, and walked to the back door and down the steps. The horses were in the pasture nearest the barn, and they were coming up to the trough to be fed. There was a cool breeze blowing and Harry took in a deep breath and blew it out. Arthur, a tall black male in the group, was prancing around, which meant one of the mares was in heat. Harry walked over to the gate and grabbed a bridle and headed towards one of the pregnant mares. He didn't even stop to think about what he was doing. He just knew he wanted to ride this morning. No coffee. No breakfast. He just wanted to get on a horse and ride.

Trixie stood still while he bridled her and threw a saddle on her back. She was the calmest one, besides Belle, and he felt like he could handle her easily. He was nervous about his leg. He wasn't sure if he could feel her like he should. But he wanted to take the risk. His life was up in the air and he just needed to burn some energy. He put his left foot in the stirrup and pushed off with the metal prosthesis. He almost overshot the saddle, but he grabbed the horn and held on, while he swung his other leg over the horse's back. He sat up and centered himself before he took off. His balance was a bit off and he felt like he might fall off at any moment, but it felt so good to be moving with the horse that he almost forgot about his leg.

He rode out of the pasture in a slow trot, moving down three pastures to an open gate that opened up the largest field. He kicked up the pace a little to see how he would handle it. It felt like a million dollars to be running in the field. It was a beautiful time of morning and his head began to clear. He had to make some decisions that were life changing, but he wanted to take his time and not make a mistake.

He turned around and headed back to the barn. He didn't want to overdo it on his first ride. As he was nearing the gate Sam Pendleton drove up, so he got off the horse and tied her to the first post and headed toward Sam's truck.

"'Morning, Doc. How's it going with Belle?"

"She's coming along nicely. That's just why I stopped by. I was in the neighborhood and thought I'd bring you the good news in person. I think she's going to be just fine."

"That is music to my ears. She's such a good mare. I'd hate to have to put her down. I think she's got some good years left in her. You agree?"

"Yes, I do. I see you've taken a short ride this morning. How'd that turn out?"

"Frankly, I didn't know if I could ride or not. But this morning I needed it badly, so I just hopped on and held on. You have no idea how good that felt to me."

"I know how much I love riding, so I think I do understand. But you've overcome something that most people don't have to deal with. I'm surprised you did so well with your leg issue. Looked like a pro sitting on Trixie."

Harry laughed. "Not hardly. But at least I didn't fall off. I think she knew all about me as soon as I put my good leg in the stirrup."

"Probably right. Horses are pretty intuitive."

"You want to come in for coffee? I haven't had breakfast and I make some mean eggs and bacon."

"I'd better head out, Harry. But thanks, anyway. I got lots to do this morning. But glad to have good news for you. I'll let you know when I'm bringing Belle back home."

"Sounds good. Great to see you, Sam."

Harry watched as he pulled down the long driveway. Then he walked over and unsaddled Trixie and led her into the pasture closest to the barn. He hung up the bridle on the nail near the tack room and walked back into the house with Hack on his heels. He was starving and threw some bacon and eggs on the stove and stuck some biscuits in the oven. Hack ate his food down in two seconds and sat waiting on the bacon.

Harry looked at his watch. It was nearly 10:00. He was going to call Anna and see if she wanted to come over for dinner at the farm. He'd decided to see her again, even though the call from Murdock was probably going to come Monday or Tuesday. He knew in his gut that it was too late to pull back now. He felt something so strong for her, but he didn't want to be selfish about it. They weren't kids anymore.

He sat down and ate a quick breakfast, feeling frustrated. This wasn't how things were supposed to have played out. Seeing her again was the greatest thing in the world. He was so thankful. But he wasn't thinking clearly anymore. She had a son. That was a huge responsibility. She took it so seriously that she wouldn't even allow him to meet the boy. He felt like a jerk. Surely there was a better way to deal with this situation. If he had her over tonight, what in the world was he going to say to her to make it any better?

He grabbed his phone. There really was no way out of this nightmare. He cared so much for her. It rang four times and finally she answered.

"Well, hello, Soldier! How are you this morning?"

She sounded so cheerful. She didn't know a boulder was going to fall. "Hey, lady. So good to hear your voice. You got a busy day today? What's your schedule look like for tonight?"

"I have errands to run today. And Zach wants to go bowling with a friend, so I will drop them off at the bowling alley for an hour or so. What were you thinking about?"

He wasn't ready to tell her what he was thinking. "I was hoping you could come over tonight and have dinner with me here at the farm. Is that option still on the table?"

"I'd love to, Harry. Just tell me what time and I'll be there."

"I'd kinda like to pick you up, if that's okay."

"A real date. That sounds wonderful. I haven't been on one of those in a long time."

He smiled. She was adorable. "I look forward to seeing you. I'll pick you up at 6:30."

"I'll be ready, Harry. Casual, of course?"

"Yes. Very."

"Do I need to bring anything?"

"Not one thing but yourself. This is our time together and I plan to make the most of it."

"Thank you, Harry. See you soon."

Harry put his head in his hands. He was so messed up. But there was no turning back from this path he chose. He had created an impossible situation and he knew he would have to see it through. He imagined how Anna would react when he told her that he wanted to go back into the military. How unfair of him to mess up her life again!

He felt sick. And he felt lonely. He needed her, too. She wasn't the only one who had been lonely during the last ten years. He had kept her photo in his pocket and it was getting frayed on the edges it had been pulled out of the tight slot so many times. He'd dreamed about her so often over the years. And then he had let her go, because he knew she wouldn't have waited for him that long. He wanted her to have a good life, but he wanted to be a part of that good life.

He stood and cleaned up the dishes and headed out the door to the grocery. He'd made a short list in his head of what he wanted to cook, and he decided he was going to make the best of this night if it killed him.

Hack hopped up on the front seat of the truck and he pulled out of the driveway, heading west to the closest Kroger. Hack stayed in the truck with two windows partially down as Harry ran in and picked up steaks, potatoes, broccoli, an apple pie, and vanilla ice cream. They might as well enjoy a good meal, as that might be the only thing about the night that they liked. He got back in the truck and drove home, his mind a million miles away. After unloading the groceries, he cleaned the house, thinking through what he would say to this lady he'd loved a long time.

He wanted to take care of her but he also wanted to be fair. .. At the same time, he realized he needed her more now than ever. How would he ever say the right thing that would make it good for both of them?

He wanted to go to war. He wanted to love her. It felt like a runaway train with no brakes. He only hoped that Murdock didn't call him tonight. Because the way he felt right now, he wouldn't be able to take the call.

CHAPTER THIRTEEN

Mike Murdock was not a man anyone would want to meet in a dark alley. He was short, stocky and built like a tank. He had a mind like an elephant and a photographic memory that could drive a person insane. He had a great smile and a set of large white teeth that showed every time he grinned. But he had a fiery temper inside him that no one wanted to witness. The men under him saw that fire from time to time, but they only provoked it once. However, a few men, a very few, knew Mike had a soft heart underneath all that fire. He hid it well.

When his phone rang and he saw Harry Down's number across the top of his phone, he nearly died inside. Harry was one of his men. He loved the guy. There was no other person under him that could shoot like Harry Downs. And his mind was from another universe. He wasn't normal. He could do things that seemed near impossible with computers. If you wanted him to track someone down, you better believe he was going to do it, and it would usually be by some way that wasn't on the books. No text book contained what Harry Downs could do. Or would do. The phone call was dope. Harry wanted back in. How could you turn a guy down like Harry? And his buddy Max was equally as lethal.

Mike sat at a huge oak desk with the moon shining through the window in front of the desk. He had a big decision to make that would affect the military, the other men involved, if there were any, and it would affect the two soldiers who wanted back into the middle of things. This never happened. Not in his time served. But here it was, and he had to be the lucky one to make the decision. From where he was standing, he had three choices. He could turn them down flat, he could put them in counterintelligence where the threat of death was low, or he could put them in the heat of things and use their unmatched abilities as snipers. He loved both men. He loved what they had done already. But now he had to decide if they could continue in the direction he knew they were meant to go.

His head ached. He felt nervous but excited. He didn't want to make the wrong call. These two men had the strength of Goliath, but they also had hearts. And he didn't like being responsible for keeping those hearts beating.

It was going to be a long night, and he was alone. He got up and made a pot of strong coffee and stood looking out at the clear night. What he yearned for now, what he needed the most, was a clear answer. And he wasn't moving out of his office until he had it.

CHAPTER FOURTEEN

The Chevy pickup had been washed and spit-shined. Harry had cleaned himself up and rechecked his hair as he pulled onto Walnut Grove Road. It was taking him longer to get there because of the traffic, and the length of time didn't quiet his nerves.

Who would have ever thought that he and Anna would be able to have any kind of relationship after all this time? He had about given up on that dream. And maybe she had, too. He turned down Highland to Poplar Avenue and found her house. It was an older home, but nice. She had kept it up well, and the neighborhood had held its value. Amazingly. He slowly pulled into her driveway and turned the engine off. He couldn't wait to see her, but he wasn't sure how the night was going to turn out. *Sometimes even when you're doing a good thing, it backfires.*

He rang the doorbell and stood there waiting. In a few moments the mahogany door opened and Anna stood there with her captivating smile. The kind of smile that melted his heart in five seconds. Harry's legs were weak but he stepped forward and gave her a quick hug. Somehow he found his voice.

"Hey, girl. You look fantastic! Am I too early?"

She brushed the hair out of her eyes. "No, I'm ready. Just need to get my purse. Come in for a moment."

Harry stepped into the foyer and stood there like a wooden statue. He didn't know if he was supposed to follow her or just stand there. She walked into the living room and picked up her purse and turned off the television.

He had moved closer to the doorway of the living room and was looking around the room. It was so her. Wooden built-in bookshelves absolutely crammed with books. She was a reader. He remembered that about her. Everything looked warm and inviting. It had her touch everywhere. It felt like home. That was the best way to describe Anna's house. It felt like home.

"Okay, I'm ready." She smiled again. He nearly grabbed her but refrained.

"Where's your son?"

"He's at a friend's house for the evening. A baby sitter will pick him up and bring him home and she will stay here until I get back. They're good buddies."

"I have dinner waiting for us at the house."

"How nice. I really have been looking forward to this night."

He took her hand and walked down the driveway to the truck, opened the door, and watched her slide into the soft blue bench seat. He hadn't been around a woman in a long time. Seeing her the other night was way over the top. But tonight was different. He picked her up. It was like a real date.

He closed the door and walked around the truck. He knew he needed to get a grip because this could be a tough night. He needed his emotions in check. Because she was probably going to get upset and he had to be ready for that.

"I have, too, Anna. Just a relaxing night for the two of us. I'm so glad you could come. How is Zach doing?"

"He's great. He got to go bowling, so that made him happy."

"Does he know you are going out on a date?"

"I told him an old friend had asked me to dinner. He was fine with that and didn't ask any questions. I haven't dated that much, so he didn't think that much of it."

"I would have liked to have met him. I bet he's a great kid."

"I like to think so." She leaned her head back and laughed. He almost ran off the road.

"You say he's ten?"

"Yes. That's what I said."

"Perfect age for a boy. Old enough for you to loosen up on the strings a little. But not too old for you to worry too much about what he's up to."

"They know more than you and I did when we were their age."

"No joke. I don't want to know what that boy has learned about life. It would be scary. But the sad thing is that they have too much information and not enough experience. They think they know. That can be dangerous."

"I have seen that in my teaching. Too many times kids have seen or heard something and act on it without the real facts."

"Like drugs?"

"Yeah, that and alcohol. Even sex. You wouldn't believe how young they learn about all of that."

"Makes my head spin. I haven't had kids, but I want them one day. I'm not sure how that will all play out in my life."

"It will come, Harry. You'd make a wonderful father."

He smiled this time. That was a kind thing for her to say.

He took her hand and held it the rest of the way home. Like a school boy. Like a first date.

The farm was a welcome sight. He parked the truck under his favorite oak tree near the house, opened her door, and took her arm.

"Okay, lady. Our dinner is waiting."

Anna climbed out the truck and hooked her arm into his. "You know how to charm a girl."

"I can hear Hack barking in the kitchen. He's excited that you're coming."

"Can't wait to see what we're having for dinner! I didn't know you could cook."

"There's a lot you don't know about me. It's been a while, you know."

Harry walked her up the steps and into the kitchen where they were greeted by Hack, who immediately took up with Anna.

"See? I knew he was waiting for you."

Anna laughed that golden laugh and his heart nearly burst in his chest. He was nervous about telling her his little secret, but he was distracted by how delightful she was. He was determined to make this a good time, because it might possibly be the last time.

"Anna, take a seat in the living room and I'll get dinner ready for us. On the other hand, why don't you sit on the porch and watch the sunset? It is lovely this time of day on the porch. I'll bring you a glass of tea."

Anna reached down and patted Hack and he followed her to the porch, where she sat down on the swing with him. The sun was lowering its head behind the barn and streaks of orange light were coming out from behind the barn's metal roof.

Harry watched as she leaned her head back against the swing and pushed off with her foot to gently move the swing. She looked totally relaxed. She looked like she was happy. And she looked like she could stay forever, but he knew better. After she heard his news, he was almost positive that she would run like a deer being hunted. It would feel like a repeat performance from years ago. Only this time, she wouldn't be willing to forgive.

CHAPTER FIFTEEN

The small dining table was lit up with candles and a bottle of wine, two glasses, and silverware that didn't match. Harry had bought some wonderful-smelling bread that was heating in the oven. The steaks were done and the pie was warming in the drawer. Harry pulled out a chair for Anna and she sat down, reaching to pat Hack like it was second nature. The two of them were bonding fast.

"I hope you like your steak medium. I was guessing."

"You guessed correctly."

"Great. Don't be shy. The potatoes and the broccoli are on the table. I'll bring the bread out. It's what's been feeding our grizzly bear appetite."

"I am starving. This is nice, Harry. You've gone to so much trouble."

"I wanted us to be able to talk, and a restaurant isn't conducive to a good conversation. Especially if one wants it to be intimate."

"Ah, I see. Well you have outdone yourself with the candles and the sunset. I wonder how you ever got all that together?"

"It took some doing, but I pulled it all off. I've heard that timing is everything."

They both laughed and Harry sat down and cut his first bite of steak. Hack was staring a hole through him.

"So Anna, tell me all about Zach. Is his father involved in his life at all?"

Anna nearly choked and grabbed her water glass, swallowing half the glass before she stopped coughing.

"Um—no. He isn't around at all."

"Are you saying he chose not to be involved in Zach's life?"

"No. Well, in a roundabout way."

Harry stopped eating and looked at Anna. "Did I overstep?"

She paused, but he could see she was very uncomfortable.

"Anna, I'm sorry. I shouldn't have asked. I didn't mean to make you uncomfortable."

They both ate quietly, for a few minutes. Anna broke the silence. She reached for his hand.

"Harry, I didn't mean to shut you out. I—I just didn't want to talk about this over dinner. It's too serious to me and I was going to discuss it later, after we ate. Is that okay with you?"

"Of course it is, Anna. I don't even have to know anything about the father. I care more about Zach than who his father is. Just relax. Enjoy this meal. I have some warm apple pie for dessert with ice cream. I do recall you loving apple pie."

A small tear ran down Anna's face. She quickly wiped it away and smiled.

"Oh yes, I do love that pie. Not like I need it or anything. I can't eat like I used to."

"You look wonderful to me. You really haven't changed that much at all."

"I would hope that I've grown more. As a person, I mean."

"Well, we both have been through things that have caused that growth, whether we liked it or not. I was an unwilling participant in that growth. But it happened just the same."

"You certainly have been through severe trauma and have come out on the other side. I am not in your league, Harry. Not many people are."

"I don't know what league you are referring to, but if I am in one, it wasn't voluntary."

"I doubt most wounded vets recover with the vengeance you have shown. I am so proud of you."

Harry got up and cleared the table. He wasn't comfortable taking kudos for recovering from a wound. He had done it to save his own life. It was self-preservation. He was fully aware of the depression most wounded vets suffered from. He had had his share of depression. But he as a very determined individual and was highly trained to overcome. That was what he credited his fast recovery to—the unsurpassed training from Murdock. Murdock. The man he was dying to hear from.

"Let's go out to the barn to see the horses again. Maybe we'll go for a short ride. How do you like your horses? Wild and daring, or calm and slow?"

"Ride? It's been years. I am certain I better have the oldest horse you have on the place."

"I have just the ride for you. Come one, let's go."

Hack was left to watch from the porch, as they both took off down the steps to the barn. It was getting near dusk so they couldn't go far. Harry grabbed two of the older mares and saddled them up. He was excited to be on another horse again so soon. But he didn't let on to Anna that he was a little wary of his horse-riding abilities with his prosthesis.

Anna got on the horse with ease and settled into the saddle. "I guess it's like riding a bike. It feels great up here."

"I'm ready if you are. We'll just take a short walk into the back pasture and lose ourselves for a few moments."

The horses walked slowly down a well-worn path to the back pasture, kicking up some dust in their wake. The last bit of the sun's rays was peeking over the edge of the horizon, which was a small hill at the back of the pasture. The trees took on an orange glow for the last few seconds of daylight. It was a magical time to be riding. It was even a little romantic.

"So, you want to talk about Zach now? We're all alone and it's quiet at the end of the day."

"Harry, it's a long story. Should we wait for another time? I don't want to use up all of our time tonight talking about Zach."

He turned to her and smiled. Was he reading her wrong? She seemed to really be avoiding talking about the father of her son. "Anna, we've known each other a long time. Whether or not we ever get as close as we once were, you know you can tell me anything, without one smidge of judgment on my part."

Anna bowed her head and took a deep breath. "I know that, Harry. I'm sorry if I seem to be avoiding talking about it. I've spent years dealing with this secret and it has done something to my trust. Even in myself."

"We all make mistakes, Anna. I've certainly made my share. So don't feel bad at all with me around. I totally understand that life has been tough raising this boy alone. A single mom on a teacher's salary. I don't know how you've made it so well. And you have a nice home. A safe place to raise your boy."

"Harry, stop. You don't know the whole story. Yes, it's been difficult to raise my child alone. But it was something I chose. I did this to myself."

"I hardly find it a horrendous choice for you to raise your son alone. You must have had your reasons, Anna. I trust you. I know you would have done differently if you thought it would have worked out."

"That's just it. I don't know how it would have worked out. I never told the father that I was pregnant. He doesn't know to this day."

Harry stopped his horse and looked at her. "You didn't tell him he had a son?"

"No. I chose to keep it to myself because he was gone and I didn't know if he would ever come back."

"So he's out there somewhere, and his son is living without knowledge of his father?"

"You're judging me and you don't know all the circumstances."

"I'm just asking you to think about this. That's a huge thing that you didn't tell him. You never gave him the chance to jump in and help or to disappear. What kind of man was he, anyway, that you would leave him in the lurch like that?"

"He was a good man. He was the best man I've ever known."

Harry got off his horse and tied it to a small tree. He reached for her and pulled her down and tied her horse on another branch.

"Anna, who was this man that you have kept this secret from all Zach's life? Did he hurt you? Why did you make this difficult decision that could affect Zach for the rest of his life?"

Anna walked away from Harry and leaned against a tree, looking in the direction of the sun that had just set for the night. It was dusk and he could barely see her face. But he could see well enough to tell that she was crying. He walked up to her and put his arms around her, lifting her face up to his. He kissed her softly and moved a lone strand of hair away from her face.

"Baby, I wouldn't hurt you for the world. I'm just trying to understand why you would keep this news from the father. In my estimation, he would have to be pretty ruthless for you to have made that decision."

She whispered low in his ear. "He wasn't horrible. He was the most valiant man I've ever known. But I'didn't know if he was dead or alive. I had to make that decision alone. I had no way to get in touch with him and I thought he was dead. I heard nothing for years. Nothing. Until recently."

Harry felt nausea coming up into his throat. He didn't even know what he was thinking. He was afraid to think at all.

"Anna, who is this man? Tell me now."

"Harry, no. This isn't the way I wanted to do this."

"Tell me now, Anna. I have to know who the father is."

She blew out a sigh and stepped away from him. "I'm going to lose you again if I tell you. I just got you back into my life, Harry. And if I tell you who the father is, I will lose you forever."

"You are talking crazy, Anna. Why would I do such a thing to you? I'm thrilled that we have found each other again. There is nothing that would make me that angry that I would just walk away now."

"Oh you don't know that, Harry. You don't know the hell I've been through for the last ten years. It was very difficult for me. You have no idea what I've been through."

"Well, get if off your chest, then. Tell me. The one person who you can trust with anything."

She stepped away from him, and had a resigned look on her face. He could barely see her and knew they needed to head back to the barn before it got pitch black dark. He walked up to her again and lifted her face to his. "Who is it, Anna? It's eating you alive. I can see it, now."

She whispered so low he could barely hear her. "It's you, Harry. You are Zach's father."

Time must have stopped. His ears were full and he couldn't think at all. He felt his knees buckle. Or the one good one. "What? What did you say?"

"I said that you are his father. This was difficult, Harry. I thought you were dead. When I found out I was pregnant you were overseas. I had no way to get in touch with you. You had stopped communicating with me totally. What was I supposed to have done?"

Harry was speechless for possibly the first time in his life. What he heard her say, what he understood her to say, was that he had a son. Zach was his son. And he had missed the last ten years of his life. Because she had been afraid to tell him? Because she thought he was dead? He faltered and caught himself on the tree where the horses were tied. "Anna, what have you done? Zach doesn't know I'm his father. How can you ever tell him, now? Were you ever going to tell me?"

"Of course I wanted to tell Zach. But there was no point if you were gone. And we just found each other a week ago. I didn't know where to begin. I had no idea you would pop into my life again. Harry, I know you're angry. I'll go. I don't have to stay here tonight. I understand if you never want to see me again. Just know that I always loved you. I always wanted you to be a part of his life. But for all purposes, you were gone. I never heard from you. Never."

Harry grabbed her and held her close. He started to cry and it seemed like the ten years of pain all came out in the next five minutes of tears. "Anna, oh, Anna. I don't know what to say. I feel angry and happy all at the same time. I have a son. It's your son. We have a son together. I can't wrap my mind around this. It's insane. How did you keep this secret inside of you without losing your frigging mind?"

"I nearly did. I was dreading this conversation, Harry. You don't know how I was fretting over how in the world to get the words out. I wanted you to know so badly, but I also knew it was going to hurt more than me keeping it a secret."

"I don't know how you kept this inside. That wasn't fair to you. I wish I could have been there when you had Zach. My head was somewhere else. And I belonged to the military. I still do, in a way. What do we do now, Anna? Where do we go from here, because I hate this place we're in right now."

Anna stepped back and shook her head. But Harry couldn't see it. It was too dark. He untied the horses and they rode back to the house in silence. The weight on Harry's heart hurt more than his leg, which was tired from riding. His thoughts were broken and running in ten directions. He had a son. He really could not think past that thought. And how in the world was he going to ever make a decision about reentering the military after finding out this bit of news? He had a son.

CHAPTER SIXTEEN

A slightly cool breeze was blowing across the porch, and the moon was perched in the dark sky to the left of the largest oak tree in the front yard. The glow from the moon seemed to put a fuzzy haze on everything, including Anna's face. Harry had his hand on hers but his mind was racing. He could tell she was worried. But he didn't have the words in him to calm her down. Finally she spoke to break the awful silence.

"I don't know what to say to make this any easier. But in a way, I'm glad the truth is out. I've been sick for so long about carrying this secret inside me, and now it's out. Now I can face you and not feel like I'm hiding the most important thing in the world from you."

"I feel angry, Anna. Sort of angry. Well, I really don't know what you would call it. Too many emotions involved. But I am happy I know now. I haven't met Zach yet but I've seen him on Facebook. I know he favors me. But I don't know how in the world you're going to tell him."

"We're in a mess, all right. I'm so sorry to do this to you, Harry. It wasn't how I dreamed it would be. But I thought you were gone. Please don't forget that."

"I'm trying to keep that in mind. But did you try to find out? Did you call my parents to see if they'd heard from me?"

"I haven't spoken with your parents for so many years; there was no way I was going to call them. When we broke it off, I was so embarrassed that I was pregnant; I didn't want to tell anyone. I am so sorry."

"I know, Anna. But you have to stop saying you're sorry. You've raised Zach alone for the last ten years. Now I'm in the picture and we have to figure out how to tell Zach without ruining his little heart. In my estimation, it could go either way."

"Harry, I told him that his father was probably dead. I didn't really talk to him about you at all. He accepted it and never asked questions."

"I'll have to meet him. It will have to go slowly. Maybe let him get to know me a little. I don't think we should tell him right off the bat."

Anna walked over to the railing on the porch and stood there. He could see that she was upset. He stood up and walked near her, putting his arms around her.

"Hey. Let's let this ride for tonight. We aren't going to solve it in one day. You've been carrying this for a long time. Years. Just because I know doesn't mean it is over. I can handle anything, but Zach is just a kid. He is fragile. I have to earn his trust. It won't—"

Harry's phone rang. He checked to see who it was, and saw Murdock's name. He didn't feel like taking the call, but he also knew if he didn't, it might be the worst mistake he'd ever made. And Max would never forgive him.

He looked at Anna and shrugged, as he punched his phone and said, "Hello."

"Harry? Murdock here. I know you've been waiting for my call, so I tried to make this as quick a decision as I could. Not all that common to have men return to duty after suffering what you went through. You and Max both. But I want you to come in and let me put you through some tests. Psychological and physical. I have to be dead sure you both are ready for combat, even if we just put you back into counterintel. You never know when your sniper skills will be called up. You know that better than I do. But I'm not going to risk your life unnecessarily just because you want to go back to war. I have to know you both are fully capable."

"I understand, Sir. So what is the next step?"

"Report to me in a week after you've gone through your screening and re-qualifications. We'll see how it goes."

Harry stood there with his phone in his hand, not sure what to say. Anna had heard his side of the conversation. She wasn't stupid. He turned to look at her and she was shaking her head.

"I cannot believe this! You're planning to go back to battle. Even after you nearly lost your life! I should have known you weren't done. I should have seen this coming. You have rebuilt your body; you look like you're in perfect shape. I bet Max has done the same thing."

"Don't be angry with me, Anna. I was going to tell you after I got the call from Murdock. I was afraid this would happen. Right in the middle of a very critical conversation about Zach. The timing couldn't have been worse."

Anna sat down and stared at him. "I just found you back. After ten years. And you want to leave me and your newfound son and go back to war."

"I didn't know you were around. I sure didn't know about Zach. You know I not only love the military, I am military. It is what I do. Surely you can understand my going back, Anna. I don't even know what position I will be in. We just want the chance to do what we are good at. Just like your teaching position. It's what you do. It's what you are."

She surprised Harry and put both her hands around his face and pulled him forward to kiss him. He was sweating profusely.

"Harry, I love you. I have always loved you. I'll be here when you get back. But how will you ever get to know Zach? You cannot wait any longer to meet him. I want him to know you before you leave for overseas. I don't even want to know what you'll be doing. I just want Zach to know you're alive and that you care about him."

"That's going to be tough at his age. He may not trust what we are telling him. That you thought I was dead. And now I show up wounded and reentering the military, like I'm not interested in being around him at all. I hate the timing of all of this. I want to know my son."

"We'll make it happen, Harry. Do you love me anymore?"

Harry sat there looking at her. He took her in, all of her. "How could I not still love you? The most beautiful woman in the world. You haven't changed much, except to get wiser and prettier. I just didn't think we'd have a chance to start over. And now I find out we have a son together. It jolted me into reality, Anna. I do love you. I feel so torn."

"You have a lot on your mind. I need to go. But I want you to meet Zach tonight when you take me home. He needs to see who I had dinner with and see that I am interested in you. I think he will be relieved because he hasn't really had a man in his life at all. Just go easy. Don't expect too much of a reaction right off the bat."

Harry smiled a weak smile. He was overwhelmed with the knowledge that he had a son. And who was this incredible woman in front of him? She didn't back away one single inch after over-hearing the phone call with Murdock. He was blown away by her strength. His feelings had been buried for years, if he were totally honest with himself. And all of these thoughts were going through his mind in a nanosecond.

"First of all, sweetheart, I want to thank you for being so un-derstanding. You could have reacted a zillion different ways but the one you chose was total understanding. How did you manage that? We have so much going on and I'm adding additional stress by springing this on you now. Please forgive me. I am still shocked over the news about Zach. I'm dying to meet him and put my arms around him. But I know I can't do that just yet. I'll have to spend some time with him and win him over. I hope I have that kind of time before I go."

He grabbed her and hugged her, kissing her hard. "Let's take you home. I want to meet my son."

CHAPTER SEVENTEEN

Life had a way of throwing some balls at you; "curve balls" they were called. And Harry felt like he'd been hit in the gut as he pulled the old truck out of the driveway and headed over to Anna's house. It felt like time was going in slow motion. Nothing in his world had prepared him for this moment when he would meet his son. A boy he didn't even know existed if it weren't for Facebook. No wonder he thought the boy looked familiar. He chuckled and Anna looked over at him and smiled.

"What are you laughing at, Harry?"

"I can't believe what has happened tonight. I never for the life of me saw this coming. And I consider myself intelligent."

"I know, Harry. I know. It's not been a normal first date at all. In fact, we'll probably remember this for as long as we live. But we can't sit here all night. You ready to meet Zach?"

"What do I say to him?"

"Just say 'hello.' He's meeting the man I went out on a date with tonight."

"Okay. I'll just relax and try to act like I'm just your date. But it will be nearly impossible not to hug the boy. I will be looking at my son for the first time. Do you realize what I'm going to be going through?"

"I do, Harry. Of course I do. But we can't spring it on him right now. You just can't blurt out that you are his father. That would not work at all. He'd never believe it, I don't think. He might reject you totally. We may not know exactly when to tell him, but I do now it's not the first time he meets you."

"I'll tell you what, Anna. Let's not plan this out too much. I want to go in and meet Zach and talk to him. Let's just see how things play out. With a ten-year-old boy who isn't stupid, he might just figure this whole thing out himself."

Anna raised her eyebrows and smiled a slow smile. He brushed her hair off her face and kissed her. "I know this is hard for you because you are protective of him. But I will be careful. I'll watch you for cues. But let's not worry too much about it until we see how Zach reacts to me."

Harry got out and opened the door for Anna. He helped her out of the truck and they walked to the front door arm in arm. Anna used her key and unlocked the front door and they walked directly into the living room where Zach and Jennifer were watching television.

"Hello, guys. Jennifer, I'm sorry we're so late. I really appreciate you staying so long tonight."

Anna handed her some money and Jennifer skipped to the front door. She looked glad to be leaving.

"I enjoyed it. Just let me know if you need me again.."

Zach yelled out. "Bye, Jenn. Thanks for coming."

Harry walked in and sat on the sofa near Zach. "Hey, Zach. I'm Harry. You have a good time tonight?"

Zach looked at Harry, nodded, and went back to watching television.

"Zach, we went to Harry's farm tonight for dinner. You should have seen the horses. They were beautiful! We actually went on a short ride after we ate."

"Cool." Zach seemed unimpressed.

"I'd love to show you the farm if you like the sort of thing, Zach." Harry was determined to get a connection somehow.

"Sure. That's cool."

"You like that word 'cool,' don't you?"

"Yeah, sort of."

"So Anna, how long you been in this house?"

"All of ten years. Zach was born here. So it really feels like home to us."

"I love the house. Can I see the yard? I know it's dark but I'd love to see what kind of yard it has."

"Sure, come on out. I'll turn on the back lights."

"You got a glove and ball, Zach? You like to pitch?"

"Yep. I'll get it." He put the remote down and headed to his bedroom.

Anna rolled her eyes. It wasn't going so well. Zach was clamming up and not being very social. But maybe he suspected something. He seemed uneasy to Harry.

"Honey, don't worry. We've just gotten started. I'm going to try to get him to open up to me a little. I know it's late so I won't stay long."

"You're the man. Do whatever you think is best."

Zach came back with two gloves and a ball. Anna switched the outside spotlights on and Harry took a glove and started pitching to Zach. He held back throwing hard until he saw how good the boy was. He was pleasantly surprised at Zach's aim.

"You're pretty good for a ten-year-old, Zach. You play ball?"

"I tried once, but didn't have anyone to practice with, because Mom was always working. So I dropped out. But I do like to play."

Harry threw a few more balls and called it quits. "I just wanted to throw a few. It's been a while for me, too."

Anna was sitting on the patio watching, keeping quiet.

"You've got a great backyard. Larger than I thought it would be and you've done a good job with the landscaping. It's big enough back here to play a baseball game. I see the basketball goal. You like that, Zach? Or are you a hunting man?"

"I've never been hunting, but my friend Josh said I might be able to go with them sometime."

"It's something you either love or hate. I hope you end up liking it."

When Harry sat down, his pants leg came up a little and Harry felt Zach staring at his foot.

"So, Zach, your mom told me that your dad may have died in the war."

"Yeah, I guess. She doesn't talk about that much. Do you, Mom?"

"No, I guess I don't." Anna sounded nervous.

"Your mom told me that he was wounded in the war. But she had not heard from him in a long time."

Zach seemed suddenly interested in what Harry was saying.

"What happened to your leg, Harry?" Zach was shooting straight from the hip.

"Our jeep hit an IED and exploded, killing some of us. I got my leg blown off. My buddy lost an arm and a leg. It's been heck trying to recover from the injury. But they got me the best prosthesis made and it really helps me live a normal life."

"Can I see it?"

Anna winced.

"Sure you can. Come over here and I'll let you see it." Harry was sitting next to Anna and reached over and squeezed her hand.

Zach walked over and knelt down and stared at the prosthesis. He reached over and touched the foot.

"Does it hurt to wear it?"

"No, I'm used to it now. My leg was sore at first but when it healed, I really was thankful I had a way to walk again."

"So did you know Mom before?"

"You mean before I got injured?"

"Yep."

"I used to date your mom. She was the first girl I fell in love with."

"Really? You dated my mom?" Zach looked surprised.

"I did. We were going to get married when I left for the war."

"Um . . . you were going to marry my mom? What happened? Why didn't you marry her when you got back?"

Here it goes. Harry took a deep breath.

"Things happen, Son. Your mom thought I was dead. And I was so overwhelmed with recovering from a near death experience that I didn't have the ability to think about her or a relationship then."

"So she thought you were dead?"

"Yes, she did. We haven't talked in ten years."

Anna interrupted the conversation and asked Zach to help her in the kitchen.

"Come on, Zach. Let's get some iced tea for Harry. I'm kind of thirsty and I bet you would like some ice cream."

Zach stood up slowly and walked into the kitchen. "Mom, you told me my father was dead. Did he fight in the same war as Harry?"

"He did, Zach."

"Did Harry know my father?"

Anna knelt down and hugged Zach. "Come here, Son. I need to talk to you about something."

Zach came close to Anna and looked at her. "What is it, Mom?" His eyes were watering.

"Honey, you remember I told you I thought your father was dead?"

Zach nodded.

"Well, Harry is your father, Zach. I thought he was dead, so I never got to tell him about you. He didn't know he even had a son. He didn't know about you, Zach."

Zach started crying. "Harry is my dad?"

"Yes, Son. He is. And he wants to get to know you. He is so excited that he has a son."

Zach ran into the living room where Harry was sitting and wrapped his arms around Harry's neck. He was sobbing. "I knew you were my dad. I just knew it. You look like me."

Harry wiped his eyes and hugged his son. It was the best feeling ever. "I love you, Son. I'm so sorry I've missed so much of your life. I want to make it up to you. But we have a small issue I need to talk to you about. Can you listen just a minute?"

Zach wiped his face on his shirt and stood there in front of Harry, shaking a little, but quiet.

"I know we've just found each other, and it is the best feeling I've had in years. But I may have to go back to war. Not like fighting in the middle of things. But it will still be dangerous. I'll be back. But I want you to take care of your mom while I'm gone."

Zach pulled away. "You just met me, and now you're going away?"

Harry got on the floor and hugged his son. "Don't worry about it right now. We don't know for sure when I'll be leaving, so let's not even worry until it happens."

Zach wiped his face on his shirt and went over to Anna and sat near her on the sofa. "I thought he was my dad. Why doesn't he want to live with us, Mom?"

"You have to understand that we haven't seen each other for ten years. That's a long time to be apart. We have to catch up with each other. He missed all of your childhood, Zach. He needs to get to know you."

"Can't he live here? I'll share my room with him."

"No, he can't share your room. But we will be seeing as much of him as we can, before he leaves. I promise."

That seemed to settle Zach for the moment. He walked over to Harry and leaned against him, closing his eyes. It was late. Harry leaned back against the sofa and let the boy fall asleep on his arm.

It was the greatest feeling in the world, but he was aware that it might be the last time he would feel his son against him for a long time. At that moment, he hated the decision he'd made. But at the same time, he felt compelled to do it, anyway. That alone made him question where his loyalty was. He had a woman who loved him still, and a son he wanted to get to know. Why in the world would any sane man leave all that to go back to war?

Anna put Zach to bed and walked back into the living room. Harry was standing near the window that looked out into the back yard. She walked up and put her arm around him.

"Pretty tough night, Harry."

"An emotional roller coaster. I found out I have a son. You found out that I want to go back into the military, and I had to tell Zach that I wasn't going to be around for a while."

"Does that make you question your decision?"

"You bet it does. But I still feel the need to go. I'm so sorry, Anna. Can we live through this?"

Anna smiled and looked at him closely. "I think this time we have to survive this. I don't want to lose you again, Harry."

He turned and held her in his arms. "I don't want to let you go. Believe me, knowing you both are here waiting on me will give me the strength to do my job and come back home."

He kissed her several times and walked to the door to leave. "Anna, thank you for not walking out on me. I'll never forget that. I promise I'll come back home."

"I don't think I could take it if you didn't."

CHAPTER EIGHTEEN

Harry sat on the steps outside of Anna's front door, watching the clouds pass over the moon. He couldn't get the energy up to walk to his truck. His head was spinning and he hated to admit he really didn't want to go home. He turned to look at the window behind him and Anna was standing there watching him. He motioned for her to come outside. She opened the front door and sat down beside him on the steps.

"Harry, what's wrong?"

"I don't know, Anna. I feel strange right now. I thought I had my life all planned out. Murdock has made his decision, except for a few tests he'll run us through. I believe we will be sent out on a mission within the next month. But all this was discussed before you and I found each other again. And then I find out about Zach. It's just too much to process."

She put her hand on his shoulder and leaned against him. "It's okay, Harry. Don't put so much stress on yourself. Zach and I have been alone for all of his life. It's nothing new to us. In fact, it feels normal. We will be fine while you are away." He could tell she was lying through her pretty white teeth.

"Anna, he just met his father. The last thing I need to do is disappear. I didn't realize it would be this tough. He's such a nice kid."

"I'll take some credit for that!" She managed a weak grin.

"You can take all the credit. You've done an incredible job by yourself. But now I'd like a chance to influence him in some way. He needs a man around, too. He needs his father."

"That is why we just went through this nightmare, so that he could know who you are."

"I really don't want to leave you again. Do you know how hard that is for me?"

"It's hard for me, too, Harry. I just found you again. I thought you were gone."

He leaned over and kissed her nose.

"I promise I'll be back. I wouldn't miss this for anything in the world. Just don't give up on me now."

"Do you see me moving away, Harry?"

"No, and I've done nothing to deserve such loyalty. But I am forever grateful."

She smiled. It shot something straight through him. What a beautiful soul she was. And she was willing to wait for him.

"Go get Zach. I need to talk to him a minute."

Anna got up and walked to the foot of the stairs and called for Zach. He came running out of his room smiling from ear to ear. They walked outside where Harry was waiting on the steps.

"I was hoping you hadn't left yet, Dad."

Harry was speechless. *He just met me and he's calling me Dad.* "Sit down, Zach. Let's have a man to man talk before I go."

Zach squatted down in front of Harry and looked at him with dark brown eyes that spoke what the boy was too young to say out loud.

"Son, I told you I may be going back into the military. It's not something I really want to do, since I found out about you. But I want you to know I will do everything in my power to return home safely. I want you to take care of your mother and not give up on me. Is that a deal?"

Zach smiled. "Dad, I'll take care of Mom. She's easy to take care of. But I wish you weren't going. I can't believe I've found you at last! I never thought I'd have a dad. So if you have to go, just know we will be waiting for you. I'm just a kid. But I know all about waiting."

Harry shook his head and smiled at Anna. "This kid's going to kill me. I can see that now."

Anna stood up and grabbed Zach's hand. "I need to get this guy in bed. You want to help?"

Harry walked into the house behind them and followed Anna to Zach's room. Zach dove into bed and turned over with the biggest grin in the world.

Harry sat down on the bed and brushed Zach's hair off his forehead. He had a slew of freckles thrown across his nose and his skin was darker than his mother's. Even though it was so new to him, Harry leaned over and kissed his face and whispered into his ear. "I love you, Son. Sleep well, and I will call you tomorrow." He felt nervous saying it, but it just came out of nowhere.

"This is the first time my father has put me to bed. I'm not gonna forget this for a long time."

"Me, either, Zach. Me, either."

Anna kissed Zach and walked out of the room with Harry. They held hands.

"I know you need to go but this was worth the wait."

"I wouldn't have missed this chance for anything. I'll call you tomorrow after my meeting with Murdock. Thanks for everything, Anna. What a night."

She smiled again and reached up on her toes and kissed his mouth. They were slipping back into their old ways, like a pair of old comfortable shoes. These shoes hadn't been worn in a long, long time, but there was still a lot of good wear left in them.

"I'll be waiting to hear, Harry."

Harry left in his truck, squealing the tires. He looked back in the rearview mirror and saw her standing there. Her smile had faded and he thought he saw her wipe her eyes. He almost turned back, but decided not to. He knew that it wasn't that uncommon to make quick decisions that we later regret, This was one of those. Ten years was a long time to be away from a person. But after to-night, it had felt like they'd never been apart. With him leaving again, it felt like they were reliving the very moments that sepa-rated them in the first place. Was that the hand they were dealt? Or was he afflicted with a death wish?

On the drive back to the farm he dialed Max's number. Hopefully this conversation would go well. He needed something to pick up his spirits. Although nothing was going to top finding out he had a son.

"Hey, Buddy! What's up?"

"Got a call finally from Murdock. He wants us to report to him tomorrow morning."

"That soon?"

"Yep. We're going to be put through some tests, which I am sure will be grueling. But I think we're ready. Don't you?"

"Hell, yes. We made it through that last explosion, so we can live through anything the military can put us through."

"No kidding. I'll meet you there at 7:00. Here we go, Max."

"I'm more than ready. See you early."

Harry ended the call and pulled up in his driveway. The farm seemed empty without Anna there. He walked inside and Hack greeted him. Suddenly he felt tired. His mind was worn out with emotions he'd not allowed anywhere near his heart for years. He was more than overwhelmed. He didn't know what else to do but climb in bed, because tomorrow was going to be tough on him physically. But in the back of his mind would lay that picture of Anna standing there in the yard waving, with that look of sadness on her face. All because he wanted to play soldier again.

He swore he would come home to them as a whole man. No more limbs missing. Zach needed him now. And that boy was enough to motivate Harry to make it back. He didn't know what was ahead of him, but he did know what he was leaving behind. And nothing or no one was going to take that away from him.

He fell into bed with Hack by his side and slept hard and fast. He hoped he was as trained a machine as he thought he was, and he hoped Anna would be there when he came home. He hoped.

CHAPTER NINETEEN

The meeting with General Murdock went better than expected. Their requalification wasn't as tough as they thought it would be. A mission was already planned and Murdock wanted them to report tomorrow.

There was no time for Harry or Max to plan or even think. It was now or never. Harry was taken back by how quickly this all had fallen in to place. Max was single and he had no issue with the time frame. Harry's mind was racing to get things sorted out. He would have to take Hack over to Anna's house and ask if he could remain there until he returned from the mission. He was pretty sure Zach would be excited to have Hack around. But inside he wished Hack was going with him. He pulled up at the farm and got out, breathing in the fresh air and taking in the place he called home. It would be a while before he came back.

He made a quick call to the vet to see if he would take care of the horses. It was a stretch, but that was his only choice.

"Dr. Pendleton? Sam? It's Harry Downs. Hope this isn't a bad time."

"Never a bad time for you, Harry. Got another issue with your horses?"

"Not this time. It seems I've gotten myself into another military situation, and need your help."

"How can I help you, Harry?"

"Can you watch over my horses while I'm gone? I know that's a tall order, but I really don't have anyone else to turn to. I'm not sure how long I'll be gone this time, but it shouldn't take too long to carry out this mission."

"I had no idea you were still in the military."

"Well, I am still considered active duty, and it was my goal to step back in. It happened sooner than I thought; I'll be leaving in the morning early."

"I've got some spare time and it's the least I can do while you are serving our country. Sure, I'll take care of your horses. I'll make sure they're fed and watered. I have a part-time guy that would probably love to make some extra money cleaning out your stalls and feeding the horses. Between the two of us, we should be able to cover it."

Harry blew out a sigh of relief. "You have no idea how much that means to me. I love those horses, and would die if anything happened to them while I was away."

"They'll be in good hands, Harry. You will have enough on your mind without worrying about the horses."

"As soon as I land here I'll call you to let you know I'm home. Thanks so much, Sam. I can leave now without worrying about the welfare of my horses."

Harry grabbed Hack and wrestled with him on the floor. He was going to miss the dog terribly. They had become almost inseparable. He gathered his leash, bowl food, and favorite toys and threw them in the truck. He suddenly felt rushed. He had no idea they would be sent out so quickly. He felt like he hardly had time to get his house in order before he was gone. And he had no idea how long this mission would take. He got into the car and drove over to Anna's. Hopefully she wouldn't be planning a long trip somewhere. Keeping Hack wouldn't be an issue as long as she wasn't too busy. He parked in her driveway and rang the doorbell. Zach answered with the biggest grin Harry had ever seen.

"Hi, Son! How you doing?"

Zach ran to Harry and wrapped his arms around his waist. "Hey, Dad. I wasn't expecting you today."

"Well, I'm kind of surprised, too. Is your mother home?"

Zach yelled into the house. "Mom? Dad's here."

Harry grinned and shook his head. He just wasn't used to being called 'Dad.'

Anna came running into the living room, out of breath. "Harry? Is everything all right? What are you doing here in the middle of the afternoon?"

"I have some news and a favor to ask of you."

Anna looked at him straight in the eye and frowned. "I don't like the first part of that statement."

"I knew you wouldn't."

"Come on in and sit down. I'll get you some tea."

Harry sat down on the sofa and Zach piled in beside him, petting Hack on the head and smiling.

Anna returned with the tea and a weak smile. "Okay, let's hear what's going on. And I already know it's not good."

Harry got to the point. Mainly because there was no time to waste. His emotions were creeping in, and he knew he was going to have a tough time leaving the house without the two people he cared so much about. "Max and I met with the general today. It was a fast meeting. We were approved to reenter the military and were assigned a mission today. It sounds exciting to us, but dangerous. I know you don't want to hear that, but I have to be honest with you. It will be very precarious, but I feel we can accomplish the goal and get things done without getting hurt. I cannot promise that, but after hearing what we are doing and studying the charts, I think I'll make it back home safe and sound."

"Where are you going?"

"I cannot say right now. And we will be off limits while I am on the mission. You can understand why."

Anna sat back and leaned her head against the sofa. "Harry, we just found each other. It feels like we have reentered the place where we left each other cold."

"But this time you will have my dog with you."

She looked up and grinned. "Oh, so that's why Hack is here. You're leaving him with us."

Zach jumped up and down. "I'm going to keep your dog? Hurray! I'm so excited. Mom, did you hear that?"

Anna laughed for the first time since he came into the house. "I heard it. Harry, of course you can leave Hack with me. I would love to have him. He's no trouble at all. Zach will sleep with him and feed him, won't you, Zach?"

"Sure, I'll take care of him. I love this dog."

"In fact, why don't you take Hack outside while your dad and I talk?"

Zach frowned, shrugged his shoulders, and walked out of the room, dragging Hack's leash behind him.

Anna waited until Zach was outside before she spoke. She moved up closer to Harry and kissed his cheek. "How do I handle you being gone? Can you tell me that?"

Harry winced. "I need you strong this time, Anna. With me on this. I know it sucks and I'm trying hard to control my emotions, especially since Zach is in the picture. It would be difficult enough leaving you. But now I have to leave Zach, too. All I can say is that I will be back. I don't have any way of knowing how long this will take."

Anna shrugged. "I don't mean to make it harder on you, sweet-heart. We have moved so quickly in this and I still am not sure where we are. Do you know?"

He leaned in and kissed her. "I would have loved to have been able to get to know all of you again. To spend more time with you before I had to leave. I was so happy when I found you on Facebook. Damn. I never thought I'd thank social media for putting my life back together!"

She laughed out loud and shook her head. "I don't go on there much these days. It's a wonder you even found me."

"You're much prettier in person, I might add."

She raised an eyebrow. "That's a line."

"Yes it is. But it happens to be true. Come here to me." Harry stood up and held her in his arms. He could feel her crying softly. He rocked back and forth, trying to soothe the both of them. But nothing would quiet the feelings that were sitting in the bottom of his stomach. The sick feeling that maybe they weren't meant to be happy together.

His obsession with the military was overtaking the love he felt. It shocked him to see it so clearly. He loved her and he was excited about his new love for Zach. How was he supposed to juggle the two things he wanted to do in life? How could he leave her after ten years of being apart? It was hell to have to make that decision and not make her feel like she was second choice.

"Anna, listen to me. I don't have all the answers in this. I am as confused as you and hating myself for wanting to go to battle when I have found the love of my life again. Do you know how much I thought of you during my recovery?"

She remained quiet but blew her nose a few times.

"Here. Look in my wallet." He pulled out the photo of her that had bent corners.

"This is what I looked at for years. It kept me going. I guess I didn't tell you that the other night."

"Oh, Harry. I had no idea you had that photo with you. How old is that photo, anyway?"

"Pretty old. You were very young in this picture. But it kept me hoping. Fighting to stay alive. And later, fighting to recover from all my wounds."

"That is the most romantic thing I've ever heard." She kissed him softly and hugged him. "I'll be brave while you're away. Zach and I will keep each other strong. We have Hack. He will remind us daily that you are fighting for America and coming back to us. You're a hero, Harry. An American hero."

"Hell, I'm an idiot for leaving you. I'm no hero, Anna. From the look of things I am a guy who just can't let go of the military, even when it would be better for me to stay home. You are everything any guy would want in a wife. I don't have anything to give you to remember me by." He paused as he remembered something. "Wait a minute."

He reached into his pocket and pulled out a cross that his grandfather had given to him as a child. He had kept it with him in Afghanistan and into recovery. He hated to part with it, but he loved her more. So he handed it to her. "I want you to take this cross and put it in your purse so that you can have something of mine to remember me by. This is tough, Anna. But we can make it through this if we stick together. You want to order something in, because I'm going to have to make this an early night. The house needs shutting down. I'll leave you this key so that you can check on it from time to time. Like I said, I may be home quicker than we think."

Anna took the cross, kissed it, and put it in her wallet. He could tell she was upset, but she was trying to be strong. She called Mac's Barbeque and ordered dinner, and they sat outside waiting on the delivery boy to come with their meal.

Soon the doorbell rang and Hack ran inside barking wildly. Harry paid the young man at the door and took the food to the backyard. Anna had already gotten the tea, the forks, and plates and they sat outside on the picnic table with a gentle breeze blowing.

"Dad, why do you have to go back to war? I thought you were done." Zach laid his head on Harry's shoulder.

"I have to do my job as a Marine, Zach. One day you will understand."

"I don't want to understand, Dad. I just want you home."

Anna raised her eyebrows and winked at Harry. She knew that was a hard hit.

Harry kissed the top of his head and put his strong arm around the boy's shoulders.

"I'm counting on you to hold the fort down until I get back. We're men, Zach. We have to protect our country and our loved ones. One day you'll be a Marine and you will feel the same way I do."

Tears streamed down Zach's face as he turned to face his father. "I just don't want you to die for America, Dad. I want you to come home to me."

CHAPTER TWENTY

S itting outside his parents' house, the house he grew up in, Harry sat staring at the front door. He was remembering all the summer days he had spent on that porch with his brother, David, especially when a rain was coming up and the trees were blowing hard. He loved that smell of summer rain. He also loved the baseball games they played in their backyard with all the kids on the street. The house looked suddenly small.

He knew this talk wasn't going to go well with his mother. She nearly didn't make it when he came home from Afghanistan with a leg missing. It would make no sense to her that he wanted to go back into war. It might not make sense to anyone but him and Max. Maybe you had to be there and experience what they saw, what they did, and what they felt, to really get it. A Marine is a Marine to the bone. They pretty much rip out any human qualities you have running through your veins. You think like a very highly focused predator. Like a lion. And that doesn't go away easily just because you are out of the service, and not just with Marines. All soldiers have to be this way or they wouldn't be able to carry out orders which normally would seem inhuman but are required in times of war.

Things weren't going to get any better the longer he sat in the car, so he got out slowly and walked to the front door. They were not expecting a visit from him. He used his key and opened the door, looking right into the living room where they both were watching television. His father looked up and smiled. But his eyes told Harry that he knew what the visit was about.

"Hey, guys. Hope I'm not interrupting your evening by popping in like this."

His mother got up and hugged him. "Heavens no, Harry. Always love for you to come over. What do we owe this surprise visit to?"

Harry sat down between them and let out a big sigh. There was just no easy way to say it.

"Mother, I've already spoken with Dad about this. But I wanted to be the one to tell you to your face about a decision I've made."

His mother sat down but the look on her face was somber. Harry saw a little fear dancing across her face.

"Of course, Son. What's on your mind?" Joseph spoke up gently.

"Dad is aware that I have spoken with General Murdock and I will be leaving in the morning early for my first mission. My friend Max McIntyre is also going. We trained under Murdock, if you will remember."

Martha Downs sucked in a breath and walked over to the window facing the backyard. "So you just couldn't be happy in the civilian life, making your beautiful farm your home."

"I love the farm, Mother. It's not that. I just feel like I'm not through serving my country. I still have a lot in me that I need to use in the military. Max feels the same way. We both have been training for the last two years of our lives to prepare us for the possibility that we might get back into counterintel again. We are two of the best snipers in the Marines right now, and Murdock seems to think we are the best for this job. So we are going."

Martha began to sob and Joseph walked over to her and put his arm around her. "Now, Martha. He's a man. He has to make up his own mind about his life."

She turned to face Joseph with anger written in bold letters on her face. "Don't you think I realize that? I gave birth to him. I know he's a fighter. He doesn't quit. I just thought with the last injury, he might be able to put himself into something else that wouldn't take his life. He came so close to dying."

Harry walked over to her and hugged her. "I don't have a death wish, Mom. This is just what I do."

The three of them walked over to the sofa and sat down again. Harry grabbed a Kleenex out of the box sitting on the end table and handed it to his mother.

"I have some other news that you might find a little more palatable."

Joseph glanced up and grinned halfway. "I think this would be a perfect time to insert some good news, Son."

"I know you both remember Anna Shaw. I used to date her years ago. In fact we spoke of getting married and then I enlisted."

Martha gave a weak grin. "Yes, I remember that pretty girl. I was angry at you for losing her."

"Well, we have found each other again. It's hard for even me to believe, but I located her on Facebook and we have been seeing each other."

"Harry, that's wonderful! What delightful news," Martha said.

"Well, there's more to the story. We have had an interesting time getting to know each other again. Quite a few years to catch up on our lives. But I have something grand to share. I know you're not going to be ready for this, but it has changed my whole life and I know it is going to change yours."

"And?" Joseph grabbed Harry's arm.

"Anna has a son named Zach. He is ten years old. And the last time I saw Anna was ten years ago."

Joseph's eyebrows went up.

"Zach is my son, Mother. I have a son ten years old."

Joseph and Martha both cried out at the same time. "No! This can't be true!"

"Yes it is. And he is the bravest little guy I've ever met."

"Anna told her son that you are his father? After all these years?"

"She did. It took some time and neither of us was sure how he would handle the news. But just like a trooper, he was so brave. It actually made things better for him. He thought his father was dead. To know now that I am alive and love him, well, that just makes his whole life better."

Joseph stood up and raised his hands up in despair. "And you can walk out on them now, after all these years of being without them? How in the world could anyone in their right mind do that?"

Harry stood up and rubbed his head. "Dad, I didn't say this was an easy thing to do. I had already contacted Murdock before I found this news out. I had already made up my mind to go."

"How did Anna take this wonderful news that you threw at her?" Martha's anger was returning.

"She was upset, of course. But I am leaving Hack with her and Zach to take care of. Zach is excited about having a dog with him. Especially my dog."

"Oh, Harry, how could you do such a thing? How could you leave Anna after being without her for ten years?" She was tearing up again.

"I hate leaving them, Mother. I already love Zach, and Anna and I have reconnected, almost as though no time has passed. It is the greatest thing in the world for both of us."

Both parents shook their head. Joseph spoke up first.

"I'll never totally understand you, Harry. Right when I think I have it down, you surprise me. But this is your life, your decision. We have always supported you in everything you do. I would say this is pushing the envelope some, but you know we are here for you. Do you know how long you'll be gone?"

"I have no idea. But I will be amongst the best of the best, so it should ease your mind a little to know that. I am trained for this and I love doing it. You have to trust me, Dad. I'll come back home. I have to. I have a son now. And a girl I want to marry."

"We want that for you, Son. I just wish you were happy working here and having a family. At some point you will have to settle down. The military cannot be your whole life. Surely."

Harry paused. He would not make any promises to them that he could not keep. So he didn't respond to his father. He hugged both of them and tried to make the goodbyes short.

"I'll keep in touch when I can. I'll send you Anna's cell phone number in case you want to meet your grandson. I would love to see that meeting. You'll fall in love with him. And Anna would be delighted to see you again."

Harry walked to the door and opened it. "I love you. Pray for us as we leave in the early morning. It is a dangerous place we are headed. But all of us are highly trained. Trust me this time. I'll come back home soon. Love my son while I am away. And please call David and let him know."

He turned and walked out of the house and closed the door. He knew they would be upset and he just couldn't take the tears right now. He had to harden himself to prepare for the dangerous situation he was about to enter into. His emotions needed to be compartmentalized so that he would make quick decisions and have perfect reflexes. A clear mind was critical to remaining alive.

CHAPTER TWENTY-ONE

Harry sat up in bed, propped up by pillows against the headboard, in a dark room with only the light of his cell phone. He hesitated for a nanosecond and then dialed Anna's number. It was really too late to be calling her but he was betting tonight would be different. Anyway, he hoped she was as miserable as he was, sitting up in her bed thinking of him. It rang and rang, and just about the time he was going to disconnect, her sweet sleepy voice answered.

"Hello. Harry?"

"I'm so sorry. It sounds like you were asleep."

She sighed. "I was, barely. Zach is in his bed with Hack. They rhyme, you know."

He laughed. But the seriousness of tomorrow was coloring his tone. "I just wanted to talk to you before I went to sleep. Morning is going to come very quickly and I will be gone. I'm not sure when I would be able to contact you again."

"I'm trying hard not to think about it."

"Anna, I have to thank you for telling me about Zach. That had to be a tough thing to do after ten years of hiding it."

"I had gotten used to the fact that you were gone. Dead. So it got easier as time went by, until Zach started asking questions. Then it brought the pain all back again."

"I take all that seriously. I want you to know that. I had no life until you waltzed back in. And to know I have a son, well, there are no words."

He could feel her smiling. "I was so glad for Zach that he got a chance to meet you before you leave. It was the right thing to do, and he seems perfectly fine with this new revelation."

"I sure want him to be good with it. Not easy for a young boy. I was scared at first that he might just reject me. But he didn't. Not even for a second. He had plenty of questions, but I was expecting that."

"He has not brought up anything to me since you left. He had a smile on his face all night."

"Seriously, Anna. I will be thinking of you both the whole time. It will be what brings me home."

"I am counting on that, Harry. We just found each other again. I want the chance to get to know you more."

"I will give you that chance soon."

"Harry, I hate you going. Now, of all times. Crap. It's just crap."

"You are adorable when you get angry. But I hate the timing of all of this, too. I wasted too many nights staring at your photo on Facebook when I should have picked up the phone and called you, Anna. I was scared."

"Scared? Of what?"

"Scared of you not forgiving me. For us losing each other so long ago. Maybe it was too late. So many maybes. But most of all I was afraid you would not be able to handle my leg. Or the lack of my leg."

"I don't even think about it, Harry. I would not have noticed except for the fact that your pants leg was up a little and I saw the metal. I mainly was worried about the adjustment you had to make. I wish I could have been there for you during your recovery."

"I had you in my wallet. I took that photo out so many times that the edges are frayed."

"That makes me sad and proud at the same time."

"I loved you so much, Anna. Ten years had gone by and we'd both been on our own journeys. Sometimes that type of space between two people is too much."

"I agree. But I never thought I would see you again."

"Well, this surprised us both, then. Do you regret anything about my calling you?"

"Only that you didn't make that frigging call sooner."

He laughed. Oh, how it felt good to laugh. "I have you in my sight now."

"Harry, I will be waiting to hear some kind of word from you. I will text you, but I won't know if you got the text or not."

"If I have a signal, I'll text you back. But there will be times when I'll be completely off the radar. And you will have to just trust me during those times."

"I understand, but I won't like it one bit."

"Sweet Anna. Let's agree to stay close. Tell Zach I love him. I better get some serious sleep because we are heading out around 4.00. You will hear from me as soon as possible."

"Bye, Harry. I'll take care of Hack for you."

"Actually, I left him there to take care of you."

The line went dead. He felt so cut off. But not near as cut off as he would feel when that C-130 left the ground.

CHAPTER TWENTY-TWO

In the belly of Iraq there were tunnels that branched out like tree branches, hiding things from the world above. There was a layer of thick fog as a plane landed on the outskirts of the city of Mosul, and behind the curtain of clouds a team of men, unseen by the human eyes that were watching, departed the plane and headed for a Blackhawk Special Ops that was waiting in the dark. The stealth drones were overhead, hidden somewhere above the clouds, with only a corner of the moon showing any life at all on the ground.

It was the middle of the night when most people were sleeping, but these men seemed to live without sleep. For they were called to a mission and that was their food and drink for the next days ahead. They were so highly trained that they moved as one. Their skills were off the chart, and each one had a specific purpose that if uncompleted could cause loss of life and a failed mission. But that pressure was nothing to the Navy Seal team or the two Marine Counterintel men who climbed into the Blackhawk. They had been pressured so much in their time of serving in the military that they hardly felt the weight of what they were walking into.

The amount of military power behind this mission was mind boggling. Most of it was hidden, waiting, like a great white shark lying at the bottom of a deep ocean. ISIS had stretched its claws out too far, taking too many cities, with total disregard for human life. It was past time for someone, some country, America, to take back the security of the United States and Europe, and for the moment, restore some semblance of order to the Middle East.

Harry and Max were at the forefront of this mission. Even with their handicaps, they were the two most valuable players in this venture. Their sniper abilities were laser sharp. They never missed their target, no matter how far away they were. No matter how deep the enemy hid, these two men would find them and take them out. That was exactly what had to happen on this mission. Mustard gas was being used and spread all over Iraq in the tunnels below the ground. In spite of the concrete buildings and streets, tunneling was the road system ISIS was using to move the gas to other locations. They were good at what they did. But they were not as well-armed as the military force that was about to retaliate.

The Blackhawk landed outside of Mosul, and all the men departed the chopper, whispering their directions and talking to their command. Because things were changing constantly, the communications officer, James Pelham, had to be relaying location information as it came in. Harry and Max were seeking out the bunker where the chemists had been seen. An informant had given info to two of the American soldiers who were fighting at the front with the Iraqi troops. The information was only good for a short time, as the chemists and the gas were on the move.

Harry was hoping to find some of the chemists at a bunker warehouse on a side street in town. As they walked towards their destination, they stayed hidden against the buildings and crept in the darker areas on side streets so that they would remain unseen. It was critical to their mission to hold the element of surprise. As with all missions, once you were seen, you no longer had the upper hand. Information spread quickly in war now because of drones and high-tech forms of spying, so it was a slim chance that they would even find the chemists at the bunker they were heading towards. They only hoped to move faster than the words that were being whispered throughout Mosul.

There was sand blowing, and buildings that were partially destroyed lined the streets. In the near distance the men could hear the sound of gunfire. It seemed to be getting closer. After checking the map, they reached the side street that would take them to the bunker. The SEALs moved slowly towards the building and saw a tunnel opening on the side of the road. They nodded to each other without speaking and crept towards the door of the bunker.

Harry and Max were behind the team, watching closely, with rifles ready to shoot. The team leader, Fletch, motioned for Harry and Max to circle around the back side of the building, which was totally in the dark. They spotted a small door on the back of the building. Scanning the area, Harry spotted a concrete wall that had been partially knocked down. He motioned to Max and they jumped behind the wall and they set the guns up on top of the wall, aiming them at the door.

The SEAL team took the building, opened the door, and rushed in with guns loaded. At the same time, Harry and Max spotted two men sneaking out of the building in the darkness. They both took a shot, taking down both chemists. The SEAL team ran out the back door and saw the two men lying on the ground.

"I thought we'd find more here. I think they were tipped off and left. What did you find in the bunker?" Harry asked Fletch.

"Nothing but a couple of computers and a few maps. You might want to take those, Harry. We could get some pertinent info if we studied those maps. These tunnels are everywhere in the city."

Harry and Max hit the bunker and grabbed the computers and maps. "We need to find out where they've moved the gas. There's no telling where they are. What info are the drones giving us?"

"Not much at this point. What we need from them is information about the location of the chemists, and Harry, you need to find out where they have moved the mustard or VX gas, before they release more of it on the people."

It was disappointing to take the bunker and find basically nothing except two chemists who were taken down immediately. What they were hoping for was to find the mustard gas that ISIS was using on not only the military but the women and children. It had to be stopped and Harry and Max were determined to locate the right tunnels that led to the warehouses that held the gas.

The team moved to an empty building and Harry and Max took over a room to set up the computers they would use to find valuable information on the hard drive. Officer Pelham was in contact with the drones and General Murdock, feeding the team any information that was pertinent. The tunnels were so numerous that it was going to take a while to locate the ones the chemists used to move the gas. The sun was coming up over the horizon in Mosul so the men had to stay hidden at all costs.

Occasional explosions rocked the building that was their hiding place, but the men were determined. The whole environment was unstable and Harry knew that at any moment the building they were in could explode, coming down on top of all of them. He and Max worked quickly to check the computers, moving from one file to another, reading the code, hacking into places no one was supposed to be able to go.

This was going to take a while, but running in the back of Harry's mind was the girl he left behind. He didn't dwell on it, but her face would come up from time to time. And the face of his son. He knew he did the right thing by coming to Mosul. He knew without a doubt they would find the gas. But he paid a high price for the trip. The day would come, in a month, six months, or even a year, when he would hold his son again. But for now, he had to set it all aside and focus on the job at hand. Murdock was counting on him and Max to pull this off. So if they had to lose sleep and skip meals, they were going to get the job done.

CHAPTER TWENTY-THREE

I n offices back in the States, men were at their computers seeking intel given to them by researching drone data. They spent
hours checking out motion imagery and chats going on between
pilots. The hacking was incredibly difficult and the men were working overtime to find the gas and the warehouses. Harry and Max
were in contact with these airmen who were working the ground
intelligence systems. But with all the information flying around,
it was still difficult to nail the storage locations down. Hours were
spent with nothing turning up, except some conversation between
people involved in radical terrorism. Deciphering their language
and understanding the code took time and great effort. Nothing
was simple anymore.

The military had made great strides in their counterintelligence
working with the drones. But nothing was error free. The drones
could see in the dark but they could not see inside the tunnels. So
Harry and Max had their work cut out for them. They spent hours
bent over the computers and encrypted phones but they had to
quit when it got dark because they had to remain hidden. Dealing

with ISIS was an ominous task—the terrorist group had spread into eighteen countries after America had pulled its troops out. To have military presence again was going to need to be in a major way. No tiptoeing around.

Harry knew what had to be done, but to accomplish his task would take some time. And maybe he didn't have that kind of time. The forces of ISIS were being held back by the Iraqi troops, with U.S. forces backing them up. The U.S. had the power to blow them off the map. But the job of these two men was only to find the gas and the chemists who were making it. The storage of the gas had to be in a warehouse not too far from where they were. The chemists didn't have that much notice that a chopper was landing or that they had been discovered. So they couldn't be that far away.

Sleep came with difficulty as Harry and Max settled down in sleeping bags on a hard floor, listening to the lulling sounds of battle somehow muted by the thick fog that had settled in around them. Lying on the floor beside the two warriors were the prosthetics that they had taken off to give their limbs a rest. Harry blew out a sigh of relief as he laid his head on the makeshift pillow.

"You disappointed?" Max said in a low voice.

"What do you think?"

"I think it sucks that we only got two men."

"That. But also we are left here to figure this mess out."

"What?"

"The SEALs left. They were called out on another mission."

"Seriously."

"I wouldn't joke about that. Looks like we're going to be around for a while, Buddy."

"I figured, when you took your leg off."

Harry smiled. "I couldn't have left that on one more second. We've been on our feet for a long time today, pushing it."

"It felt kinda good, though."

"It's what we asked for."

"What is our next move?" Max yawned.

"Murdock wants us to find the other warehouse. That has to be destroyed and so do the other chemists if we can locate them."

"It is what we do."

"Yep."

"We better get to sleep, Harry. Tomorrow could be worse as far as the fighting goes."

"'Zactly. Keep one eye open. We aren't safe in here."

"Harry, you know it's going to get bad around here."

"I am aware of that."

"I realize we bought this. What do you think?"

"I think I'm gonna have your back no matter what, Max."

Silence. "We were trained for the worst and we've pretty much experienced it."

"It always can get worse. There is no boundary on worse." Harry shook his head in the darkness.

"True."

"Sleep, Max. If I have to carry you home, we will make it back to the extraction site."

"Or I'll be carrying you on my one good leg and arm."

"We are sounding like girls."

"I think we can find these suckers and take them out. I'm prepared to do whatever it takes."

"Ditto. Good night, Max."

Harry lay there with his eyes open staring into pitch black, listening to the random incoming fire and explosions. They sounded closer in the dark. But somehow he wasn't afraid. He almost felt like an animal that was trained to protect. Like Hack. He wished now that he could have had Hack with him. But instead, lying on the floor in sleeping bags were the two best snipers in the military. And he was one of them. He smiled. No one saw it, but it helped to strengthen his insides for what was to come. Maybe not tomorrow but soon.

CHAPTER TWENTY-FOUR

Fall was in the air. The beginnings of that crispness, that smell in the air that no human being could recreate. Anna woke, immediately thinking about Harry. It was going to be difficult to keep her mind on other things. She lay there watching the curtains moving to the cool breeze and pulled the blanket over her shoulders. It felt good for a moment to just let her mind go.

It was nice to have a day off. Zach and his favorite dog were still asleep upstairs, so she had these few moments of quiet to just think about her life, Harry, and everything that had transpired in the last few days. She could write a book about her life, and no one would believe it. The greatest love story ever told. Very cliché. She really wasn't dead sure that they would marry, she and Harry. But she sure liked the sound of it. They had just started reconnecting, but things had moved pretty quickly between them. She had almost forgotten the ten years that were lived without him in her mind. Her life.

And Zach had handled things like a pro. She was so surprised at how easily he accepted Harry as his father. She knew he had yearned for that day for all of his young life. But still, it was even difficult for her to process. His mind just accepted what was in front of him. Maybe it was his youth. The young are so free thinking; they believe what they see. Adults have to have proof, and even then, they falter.

She didn't like to picture Harry in battle. She had not known all that he had suffered and had not walked with him in his recovery. It was impossible to know the magnitude of his efforts and how powerful his mind was to have overcome such injury. He set his sail and he adjusted it to the direction the wind blew. She had read that somewhere and now she knew someone who had actually lived it.

Just as she was about to raise her head off the pillow, the phone rang. Her stomach went up in her throat, fearing bad news. "Hello?"

"Anna? Is this Anna Shaw?"

A female voice she didn't recognize. Or the phone number.

"Yes, it is. Who is this?"

"This is Harry's mother. Martha Downs. Do you remember me, Anna?"

Anna sat up with her mouth open, but no words would come out.

"Um . . . of course I remember you, Mrs. Downs. Is everything all right? What a surprise to hear from you."

"I hope I didn't wake you on this lovely Saturday morning. I wanted to call you before you made plans for the evening."

"I was just lying here enjoying some quiet time before Zach woke."

"I will get to the point. We have spoken to Harry, or did before he left. He told us all about you and Zach. We would love to meet Zach and see you again. It has been a very long time."

"Yes, it has. What were you thinking, Mrs. Downs?"

"Please call me 'Martha.' I wanted you and Zach to come over tonight for a casual dinner. I hope he likes hamburgers. We could cook out since the weather is still warm enough. And please bring Hack. Joseph has taken a liking to that dog."

"What time would you like us to come over?"

"We would like to eat around 6:00. But please come a little before that, so we can visit. I have so much to talk to you about, and I want to hear all about you and your son."

"That is so kind of you, Martha. We would love to see you. We will see you at 5:30, if that's okay with you."

"That will be perfect! I can't wait to see you both."

Anna lay back on the pillow and brushed the hair off her face. What a surprise that was! So they wanted to meet Zach. She wondered how they took that news about her being pregnant and not telling Harry. This would be an interesting night, but inside she was elated about Zach having grandparents. The more family the better at this point. They had pretty much been on their own for so long that she was starving for family. Her parents had not taken the news of her pregnancy well and had ignored them for years. Maybe now, with Harry back in the picture, they would come around. They had missed all of Zach's early years, but it was never too late to catch up.

She got up and went into the bathroom to wash her face and brush her teeth. She quickly threw some old comfortable clothes on—her "grays," as she called them, gray jogging pants and a black t-shirt. That was her uniform when she wasn't at work. She walked into the kitchen and made coffee and yelled up the stairs for Zach to come down. She could hear the dog barking and growling, so she knew they were playing in his room. Zach slid down the railing and Hack came bouncing down the stairs. They both ended up at the bottom at the same time, with Hack nipping at Zach's heels.

"Let's get breakfast, Zach. I bet Hack is hungry."

"He didn't sleep that well last night, Mom."

"Why do you say that?"

"He sat on the edge of the bed as though he was waiting for Dad."

She was taken aback for a moment at the word "Dad."

"Well, we all would like to see him come through that door."

"I know I sure would."

"Maybe it won't be too long. Now eat your cereal, and I'll fix Hack some food."

"Who were you talking to on the phone?"

Anna knew he was hoping it was Harry. "Well, I was going to talk to you about that after breakfast, but I suppose now is as good a time as any. That was your father's parents. Actually, your grandparents."

"Grandparents? Where have they been all this time?"

"No one knew about you, Zach. I hadn't told your father because I thought he was gone, so I had no reason to tell anyone."

"Oh."

"Joseph and Martha would like us to come for dinner tonight. With Hack, of course."

"Okay, cool."

"That's all?"

"What?"

"So you're okay with going to see them? I thought you might be uncomfortable."

"Mom, they're Dad's parents. Besides, we need some family. It's kinda boring with you and me all the time."

Anna raised her eyebrows. "Oh, really?"

"Well, my friends all have big families. It sorta feels weird that it's just you and me."

Anna shook her head. "I can see why you would feel that way. So, dinner is at 6:00 but we'll go a little earlier to visit. They are going to have a million questions."

"Mom, you have all the answers inside your head, so that's no problem."

She laughed. "You are right again, Einstein."

Anna poured Zach some cereal and juice and Hack already had eaten his bowl of hard food. He seemed to fit right in with Zach. She almost felt like she was in a parallel universe. Nothing seemed real, since Harry left. She just hoped she could hold things together until he got back home. She wanted a real life. Real time with him doing everyday things. Right now she just had to get through today. And with the evening looming over her with Harry's parents and the twenty questions they would have about her life and about Zach, that was going to be quite a task.

CHAPTER TWENTY-FIVE

S tanding at the front door of this older home in Memphis that was surrounded by huge oak trees and with one side of the house covered in green ivy, Anna felt very small. Zach was next to her, holding the leash of a giant German shepherd, fidgeting because he was excited to meet Harry's parents. His grandparents. In a way she almost felt like Cinderella, because of her past; the pregnancy out of wedlock, and her choice to remain silent. But inside, she was remembering that last moments with Harry and his lovely voice and strength. So she stood tall and rang the doorbell, preparing herself for the questions that they had a right to ask.

It took a moment and then the large mahogany doors opened and Joseph stood there with his arms reaching out to them. Anna walked up to him and hugged him, and he knelt down and spoke to Zach and his now-favorite dog, Hack. His gesture was disarming and she felt herself relax a tiny bit. He seemed genuinely glad to see them.

"You must be Anna, and this is Zach, whom we have heard so much about!"

"Hello, Mr. Downs. It's wonderful to see you after all these years."

"Please call me 'Joseph,' Anna." His voice was very deep and warm. Not unlike Harry's.

They walked into the foyer and Martha came rushing in, hugging Anna and kneeling down to see Zach.

"Oh, I couldn't wait to see you, Anna. You haven't changed one bit since high school. Please come in and I'll get us some tea. I am so anxious to hear all about your lives and get to know Zach."

"Thank you so much for having us over, Martha. It is very kind of you, and I am so anxious for Zach to meet his grandparents. It's just been the two of us for so long."

They walked into the hearth room, which was connected to the large kitchen. There was a wall of windows that looked out at the backyard, which was covered in all kinds of trees and blooming shrubs. There was a deck built off the back, and French doors looked out over a beautiful fire pit with a grouping of furniture surrounding it. Such a welcoming sight as they sat down on the sofa.

"You have an absolutely lovely home here, Martha. So warm and inviting."

"That was what I was shooting for, Anna. I can't tell you how happy I am to see you again. Now I want to hear all about your life. What in the world have you been doing for the last ten years or so besides raising Zach?"

Anna swallowed some cold iced tea and took a deep breath. "I've been teaching most of that time. I was able to stay home two years with Zach before I went back to work. It felt good to be able to take that amount of time off to spend with him as a baby, before I put him in a day care that the school provided."

"I know that had to be difficult for you as a single mother. Can I ask why you never told Harry about the child?"

"I had not heard from Harry after he left for the military. I thought he was dead. So I basically raised Zach by myself. My parents were angry at the situation, with me not being married. So Zach has had no grandparents in his life at all."

Zach had taken the dog outside and Joseph was throwing a ball for Hack to chase. It was nice to have a quiet few moments with Martha without worrying about Zach overhearing what they were saying.

Martha nodded as though she totally understood. "I am sorry about your parents. I'm sure they'll come around. Things happen in life that we do not expect. Harry was so committed to the military that he failed to communicate much at all with us, either. There were times I thought he was not coming back. I am praying this time won't be an echo of the past."

"I think Harry is aware now of how important communication is. He was shocked to hear about Zach, but I thought it best to let him know before he went out on this mission. It was his right to know as the father, but also, I wanted to give him another reason to come back home."

"That was smart, Anna. He has lived by himself for so long, and has not had to think about anyone else. I can guarantee you that his mind is on what he is doing, but somewhere back there, he is thinking about his son. And you, of course."

"I don't want to ever be a distraction to him, but we do need to establish a solid relationship because of Zach."

Martha nodded and drank some tea. "So Anna, I know it is a bit presumptuous of me to ask this, but after seeing Harry after so long a time, where do you see this relationship going? I mean, do you still feel anything for Harry?"

Anna was surprised at Martha's frankness, but then she remembered. Martha was an attorney.

"Of course, I have feelings for Harry. We were planning on getting married back when we were dating. And when we got together this time, many of those same feelings arose in both us, I think. But it will take time to know if we are right for each other. I don't want us to marry just because of Zach. I want us to know we love each other. We are older now, and things have happened in our lives that have changed us. We aren't the same people we were back then."

"I agree that you shouldn't jump into things. Harry was so blown away to find you in the first place, and then to hear that he had a son with you was almost incomprehensible. But when he shared it with us, I wish you could have seen his face. I haven't seen him that happy in a long time. If ever."

"That's so good to hear. I know how he was with Zach at my house. He was so gentle and kind. He was overjoyed to know Zach was his son. I feared that he would be angry. I saw none of that. He had questions, of course, about why I hadn't tried to find him. But he never sought me out, either. The longer I waited the harder it became to ever think about telling Harry, if he was still alive, that he had a son. Zach is ten years old."

"How did Zach take it?"

"He was amazing. He still is. I am learning from Zach to just accept. He didn't question things at all. He was so happy to find out his dad was alive that it seemed to take care of any questions he might have had. They bonded very quickly. Zach thinks they look alike, and I admit they do favor each other a lot. I am thrilled at how all that went. And look how he loves Hack! They are best buddies."

"Harry wanted to take that dog with him to war. He believes he is a trained military dog."

"I think so, too. But that wasn't meant to be, I guess. We love having him around, and it will be tough when Harry comes home to give the dog back to Harry."

"So, changing the subject, do you love teaching?"

"Yes, it is what I do best. And it gave me summers off with Zach. Our budget is tight, but it was worth the time I had with my son."

"I wish I could have been around to help you, Anna. I could have kept Zach some while you worked. I have my own law practice, so I can make my own hours. Remember that, if you ever need me to watch him. We want to get to know him and I know that takes time."

"He was so excited to meet both of you. To have more family in his life. That's what I am talking about, with Zach. He is amazing for his age. I think he is an old soul."

"Then he is like his father. Harry was an old soul, too. And he still is."

Zach and Joseph and Hack came in the open doors, laughing and brushing leaves off their clothes. Dinner was served and Zach hurriedly took his place near Joseph at the table. It didn't go unnoticed by Anna.

"Anna, you've got quite a boy here. He's full of energy and questions." Joseph smiled and patted Zach's hand.

"I noticed how much fun he was having out there with you. Hack has been such a joy to us and is such a gentle dog for his size."

"Don't be fooled by his gentleness. Behind that sweet spirit is a lion of a dog. I wouldn't want to punch that button for the world. I think this dog would take someone down, or possibly kill them if he had to. He's very strong. And I think he will be very protective of Zach, the way they have bonded."

"It does make me feel very secure at home with Hack around. When he barks, I know it would scare most burglars away. I have to cover my ears."

"He's definitely trained. I would love to see him in action. Harry absolutely loves this dog. How in the world are you going to give him back when Harry comes home?"

Martha interrupted. "Well, maybe she won't have to, Joseph."

Anna raised her eyebrows and they all laughed.

"I just want Harry home. I don't care what we have to give up. And I know you two feel the same way. His obsession with the military is almost scary. He is so trained that I wonder if he's human anymore. But I told him I would support him in whatever he wanted to do. I just hope the trips overseas won't last forever. I want him to get to know Zach and be able to spend time with him. And I wouldn't mind a little of that, myself."

Joseph smiled. "I understand your viewpoint, dear. But we have to realize that the military is all that Harry has had for years. It is what he is, and what he does. A Marine is so highly trained that is sometimes removes some of the human qualities that we all look for in a man. On top of that, Harry is one of the best, if not the best, snipers in the military. If you get that good at something, you're compelled to use your ability as long as you can. At some point, he will lose his edge. I hope he quits before that happens."

Martha signaled to Joseph to back off a little. Anna grinned and finished her hamburger and potatoes. Zach broke the silence. "I think Dad should do what he loves. I miss him, now that I've found him. But I want to be just like him, one day. I wish I could see him shoot. That would be so cool. But I want him home, first."

"You have a wise heart, Zach. I think that would be the highest compliment you could give your father. That you want to be just like him." Martha said with a gentle smile.

"Martha, do we have some of your special ice cream and chocolate chip cookies?"

"Yes, we do, Joe. I'll get them right now. Anna, can you help me clear the table?"

Zach jumped up quickly and grabbed some plates. "I'll do it, Mom. You sit and talk with Grandfather."

Anna reached over and touched Joseph's hand. "I think you've won him over, Joseph. Don't you think?"

Joe kept quiet for a moment, while a single tear found its way down his wrinkled face. He opened his mouth to speak, but nothing came out. He just shook his head and patted Anna's hand. The word "Grandfather" had made ten years vanish in a single second.

CHAPTER TWENTY-SIX

The war in Mosul was escalating. Harry was awakened by the sound of explosions and gunfire. He checked out the surroundings to see if the building they were in was too close to the front lines. He decided at first light they would need to move to another location. When Max woke, they grabbed the computers and all the maps the chemists had left behind and crept outside, staying against the walls of the buildings behind the scruffy shrubs that were a weak but only source of cover. There was a thick fog remaining in the area that helped to disguise them as they looked for another building a few streets down. Harry spotted what appeared to be tunnels beginning at the curbs of the roads as they walked, and he wondered where they led.

Harry looked back at the building they just left and suddenly it exploded, shaking the ground, showering the air with metal, glass, and concrete. "Too close for comfort, Max. Did you see that?"

"No joke. We need to find these dudes and get the heck out of here."

They found an empty building not too far away and opened the door. All but three of the windows were blown out from the explosions that had taken place during the night. The ground shook under their feet as they moved to enter the building and check to see if it was a safe bunker. With guns ready, they went through all the rooms and also checked out the buildings surrounding them before they finally agreed they were safe.

Incoming information from the drones was incredible. Motion imagery and still images were helpful in locating the tunnels. Harry was waiting on any image of men exiting tunnels or warehouses so they would know what direction to move. He set up their computers and laid out the maps that were applicable to their location. He turned on his computer and watched the images coming through, trying to find their location on the maps.

"I think we need to take this into our own hands and explore the buildings on the side streets. At least we can be doing that while we are waiting for any info that comes in from the drones."

"I agree. I'm ready when you are. We can contact air support if we find the warehouse. Let's get moving."

They ate some food and drank enough water so that they wouldn't be dehydrated, also carrying water in their backpacks for later. They decided to leave the computers that belonged to the chemists as they had downloaded most of the pertinent information onto their own computers.

The situation was getting worse by the moment. While moving from one building to another they would feel rocked by the force of explosions so strong that they would have to hunker down to protect themselves. It felt like the fighting was right on top of them. It was critical that they find the gas, as it was being used against the Iraqi troops and any civilians that ISIS came across. Time was of the essence. The fighting was very active with increased presence of U.S. troops. Heavy tanks were on the roads, explosions happening every few minutes, and incoming fire from all angles.

As Harry and Max were moving along the roads, keeping hidden from sight, they heard something overhead and in front of them one of the buildings exploded, sending huge chunks of concrete, glass shards, and metal flying through the air. Harry had managed to move away from the explosion quicker than Max. As Harry turned around, he saw Max on the ground with crumbled concrete and metal on his good leg. Harry ran to help, lifting as much of the metal and concrete away from Max's leg. He was bleeding profusely, so Harry grabbed his back pack and pulled out a packet of Quik Clot, which would stop the bleeding. He wrapped it around Max's leg, trying to ignore his screaming.

He gave him shots of morphine and pulled him away from the building to avoid incoming fire. Harry ducked into a building on a side street, dragging Max as fast as he could. The bleeding had subsided and Max was calming down a little with the help of the pain meds Harry had given him. He tried to stand but Harry could tell that he felt faint.

"Don't stand yet, Max. Give your body time to get over the shock. I can't see what damage was done to your leg yet. We had to stop the bleeding first. Are you okay everywhere else? Are you losing blood anywhere else?"

"No. I think it's just my leg. Why couldn't it have landed on this prosthesis? I would be good to go."

"When does it ever happen like that, Max?"

"I know. I'll be good as new. Just give me a few moments to get over the shock. Can you get water out of my backpack?"

Harry gave him a long drink and walked to the window to see how dangerous things were getting.

"Max, I'm going to set up my computer to see if I'm getting any more information from the drones that are overhead. We are really taking the heat right now. It might be best to wait until dark before we move around again."

"Since I'm hobbling on my one good leg I think that's a brilliant idea. I know I'll be ready to move by then. When you're finished checking the drone information, let's take a good look at my leg. I think it's a puncture wound. But let's make sure so I can be ready to go when you think we're safe."

"It says we are surrounded by fire, but the side roads seem to be clearer. I still don't see any images that would help us know the location of the warehouses where they are making the gas."

"They are out there somewhere. We need to take them out and also find the chemists, or ISIS will destroy everyone in their path."

"Rest for now. I'm going to sit here and watch the computer images to gather as much info as I can while you rest. As soon as the sun goes down, we're out of here."

Harry checked the wound on Max's leg, which seemed to have clotted well. He was hoping that Max would still be able to walk without starting the bleeding again. It was about to get dark, and it would be time to move.

"Max, how do you feel? Is your strength back now that you've had a bite to eat and plenty of water and rest?"

"I'm sore, but I think once I stand up I'll be okay."

Harry helped him up and noticed that he was a little unsteady at first. But after walking around the room for a few moments, he gave the signal that he was okay.

"Let's get out of here. I don't trust this location anymore. The battle is moving our way fast. I think we need to move now before it's on top of us."

Max walked towards the door. "I'm waiting on you."

They headed out of the bunker towards the street, watching for any sign of movement. They walked four blocks without seeing anyone. Harry was staying off the main roads because a young man he spoke to on the street said the chemists were hiding on the back streets. As they approached a row of empty buildings, half of which were nearly destroyed, Harry spotted some men moving along the side of a building. As he and Max approached them he noticed they were about to enter a warehouse a block away.

"I think we may have our men." Harry whispered.

"We're not gonna let these guys get away."

They walked silently towards the building, spotting two men on top of the warehouse with guns. They ducked into a building close by, hiding in the doorway. Harry phoned Air Control to let them know the location of the warehouse. They immediately contacted an F-18 ground support aircraft to take out the building. Harry was told to clear the area and watch for any attempts of the men inside to leave the building. Harry and Max moved back about four blocks and set up their rifles aimed at the building. They could easily take out anyone who tried to leave.

Sitting in silence with serious battle going on around them, Harry and Max waited for the building to be taken out. It wasn't long before the F-18 released an air-to-ground missile and wiped out the building. It took a while for the dust to settle. The noise was deafening. They knew there would be no survivors after that explosion, but what they didn't know was how many people were in the building. They still had no reassurance that the chemists were dead. They could have escaped through one of the tunnels.

"Let's head back to the building and get our computer and all the maps. I think we're done here, Harry."

"You need someone to look at your leg. We don't want infection to set in. It's your good leg, Max. Got to be careful with it."

"It feels kinda numb right now with all the shots you have given me. But I know you're right. Call the Hawk and tell them to come get us. I'm as ready as you are to get outta here."

Smoke was covering the air everywhere they looked. Explosions were going off, tanks were rolling the streets. It was beginning to look like ISIS was losing ground in a big way. The Blackhawk was on its way, and Harry and Max were walking to the extraction point, being careful not to be seen. It wouldn't do to be shot down on the way out of town.

"We got what we came here for. Only we don't know how many more warehouses there are that are full of mustard gas. I wish we could have destroyed it all." Harry held his hand up for Max to punch it.

"I think some of the warehouses were blown up with all these explosions going off. But there's no way to know if all the gas has been destroyed. I wish there was. The drones can still be working for us, even when we go back home. If we have to come back, we will."

"You're in no shape to return real soon. That leg will have to heal, Max."

"Hell, I'll be ready if we have to come back. Nothing stops a Marine."

Harry grinned and slapped Max on the back. "You got it, brother.

They continued on to the extraction point, dodging gunfire all around them. Things were definitely coming to a head in this war against ISIS. But Harry knew they were not safe until they were on the Hawk. Even then, the chopper could be shot down, but it was highly unlikely with all the weaponry on board.

Max saw the massive chopper coming and began to lightly jog across the open field in spite of the sharp pain in his leg. Harry was running behind him with his gun loaded. Suddenly the Blackhawk was hit with a surface to air missile and the chopper went down right in front of Harry and Max. The escort chopper was in the distance spraying the area with Hellfire missiles, right over the heads of the men on the ground. This gave Harry and Max time to pull the wounded men together as soon as the chopper barely touched the ground. It took Harry a few minutes to load the four wounded men and the pilot who had somehow made it into the chopper, and it took off as Harry's feet hit the step.

As the Blackhawk lifted into the air, the landscape of Mosul was nothing but smoke and ruined buildings. Harry looked at Max and spoke in a low voice. "It feels good to be out of the hell hole."

"Are we stupid to want to do this, Harry?"

"No, friend. We are Marines."

CHAPTER TWENTY-SEVEN

The ride back to base was a blood rush for Harry, but they were busy helping to take care of the men who were slightly wounded from the crash. Everyone's spirits were high, and Max and Harry found out that the U.S troops were making big headway in the fight against ISIS alongside the Iraqi troops.

It felt good to be a part of a bigger picture, and that is what Harry had wanted all along. Nothing seemed more right than being in uniform and fighting for his country. But his thoughts did drift to Anna and Zach, and he felt an excitement welling up inside for the time when he would see them. He couldn't promise her he wouldn't do it all over again. But at least this time, he came home safe. Not many women could live with that, but he was hoping Anna was one of them.

On the ground, the troops went through debriefing, which could be lengthy if there were complications either emotionally or physically. Harry and Max were familiar with the routine and went through the steps without a glitch. That isn't to say they both didn't have residue floating around in their head about losing limbs and watching their fellow Marines get slaughtered. No one got over that during debriefing. Sometimes, they never got over it. But it was hoped that most soldiers could go back to civilian life and be productive citizens without carrying the battle with them all the time.

Harry was excellent at compartmentalizing. So was Max. But somewhere down in there, it did bother both of them that they had given up limbs. It also gnawed at them that they survived when others did not.

The flight back home to the States was long but quiet. Both men were lost in their own thoughts, tired and ready to take a break from all the bloody fighting. They slept most of the way, talking occasionally about anything that didn't relate to the battle they just left. When they landed, they had another short debriefing with the General and then they were released. It was a good feeling to know it was over, at least for the time being.

Harry walked out of his last debriefing session and saw Max leaning against his car. He waved and ran towards him, feeing elated that it was all over.

"So, Max. Where you headed?"

"I've got some healing to do before I can work this leg. But luckily it wasn't that bad, thanks to you. I thought we did a pretty good job over there."

"I feel good about it. But unfortunately there seems to always be war overseas. I was wondering while sitting in that last debriefing session if we would get another phone call down the road to do this again."

"Would you go if we did?"

"Heck, yes."

"You say that now. But you haven't seen Anna and Zach yet. That looks like a commitment to me, Buddy."

"It may just be that. But we're not going to rush things. And she understands my love for the military. At some point I will be too old. You and I both will. I don't want to look back wishing, Max. However, I also want to be around to see Zach grow up."

"It's a Catch-22, I think."

"Probably. Just keep in touch. I will let you know if I hear anything."

Max pulled away, waving as he turned the corner to head towards home. Harry climbed into his truck and sat there holding his phone. He wanted to call her. He wanted to hear her voice. But instead, he drove home in silence, thinking of all the things he'd seen. He needed time to separate himself from the scars of battle and life-threatening situations so that he could be there one hundred percent for her and for Zach.

It was a bit of a letdown coming back to civilian life. The everyday routine on his farm could not compare to the intensity of battle. It could almost become addictive living at such a high place of danger. He didn't crave the adrenalin rush, but he did crave using his abilities to make a difference. When he was working as a sniper or using his skills in counterintelligence he felt like he was being productive. It was a high; there was no way around it.

In real life, when he came home and saw the horses and the peaceful atmosphere, he had two reactions. One was a sigh of relief and the other was a restlessness that was difficult if not impossible to explain to those around him. Harry was certain he wasn't alone in this adjustment. It just felt good to know that he was able to come back from a life-altering injury and still be considered valuable in the military. He did enjoy working on the computers at Glassco but it wasn't what he wanted to do the rest of his life. He wasn't sure how he would provide for a family if Anna and Zach became a real part of his world. He actually could get disability because of his injury, but he wouldn't ever do that. He was capable of much more. He would like that "more" to be used some way, somehow, in a uniform serving his country.

He parked his truck underneath his favorite tree and walked to the gate, calling the horses. They came running, as they knew the sound of his voice. They all looked healthy and well-fed. He hadn't been gone that long, so things pretty much looked the way they did when he left. He fed them and phoned Sam to let him know that he wouldn't have to tend to the horses for a while. It hit him that the fact that he even thought "a while" to himself meant that he really hoped he would get a call from Murdock soon.

"Glad to hear from you, Harry. I might add that I was a bit concerned about your well-being with you having already sustained a tremendous injury on your last mission."

"We Marines are a pretty rough group. But thanks so much, Sam, for overseeing these guys. They look very healthy and happy."

"You gonna be around for a while or is this something you plan on doing for a few years?"

"I hate to admit it, but I do love being out there where the action is."

"A dangerous way to live, Harry. You have such a great place to call home."

Harry looked around the farm and smiled. "Yes, I'm very grateful. But for some reason, I feel compelled to do something with my abilities. I wish there was another way to use them other than the military."

"I'm sure you'll figure something out. You could go into law enforcement or work for the FBI. Are either of those an option?

"Anything is an option at this point. But I don't want to tie you up talking about what I'm going to do with the rest of my life! Thanks, again for watching the horses. It sure kept my mind free to concentrate of the job at hand."

"You take care, Harry. Glad to have you back home."

Harry walked inside and sat his gear on the floor. The house felt so empty without Hack. He went to his office and dialed Anna's number.

"Harry! You're home!"

"Yep. Just walked through the door. How are my favorite two people doing?"

"Oh my gosh! We're doing great now. I'm so glad you made it home. Are you okay?"

"I'm doing fine. We can talk about it when I see you. How about I come over for dinner?"

"Of course you can. Zach will be so happy you're home."

"Don't tell him. I want to surprise him at the door."

"Okay. Harry, you don't know how much I worried about you."

"I know it can be difficult, Anna. But I'm fine. I think we accomplished most of what we needed to get done. You never get it totally done."

"We'll see you around six, then?"

"Look forward to it, Anna. I've missed you, too."

The truth was, when Harry heard her voice it brought back all the feelings he'd felt before he left. Her voice did that to him. And the joy of seeing his son again was suddenly overwhelming. He unpacked his bags and did laundry, went out and cleaned the stalls in the barn, and took a short ride on Trixie to check the pastures on the east side of the property.

He did have a good life here. He just needed to settle down and figure out what to do with himself. But if he were honest, he knew he would take the call if Murdock needed a sniper. Two worlds colliding. Anna, Zach, and the United States Marine Corps. It was a mystery but he didn't have to solve it now.

He got in the truck and headed towards Anna's house, dialing his parents to let them know he was home. "Dad? Good to hear your voice. I just wanted to let you and Mom know that I made it home safely."

"That's great to hear, Son! I want you to know we really enjoyed seeing Anna again. And meeting your son. What a great kid Zach is. It was a shock for us to hear you had a son, but we are so happy to have him in our family. Did Anna get a chance to tell you they came over for dinner?"

"I haven't seen her yet, Dad. But I'm sure she will tell me all about it. I'm going to let you go, but tell Mom I'll be by tomorrow and we can catch up on everything."

"Okay, Son. Glad you made it home safe. We sure worried about you. I'll tell Martha. She'll be so happy to know you are back."

Harry hung up and sat back in the seat, staring at the front door. A whole other life was waiting for him. He took a deep breath and walked to the front door and rang the doorbell.

CHAPTER TWENTY-EIGHT

Harry could hear Zach running across the wooden floor to answer the door. Hack was barking loudly. When he opened the door, Zach screamed out. "Mom! Dad's home! Dad's home."

Harry bent down and hugged Zach, picking him up and swinging him around. "It's so good to see you, Son. Have you taken good care of Hack while I was gone?"

"I sure have. He's a great dog, Dad. He slept with me every night."

"I bet he did." Harry bent down and wrestled with Hack for a few minutes, letting Hack lick his face.

"I missed you, too, boy."

Anna walked up and waited her turn. Harry grabbed her and hugged her. He had barely set foot in the house, so they moved away from the door and walked into the living room.

"So! How you guys been since I've been gone? Having fun without me?"

Anna laughed. "You don't know how hard it was knowing you were so far away and in danger. We did our best to distract ourselves but you came up in nearly every conversation. Zach couldn't wait for you to get back."

Harry kissed her and they sat down on the sofa. "It's nice to be missed, Anna. I missed you guys, too. I wasn't gone that long this time, but it seemed like forever."

"Where were you, Harry?"

"I was in Iraq. Not sure what else will come up, but at the moment that was the most pressing situation. We took care of things and made it out alive. But it was close. I wouldn't want you to know how close it was."

"Unfortunately, they show too much on television. We saw the tanks, explosions, and ground fire going on. I'm sure it was much worse than they showed us on the screen."

"Yes, because when you're there fighting, you see actual people dying. Women and children suffering from the effects of mustard gas. It is horrific. But we did what we could. I don't think we solved the bigger problem, but so far no one has been able to do that."

She patted his leg. "It feels so good to look at you in person. I thought of you a hundred times."

Zach was sitting right next to him, touching his arm. Harry put his arm around the boy and pulled him close. "I missed you, Zach."

"What's it like, Dad, to be a Marine?"

"It's hard, Zach. Real hard. One of the toughest things a man can do in his life. But it is so worthwhile. I hope you get a chance to do what I do, and even more, if you want to."

"I want to be just like you."

Harry looked at Anna. He could see that she was frowning and she shook her head.

"Well, there are tons of things you can do when you grow up. This is just one option, Zach."

"If it's good enough for you, it's good enough for me, Dad."

Anna broke the conversation and headed them into the kitchen where they ate a light dinner of hamburgers, kettle chips, and pickles. She took a long drink of Sprite and touched Harry's hand. Zach was sitting on the floor playing with Hack, a distance away from the table.

"You have been in another world, Harry. I have no idea what you've seen or heard. Even if you shared it with me, it wouldn't be the same as experiencing it like you have. The same goes for my world. Zach is very easily influenced right now, especially by you. You are his hero right now. Well, actually our hero." She smiled and blushed, but continued.

"He listens to every single word that comes out of your mouth. So be careful what you say. And I promise you, he forgets nothing. That ten-year-old mind is incredible. Not at all like we were as children. He knows so much more. He understands more, but he's still ten years old. I'm not saying he can't be a Marine, but after seeing what you've lived through, that wouldn't be my first choice for him. In saying that, I realize he'll make up his own mind as he gets older. And I will not try to talk him out of it, no matter what he wants to tackle."

Harry wiped the mustard off his mouth and drank some tea, swallowing hard.

"A hamburger never tasted so good, Anna. Gosh, I've missed eating real food."

"Did you hear a word I said?"

"Yes, every single word. I am taking it in as we sit here watching Zach. I'm not used to being around kids, but I have always loved them. You will have to teach me a little, and be patient with me about being the type of dad he needs. Mainly I just want to be there for him. I think that's what he wants right now."

"Exactly. He has told everyone about you, at school and all his friends here in the neighborhood. You will have to come by and play basketball with Zach and his friends so they can meet you. Of course, to Zach you are Superman. Larger than life. And even though that may make you a little uncomfortable, he needs that right now."

"I understand, Anna. I had guys I looked up to as a child. My dad seemed larger than life most of my childhood. So I'm okay with giving him that. It is an honor to give him that for a while."

"Harry, how was it over there? How bad was it?"

"I can only tell you that what I saw was like the worst horror show as far as the chemical weapons. I don't know how anyone will be left alive with all the explosions, although they have probably evacuated most of the area. No one in their right mind would stay there with all that fighting. But many have died. Innocent people have died. That is what I hate about war."

"How did you eat? Sleep?"

"The food is basic MREs. It's fair. It gets the job done. But it doesn't taste anything like real food. It gives us the energy and nutrients without much taste, if that makes sense. As far as sleeping, when you are as tired as we were, sleeping comes without struggle. But I also slept with one eye open because of the high risk of attack. We didn't want anyone to know we were there. We did everything we could to remain invisible."

"Were there just the two of you?"

"I can't tell you that, Anna. I've really told you too much already. But we had the whole military behind us. At our fingertips. Trust me. They know what they're doing."

"I feel so ignorant about all of this. The general public has no idea what's going on."

"It's best they don't. We have to have complete secrecy in what we do, because it is classified. U.S troops were there fighting alongside Iraqi troops and that is all over the news. But what is going on behind the scenes has to remain there."

"I know you are highly trained. I am just learning about what all that entails. How does it feel to be home? Do you know if you're going back out?"

"That's up to the military. I think I want to go back, but not in the same capacity as this last trip. Let's not worry about it until I get that phone call, okay?"

Anna smiled but he could see the worry lines on her face. "Relax, baby. It will be okay. My goal right now is to spend more time with you and Zach. Now let's not talk about me anymore. What have you been doing? Is Zach doing okay in school?"

"My life is pretty much the same thing each day. But Zach has miraculously raised all his grades since you came into his life. I didn't want to tell you that, but since you asked, well, there it is. He really did want to find his Dad. So just these few months have made a huge difference in your son."

Harry squirmed a little and laughed. "I'm still not used to having a son, Anna. You will have to help me with this. What a shock it was when you told me. But I'm so glad you did."

"Time, Harry. It will take some time. I've had ten years with him, and I still get surprises."

"Hey, Zach? You ready for bed? It's nearly bedtime for you and I thought I would go up with you and we could talk, just you and me."

Zach looked at Harry and grinned. "Sure, Dad. What about Hack?"

"He'll be coming home with me tonight. But we'll be seeing a lot of you now that I'm home."

Zach raced upstairs and Harry grabbed the short moment to hug Anna and kiss her. "I have waited a long time to do that. I missed you, Girl. I'll be right down. We boys need to have some 'male bonding.'"

"You go right ahead. I'll clean up the kitchen."

Harry raced up the stairs, making a racket as he hit two steps at a time. Zach was already in bed with the covers pulled up to his neck.

"What you want to talk about, Dad?"

Harry sat down and looked at his son. He was beautiful. He almost got choked up looking into his dark brown eyes.

"I just wanted you to know I thought of you while I was gone. Every single day. I'm so glad I'm home so that we can spend more time together. You, me, and Hack. Would you like that?"

"Sure, Dad. But what about Mom?"

"She'll be there, too. But sometimes I want you to myself. Is that okay?"

"I guess so. What would we do?"

"Horseback riding. Fishing in my lakes. Do you like that?"

He grinned and nodded. But he yawned, too.

"I know you're tired, Zach. Sleep well and I'll pick you up from school tomorrow. We'll go get an ice cream or hamburger. Whatever you want."

"Who can turn down ice cream?"

"No one I want to know." Harry smiled and Zach laughed.

They hit knuckles together and Harry stood up. "I love you, Son. See you tomorrow."

Zach was quiet for a moment. "Love you, too, Dad."

Harry didn't want another sound to erase those words out of the air. So he left the room and went downstairs to see Anna. All they did was stand in the living room, holding each other in silence, moving to a song that only lovers could hear. *For such a tough guy, I'm crumbling way too easily.*

CHAPTER TWENTY-NINE

It was a windy Sunday, and the leaves were beginning to turn. Harry was driving to his brother David's house to visit the family. His mother and father would be there. It wasn't what he wanted to do but needed to do. He hadn't seen his brother in a while—he had only spoken to him on the phone. They needed to reconnect and catch up with each other. Growing up, David was the one with the outgoing personality. For him to have landed in life as a realtor was perfect for his personality. And he had done very well with his career. He owned his own real estate company in Cordova, Tennessee, just on the outskirts of Memphis. His two children were growing like weeds. Jack had the same personality as David and Sara Jane was like Taylor, her mother. It was going to be interesting to see how they turned out as adults.

Pulling into the driveway, he pulled the truck over to the side so he could get out if he decided it was time to leave. Not that he didn't love his family. But family gatherings made him restless for some reason. His father was standing in the doorway watching him get out of the truck with Hack. When he walked up the steps,

Joseph opened the door and gave Harry a bear hug, patting Hack on the head at the same time.

"Gosh, it's good to see you, Son. You look great. I guess you've recovered from your last mission?"

"Yes, Dad. Thanks for asking. It was tough but nothing we couldn't handle."

"And Max? Did you both make it through unscathed this time?"

"Max took a hit when a building exploded near him. He wasn't able to move away fast enough, so the broken pieces of concrete landed on his good leg. But he is recovering as we speak and will be good as new soon."

"I know you boys are a tough breed. I don't understand your desire to put yourself in harm's way, but as long as you come home, that's all we care about. I know the kids are going to want to see you. Let's go inside."

Harry walked inside and both kids ran up to him, hugging him and laughing. They had grown a foot since he'd seen them last.

"Uncle Harry, Dad says you've been in the war again. Did you shoot anybody?"

Harry laughed. "There is a lot of shooting going on in war, Jack. I don't look forward to firing my gun unless it is for protection."

Sara Jane frowned. "I hate guns." She reached over and touched his leg.

"How's your leg, Uncle Harry?"

"It's doing fine. I'm used to it now."

They both ran off, laughing and racing Hack through the house to the backyard.

Harry found David in the backyard cooking chicken on the grill. He looked the same, only he was going to be bald early. His hairline was moving backward in spite of the partial comb over.

"Hey, brother." David slapped Harry on the back.

"Hey, yourself. How are things in the real estate world? Selling tons of houses?"

"The market is great right now with a new president in office. We're hoping for better rates and easier lending from the banks. You look terrific, Harry."

"I feel good. Rested up."

"Any idea what you'll be doing now? Is this a permanent entrance into the military again or do you have something else up your sleeve?"

Martha walked up with Taylor, David's wife, and hugged Harry.

"We don't want to interrupt, but it's so good to see you. It's been a while since you've been to our house, Harry."

Harry smiled at Taylor. "Yes, it has. I've had my hands full, you might say."

"I see you have a dog. David didn't tell me about Hack."

"He's the best thing that's happened to me, Taylor. You can see how the kids love him, and Mom and Dad have practically adopted him. He's such good company to me, and so well trained."

"Did you take him with you on your last trip?"

"No, that wasn't allowed."

"Where did he stay while you were away, Harry?"

David had walked up, and Joseph and Martha were standing there.

"Do you remember Anna, David? A pretty girl I dated in high school and was going to marry before I joined the Marines?"

"I think I do. Brunette. Very nice." Taylor rolled her eyes and laughed.

"Well, we found each other again. That is to say, I found her on Facebook and finally got enough nerve to call her. We 've reconnected in a big way."

"That's wonderful, Harry. I bet you two had so much to talk about after all these years. Was she married? Any children?"

"That's just it. She hadn't married, but she had a son. One son named Zach. He was ten years old. Come to find out, he's my son."

"And you're just finding out about him? What's that all about?" David asked with a frown. He grabbed the chicken off the grill and motioned to Taylor to carry it into the kitchen.

"It's a long story, but we faded away from each other after I went into the Marines. And after a time, she never heard from me and thought I might be dead. She also didn't want to burden me, if I was alive, so she raised Zach alone, by herself, supporting the two of them on a school teacher's salary. You know how tough that had to be."

"Yes, I do, but I cannot believe she didn't try to contact you."

"Take it easy, David. Everything's fine. I've met the boy and he is brilliant. We even favor each other. He wanted to meet his father so much that when Anna brought me to the house, he readily accepted me and we are best buddies now. I think it's all going to work out."

"That sounds all great, but what about you and Anna?"

"Boy, you are really hammering it tonight. Will you cut her some slack, David? She and I are finding our way back to each other. I kept a photo of her in my wallet all these years, always wishing we hadn't broken it off. But things happen, time passes, and sometimes you just don't make the effort to reconnect with someone. It could have been too late. She could have married, and so could I. But we didn't. So we've had a few dates and talked very seriously about all of it. I want to be a big part of Zach's life. I don't know at this point if she and I will marry, but I wouldn't be surprised if that didn't come down the road not too far in our future."

"Wow. You do have it all worked out. Well, we are happy for you, Harry. Never dreamed you would settle down long enough to have a son. We'd love to meet him. You should have brought them with you tonight."

"Wasn't sure how that would go. Mom and Dad have met him. While I was away, they asked Anna and Zach over for dinner."

Harry followed David back outside so they could talk in private. He could hear Taylor and his mother talking ninety miles an hour about the whole situation. "I don't want to be the topic of conversation tonight. It is just good to see all of you and be home again for a while. I'm not sure what is coming next."

"I'm sure you will figure it all out. Nothing is ever easy for you, Harry."

"I'll agree with you there, David.

Dinner at the table was filled with talking and laughing. At least Harry could sit on the sidelines now that his secret was out. He wanted to just soak in the family and watch the kids playing with Hack. With his future up in the air, he didn't know how much time he would have to spend with family, much less Anna and Zach. The chicken and potato salad, green beans, fresh rolls, and brownies and ice cream were perfect for this first fall night together.

Joe walked over and sat down near Harry, putting his arm around his son.

"I really like your girl, Harry. She's all right."

"Thanks, Dad. That means a lot. I really like her. And I'm so happy about finding out about Zach. It freaked me out at first, because she had raised him alone and not told me. But after I spoke with her, I totally understood. She was put in a precarious situation and she made the best of it. She has raised a great kid. He is so courteous and smart. I want to spend more time with him and hopefully be a good influence on him as a male."

"I think that's great. Let me know if I can help any way. Your mother and I fell in love with him at first sight. He is you made over. If you need us to keep him and Hack, let us know. They brought life back into our house, Son."

"I know the feeling, Dad. They do the same for me."

After three hours of family chatter, David walked Harry outside to his truck.

"It almost makes your head hurt, doesn't it, brother?" David laughed as he leaned against the old truck.

"I can only take so much. But it was great seeing your kids again. And Taylor just keeps getting prettier. You must be doing something right"

"I take that as a compliment. You don't give them out too easily, Harry."

"I guess I don't. But now that I have a son, I realize how much work it is raising kids to be responsible."

"That is a challenge that never stops until they leave home."

"I think you're doing a great job."

David paused. "Harry, what you going to do with your life? Are you going to spend the rest of your life in the military, running covert or other very dangerous missions? Will you ever marry? I know you are good at what you do and I get that. I so get that. But don't you ever want to settle down and live a normal life?"

"Normal for you may not be normal for me. I know that sounds cliché but it is true for me. I don't think I could be happy sitting at a desk all day long after the life I have lived. It isn't that I crave dangerous situations. I don't want to die. But I do love using my skills. Intelligence work and sniper skills don't do well in the mainstream corporate world. I'm either staying in as a Marine or going to work with the FBI. One of those things will be my life. That's not to say I won't marry."

"The question is, will Anna be willing to have you part time? Not many women will settle for that life."

"That all remains to be seen. I'm not rushing anything with her. She is a wonderful mother and teacher. She is happy with her life. I sure don't want to come in suddenly and turn her world upside down and then leave and be gone all the time. I'm just not sure how all this will play out, David."

"Well, the bright side is that you have a son. I can't wait to meet him. If he is anything like you, I know I'll like him. You do have a way, Harry, of making me want to be braver. Of stepping out or pushing myself. I think you do that to people because you have pushed yourself so far."

"I'm just trying to survive, Dave. That's all it is. I do have a drive in me to be the best I can be. The problem with that drive is that no one knows where the line is. So I just keep on pushing."

David shook his hand and gave him a hug. "Don't wait so long to come over, Harry. My kids love to see you, and it's good for me, too. I need to see you more often."

"Thanks, David. Means a lot coming from the older brother who used to try to drown me every summer in the neighbor's pool."

"You still hanging onto that story, little brother?"

Harry jumped in the truck and pulled away with Hack in the front seat, waving at his brother. Yes, he did remember only too well how his older brother used to hold him down under the water until he thought he was going to drown. Perhaps that was why he had such a drive to be stronger. Skeletons clanking in closets.

CHAPTER THIRTY

Anna was finished with her day at school and walked to her car exhausted. It felt good to be going home. Zach was already waiting by the car, leaning against it, scrolling his IPad. It was a typical Monday with tons of homework sent home, so his backpack was on the ground.

"You have a good day, Zach?"

"Yeah."

"Looks like you got homework."

"Yeah."

"You want to stop for something to eat? I know you are starving. I always was, after school."

"Yeah."

"Zach! Are you even listening to me? Put that IPad down. Good gosh!"

"Sorry, Mom. I haven't touched it all day. Was just checking out my game from last night."

"I know you're in your own world, Buddy. But step into mine for a moment and let's talk a second."

"What's up?"

"Nothing on my end. I just wanted to know if you were hungry."

"I'm always hungry, Mom."

"Okay, I give. What do you want?"

"Relax, Mom. I can eat something at home. A sandwich or something."

Anna rolled her eyes. "Okay, remember this conversation after you go home and swear there is nothing in that refrigerator to eat."

Zach was already on his IPad, in his own world. Anna drove home thinking about Harry and how fast things were moving. Her life had been calm, although boring, for the last ten years. His coming back into her life had thrown her for a loop. Now she wasn't sure what she wanted or what was best for Zach. She was thrilled that Harry knew about Zach. It was such a huge relief. But where did it go from here?

She pulled into her driveway and there sat Harry's truck. He was leaning against it with his arms folded. If he wasn't so darn good looking, she probably wouldn't have such a dilemma on her hands. Zach ran up to Harry and hugged him and walked inside the house.

"What a nice surprise."

"I was in the neighborhood." He gave her his best Boy Scout smile.

"I see. Well come on in and I'll fix you some coffee."

"I was hoping for a kiss."

"Oh you were, were you?"

"Yep. A single kiss. How was your day?"

"It was busy and full of kids yelling and griping about their homework. They all hate homework."

"So don't give it to them. Teach during the day, give them tests every other day, and see how much they are retaining."

She looked at him with her eyebrows raised. "So when did you get your teacher's certificate?"

He smiled. He knew when to be quiet.

"Seriously, Harry. What are you doing in my neck of the woods this afternoon?"

"I wanted to see you and Zach. You feel like family."

She raised her eyebrows again. He was full of surprises today.

"Okay. I had nothing to do after I fed the horses and put my laundry away. I've worked out and played with Hack. I got bored. Is that a crime?"

She laughed. "No. You just need to be around Zach a little. There is no dull moment."

"That's what I was hoping for. It's hard coming off a mission. I am restless for a long time and don't know what to do with myself. I have avoided a text from Max because I know he is going to want to talk about the next thing."

"Which is?"

"I don't know what it is."

"So you guys are wondering what you're going to do with the rest of your life?"

"That pretty much sums it up."

"Let's go sit in the hearth room. I'm sure Zach will go up to his room for a while. We can talk more about this without ears bending around a corner."

He smiled at her sarcasm. He followed her to the hearth room and took a seat on the sofa next to her. For a while he just sat there looking out the window into her backyard. He also stared at her beautiful face, which became the most important thing for a second. His mind was going in ten directions and he wasn't including her in any of them.

Finally she interrupted what she thought was his train of thought. "You look like your mind is going in ten directions. Harry, where are you?"

He shook his head. "I'm sorry. I got lost for a moment, thinking about you and all my options."

"This is serious, isn't it?"

"It's the rest of my life."

"Do you have to make that decision right now? What's pushing you so hard?"

"Well, we can't say we want back into the military, run one mission, and then duck out of sight. They just don't operate that way. The mission was partially successful, and we did an okay job. But now what? Do we stay in as Marines or do we get out and do something else?"

"What does your gut tell you?"

"I feel like I want to use my skills. That is as far as I can get with it. I haven't talked to Max; he may have some suggestions. I feel like it will have to be with the FBI, but I'm not dead sure. I have allowed that to cross my mind, but I don't know where to go with it."

"You need to relax. Is the general putting pressure on you?"

"I expect a call from him any day asking if we are ready to report back."

"You just got home."

"Yes, and I am perfectly healthy. They will want me to report back for duty. There is something going on all the time that I could be a part of. I'm not the only sniper in town; there are many in the military. But they know I can handle intel as well as being a sniper. Max is the same way, and we work well together."

Anna paused and rubbed her face. "Okay, let's talk about where that leaves me in all of this. And Zach."

Harry blew out a big sigh and leaned his head back on the sofa. "Don't think I haven't already touched on that subject a zillion times since I saw you last."

"Oh, really?"

"Yeah, really. Look, Anna. I hate that everything is happening so fast with the military. I didn't plan it this way. Meeting you again and finding out about Zach has turned my world upside down. I was planning on getting into the military before I made that phone call to you. Now this relationship with you and Zach makes my decisions even more difficult."

"Look, Harry. We were just fine before you came into our lives. I'm not putting any pressure on you with Zach or myself. I want you to feel free to make all your decisions without putting us into the mix. This is your life. We only became a part of it recently. Please don't let us interfere with what you want to do with your life."

"You haven't changed one single bit. But no, this time, sweet girl, I am taking you into account. It does matter to me how you feel about my being in the military. Or the FBI, for that matter. I told you after I met Zach that I wanted to be a part of his life. I also want to be a part of your life. You and I have to figure out what all that means. I want us to have time to do that. I don't have to rush here to make the decision, but we are fast approaching a time when I will have to decide."

Anna stood and walked into the kitchen, stretching and bracing her back. "I've had a long day at school. It probably isn't the greatest time for me to be talking about something as serious as the rest of your life."

Harry walked over to her and held her in his arms. "Anna, listen to me. I'm sorry I showed up this afternoon and dumped all this on you. I haven't given you time to relax and come down after a busy day at work." He pulled her face up to his and kissed her.

"Harry, I—"

"No wait. Just listen. I didn't do you right ten years ago. I am not saying we would have gotten married but that was where we both thought we were headed. I want us to have time to see what we have now. We are older and wiser. I love having you back in my life. I just need to see where I fit into your life and Zach's. I know we have to be careful with him. He is really glad to have me in his life, but I cannot just walk in and out whenever I please. I have to be all in."

Anna put her head on his chest. She could hear his heart beat. "I had become pretty independent while you were away. I had to. I had no one to lean on. My parents didn't like the situation with my being pregnant and all. They were embarrassed. So I am used to being on my own. It is a little bit scary to allow someone else into my world. I almost feel like I am losing control."

"I can see how that would happen. You've done such a great job. It would be an honor for me to be allowed in. But nothing is set in stone yet. Except that I care and really want there to be an 'us.' I will keep you posted on anything that transpires concerning my career. Is that fair? We will talk about all of it, and I won't make a commitment until we have talked it over. No more surprises."

Anna smiled. Damn, he was handsome. She tiptoed and kissed his mouth. "That sounds pretty good to me, Harry Downs. Now you better go so I can tackle some homework with Zach. Let me know when you speak to the general. In the meantime, text me to let me know I'm on your radar."

Harry walked to the stairs and hit them two at a time. He stuck his head into Zach's room and smiled. The boy was sitting on the bed with headphones on, playing a game on his iPad. He walked over and pulled the headset off his head and sat on the bed.

"Hi, Son. I missed you today. Everything going okay at school?"

Zach grinned. "Yeah. It's cool."

"Work hard. You're gonna need it to be a Marine."

"I told you, Dad. I'm gonna be just like you one day."

"Then it starts now, boy. Right now. By doing your best every single day at school, you are preparing your mind to be a Marine."

Zach thought for a moment and shook his head. "I'll try, Dad."

"The difference in a Marine and a regular guy is the Marine never does just enough to get by. Always do more, Zach. Remember that. Always do more than you are asked to do."

Harry walked down the stairs and kissed Anna goodbye.

Anna walked him to the door and watched him get into his truck. For some reason she felt sad. The decision about being in the military was facing them again. Only this time she knew what it was like to be left. Would she ever really have Harry? Or would he always choose the military first over family? She knew that because she wasn't raised with the military, she didn't understand the pull. But she did understand the pull she felt to love him again. And that perhaps scared her more.

CHAPTER THIRTY-ONE

Harry sat in the parking lot at the base in Millington holding his cell phone in his hand. He'd been working all day with Max, sniper training. Working on breathing, checking wind speed, heart rate, and distance. It was nothing new to them, but it was required for all snipers. He pushed himself to the limit, always striving to beat his best.

He knew another mission was headed his way. Their senior commander had hinted as much to the both of them after lunch. He was torn in several directions and he knew Anna was not going to be that happy about his leaving this time. He was sick about the timing of everything, but what was he supposed to do? He still didn't have it figured out.

He dialed her number and waited. She should have been home from school by now.

"Anna, it's me. I'm leaving the base. It's about 5:15 and I'm headed home to take are of Hack. Please call me when you get this message. We need to talk."

Harry drove home thinking about Zach and how Anna was going to handle this next trip. This might be one of the toughest decisions he'd made in his entire life. Leaving the woman he had loved for so long and his newly-found son. Maybe he was being selfish. Maybe he'd been single so long he couldn't manage to think of someone else. Or what would be best for the three of them, instead of just him. But this was his career, just like Anna's teaching. Granted he was in a high-risk position and she was teaching children how to read. But in his defense, he was fighting for his country. Saving lives. Oh, these rabbit trails could go on and on all night, and he wouldn't feel any better about going away than he did at the moment.

Hack was eager to see him after being home all day alone. Harry wrestled with him after taking him out to run while he fed the horses. Once inside, he ate a ton of food and stayed by Harry's side all night.

Harry spent three hours on the computer checking out different areas where ISIS was establishing cells, trying to determine where he would be sent. It really didn't matter. He knew no matter where he went it was going to be dangerous. But it helped him to read as much as he could about current attacks in Afghanistan, Syria, Iraq, and the surrounding areas.

By ten o'clock he was ready to get some shut-eye. He took Hack out one more time, checked the horses, and jumped into bed, puzzled as to why he hadn't heard from Anna. He debated calling her but gave her the benefit of the doubt. Maybe she was snowed under helping Zach with homework. He lay back on his pillow hoping against hope the phone would ring. At 10:30 he sent Anna a text. He stared at the phone, almost willing her to text him back. What was wrong? It wasn't like her to avoid him.

He closed his eyes and thought about their last conversation. He almost fell asleep because his body was worn out. Suddenly the phone rang and he knew it was her.

"Damn. I thought you'd never call me back."

"I'm sorry, Harry. We had a game to go to and then homework. Bath. I had some washing to do, so this is the first time I've sat down and had a moment to call."

"I thought it might be that. I just think we need to have a talk tonight. Are you in the mood? Are you too tired?"

"Let me get some coffee and change into my pajamas. I'll call you back in five minutes."

Harry yawned. "Okay. I'll be waiting."

It took everything he had not to fall asleep in that five minutes that seemed like an hour. He was so tired he could hardly keep his eyes open. But finally she called back. And it was worth the wait.

"Hey, Sweetie. Sorry it took me so long. Are you okay? Did you have a long day at the base?"

Yawn. "Yes. I'm worn out. We practiced all day, sniper training. Not that I'm not used to it, but for some reason I worked harder today and it has kicked my butt."

She laughed lightly. It made him smile. "We had a long day at school, too. Testing the kids. A fire drill. Had to send two boys to the principal's office. I hate having to do that, but we have no form of discipline anymore. It's all I have in order to retain some semblance of order in the classroom."

"I don't know how you do it day after day. You deserve to get paid a lot more than you get, Anna."

"We aren't going to change that tonight. So what's on your mind, Harry?"

"Anna, things are moving quickly again. I can tell that we're going to get pulled out on a mission soon. I just had to talk to you about it."

"We've talked a lot about it, already, Harry. I know you want to do this, and I've told you that I am behind you one hundred percent. But I don't like it. No woman would. I worry about you. I want you here. We've just found each other again, and we need time to see where that's going. You really haven't established a strong relationship with Zach yet. Those are the things that run through my mind."

"Don't think that I haven't thought the same damn things. I don't want to lose you, Anna."

Anna was quiet for a moment. "You there, Anna?"

"I'm here, Harry. I'm here. I just need you to hold me sometimes. Like now. When do you think you will be leaving?"

"Not sure. But soon. I want to see you before I go. I'll know more in a few days, but for now, I'll see you tomorrow. We have to go in and train again, but when I get off, I'm headed your way. I'll pick up Hack and we'll have dinner together, the four of us. I say four, because Hack and our son are inseparable. Even at dinner."

Anne spoke in a quiet tone. "Harry, can you believe we are going through this again? The leaving part? It seems like a dream. I didn't think I would live through the first time you joined the Marines. And when I didn't hear from you, a part of me died inside. I was so in love with you. Ten years I lived alone with Zach, and now you're back in my life again. God only knows, you better come home this time. You better not dare leave me alone to raise our son after having these wonderful moments together."

Harry sighed. He barely had the energy to speak he was so tired. "Anna, Darling. I'll be back if I have to drag myself home. Trust me one more time. I won't let you down. Now let's both get some sleep. We both are tired. I'll call you on my way home to get Hack so you'll know we're on our way. I love you, Anna. Do you hear me?"

He could hear her crying softly. "I love you, Anna. Please let me know you heard that."

Choking back the tears, Anna whispered. "I love you, too."

CHAPTER THIRTY-TWO

The huge trees that lined all the streets were dropping their leaves, baring their limbs that stretched out across the yards. There was a definite coolness in the air, and the fragrance of smoke coming out of fireplaces at night was one of the sure signs that winter had arrived.

Harry and Hack were piled up in the truck with the heater on low and the music playing a little too loud. After last night's conversation, Harry was going for a more cheerful atmosphere, looking forward to some time with Zach. He was still surprised at how the young boy accepted him so easily into his life. They seemed to develop a bond so quickly and Harry wanted to set that in stone before he left on his next trip overseas.

He sang with the radio, and Hack stuck his nose out of the small crack in the window on his side of the truck. Soon he turned into Anna's driveway, glanced at the window by the front door, and saw Zach watching for his truck. He was such a handsome kid. Harry got out with Hack and they jogged to the door. Zach opened it and Hack jumped all over him with excitement.

"We're here! I guess you could tell already." Harry shouted as they walked into the hearth room.

"We've been waiting for you." Anna walked out of the kitchen and smiled.

Harry pulled her to him and kissed her. "Gosh, it's good to see you."

"You must have had a good day."

"I have now. What smells so good?"

"Just hamburgers I cooked on the grill. Let's sit down and eat while it's hot."

Hack sat near the table and Harry absentmindedly dropped his left arm to pet the dog while he was eating. It was a bad habit but one he didn't see the need to drop.

"Zach has a science project to do this week. I always hated those things as a child."

Harry rolled his eyes. "The worst. I had a difficult time coming up with something that hadn't been done a million times before. It's very hard to be original in a science fair."

"No joke." Zach spoke up with his mouth full of food, which got a rise out of his mother.

"I wish I could say I had some great ideas, but I'm plumb out of them, Zach. What did you decide?"

"That's just it. I haven't got any ideas yet. I am going to look on the Internet after dinner to see what I can find."

"Do you have lots of friends, Zach?"

"Yeah. Sorta."

"'Sorta?'"

"I have friends at school, but not where I live. Mom lets me have a friend over on the weekends but during the week I am pretty much on my own." Zach finished his burger and got up from the table to play with Hack.

"Why don't you take the dog outside for a few minutes before it gets too cold?" Anna smiled and pointed towards the back door.

"Sure, Mom. He loves playing ball with me."

Harry looked at Anna and winked. "Were you trying to give us time alone?"

"You're very intuitive tonight."

Harry laughed. "Anything you want to talk about while we have the chance?"

"Let's move over to the sofa where we can watch them playing."

They got up and took a seat on the sofa next to each other, and Harry took her hand.

"Come here, Anna. Let me hold you. I don't know if I want to hear what is going through that mind of yours. Because I'm having enough trouble coping with what is going on in my own mind."

Anna snuggled into his chest and sighed. "Harry, I can be brave for you. I can last a long time without knowing if you are coming back or not. But it's really getting to me that we've done this before. I swore I wouldn't put myself in this situation again. And yet, here we are."

"I know. I know. I feel like a dog about it. There's nothing I can do to make this better or okay. It stinks and I'm the first to admit that it's not going to be easy on either one of us. We don't know yet if I'm going to be put in harm's way or just do intel work. Let's not assume that I have a bullet out there with my name on it."

"I don't necessarily think that. But I do think you are playing Russian roulette if you go enough times into battle. Eventually you will find that bullet. Or it will find you. The odds go up the more times you go. That is a teacher's opinion."

"I am good at what I do. I have Max with me at all times. I will not hesitate to shoot to kill to protect myself or Max, or the rest of a team that might be with me. So let's talk about dealing with the time frame and not whether or not I am going to live through this. I am confident I will make it back home, I just don't know how long I'll be gone this time."

"I have pretty much told Zach that you are a Marine and this is what Marines do. They protect our country in any way they can. He seems okay with it, but he really wants to spend more time with you. I told him that when you get back, you will be there for him. But you, Harry, will have to show him that on your own. All the words I speak will fall on the floor if you don't live it out. He really needs a dad now more than ever."

"I know that's true, and I feel the responsibility. But you just now let me into your world. I haven't known that long that I have a son. I am happy about it, but these plans were made before I met you this time. I already knew I wanted to go back into the military. I want to be in your world, Anna. And I want you in mine. But we have to give this time."

Anna laid her head on his shoulder and grabbed his hand. "I'm just afraid I am going to lose you, again, Harry."

He took her face and turned it up so he could look into her eyes. "Do you still have that cross I gave you? Keep it with you. And Anna, we don't know when I'll be going. I may be around for the next week. We are training hard, so that makes me think it's soon. But whenever it is, I will do all that I can to get back to you as fast as I can. Zach means the world to me. Look at him out there playing with Hack. He's adorable. He's going to make a fine young man. And I think he might be tall like I am. He's tall for his age, isn't he?"

"Yes. He's the tallest kid in his class."

"I can't wait to see how he turns out. What his interests are."

"It will come soon enough. I'm not going to rush his childhood because I'm not sure we're ready for puberty with this kid. And all that comes with it."

Harry laughed. It felt so good to laugh. He stood up and grabbed her and danced slowly with her, holding her close to him.

"You are the one I've waited all my life to be with. I'll never love anyone but you. So hold on, Anna. We're in this together."

Anna pulled away and looked at him. "Even looking at you now, it's hard to believe you're really here with me. In this life I have with Zach. It's wonderful, Harry." She pressed her face against his, smiling.

The lights had come on in the back of the house and it was getting late. Zach was staring at them through the glass. His nose was pressed against the window pane; Hack was standing next to him with his tail wagging and his tongue out. Harry noticed and pointed to Zach laughing.

"We just think we are talking in private. He's not missing anything, Anna. That kid is something else."

"He's a little you, Harry. Remember that."

"That's what I'm afraid of."

Harry walked Zach up to his bedroom and tucked him in. As Harry reached over to turn out the light Zach looked up at him.

"You going soon, Dad?"

"Yes, Son. I'm not sure how long I'll be gone. You'll need to take care of Hack for me."

"I know. Mom told me."

Harry leaned over and spoke to Zach in a low voice. "I'll be back, Son. Remember that, will you? I'll be back and we'll pitch in the backyard, we'll go fishing, and I'll teach you how to throw a football if you don't already know how. I'll do anything you want to do."

Zach hugged Harry and didn't want to let go. "We don't have to do anything, Dad. I just want you home."

Harry stood up and kissed his forehead and walked out of the room. But inside he was shaking. If he stayed one more minute he knew he wouldn't be able to leave at all.

Anna was waiting in the living room and stood up when he walked into the room.

"Tough duty?"

"Yeah. You might say that. I got to get out of here, Anna. It's not making it any easier on all of us."

He reached out for Anna and held her one more time. "This has to last me until the next time I see you. If I don't leave in the next day or two, I'll be back over here and we'll go through this all over again."

"We'll be fine, Harry. Hack will be fine with us. You do what you have to do, and we'll be waiting here. I'm just going to stay so busy that I don't give my mind time to think. Because if I do, I might not be able to handle your being away from me. And why don't we let Zach feed the horses for you and let the vet check on them from time to time. Would that work?"

"That would be terrific. And Zach would learn a lot by feeding those magnificent animals. I have a feeling it won't be long, Anna. I did not find you again to be separated from you. So let's trust that feeling and look forward to the next time I walk through this door."

Anna kissed him and opened the front door. Harry walked out without a word and never looked back.

CHAPTER THIRTY-THREE

With memories of the last night he spent with Anna floating through his mind, Harry sat on the transport plane across from Max, staring out the window. His life was about to change again. He would have to compartmentalize anything to do with his normal life and prepare himself for what was ahead.

They were headed into Turkey at the military base in Adana. There they would be able to do intel work to find an ISIS cell in Pakistan. Harry knew it was going to be a long trip, so he closed his eyes and tried to sleep for a while. Max had already dozed off, so all he could hear was the hum of the engines in the background. There were no storms in the forecast for the flight over, so they expected it to be a smooth flight.

Once they landed at the base, Harry and Max were taken to their rooms, where they left their baggage and personal items. Then they headed over to the offices where they would be doing their intel work and set up their computers. It was evening when they arrived and time for dinner, so they walked to the mess hall and got their meals and sat down to eat.

"That was quite a flight, Harry. And I don't know about you, but I'm starving."

Harry nodded, with a mouthful of food. "No joke. I didn't think we would ever get here. We should be used to these long flights. I guess I'm anxious to get this thing done."

"I thought you wanted to get back into the thick of things."

"I did. I still do. But I have a conflict, as you well know."

"The food's not too bad, you agree?"

"Not bad at all. But at this point I would have eaten pretty much anything to get rid of those hunger pangs in my gut."

"We need to pick up some snacks to keep at our desks. I think we're going to be leaning over our computers for a long time. This should be interesting."

"I cannot wait to nail those animals. For too long they have been ravaging this whole area. And nobody has been able to stop them. We can do our part and get rid of this one cell, although I fear it has grown since we were contacted."

"I think we can count on that fact."

"Let's get a good night's sleep, Max, so that we can tackle this thing with a fresh mind. We were told to check out this isolated situation and see what kind of threat this cell is so that we can call in support when we need it. And we already know we have to locate our contact that will have valuable information about the location of this cell."

"Right. I'm ready if you are. Let's hit the sack and jump on this first thing in the morning."

Harry reached his room, undressed, and lay down on the bed, feeling a little jet lag. He took an aspirin and a small amount of melatonin to reassure a good night's sleep. But his mind left Turkey and the ISIS situation and went back to Zach and his moments with him before he left Anna's house. The kid was really getting to him. He seemed older than his years. Maybe living without a father had caused Zach to feel like he had to take care of Anna. He was the man of the house. Harry smiled. He was so fortunate to have found Anna after so many years. His life had meaning now, more than ever.

He sent Anna a text through the military letter box, letting her know he was okay. He knew she would not be expecting a text, but he also knew it would let her know he was thinking of her. He closed his eyes and was asleep in seconds.

Morning came and like a thief, stole the moments of peaceful rest that both men would need to pull from in the days ahead. Harry and Max both hit the floor running, dressed, and ready for breakfast, which was served in the officers' mess hall. When they arrived, it was full of men talking. They recognized Lt. Michaels, who had gotten them settled into their offices last night after they landed. They sat down and ate, and the lieutenant outlined the situation in Turkey and the surrounding area.

"Men, I know you realize things are active in this whole area. Both ISIS and the Taliban are everywhere. It's gotten so infiltrated that we can't take for granted that anyone is safe. Of course you can't get on base here unless you are vetted to the bone. But outside here, it's mayhem. Absolute bedlam. It wasn't this way in the beginning. There was a clear division between who the enemy was. But now they move in and grow up in your town or city and you think they are one of us. But they are waiting. Waiting for that right time to blow up the whole city. Block by block if they have to. I've never seen anything like the ruthlessness and the extent to which they will go. Even blowing themselves up to prove a point."

Harry nodded. "We see it in so many countries, but what grates me to no end is that we have allowed this infiltration of radical Islam to spread without doing anything much to stop them. I have hopes for this new president we have that things will change. But we have hoped for years and nothing has changed."

"We're glad you're here. If I can be of any help to you, let me know."

Lt. Michaels got up and left the hall, leaving Harry and Max to discuss their plans for the day.

"I guess we won't know how long this will take until we get inside our computers and see what's going on. I've communicated with Colonel Hamilton to let him know we're here and that we'll keep him posted on our progress." Harry rubbed his eyes.

"You up to this, Harry? I know you have had a lot on your mind lately."

Harry forced a smile. "I trained all my life for this. I better be ready."

"I meant mentally."

"Yeah, I'm okay. Just weird the timing of things. But life is kinda like that. Things hardly ever go easy for anyone. You just can't plan too far in advance because you never know what's going to come up."

"That's for sure. Let's get out of here and head to the office. I'm ready to see what's going on out there in cyber land." Max stood up and walked towards the door.

"Right behind you. I'll dump our plates and follow you."

Once inside their office, Max and Harry sat at their computers the rest of the day, taking in intel from drones in Pakistan. They were also intercepting conversations, sitting with interpreters and taking notes and then communicating with Command. It was a busy afternoon and a productive one.

"Max, we are finding out some valuable info for Colonel Hamilton. We both know he wanted us to find out what kind of threat this ISIS cell was and that is just what is showing up. It looks like it is massive. Not just a small thing. But from what I am seeing, there are broken off parts of that cell that are moving around, destroying small towns and killing women and children. This cell seems to have hundreds of men who are willing to sacrifice their lives for the cause. We would be insane to enter that battle without huge backup forces. Air and ground. Agree?"

"You summed it up nicely, Harry. We're looking at a horrendous battle and we need to find out how Command wants to approach this."

"It's late. Let's quit for the night and in the morning we will
have answers so that we'll know how to proceed. This is bigger
than we all thought. But at least we are finding that out."

Both men ate a quick meal in the officers' mess hall and hit
their beds quickly to get some rest. Tomorrow would be another
busy day. Harry closed his eyes and was asleep before he could
even think about home. And that was a good thing. The further
he could separate himself from his world in the U.S, the better and
more focused job he would do where he was. Harry was told in his
training that he would never be the same person. He was finding
that out the hard way. But hard or easy, it was a fact that wasn't going to go away. Ever.

CHAPTER THIRTY-FOUR

Morning came fast and hard. The two men hit the ground running and were met with a phone call that would direct their actions forward. It was clear and to the point: At least until they found their contact in Pakistan, they were to further open up the locations of the enemy.

"I understand you have located some of the cells that ISIS has placed throughout Pakistan, mostly in the mountainous areas," Colonel Hamilton said.

"Yes. It's bigger than we thought. The major ISIS cell has gotten so large it has broken off into about five smaller cells. Highly armed. We're going to need some major help to get this done."

"We've got you covered. Navy SEALs and Rangers will be at your back door with every form of ammunition known to man. But don't think for one minute that this might not be one of the most dangerous battles of your life. These people are used to the mountains and we are not. We don't know our way around like they do. You'll have guides and interpreters, but this will take all you know and some things that you will learn on the job."

"We understand the seriousness of this mission, Sir. We are ready to head to Pakistan and locate our contact. We will be in contact with you at all times to let you know if anything changes. I'm certain there will be changes in locations as we move towards the different cells."

"As soon as you land, you'll meet up with a Navy SEAL team that will have already set up a safe house as a base for you to work from. Your contact's name is Saber Hassan."

"We will report in as soon as we arrive at the safe house and will seek to locate Hassan immediately."

Harry hung up the phone and looked at Max. "We're in for a run this time, Max. I think this is much worse than we first realized. We leave tomorrow morning for Pakistan before first light. It's not like Mosul, where we'll walk into ground fire immediately. But once we locate those cells scattered in the mountains, we'll have to drive as far as we can and then travel on foot. It's not going to be easy."

Max sat back in his chair and winced. "My leg is healed but there is still some soreness deep inside. My guess is it's scar tissue. I'll be fine. We both are used to pushing our bodies. But we don't even know the challenges we'll have to face. We'll take it one day at a time. We'll go as far as we can go, and then we rest and rebuild ourselves."

Harry continued his take on their mission. "The rest of the today we are going to spend studying the mountainous area where we'll be travelling. We need to read up on any new posts about activity from ISIS. It changes daily. I'm certain they're on the move constantly to keep from being found. We will be pulling from the intense training that we've been through and the SEALs experience. Hundreds of hours of training in different situations; water, air, land, rugged terrain, vehicles, on foot, target practice, breathing techniques. The list is endless. We've done this for years. So have the men we'll be fighting alongside. I have no doubt about our capabilities. But what I do doubt is my knowledge of what ISIS is capable of. It is the unknown that will be our greatest challenge. Our ability to be flexible, to readjust, to think outside the box. That is what will make this mission a success."

After hours at the computer studying, both men were exhausted mentally and were ready to sleep. Night would not bring the restful sleep they needed because their minds would not completely turn off. The task ahead was daunting, but doable. But not matter how good they were, there was a respectable amount of fear that loomed in the distance and knowledge that this could be the last mission. They might not return from this one. But both men agreed that they would die using every arrow in their quiver to kill the enemy. To stop them dead in their tracks.

And it was about time that somebody stopped ISIS. Harry had seen too much destruction at the hands of ISIS, the loss of lives and the murderous treatment of the innocent. ISIS was acting like it was indestructible. And it was doing a mind game on the public, to the point where U.S. forces felt like it was nearly impossible to stop them. But the military never gave up. They found new ways of overthrowing the enemy. They had to learn to outthink them, outplay them, and the United States military could be a very ominous force to come up against. Harry and Max both knew that the SEALs would stop at nothing. They were like a wall of steel.

So lying in bed, Harry allowed himself to think for a moment about Anna. Her lovely face. Her tenderness. And how he loved her. He then remembered his last night with Zach. And those thoughts drove him to want to achieve the impossible so he could return home safe. He would not think of them again for a long time, because his mind had to be rigid. It had to be clear to think quickly and creatively and that wasn't going to happen if he was hanging onto thoughts about home. He had to be in the moment at all times.

At last sleep came and Harry did not wake until 4:30. He heard Max in the next room showering, and he jumped up and hit the shower and dressed. He no longer was attached in any way to his life. Now he moved into stealth mode, thinking ahead, listening and eyes wide open. For this mission might just be the battle of his life and he wanted to be ready to face it head on.

When he saw Max face to face, he saw the lion of a man he knew would carry them both into battle. After grabbing a quick breakfast, the men carried their bags, walking in step towards the military transport that would fly across the ocean to Pakistan.

The SEAL team members that were going with them were already on the plane, speaking in quiet voices. But you could feel the excitement in the air. Everyone was of the same mindset; this was war. They were going to put their skills together; the hundreds of hours of training now would fall into place. And they would move as one to achieve a goal that was set in stone inside each man.

Harry and Max took their seats inside the massive plane, clicking the harness and leaning their heads back against the seat.

Max looked at Harry and grinned "Okay, Buddy. We're ready for this."

CHAPTER THIRTY-FIVE

In the dark of night a Blackhawk landed near the base of the Himalayan mountain range in Pakistan, and ten men hit the ground running towards a group of abandoned buildings. Max and Harry stayed behind while the SEALs went to recon the area. After about twenty minutes, Harry and Max were notified that it was a safe place for them to set up a base. Harry unpacked their computers and set them up on an old cracked table, placing their maps on the floor with all the equipment and guns and MREs. The SEALs left and scouted out the area and found a market shop that had remained open even though the whole area had been wiped out. They found water and other supplies that they needed and brought them back to the base.

It would take hours for them to set up everything and locate at least one of the cells in the mountains. Because it was already dark, and they were worn out from the flight, they rolled out their sleeping bags and lay down to get some much needed sleep. The SEALs alternated sleeping and guarding the safe house. It was going to be a long night.

Before Harry closed his eyes, he checked in with Colonel Hamilton on a secure phone to let him know that they had arrived at the safe house. "Colonel, we have arrived and have taken over a small building near the base of a section of the Himalayan Mountains. The SEAL team has secured the area and we are bedded down for the night."

"You have everything you need to get this job done."

"We will get it done."

As soon as the line went dead, Harry crashed. Max was already asleep, and two of the SEALs were down for the count. It was cold and the insulated sleeping bag felt warm enough to forget for a moment what was ahead of them. Harry did not allow his brain to think of anything except what he would need to do in the morning. Everyone in the safe house had to live in the now, to keep alive.

Early in the morning a fog had settled in over the area, causing an eerie kind of quiet, but the SEAL team was active, searching the area for any signs of the enemy. There were some lone travelers with pack animals moving upward at the base of the closest mountain. But they were in another world, carefully making their way somewhere. Only God knew where. Most of the area had taken a beating, but somewhere in these mountains ISIS was hiding, planning its next move. It was Harry's and Max's job to find out what that move was.

After eating some food which was filling but lacked much taste, Harry and Max turned on their computers and poured over the maps. They were receiving incoming information from drones flying near the area, but as of yet, nothing was shaking loose about the ISIS cells. An interpreter showed up in the late morning and helped them as they listened to conversations that were broken up and scattered, hoping to find something that would lead to the location of a cell or any activity.

Suddenly, information came in from the drones showing a cell three miles from the safe house on the side of a mountain. They had spotted movement around the cell. Noting the location of the cell, Harry spoke with the SEALs and they immediately headed out the door to recon the area surrounding the cell. The fog was an excellent cover for checking out the area without giving away their presence. Harry and Max followed with their sniper rifles, staying in contact with the drone for more information.

The SEALs moved quietly through the rough brush on the ground as the fog lifted. There wasn't much vegetation but they used what was there to hide their presence. Harry and Max stayed behind the men, ready to shoot at a moment's notice. At about a two-mile range, the SEALs scoped out the area, noting that there was movement near the cave on the mountain side.

After checking out the situation, Harry and Max set their guns on a huge foliage-covered boulder, aiming their sights on the men guarding the camp. It was obvious to them that if they fired their rifles to take the men out, their cover would be blown. It would have to happen simultaneously; the SEALs would attack at the same time that the shots were fired, realizing that there was no way to know how many men were inside the cave.

Harry and Max fired their guns, the sound echoing in the distance. Two men dropped from the side of the mountain and hit the ground. As they fired their guns again, killing two more men, the first two SEALs headed across the grass covered ground in front of the cave. Immediately an IED exploded, sending one of the men up into the air. The other man was knocked down, suddenly aware that the ground was loaded with IEDs to protect the entrance into the cave where they were hiding.

Everyone was caught off guard to see proof that there were IEDs in the field. The leader of the SEAL team contacted Command and requested assistance from the Rangers, who were waiting across the border. A Blackhawk gunship full of Rangers was sent to handle ground cover. Another Blackhawk came and lowered a gurney for the man who was killed, and the SEAL who was still on the field managed to retrace his steps and helped load the body of his friend into the gurney so he could be lifted up to the chopper. Another rope was dropped, and the soldier clipped himself to the rope and was moved across the field to safety, where he joined the team.

Harry was informed that an air to ground missile was going to be fired and he immediately aimed his laser at the entrance of the cave. What seemed like seconds later, the missile was fired into the cave and the explosion was massive. The whole side of the mountain seemed to crumble.

All of this took place quickly and then it was over. The loss of one of the SEALs was devastating to the team. They also knew it would be impossible to retrieve any records from the cave that would help Harry and Max locate the other cells or know what ISIS was planning. The men moved back into the safe house immediately to rest and regroup. There was a sadness in the room that each could feel. But nothing that could be spoken would fix it.

Before the dust had settled from the explosion, Harry and Max were on it with the drones, seeking to locate another cell in the barren landscape of the mountains in Pakistan.

"That didn't go as planned, Max. I hate that we lost a team member. I feel like we should have known there might be IEDs present. I bet Hack would have smelled them." Harry put his hands over his eyes. He suddenly felt weary.

"It sucks, Harry. I would hate to have to be the one to deliver the news to his wife. But that is the price of war against ISIS. It will make us more aware when we try to take the next cell out."

"High price to pay. It could have easily been you or me that died."

"You and I have seen this over and over. You never get used to seeing someone die like that. But he was a hero, just the same. Those two men were the first two to lead in attacking that cave. We could just have easily faced severe incoming fire from that cave. They had the advantage of being on higher ground. We had the advantage of surprise. Even then, we lost someone."

"We need to plan better next time. His death was not a waste. We took them out. But let's use this to know next time that the terrorists will use anything to guard their cell."

"And we will use anything to take them out."

CHAPTER THIRTY-SIX

The farm seemed terribly quiet as Anna pulled up in the driveway. It seemed like a year since she'd seen Harry. He seemed so far away. She looked at Zach, seeing Harry in his face. His whole demeanor.

"Well, we've got work to do. Those horses aren't going to be fed unless we do it, you know."

"I know, Mom. I'm ready if you are."

"It's cold out so pull on your jacket. I think winter is officially here."

"I wish it would snow, but that might be hard on the animals."

"Don't even think it. We have enough on our hands without several inches of snow on the ground."

Zach looked at her with a serious expression on his face.

"Do you think Dad will be home for Christmas?"

Anna paused. She didn't want to say the wrong thing. "I sure hope so. That would be such a great Christmas present."

"It would be the only present I want for Christmas."

"That was sweet, Zach."

"I wasn't tryin' to be sweet, Mom. I just want him home."

Anna opened the car door and stepped out into the cold night. "I'll unlock the gate and you go in and start feeding while I check the house."

Zach walked through the huge gate and shut it behind him, and picked up a handful of hay and shredded it in the small pasture beside the barn. He also put out feed in the trough so that they would get enough nutrition. He watched as the beautiful animals lined up at the trough to eat.

Something was moving outside the pasture that was beginning to scare the horses. Zach crept slowly, trying to see what was outside the fence. The sun was almost set and it was difficult to see in the dark. He squinted but still didn't see anything.

Just as he walked around the trough towards the fence, the horses got spooked and ran, almost trampling Zach, He yelled at them as he fell, twisting his ankle.

"Ouch!" He cried out in pain, and Anna came running out of the house. She pulled out a flashlight from her purse and shined it on Zach. He was sitting on the ground holding his left ankle.

"Zach! What happened? How did you hurt your ankle?"

"The horses got spooked and ran. They knocked me over and I twisted my ankle. They didn't mean to, Mom. It wasn't their fault."

Anna laughed. "I know it wasn't their fault. But you still hurt your ankle. Does it feel sprained?"

"I think it's just twisted. Let me try to get up and put weight on it."

Zach used the trough to help himself get up, and slowly he tried to put weight on his foot. He winced in pain and hobbled to the gate.

"I think you need to get off that foot, Zach. We'll get some ice in a baggie and put it on your foot when we drive home. I'll finish with the horses; you just sit in the car. It won't take me long to make sure the stalls are clean."

"I didn't want you to have to do anything. This was my job, Mom."

———

Anna hurried and checked the stalls and made sure the horses were eating and had fresh water. Everything looked okay. She worried a coyote was out there in the dark, but there was nothing she could to except hope that things would be okay. This was the frustrating part about Harry being gone. She had no one to ask about things if they went wrong.

She went into the house and got some ice and shoved it into a baggie, locked up the house, and got into the car. Zach laid the ice pack on his ankle and leaned back in the seat. Anna could tell he was upset.

"Zach, don't feel bad about your ankle. It will probably be sore for a couple of days and then you'll be fine. Accidents happen."

"We don't have time for that, Mom. Dad is relying on us to do his job. We can't let him down."

"I know, Honey. We won't let him down. Just relax. We'll be home in a minute and you can do your homework and get into bed. I'll keep that ice pack on you when you get in bed, and by morning it may be okay for you to walk on it."

"It better be. I don't have time for this. "

———

Zach finished his homework and Anna got him into bed and settled down. She turned out the light and pulled his door shut. Another day gone without hearing anything from Harry. This was going to be tough.

It was one thing to not know where he was. But to not be able to have contact with him was almost unbearable. She wondered if he had any thoughts about home. About her and Zach. She wondered what he was going through and how much danger he was in. She wasn't used to having a soldier in her life. She was becoming rudely aware of just how difficult this was going to be. And she had no idea when he would be coming home.

The phone rang and startled her. It was Martha.

"Anna? We were just wondering how you are doing? You and Zach making it okay?"

Anna blew out a sigh. "I thought we were. We went to Harry's to take care of the horses tonight and Zach twisted his ankle. He is so upset that he wasn't able to finish taking care of the horses. He really is taking this promise seriously. He misses his father."

"We all miss Harry. It's a nightmare when he's out on a mission. We don't know where he is or when he will be back. I was hoping we were done with this kind of life, but apparently we are not. This is what he loves to do, but I don't think he's aware of how tough it is on his family back home."

"He probably isn't able to think about all that, Martha. But I want to be strong for him. He has one good leg, and his friend Max is over there with one leg and one arm. If they can survive whatever they are going through, then I should have no problem being here in the lap of luxury all safe and warm."

"We all have those thoughts, Anna. But we're human. It's okay to worry and miss him. We just have to trust that he's doing what he loves and will come home to us when it's over."

"Have you been busy at work, Martha?"

"Way too busy. But that's good because it keeps my mind occupied."

"We'll come to see you this weekend. We could use the company."

"That would be great. I'll let you go, Anna. We love both of you and just wanted to make sure you were safe."

Anna hung up and walked into her bedroom to put on her pajamas. She turned the heat up and started a fire in the living room.

Sitting on the sofa with a blanket wrapped around her legs, she leaned back and thought about all the years she'd lived alone, just she and Zach. She had dealt with her feelings about Harry and had begun to enjoy her single life with her son. It was hard work and sometimes she was lonely, but it wasn't a bad life. She loved teaching. But Harry was back into her life, and he knew about his son. And here she was again, mourning him because he was off fighting somewhere. And she was alone again. Only this time was different. She loved him. She loved him all over again. Some people would say that was insanity, but she would disagree. She thought it was fate, or something more. Something meant to be. But it hurt like hell.

Her phone sat in her lap and it was useless. She couldn't send him a text. He had told her that when he went on a mission, it was like he fell off the face of the earth. That was exactly how she felt now. It was like he had vanished all over again. She would have killed to have one word from him. One single word to let her know he was alive. But instead, she had the silence that drives people over the edge. And he'd only been gone two weeks. Two frigging weeks. It felt like a month, and she was pretty sure that it would be at least a month, maybe longer.

She leaned over on the two large pillows at the end of the sofa and covered herself up. The fire kept the room toasty, but she felt chilled inside. She had to teach tomorrow. She needed to be rested to deal with a room full of kids. But her mind would not let her rest; she could not stop thinking about Harry. Without knowing it, she fell asleep with her cell phone in her hand, almost as though she was hoping that some word would come through.

What she didn't know, what she couldn't see, was that Harry was across the world on the other side of nowhere, holding his cell, and thinking of her. Wanting to text her. Shoving all thoughts aside as he searched the computer for some clue. He would have died to have texted her once. She would have died to have heard from him tonight. That was love. That was the kind of love books were written about. But the phone remained silent just the same.

CHAPTER THIRTY-SEVEN

David Downs was planning a trip of a lifetime for his family. Taylor had been after him for years to take the kids to Paris, and he had purchased the tickets as a surprise for them, for Christmas. This was the year they would live their dream. He was going to keep it a secret until the kids got out for Christmas break. Taylor would freak out, and David knew it was going to be the best surprise he'd ever pulled off. Not known for his ingenuity, he might find that this might be the redeeming gift that changed how she thought of him. He had a clumsy way of walking through life and he was trying hard to improve.

He did, however, need to tell his parents, as they would be the ones who would have to take care of the family dog, Kingsley, a King Charles Cavalier. He was easy as dogs go, but the shedding was a nuisance. He could have made a rug with all the hair that had been shed on the floors of his home. He could have stuffed a mattress with it. Instead, he'd vacuumed up the hair and filled hundreds of trash bags. It didn't seem right, but what else was he to do? And his parents loved the dog. However, they seemed to have forgotten about the shedding. He wasn't going to remind them since he needed them to keep Kingsley. They would find out soon enough.

Taylor was snooping around because she knew he was trying to surprise her this year. He had caught her in his wallet the other day. Now she was leaning over his computer. He walked up behind her, smiling.

"Hey. What are you doing?"

She jumped. "Oh, nothing. Just looking at the dust on your desk."

"What's dust got to do with my Google search history?"

"Oh, David. You know what I'm doing. I'm just trying to find out what you're up to."

"Up to? Me? I've been accused of being boring, useless, unimaginative."

"True, you have. But this year, for some reason, I feel you're planning something. I just don't know what."

He pushed the computer lid own and grinned. "Just for once, why don't you enjoy the wait?"

"I hate surprises."

"Well, it's a Catch-22 then. Because I haven't had a surprise worth waiting for since we married, and I believe I've hit the jackpot on this one. I'm not about to let you ruin it with your overzealous curiosity."

"Come on, Davie. Just give me a hint."

"I won't do that, Darling."

"Just a word. A direction."

"Zilch. Now go. Let me have my dusty desk to myself. I have some work to do."

"Oh, you're no fun. I'll find out. Trust me."

"Think what you will. But do it outside of my office. From now on, my office is off limits to you."

"You mean I can't clean in here?"

"You can't set one foot in my dust. Not until after Christmas. I'll do my own cleaning."

"You're serious?"

"Deadly."

"Wow, it must be pretty good. You must be outdoing yourself with this surprise."

"Actually, I think I am just touching the tip of the iceberg on surprises."

She looked at him with a blank look and walked out the door. He knew he was driving her crazy, but it was well worth all the looks he was going to get to pull this thing off.

David sat down at his dusty mahogany desk and hit *print* on the computer. The printer kicked on and printed out tickets for all four of them. He took the tickets and put them in the safe that was under his desk. He was the only one with the key. He wished he could swallow the key but then they would all be stuck without tickets. So he put it on his keychain and kept it with him at all times. His wife would go to any extreme to discover what he was planning. Including making him talk in his sleep. So he vowed to refrain from taking any melatonin until after the family was told of the surprise. He might face long nights of tossing and turning, but it would be so worth it in the end.

This trip was going to cost him a pretty penny. But he'd been selling real estate out the wazoo lately, and the money was pouring in. Hard work had paid off. He'd worked overtime trying to get listings, and working his Rolodex. He wined and dined prospective buyers, he went to all the social get-togethers in Memphis, and he tried to be seen at all the political events. It was boring at best and tiring. But now it was paying off. He was getting phone calls from very wealthy people who were looking for a change or to buy a second home. He knew Memphis like the back of his hand, and prided himself about being able to locate a home that was perfect for the buyer. He made friends with people easily and kept tons of business cards. He was doing so well he hired a personal assistant to do all the paperwork and research. It saved him time and allowed him to spend more time getting listings on the better houses in the most prestigious neighborhoods.

Life wasn't about money. But it took money to live a life. He had scraped by for most of their marriage, but now there was room to breathe. He was just feeling good about things, and he had opened up savings accounts for both children for their college funds. He had a healthy savings account, IRAs, and a 401K that was building nicely. He had a friend who knew all about the stock market, and as soon as he closed a few more houses, he would allow Mike to play around in the market for him. Make him some real money. He would never jeopardize his home or savings. But he was told to have a small amount to start with, and he was excited about learning more about Wall Street. He wanted to learn how to invest, because he knew that was where big money was made.

Lying in bed that evening, toasty warm, with a cold wind blowing outside, David waited for his wife to begin the conversation that he knew was going to happen. And he was so right.

She yawned. He closed his eyes and waited. It came. "Honey, there are so many things we could do for Christmas this year. We don't have to have a traditional one with dinner at your mother's house on Christmas Eve. Why don't we plan something different? Break the mold. I think the whole family would thank us down the road for showing them all how to enjoy the holidays by doing a few things differently."

She was rattling on. It was pitch black in the room. "Baby, would you relax? I know your mind is working overtime to find out what I am doing, but you're not going to make me slip. This is going to be a good Christmas; a time we will look back on and be so happy that we were able to experience it. Trust me. I do wish you could trust me."

She rolled over. "You know me. I can't let this go. Can't you tell me and we will surprise the kids together?"

"No."

"Just no?"

"I'm turning over; just say 'good night.'"

"You can't possibly go to sleep now. We're in the middle of a conversation."

"You're talking. I'm going to sleep. I don't consider that a conversation."

Sigh.

David couldn't help but laugh. "You are a funny lady. I've known you so long, and you never cease to amaze me."

"I'm determined. I will admit that."

"You are more than determined. You are crazy obsessed about finding out my surprise."

"I told you I hate surprises."

"I love you, Taylor."

"This has nothing to do with love."

"Oh, but it does. Now go to sleep before this turns into a fight."

"It already has reached that level with me."

"You're losing the fight. Now sleep."

She sighed. But he was already out for the count. She got out of bed and looked in his wallet. He opened his eyes and barely made out her figure leaning over his dresser. The moon was shining just bright enough for him to make her out.

"Taylor."

She screamed. "David! You were asleep."

"I always have one eye open, Taylor. Now get back in bed."

CHAPTER THIRTY-EIGHT

O utside the trees were barren. It was November and the wind was gusty, and there were fireplaces burning up and down the street, creating a magical landscape of smoke curling up into the gray sky. All the front doors had winter wreaths with big bows, and mailboxes were dressed in foliage and bows. Winter coats were out of storage, and hot chocolate was the drink of choice in most houses at night. With marshmallows, of course. Only the children braved playing outside, still riding their bikes, all bundled up and warm with scarves and mittens. It was going to be an early cold winter. The wind in the late afternoon might even be called a bitter wind. But indoors was another ballgame altogether.

At the home of Martha and Joseph Downs, the kitchen was full of the flavors of Thanksgiving that everyone craved once a year. A fat turkey had been in the oven for most of the day, cooking slowly in order to keep the juices intact. Cranberry sauce was cooking on the stove. It had to be homemade. Yeast rolls were rising. Four different vegetables were cooking, and there were pies on the dryer and a wonderful cider for the kids. Everything was ready for a joyous thanksgiving except for one single thing. Harry wasn't home. And that sucked some of the joy right out of the day. And everyone noticed.

Martha had outdone herself. She'd not asked for any help with the dinner. She was being stubborn, of course, but she absolutely loved doing this for her family. She had succeeded in making a very delicious, mouth-watering feast like she had done for years past. But this year, as in a few other years in the past, there was an empty chair. And the emptiness screamed so loud that it almost messed up the whole day.

Joseph saw everything. He was a quiet sort, but very in control of himself. However, unlike most men, he noticed things about his wife. He paid attention. He'd watched her slave over the stove and sit because she was getting tired. But he also saw the pain that would waltz across her face so subtly that one might mistake it for something else. A single gas pain or her aching back. But she was a mother to the bone. She adored her son. And today he was not anywhere. His chair was empty and Joe knew that Martha was dying inside to have him home.

He walked up to her and put his arms around her. "Martha, you're not fooling me one bit, you know. You are pretty good at putting up a front. But I know you too well. I know you're missing Harry today. We all are. But you, especially. Want to talk about it?"

Martha kept her back straight and her eyes dry. But inside, oh inside, she was screaming. "No. I'll be okay, Honey. Thanks for caring. I know you miss him, too. I really didn't think we would have to go through another holiday without him. But I was so wrong. I really never dreamed he would want to fight again, after all he went through. I guess I forgot what a man he was. A Marine."

"It's hard to comprehend how a soldier feels. Especially one as good as Harry. It's all he knows. Like a ball player who hurts his arm and has to stay out for a season. That player goes nearly insane waiting for the doctor to tell him he has healed enough to play ball. That's our son. He was ready to play ball again, and now he's in his element."

"I wish it was ball. I would be thrilled if he was a ball player of any sport. But sniper and master of intel? You know they need his type. Even though there are many snipers in the military. That general loves Harry. He loves how he works."

"We need to focus on Anna and Zach today, and on David and his family. Don't you think?"

"I plan to do just that."

"I think we should move Harry's chair away from the table so that it isn't so noticeable."

Martha turned and gave him the meanest look. Her eyebrow was raised. He knew he'd said the wrong thing. But he couldn't pull the words back no matter what he did.

"You know that's not an option. Harry hasn't died. He's just not home. Zach will want to sit next to Harry's chair. He worships his father. Can't you see that?"

"I see it. We all worship him in a manner of speaking. He's a pretty amazing human being."

"So, what else you got to say, Joe?"

"I think you've done a killer job on the meal, and I cannot wait to see Zach coming through that door."

Just as those words came out of Joseph's mouth, Anna and Zach came in the door with Hack running ahead to greet Martha and Joe. Behind them were David and Taylor, Sara Jane, and Jack. The house filled up with voices and laughter. After all, it was Thanksgiving Day.

"Hey, Anna. You look lovely. And how's our boy Zach?"

Anna hugged both of them and took her cookies into the kitchen to set them on the dryer. Zach ran to hug Joe and didn't seem to want to let go. It was obvious that he loved Joe.

"Grandpa Joe, can we take Hack outside? He wants to play ball with us."

"Oh he does, does he? Well, we sure can. You know where I keep our balls, so pick one out and we'll take that dog of yours outside to play. Sara, you and Jack want to go with us?"

Both kids nodded their heads yes and ran out the door with Zach. David walked outside with Joe and sat in a chair watching the kids play.

Martha took Anna's hand and they sat down on the sofa with Taylor.

"How are you holding up, Anna? I know this is tough on you."

"Just about as well as you are, Martha. I didn't know it would be so difficult. The wait is what is hard. It feels like time is moving at the speed of a sloth. The not knowing is killing me."

"It's the worst. I was dreading today at the same time I was looking forward to you two coming over. But it's even difficult to see Hack, because that's Harry's dog."

"Well, we have to tell ourselves that he isn't dead. He's just gone for a while. Hack misses him for sure. But we all keep busy so that we are not sitting around miserable all the time."

"I bet you stay busy, Anna. I would too, if Joe had to go off somewhere for a long time. I don't know how you are so calm."

"I stay busy, too. But I just wonder how long it will be. He's been gone about three weeks now. Christmas will be here before we know it. Will he be home by then, or will he be away from us? That is a tough time of year to be missing someone." Martha smiled and patted Anna's arm.

Anna leaned back against the sofa, looking out at Zach and Joe playing with the dog. She had a faraway look in her eyes.

"Martha, Harry wouldn't want us to be moping around. He is so full of life and really tries to make the most out of every situation. I know he's over there somewhere working his tail off, doing what he knows he has to do. But he's not just doing it. He is excelling in it. So that makes me want to do better. To try harder. He would be so happy today knowing we are all together in your house, having a meal together that you prepared. By the way, it smells heavenly in here."

Martha grinned for the first time that day. "It does smell good. And it's going to be a wonderful dinner. I am so glad you are in our lives, Anna. You have no idea how much joy Zach has brought us. And the thought, even the small hope that you and Harry might marry keeps me going. You would be so good for him."

Anna threw her head back and laughed. "Whoa, Martha. I don't know where our relationship is going. But I do know we are very close. And we both love Zach. Harry certainly took to that boy a lot quicker than I ever thought he would, because having a son means he also has responsibility. Yet, he doesn't seem to mind the change that has taken place in his life. I think that is honorable, seeing as how I sort of withheld this child from him for ten years, even though to my defense, I thought Harry was no longer alive."

"We couldn't have been happier to find out that Harry has a son. It has changed all our lives for the better. Look at the boy! He is such a happy child and so brilliant. I give you all the credit for how he has turned out."

Anna blushed. "He was easy to raise, I will tell you that. But meeting his father has been one of the most life-altering things that has every happened or will ever happen to Zach. He is settled now that he has his father in his life. He waited for that. He hoped even when I really didn't give him hope."

"It all worked out, even though it may have seemed an impossible thing. Let's call the boys in and sit down for dinner before it all gets cold."

Taylor leaned over to talk to Anna. "I'm proud of you for being so strong as a single mom. I know it must have been tough raising a son by yourself. It was hard enough for me to raise my kids with David around."

"It was difficult, but it was all I knew. I had no other choice that I could live with. I wasn't about to let my son be adopted. I wanted to raise him myself. You've done a wonderful job with your children. They are beautiful."

Taylor blushed. "Thanks. I know I have tough times ahead as they reach puberty. Have you had that happen yet?

Anna laughed. "Not yet, but it's coming. He is very independent already."

The table was covered with food. Every plate was piled with turkey, dressing, sweet potatoes, yellow squash, green beans, yeast rolls, cranberry sauce, and a mixed fruit salad. The talk and laughter echoed throughout the house. Martha and Joe were so happy to have their house full of family again. But Harry was there, running through the sentences. His name was unspoken but he was still there.

David leaned over to ask Joe if he knew where Harry was located. "Dad, I know he cannot communicate while he's on a mission. But does anyone have any idea where he is?"

"No one knows. It sucks, Dave. We're in limbo here, waiting for him to come home. If he gets killed, we won't know how or where."

"I was surprised that he wanted to go back in. Were you?"

"Not really. I reacted poorly to it when he shared the news with me. But inside, I knew he had to go. Being a Marine is so much a part of him that he couldn't be happy at a desk job. He worked for me as long as he could stand it. But finally, after he'd worked out for several years, he was ready to go back. He's in top shape, David. He really has overcome so much."

"I wouldn't want to meet him in a dark alley. He is very strong— always has been. But now that he's met Anna again and found out he has a son, why wouldn't they be enough to make him want to be home?"

"I think his plans were already laid out before he saw Zach. So it was nearly impossible to turn that around. I know it was tough for him to leave his son. And he and Anna were just getting to know each other again after ten years or so."

"I want to be closer to Harry. I tried to get him to come to the house many times. But he was struggling with what he saw. With what happened to his own body. I worried at times if he would pull through, but he did. And he came out better on the other side."

⟞⧓⟝

After dinner the kids played in the den with Hack and everyone else sat down in the living room to talk. It was getting late when Anna and Zach stood up to leave.

"I hate to break up the party, because this was one of the most wonderful Thanksgivings I've had in a long time. But it is getting late and Zach has a big school project that we need to start. Thank you so much for including us into your family dinner."

Martha and Joseph walked her to the door and kissed Zach goodbye.

"Please don't be strangers. You know how we love for you to come by."

Zach hugged them, waved to Sara Jane and Jack, and ran to the car with Hack following close behind.

⟞⧓⟝

The drive home was quiet. Anna was thinking about how wonderful Harry's parents were to her and how fast they had fallen for Zach. But Harry was so present in the house, it was painful. She looked over and saw Zach looking out the window.

"Son, you okay?"

"Yeah, I guess."

"What's on your mind? Let me guess. Your dad?"

"Is he ever coming home, Mom?"

"Of course he is, Zach. We have to trust him that he'll be home soon."

"Are you ever scared he isn't gonna come home?"

She paused. "Well, I try my hardest not to think that. He's very capable."

"He lost a leg in the last battle. I don't think I could take it if he lost anything else."

"I know how you feel, baby. We both feel pretty helpless. I bet there are hundreds of families like you and me who are waiting for their dad to come home."

"I don't know about that. But I do know that I'm dying to see him again. I don't want him to be a hero. He already did great things. I just want him to be 'Dad.'"

Anna had tears running down her face. She reached over and put her hand on his hand. He pulled away. She knew he wasn't mad at her. He just wanted his father. And nothing, not any word in the English language was going to make that better. Or easier.

CHAPTER THIRTY-NINE

I t was a cold winter day in Pakistan. Harry and Max were busy locating another cell that had broken off from the main group. Drones were giving them the coordinates so that they could chart the cell and pinpoint where they were in the mountains. This cell had been very active and the team leader, James Morgan, had requested a team of Rangers for backup. Harry was discussing the plan with Morgan as to how they were going to take the cell.

"From what the drones are telling me, this is an active cell. They are seeing quite a lot of movement coming and going from the cave. It is tough because we need to be able to get information from this cell so we can figure out how large this group is."

"If we attack the cave like we did the last time, then we will be forced to send an air to ground missile again. We ended up with nothing except the fact that we destroyed a cell. No info was gained. It wasn't a total loss but we took a hit with one of our men." Morgan sat down and looked at the info on the computer.

"We will be aware this next time that IEDs could be present. Not going to make that mistake again. We should have known last time. This isn't our first rodeo, Morgan."

"You're right. I take responsibility for that mistake. The men are still down over that loss."

"We need to scope this place out to see if there is any way possible that we could take these men out and still keep the cave intact."

"We need to discover about how many men are in the cave and also if there are two entrances. If there are, we can flush them out by blowing the entrance in the back. We have the manpower with the Rangers arriving today."

"I'm all in on that plan if we can find out about how many people we are talking about. I don't want to walk into a trap. We will have about eighteen men to surround the cave. But if they have fifty, it won't work. Of course we can call on the Blackhawk gunship or the Apache for ground cover. That gorilla can take out twenty-five people in one spray."

Morgan laughed. "They're the muscle car of the chopper world."

In the middle of the night, the SEAL team moved into stealth mode to check out the cave from a distance of a half a mile. They hid themselves in the scruffy shrubs along the side of the mountain, setting up a makeshift camp where they could keep their supplies and scope out the cave without being seen. They were ready and watching long before the sun rose in the sky.

It was going to be a gray day with occasional sunlight. The grayness helped their cover, but wasn't necessarily good for their long distance sight. The SEALs were highly trained to be invisible while they were trying to gather intel. This was going to take some time, so they settled in for a long night and morning. They couldn't give away their location, so they had to watch closely to make sure the enemy didn't come too close to their camp. They used night vision goggles until it was dawn, and then switched to regular binoculars to watch the cave.

It wasn't long before they saw some movement. Two men carrying rifles were walking in front of the cave. Morgan whispered, "I'm pretty sure they've been told about the destruction of the other cell. If so, this group would be alert to any movement at all in the surrounding area."

When the Rangers arrived, Morgan sent several men around the other side of the cave to see if there was a back door entrance. It was quite a hike and took a while to climb up the rocky mountain and not be seen. Daylight was fast approaching and the risk of being discovered was greater than it was earlier. The Rangers discovered that there was a back entrance and radioed Morgan. All guns had silencers on them, including the sniper rifles. They had to get this right.

The Rangers climbed down the back side of the mountain and hid in the shrubs lining the base of the mountain for cover. Everyone was waiting to see how large this cell was. The cave was rather large so it would hold quite a few people. Soon there was movement outside the cave. There were at least six men guarding the entrance. It made Harry wonder if they were aware they were being watched. Those six men were perched pretty high and had a wall of rock to hide behind while they observed their surroundings. Harry and Max could take them out. There was no question about that. But the point was to take most of the men down and retrieve what information they could from inside the cave. It might be valuable in understanding ISIS or it could be nothing at all. But the only way to find out was to get inside the cave.

After contemplating the situation, Morgan requested a Blackhawk gunship for ground cover. The timing on this raid was critical. When the chopper was close, Harry and Max took out the six men guarding the entrance. In the back, the Rangers had taken out three men who walked out of the cave. Morgan radioed the Rangers and they sent a shoulder-fired missile into the rear entrance. Immediately men came rushing out of the front entrance. Harry and Max took out at least fifteen men, and the SEALs rushed the cave while the chopper took the rest of the men.

Smoke was pouring out of the cave at this point, and the Rangers pulled back until the dust settled. Entering the cave, they found computers, maps, a stockpile of M-46 130mm field guns, RPG rockets, light mortars, and fifteen AK-47 rifles. The computers were invaluable. Harry and Max took them back to the safe house. The SEALs confiscated all of the weaponry and sent it back on the Blackhawk with the Rangers.

This raid was a complete success. No lives lost. But there were three more cells in the area. Now that they had taken this one out, it would be extremely difficult to remove the other three. Their cover would be compromised by now.

"Harry, we need to let the men have some rest. We are safe here for a short time but need to move in the next day or two. Word is spreading. We are picking up some conversation stating such. Let's spend tonight looking at their computers and using the interpreter when we need him." Max wiped the sweat from his brow, even though it was cold outside.

"I agree totally. We've had a great day today. I hate that we had to take so many down. I know they are the enemy and would take our heads off if they had a chance. But it still bugs me to take so many down. It was like a slaughter. I guess that's what war is. Somebody's going to get killed."

"Better them than us. Over time you get tougher inside. Almost a necessity."

Harry frowned. "It's hard when you go home. And someone needs love from you. I had pushed that so far back in my life that I could barely see it. We are trained to be machines, because we have to be in order to do what we are required to do. But I don't want to be a robot with no feelings. Hard to find that balance."

"Don't you know that's what screws so many vets up in their mind? Some never get over it. It took me a while last time. But the fight I had to overcome the loss of a leg and arm made me focus on something positive."

"I hear you. Let's hit the sack. Tomorrow is another day. We can pass valuable info to the military about ISIS when we dig further into those computers."

Harry unrolled his sleeping bag and lay down to rest his bones. He could hear the other men settling down for the night, talking about what they saw today and hoping the next cell wouldn't be so large. He closed his eyes and the first thing that popped into his mind was the last time he saw Zach. He had forced himself to let go of home. But as tired as he was, he had little control as he fell into a deep sleep, and the memories of holding Anna were a distant comfort to his weary body.

CHAPTER FORTY

Two weeks into December, David's plans for the trip to Europe were about to come to fruition. In spite of the constant digging from Taylor, he had been able to keep this special surprise a secret. But not without suffering many times from the looks she gave him, or the constant sighing, and the millions of questions that led them down a dead end rabbit trail. It might be the only time in his life that he would be able to carry this off. And he was going to enjoy it if it killed him.

Tonight they would have a family gathering where he would share the surprise. They had already put up a tree and decorated the outside of their house with lights and a huge sleigh with Santa and all the reindeers. The kids were excited about getting out of school in a few days, and it was a perfect time to tell them what was in store for the family this year. Taylor was in the kitchen making supper, as David walked through the door smiling from ear to ear.

"Don't come around me with that glib look on your face if you're not going to tell me what is going on."

"Well, tonight you are finally going to find out."

She turned with her mouth wide open. "Are you kidding me? You better not be joking."

"I wouldn't joke about something as special as this."

"Are the kids going to find out, too?"

"Yep. After dinner we all will go into the living room and I'll share with you what I have up my sleeve."

"Well, hallelujah! Finally I will know what in the world you've been hiding all these weeks." She walked over to David and kissed him. "It better be good, Buddy. Or you're in big trouble."

He laughed a deep laugh and turned to leave the room. "You're not going to believe this one."

Dinner was fun, with the kids talking ninety to nothing about their day, their Christmas list, and what their friends were asking Santa for. Sara Jane wanted a new bike and roller skates, and Jack wanted a new iPad and a dirt bike. Taylor was at the other end of the table chewing her food slowly, playing with the food on her plate. He could tell she was distracted thinking about what the secret might be.

"Can you pass the potatoes, Jack?" David was taking his time eating. He knew it was getting on Taylor's nerves.

"Leave room for dessert, David. I fixed brownies for tonight."

"Oh, I can't wait for that. With maybe some ice cream on top?"

She grimaced. "Oh yes, we have ice cream. It's Sara Jane's favorite dessert. Right, Sara?"

Sara was playing on her iPad at the table and she set it down, smiling. "I love brownies and ice cream. I do have a little homework tonight. Daddy, you said we were having a family meeting. What does that mean?"

That got Taylor's attention. She sat looking at David with one eyebrow raised.

"Oh, I have a surprise for you guys. So we need to eat our supper, enjoy our dessert, and then I have something I want to talk to you about."

Jack yelled out. "I bet I know! It's something about Christmas."

"You will never guess this secret in a million years. Believe me—your mother has tried for the last few weeks with no luck at all."

This started a guessing game that drove David nuts. But he had to let them try. It was part of the fun of having a secret.

Finally, after chowing down the brownies and ice cream, everyone took their plate to the kitchen and walked into the living room to take a seat. David stood up in the middle of the room, and waited for the kids to settle down.

"Hang on, kids. I have something I want to share with you. I have a surprise for all of you for Christmas. It took me a long time. I had to think about where I would want to take you, if we could go anywhere in the world. This will be a once in a lifetime event for us as a family. I am taking all of us to Europe, to Paris, for Christmas."

Everyone sat there with their mouths open. Then Taylor jumped up and screamed and ran to hug David. "Oh, my gosh! Are you kidding me? Paris?"

Sara Jane and Jack were not as excited but ran to hug David and jumped up and down, clapping their hands.

"We get to go on an airplane. Yay!"

"When do we leave, Dad?" Jack asked with a big grin on his face.

"We leave in a week. We are going a week before Christmas and staying two weeks. We will travel around, but mostly I wanted us all to see Paris. It's a changing world, and we never know how long we'll be free to travel like this."

Taylor leaned over and whispered in his ear. "How in the world did you pull this off? Where are we getting the money to do this?"

"Honey, I've been saving flyer miles for a long time and putting money back. I got the deal of the century on our tickets and hotel room. It will be fine. I just want you to relax and have a ball. We all need this. And I've been so busy lately that it made me aware of how few opportunities we are going to have to make a two week trip like this with the kids, and especially using frequent flyer miles. I hope you are happy."

"I couldn't be more surprised. And I see now why you didn't want me to find out."

He leaned over and kissed her and hugged her. The kids were running around talking excitedly about flying over the ocean. Even though they were nine and seven years old, they understood the magnitude of this trip.

"We'll need to pack our suitcases this week, taking only what we need. Your favorite clothes and a toy and your iPad. We have to pack light because we are flying. Just remember, this is a different type of Christmas. I want you all to enjoy it."

Taylor sat down on the sofa and put her head in her hands. The kids ran to their rooms to start packing, they were so excited. David sat down with his wife and leaned his head back against the sofa.

"Whew. Glad that's over. You don't know how hard it was to keep that a secret."

"I know I was dying to get you to share it with me."

"Now you see why I wanted to surprise you?"

She laughed a gorgeous laugh and kissed him in the mouth hard. "Of course I do! I still think I'm dreaming, David. I never thought in a million years we would be going to Paris. And at Christmas time! It feels like a dream."

He hugged her tightly and then looked her in the eyes. "Honey, we both work hard at what we do. You are raising our children and doing a fabulous job. I work hard to provide for the family. This is a break for us. A time to get away from all the work and stress and just enjoy the world. The kids are going to have a ball, but you and I will really enjoy the sights of Paris at Christmas. I have all kinds of brochures so that we can be sure to not miss anything."

She leaned her head against his shoulder. "I'm in heaven. You have outdone yourself."

He laughed. "The only thing bad about it is that I will never be able to match what I did this year for you guys for Christmas."

"I definitely think you've dug yourself a hole."

CHAPTER FORTY-ONE

A fire was roaring in the fireplace, but the house was quiet. Joe was reading the morning newspaper and having a hot cup of coffee while Martha was fixing breakfast. The aroma of bacon cooking always got his appetite going. She was going in late to the office, so she was enjoying making eggs, bacon, and homemade biscuits. Joseph was not even remotely hungry when he woke up, but after lighting the fire and sitting back in his favorite leather chair, smelling bacon cooking on the stove, he was starving.

Martha was just about to serve breakfast when David came waltzing through the door.

"Good morning, guys. How are you this morning? Something smells delicious. Are you making a hot breakfast, Mother?"

"I am. I'm going in to work late, so I thought it would be nice to make breakfast for Joe. Are you hungry?"

"It turns out that I am, lucky for me."

Martha smiled. "Then sit yourself down and have breakfast with your parents. What a nice surprise."

David pulled out a chair and sat down at the table and took a sip of cold orange juice. Joe got up and walked to the kitchen and took his seat at the head of the table.

"What do we owe this early morning visit to?"

"I have some news that you probably aren't going to like."

"Well that's easy. Just refrain from telling us." Joe smirked.

"I have to tell you."

Martha spoke up. "You two men are not going to play this game with me sitting here. For heaven's sake, son, just tell us. What's on your mind?"

"I'm taking my family to Paris this Christmas. We won't be home for Christmas this year."

Martha's mouth fell open. "Are you serious? With Harry gone, you are leaving us alone?"

"You'll have Anna and Zach. And Mother, this is the only time we will ever be able to take this kind of trip. I have worked hard and saved and we are going to Paris. The kids are excited and Taylor is in shock."

"I'm in a little bit of shock, myself." Martha wiped her eyes.

"Oh, Mother. Don't do that. I want you guys to be happy for us. If you could see how happy the kids are, and Taylor. We've never gone anywhere, to speak of. This will be a trip of a lifetime."

"I'm happy for you, but sad for us. We are getting older, and having family around during holidays is so important to us. You can understand that."

David could see this wasn't going well. "There is no easy way for me to tell you. I knew it would upset the both of you, but I have our plane tickets and we are going. I just want you to be happy for us."

Joseph took a bite of eggs and bacon and topped it off with a huge bite of biscuit. "Go while you can, David. With two kids that will have to go to college and the cost of living the way it is, you need to take advantage of the time you have and travel when you can while they are young."

"Thanks, Dad. I really appreciate that. I'm aware I need to be saving for college and retirement. I have already opened them a savings account. It's not like I'm not thinking ahead."

"You better, Dave. Because time will fly. They will be eighteen before you know it. I'm excited about your trip. Take lots of photos for your Mother and me to see."

David ate some of the eggs and biscuit, and drank another glass of orange juice. He noticed his Mother wasn't talking much.

"Come on, Mother. Lighten up. It's just this one Christmas."

"I'll be fine. It's just that Harry is gone; not sure when he'll come home. And now you won't be here for Christmas. I'm happy for you and your family. I mean, who wouldn't want to go to Paris?"

"My feelings exactly."

Martha stood up and took her plate to the sink. "I'm going to run, you two. Enjoy your conversation; I really need to get to the office."

Joseph spoke up, punching David in the arm. "Don't work too hard, Martha. And thanks for the wonderful breakfast. I'll call you when I leave for work."

David sat back from the table, full to the brim from eating too many biscuits. They were deadly. "Sorry, Dad. Didn't mean to cause a problem this morning with Mother."

"Your mother is sensitive, and you know that. She overreacts to things when she first hear s them. But after she has time to digest it, she will be fine. I'm excited for you. It will be a quiet Christmas for us; we are used to all of you being here at the house. But you know what? We shouldn't get into such a rut that we cannot be flexible."

"That may be asking too much when Mom is used to tradition. She holds on to that."

"We all do. And the kids have enjoyed coming here on Christmas Eve."

"They have. But I made this choice and I think it's a good one for now."

"David, I want you both to have a ball. I almost wish you and Taylor could go by yourselves. You are still young and could have a great time alone in Paris."

"When you have young kids, it isn't an option. We'll have plenty of time to do things after the kids have grown up and moved out. I don't look forward to that time, frankly."

"It's good and bad, Son. Nice to have time alone with your spouse. But too much time can be an issue, too. Your mother and I both work. I think we would kill each other if we both were home all day. I know I would go insane."

"You've got plenty of working years ahead of you, Dad. How is your company doing?"

"Great. I miss Harry there. But he will show up now and again to help out."

"Speaking of Harry, any idea when that guy might come home?"

"No, and that's eating at your Mother night and day. She doesn't talk about it much, but I know what is going on inside of her. We've been married too long."

"We all want him home. It is so dangerous out there. I still can't understand why he is so driven to be involved in war."

"It's in his blood."

"He's shed enough blood."

"I agree. But that won't bring him back."

"I know. He has his own ideas about what is important in life. But now that he has a son, well, that changes everything. I think he saw that right before he left."

"That Zach is going to change all of us, I think."

David stood up to leave. "I've got to get to work, Dad. Thanks so much for the breakfast. It was fun sitting with the both of you. Too bad I had such great news to share with you both."

Joseph laughed. "We are happy for you, Son. Go have a great time. Be safe. We don't need to have anything happen to you while you are there. Things are quite dangerous in Paris right now."

"We'll be careful. And I'll keep in touch."

⊰⊱

Joe stood at the window looking out into the backyard. His gut was telling him that something wasn't right. But he wrote it off to too much food at breakfast. He grabbed his briefcase and headed towards his office. As the day moved along, that heaviness in his stomach and chest remained.

CHAPTER FORTY-TWO

The flight home from Pakistan seemed to take longer than the way over. Harry leaned back in his seat and closed his eyes, weary from the frustration of fighting ISIS for too long. He glanced over at Max, who was already sound asleep. They had done well in their strategic planning; all the cells were gone, and many that followed ISIS were dead. But it was the tip of the iceberg and they both were highly aware. They were heading back to the base in Turkey, and after a short time of debriefing they would be flown back to the base in Memphis where they would meet with General Murdock. Harry was looking forward to that conversation. But he also felt that this might be the last flight overseas he would make in his military career. He was ready to serve in another way, though in what capacity he did not know. Finally the drive to battle was diminishing, and he was slowly finding some much needed peace inside.

After a long sleep the plane lowered through the dark clouds into Turkey. A rainy reception for a team of weary warriors. Harry was anxious to step on American soil, so these few days of debriefing couldn't happen soon enough for him. After days of meetings with a psychiatrist and the debriefing team, going over every single thing that had happened, from every angle they could think of, Harry and Max were set free to fly home. A massive amount of intel was relayed to the debriefing team and would have to be done again when they hit American soil. It was worth every minute because Harry knew they'd done their dead level best on this mission, with the least amount of casualties. In his heart he despised losing that one soldier. He never wanted anyone he was working around to be taken down.

Harry walked with Max towards the plane, both carrying their gear and talking quietly about what they'd just lived through.

"You know, Harry, after all is said and done, I would not trade this experience for anything in the world. But it was hard on me this time. I don't know why. Maybe the injury I took in Iraq. But something was taken out of me this trip. Don't get me wrong, I'm proud of what we accomplished. I think the whole team did more than what was needed to pull this win off. Yet somehow, I feel whipped inside."

Harry shook his head as they boarded the plane. "Funny you should say that, because I feel the exact same way. I told myself the other night that this would probably be my last mission overseas. I enjoyed every second, especially working with you. This is what we love and we did a fantastic job. I feel so good about what we destroyed in Pakistan. Think of the cells that were completely taken out."

"It was awesome. But it was harder this time. Maybe that is our bodies telling us that we need to slow it down. Or do something different."

"My goal now is to find something else that makes me feel equally as productive. And that is going to take some doing."

"I can't sit behind a desk, Harry. Not going to happen."

"Me, either. I am hoping Murdock has something to whisper in our ears. He won't want to let us go, I know that for sure. I just can't think of anything at the base I would want to do, unless it was training guys in the area of intel. I'm not sure that is challenging enough."

⇒⊢⊣⇐

The flight home was another long trip and they slept most of the time, occasionally talking about the mission or one of the guns they loved using. But there were hours of quiet when both men were resting their minds or thinking of things far away.

When they landed the next morning, they were driven straight to the base where they went through another debriefing of sorts and a long talk with General Murdock. "Normally I wouldn't even be seeing you guys. Because I have a soft spot for both of you and admire what you have overcome, we are having this conversation today in my office. So, how did it go this trip? Anything you want to discuss?"

Harry paused. "It was tougher than we thought it was going to be. Not that we didn't feel confident at all times that we could do the job we were sent to do. But the situation in Pakistan is crazy insane. Most of America has no idea what ISIS is doing or what they are capable of."

"I agree, Son. But most wars are that way. The public is not in the loop of what is really going on, with the slanted views of the media and what is allowed by Washington to be told."

Max stepped in. "Yet they feel free to share what tactics we are using, which helps the enemy know where we are. We were wondering where the leaks were at some point because the chemists seemed to suddenly become aware of our presence in Iraq. I wouldn't be surprised if it was the press."

"I am impressed with how you handled yourselves with the handicaps you are dealing with. Was that ever an issue?"

Both men shook their heads. But Harry spoke up.

"We were both determined after losing limbs to build up our bodies so that no one would be able to tell we were using prosthetics. We both tried hard not to allow that handicap to take over our lives. Yes, the weakness had to be overcome, and we had to make our whole body stronger. Where there's a will, there's a way. There is no room for self-pity when it comes to being a Marine."

"Do you feel like a hero?"

"The real heroes are those who gave up their lives. They sacrificed all they had for the good of the whole. We only sacrificed a limb or two. And we have proven that a person can live without a few limbs. In fact, they can not only live, they can thrive."

"Well, think about that statement when you consider what you want to do with the rest of your military career. I don't know if you were thinking about going back into battle again, or if there was something else out there that is pulling you. But consider teaching the men who have returned from battle with limbs lost, because they are full of depression, anxiety, and no hope. You could sure turn some lives around by showing them the way you rebuilt your life."

Harry looked at Max and shrugged. "That feels like we are giving up to me."

"It's quite a step down from being involved in the battle," Max agreed.

"Well, it's something for you to think about. It's badly needed. These men need someone to look at who has made it to the other side of grief and depression. The world is full of those men. You may not realize how big a problem this is within the walls of the military."

"I guess I have never thought about it, although when I was training after I lost my leg, I did see quite a few men who just didn't want to do the work. I think they thought their lives were over. That thought never crossed my mind." Harry sat back in his chair and hit Max in the arm.

"I never gave that thought room in my world. I have a fighting spirit and knew that if I wanted to continue in the military world that I loved and craved, I would have to fight my way back up. And it worked. It was well worth the hours I put in. Now I know and feel I can do anything I want to do. This handicap won't hold me back."

General Murdock leaned back in his chair. "You boys may be up for a medal or two. Just think about what I said. You have lives to live. It may be time to go about living them. I know how hard it would be to merge back into the civilian world. I'm not saying you have to. Just think about it."

⇥✦⇤

Harry and Max found themselves out in the parking lot leaning against their vehicles. It was almost a shock that they were home.

"What do you think about what Murdock had to say?" Max spit on his hand and wiped a smudge off his red Camaro.

"I don't know what to think. I do know I am heading home to see Anna, Zach and my dog. But after that, I have no frigging idea what to do with my life. I like the thought of helping men to become whole again. I know what a shock it was to find out I lost my leg. We can talk about it, Max. We have the time. But we both know we can't do a desk job just to stay in the military. And I'm not sure I want to go back to war again so soon. We have to do something and the military won't wait long for us to decide."

"Right. I'll give it some thought. We can always go back to being a sniper if this teaching thing doesn't do it for us."

"I have a feeling once we see those men and the looks on their faces, we won't be able to turn them down."

"That's something to think about. Let me know when you want to check it out. I'm outta here for now."

━◁┼▷━

Harry got into his old blue truck and grinned all the way to Anna's house. He didn't even want to go home first. He couldn't wait to see Zach, hold him in his arms, and give Anna a kiss. It was going to be so great seeing them again. Home felt good. He had missed her terribly, now that he was able to let his mind think about her again. It felt weird being home, but it felt right. He had not called her to tell her he was home.

It was Christmas Eve day. He felt sure she was going to be at her house so he pulled into her driveway and noticed her car was gone. Suddenly it occurred to him that she might be at his mother's house. It was 5:00 and the family would almost be ready to sit down for dinner. His mouth watered. He started the truck again and quickly drove to his parents' home, knowing this would surprise the whole group when he walked in. He was pretty sure his brother David was going to be there with his wife and kids. That was the normal thing at Christmas.

He stood at the front door with butterflies in his stomach. There was a curl of smoke pouring out of the chimney. He opened the door and walked in and Hack met him first, wagging his tail and jumping up to lick his face. He knelt down and ruffled his fur and hugged him hard. He spoke in a low tone so the family would not hear. He stood up and there was Anna standing in the doorway to the living room. Tears were streaming down her face. She just stood there shaking her head. He ran towards her and picked her up and swung her around, kissing her and laughing at the same time.

Zach came running and screamed out loud. "Daddy's home!" That sound echoed throughout the whole house, even the hidden places where the family skeletons lived. All the hurts and sorrows from childhood. All the disappointments. And all the meanings of what the word "Daddy" meant to Harry when he was growing up were all wrapped up in that echo. Harry picked Zach up, wrapping his legs around his waist, hugging him and laughing with him.

"I'm home, Son. I'm home."

CHAPTER FORTY-THREE

It took Harry a few hours to adjust to being home. When he came into the hearth room of his parents' house, there was a huge tree decorated like only his mother could achieve. There were decorations on the mantle and over every doorway, and there was garland trailing all the way down the stairway with huge red bows at every post. The aroma coming from the kitchen was to die for. And he knew without looking that she'd made several different kinds of cookies, along with a chocolate cake for his father and the dreaded fruit cake for the neighbors. Under the tree were presents wrapped so beautifully that you didn't want to touch them. He just stood there taking it all in. Suddenly it hit him that David wasn't there.

"Mother, where are David and his family? Are they not coming?"

Martha walked out smiling and hugged him again. "Of course you didn't know. They went to Europe for Christmas. It was David's gift to the family."

"What? He decided to go at Christmas when that's when we all get together? That seems weird to me."

"Harry, it was the only time the kids would be out of school long enough for them to make this trip. We both know that going overseas for one week isn't long enough to justify the cost. They are staying a full two weeks."

Harry frowned and shrugged his shoulders. "I would have liked to have seen them before they went. I guess that's a moot point now. He had no way of telling me what his plans were. It just doesn't feel like Christmas without them."

"Don't be upset. I was thrilled that they were able to do this with their kids. It's a chance in a lifetime for them. David has been doing well at work and saved flyer miles. I think it's great, although we will miss them tonight at dinner and later opening presents. I hate for Zach to be the only child here."

Harry walked over to Zach and sat down on the chair next to him, grabbing his arm.

"You have grown a foot since I last saw you! You got to quit growing so fast."

Zach fell out laughing and wrestled with Harry on the floor. Hack got involved and all three of them got pretty loud. Joseph got the camera out and took pictures while Anna sat on the sofa laughing and egging them on.

"Dinner is served." Martha yelled over the laughing and noise coming from the living room.

Everyone got up and walked slowly to the table, with Martha telling them where to sit. . When dinner was nearly over and dessert was on its way to the table, the phone rang. Joseph got up and walked to the kitchen to answer it. Everyone at the table could hear the conversation.

"David? What a nice surprise. We were just talking about how much we missed you guys. Everything okay?" Joseph put the phone on speaker so they could all hear.

Martha ran to the kitchen to listen to the conversation.

"Yeah, Dad. We're doing great. It was a long flight over the ocean and the kids got kinda scared a few times. But now that we're here, they have settled down. We have a great hotel overlooking the Seine River. It couldn't be nicer. Of course it's about 2:00 A.M. for us. I had to call. I knew you guys would be together."

"Well, we miss you here. Your brother made it home finally. We were so surprised tonight to see him." Martha spoke with a quiver in her voice.

"Harry's home? Can you put him on the phone?" David sounded excited.

"Hey, Son. How's it going? I can't believe you're not here on Christmas Eve."

"I had no idea you would be home. And it was the only time we could all go."

"That sucks, Dave. But I do hope you guys have a great time. We miss the kids. Zach was looking forward to spending some time with them."

"We'll be home in two weeks and will definitely get together with you guys."

"Take care of yourself, Son. And keep in touch. We'll be missing you tonight while we sit and open presents." Martha spoke softly.

"Thanks, Mom. Just wanted to hear your voices and say 'Merry Christmas.'"

They all shouted "Merry Christmas!" and the phone line was dead.

"Wow, that was nice. I know they're having a good time. Paris at Christmas! But I sure would've liked to have seen them before they left."

"Harry, I'm just so thankful you're home. We were so worried about you." Joe punched Harry in the arm.

"Thanks, Dad. Now, let's eat dessert so we can open some presents."

"Yeah, Zach is getting fidgety." Anna laughed and kissed Harry's cheek.

"It's good to be home with the family. You have no idea."

"We see enough on television to know that it's very dangerous over there. We can be thankful tonight that you have made it home without injuries. That's something to be grateful for." Martha sat down and took a bite of the chocolate cake.

Harry sat with about six cookies on his plate and a small bowl of ice cream. Zach had a small piece of chocolate cake and ice cream but his eyes were on the presents underneath the tree. Harry whispered to Anna in the lowest voice he had.

"What did we get Zach for Christmas?"

Anna grinned. "Tonight he gets one present from us under this tree. It's a new baseball and glove."

"Ah, that's cool. What did he ask for?"

"You don't want to know."

"Yes I do. Now tell me."

She looked at him and there was no smile. "He just wanted you home. That was what he asked Santa for, for Christmas."

Harry sat up straight and glanced at Zach. "Oh. This boy's serious."

"You have no idea."

"I'm catching on really fast. He is so glad to have a dad. I need to make sure I measure up to those expectations."

"You're already doing a great job, as he worships the ground you walk on, Harry."

"Well, I'll give it my dead level best. I would not want to ever disappoint this kid. He is a rare one. Very old soul."

"Living without your dad can do that to you. He thought you might be dead. Or never to be found. I'm not sure I did the best thing by telling him that."

Harry put his arm around her and kissed her forehead. Zach was watching in between bites of cake.

"You did the best you could. And so far, from what I've seen, you've raised a beautiful boy. I am humbled to be called 'Dad' by this guy. He's amazing, Anna. Really."

She blushed. "Well he does have some of you in him. So he has good genes if special is what you're looking for."

Harry's face turned a light shade of red. "I wouldn't say that. But it's nice to be included in that mix of DNA."

"Let's open presents. I think we've all eaten enough to sink a ship. Zach, you ready to open presents?" Martha was ready to see some smiles.

Zach jumped up and shouted. "Yes! I've been ready all night."

"Well, let's walk over to the tree and sit on the floor. I want you to hand out the presents with me."

Martha and Zach sat down under the tree and began to dole out the gifts as Zach read all the tags, hoping to see something for himself.

Finally all the presents were handed out and Zach was sitting there scratching his head.

"Grandpa, where's my present?"

Joseph smiled. "Go look on the back deck, Son."

Zach turned on the lights outside and opened the door. There sitting on the deck was a brand new shiny blue dirt bike. He screamed out into the cold night. His voice echoed through the whole neighborhood.

"Dad! Mom! Look what I got! It's a new dirt bike. Oh, man! I'm so excited."

Harry went outside and looked at the bike with Zach, putting his arm around his son.

"I would die for a bike like that, Zach. It's a bear of a bike. Man, that is so cool."

Zach grinned and sat down next to Harry on the deck. He leaned his head on Harry's shoulder and Harry whispered softly to him.

"You happy, Son?"

"This is the best Christmas ever, Dad."

CHAPTER FORTY-FOUR

Luckily the dirt bike fit in the back of Harry's old pickup truck. The old Chevy came in handy sometimes. It was too cold, or Zach would have asked to sit in the back of the truck with his bike. But as it was, he sat in the front seat with Harry while Anna followed in her car. It felt good to Harry to have his son in the front seat with him. It felt normal. He turned to look at Zach and noticed again how tall Zach was getting. He was growing like a weed. It looked like he was going to be tall like his dad. Harry grinned. Maybe he was in that boy somewhere.

Zach, on the other hand, was running his mouth without noticing that Harry wasn't even answering. "Dad, I cannot believe I got this bike. How in the world did Grandpa know that I wanted it? Do you think Mom told him? It's the coolest thing. And he got blue. How did he know blue is my favorite color?"

Harry laughed his booming deep laugh. It almost shook the truck. "You're going to love that bike. It is cool, and it's a rugged bike. Perfect for riding trails. We'll have to do that together when it warms up. A little too cold to hit the wooded trails now. But there will be plenty of time when spring comes."

"Will you be home then, Dad? Are you going out again any time soon?"

"I don't think so, Son. I can't promise, but it isn't likely."

Zach seemed to accept that for now. Harry was relieved. He really didn't know what he was going to do with his life in the near future. Or even long term. But he was formulating ideas so that was at least a step in the right direction.

They arrived at Anna's house and Harry lifted the bike carefully out of the truck. Zach was watching his every move.

"Where do you want the bike, Son?"

"I want it inside. I need to look at it."

Harry grinned. "Of course you do."

He took the bike inside while Anna held the front door open.

Anna smiled as Zach went into the hearth room and sat down on the floor, checking the bike from front to back. "That boy is so happy. It was the perfect gift. I had mentioned to your father that he might like a dirt bike, but I had no idea he would buy it. Zach won't pay attention to anything else he gets for Christmas. This will, by far, be his favorite present."

"I can see why. For a boy, a bike is so important. It gives him freedom, a way to move around. A bike is full of adventure. I loved mine."

"I did, too. But girls probably feel a little different. I always felt like I was flying when I rode my bike."

"I'm going to sit with him a moment before he has to go to bed." Harry walked towards Zach and sat on the floor beside him.

Anna left the room to change into something comfortable and Harry didn't miss the opportunity to talk to Zach alone.

"Hey Zach, I got something to talk to you about. Can you keep a secret?"

Zach turned slowly and shook his head. He whispered. "Yeah, Dad. What is it?"

"I have to know you won't say anything to anyone. It's between you and me."

Zach was very solemn. "I promise I won't say a word."

"I need to ask your permission, Zach. This is a very serious thing that I want to talk to you about. And I have to know you are okay with it, or I won't be able to proceed with it."

Zach sat there very quiet, shaking his head.

Harry pulled out a small blue box from his pocket and put it on the floor beside Zach.

"Hurry up and open that box. I want to show you something. But I don't want your mother to see it."

Zach grinned. It was obvious that he was glad to be in on the secret. He opened the box slowly and inside there was a beautiful ring inside, glistening under the lights of the tree.

"Wow. That's cool." He said in the loudest voice he owned.

Harry grabbed him, smiled, and shoved his face into his chest. "Be quiet, Zach!"

"I'm sorry." Zach whispered, looking pitiful.

"You got to be quiet. This is a surprise for your mother."

"For Mom? Wow. She'll love it."

"Well, it's not just a ring, Zach. I want to marry your mother. This is an engagement ring."

"Holy cow! Are you serious? You want to marry Mom?"

"Yep. That's exactly what I want to talk to you about. Would you be okay with your mother and me getting married?"

Zach sat back on his legs and rubbed his eyes. "Are you kidding? Is this for real?"

"Yes it is, Zach. I want to marry your mother. We would be a family. Are you okay with that? I know it might be too fast for you, and I need to know if it will make you uncomfortable in any way."

Zach hugged Harry. "Dad, I've been afraid to even hope that would happen. It would feel so good to have you under the same roof. All my friends have fathers who live at home with them. I never thought I would have that."

Harry swallowed the lump in his throat. "Let's hope she will say 'yes.'"

"She will, if I have anything to do with it."

"You cannot say a word, Zach. This has to be her decision, but if she asks your opinion, and she will, you can tell her whatever you want."

Harry quickly put the ring in his pocket and stood up. Anna was in the kitchen making coffee so he walked over to her and hugged her. Zach took the cue without a word from Harry.

"Mom! I'm going to bed. It's been a long day and I want morning to come fast."

Anna walked into the hearth room and hugged Zach.

"You've had a wonderful Christmas so far. How could it get any better?"

"Oh, maybe Santa has some surprises. You just never know."

Anna laughed and kissed him on the forehead. "Sleep well. We'll see you in the morning bright and early, I'm sure."

"Okay, Mom. Have a great night. Good night, Dad."

Harry waved from the kitchen and winked. He was pretty sure he saw Zach wink back. His stomach went into a knot suddenly and his mouth went dry. He was about to make a commitment that would change all their lives. But it was time. It had to come now. And he was ready, even though he was scared to death. He had not planned on marrying but that was before he found Anna again. She was turning his life upside down, and even though it might not be the best time in his life to make this kind of move personally, that seemed to be how love affected people. It just happened when you were least expecting it. His knees were weak and he didn't know what he was going to say. For such a strong man, he felt like a complete and utter wimp. But somewhere deep inside him, he was going to find the words.

CHAPTER FORTY-FIVE

The hearth room was quiet now that Zach had gone upstairs to bed. Harry glanced at the window that faced the backyard and noticed that the moon was shining right through the window. How apropos. He couldn't have planned it better.

He touched the ring box in his pocket and smiled. She was going to die. She wasn't expecting anything and it made him even more nervous thinking about her reaction. He was excited and scared at the same time. He would be getting a wife and son at the same time. It almost felt like they were married, anyway, because of the new relationship between Anna, Zach and his parents. But the thought of asking her, and committing to a relationship for the rest of his life was huge. Gargantuous.

He turned around and saw her sitting on the sofa wrapping one more gift. The tree already had a mound of gifts for Zach, and he had placed a couple there for Zach and Anna. The room was dimly lit except for the glistening lights on the tall tree. Colored lights. Like he had had when he as a young boy. When he believed in Santa. He decided to walk over and sit down beside her. But he was dead sure she would be able to read his mind.

"What you doing, Anna?"

"Finishing up this gift for Zach. It was a last minute purchase. He said he wanted a new game for his Nintendo, so I found the one he was asking for and now it's wrapped. I think he probably knows all of the presents under the tree. He has touched them, shook them, and guessed most of them already. I, of course, denied them all. But he is so smarty pants. He cannot stand surprises."

Harry laughed at that remark. *Oh, she has no idea.* He put his arm around her and hugged her.

"This is really a special Christmas. It feels so good to have you and Zach this year, and I know Mom and Dad feel the same way."

"They have been so good to us, and I want you to know that I really appreciate it. They didn't have to accept us into the family. It was so gracious of your mother. She has gone out of her way to make us feel at home. And Zach loves your father. I guess that's obvious. He was so anxious to have a family, so we have grabbed hold of yours. I hope you understand."

"Are you kidding? Mother and Dad would drop me as their child if they had to choose between me and Zach. They are head over heels in love with that little guy. He stole my heart the first time I met him."

Anna grinned and shook her head. "You're a pushover when it comes to Zach. Even I can see that."

Harry took that as his cue, but he took a swallow of iced tea she had placed on the coffee table because he felt almost nauseous, he was so nervous. Anna was staring at him like she knew something was going to happen. He took her hand and kissed her palm and looked into her eyes. He saw a tear forming, but he looked away. He wouldn't be able to take her crying just yet.

"Anna, we need to talk. I have some things I want to say and it's not easy for me to say them. It's been a long time since I had a relationship with a woman. I've been so involved with the military that I haven't even thought about dating. Like I told you earlier, I had your photo in my wallet during the times I was away, and it helped me to keep going. But I never allowed myself to get close to anyone because I had to focus on the mission. It was too dangerous to be preoccupied with anything else."

Anna gazed into his eyes. "I know it had to be a difficult time even if you loved what you were doing. Frankly, I don't know that part of you, Harry. I would think you would have to get a little hardened to accomplish what you had to do. Killing people never is easy. Even if they are the enemy."

"It wasn't all about killing. Sometimes it was gathering intelligence. But it was dangerous no matter what we were doing."

"Someday I want to hear all about it. I want to know and understand that part of your life."

"One day really soon you will know all of me. That is what I want to talk to you about, Anna." He cleared his throat. Her mouth slipped slightly open but she didn't say a word.

"When we found each other again, I had no idea, no preconception of what would happen. I just wanted to see you again. And you were open to seeing me. It took a few moments for us to catch up with each other, but considering how long it had been since we last saw each other, we moved at the speed of light. It was so great to see you and to hear how your life has been. But finding out about Zach was like winning the Super Bowl. It actually was better than that. I never dreamed I had a son walking around, and to find that out from you was just a little too much for me to handle."

"You handled it like the man I remembered you to be."

"I have no idea how to be a father, except to remember how my father was with me. But Zach is easy to love, just like his mother."

She blushed and looked down, and one tear fell from her eyes onto the sofa.

"Anna, we have something very special here. It came on us suddenly but I don't think that means anything except that the love we felt for each other when we were younger has risen to the surface again. It was perhaps the one true thing in my life that I had tucked away somewhere deep. I love you, Anna. You are the woman I want to spend the rest of my life with, if you can stand me. I know I have this strange connection with the military and I want you to believe that I will find my way with it. I will find something I can sink my teeth into, without going into battle over and over. The risk is getting greater each time I go, that I won't come home. And right now, after there is an 'us,' I'm just not willing to continue risking my chance to be with you and Zach anymore."

"I realize that is a tough decision for you, Harry. I wouldn't ever ask you to give that up for me."

"Anna, don't you see? It isn't a struggle for me now. I have what I want in you and Zach. Anna, I want you to be my wife."

He got on one knee and pulled out the blue box and set it in her hand that he was holding. She looked down and tears flowed from her face.

"Oh Harry, are you certain this is what you want to do? You know this is so serious because Zach is involved."

He looked her square in the eyes and smiled. "I'm dead sure it is what I want."

She opened the box and took out the lovely engagement ring. He slipped it on her finger and she held her hand up to look at it.

"Will you marry me, Anna?"

She grinned through her tears and he pulled her up to him. "Yes, Harry. I'll be your wife. It seems I've waited a lifetime for this."

"Well, I feel I've lived a lifetime without you. I want to grab hold of this time we are going to have together and get to know you all over again. We will have fun, Anna. We'll make it work."

He swung her around and kissed her. They danced to the music that was in the air, unheard by anyone else. Her face was lit up by the light of the moon. He felt like a school boy dancing with the prettiest girl in the class. Only this one girl was his. Finally.

Unbeknownst to Harry and Anna, Zach was sitting on the stairs peeking through the railing, watching them dance together silently. He was grinning from ear to ear, and whispered softly; "This is going to be the best Christmas ever." He had never imagined that he would find his dad, and now they were going to be a real family. He didn't know, he didn't understand the depth of what was going on inside of him, but he felt whole for the first time in his young life. He loved his mother and would always remain close to her. But there was something so special about having a father. Someone you looked like and someone you could aspire to be like. Harry was such a strong man, so tall and handsome. When he entered the room all eyes were on him. But the neat thing was, he didn't notice. He was a Marine and Zach loved that. In his dreams he was a Marine, too. He would have loved to have fought alongside his father. That would never happen. But he vowed that one day he, too, would be a Marine just like his father. And go to war as a sniper. The best sniper in the whole military. Harry made him want to be the best he could be. Strong, tall, and maybe even handsome.

He tiptoed back to bed, and as he slipped under the covers he looked out his window at the moon. He had never really believed that dreams come true. He had wished for several years now that he would someday meet his real dad, but inside he had his doubts. His mother didn't encourage any talk about his father while he was growing up. He didn't blame her. Although he was only ten years old, he somehow understood that she was trying to do the best thing for him by not looking for the man who was his father. In the weirdest way, and he would never understand how Harry found his way back to her. And the first time Zach met Harry, he felt a bond that he didn't want to let go of. Not ever.

Before he went to sleep he whispered out loud in his empty room. *"I'm going to make him proud of me one day."*

CHAPTER FORTY-SIX

Harry woke up with a grin the size of Texas on his face. He was engaged to the prettiest girl in the world. He checked the weather and it looked like it might snow, so he quickly dressed and fed the horses, making sure there was plenty of hay for them in the stalls. Hack followed him outside and chased a cat off the property. When Harry was finished with chores he called for Hack and they went inside to get dressed. He threw on his jeans and brown leather jacket and they hopped in the truck and drove over to Anna's. On the way there, Harry stopped at a Quik-Stop to pick up a newspaper, and he noticed a man with one leg missing leaning against the side of the building. He looked homeless. Something about the man grabbed at Harry's heart and he walked over to him and reached out his hand. The guy looked surprised but didn't say much.

"How's it going, man?"

"Not too bad."

Harry pulled up his pants leg. "I lost a leg in Iraq. How about you?"

The man looked surprised. "Same here."

"You don't look so good. You got a job? A place to live?"

"No. Not doing too well in that department. I feel pretty hopeless, to tell you the truth."

"I can help you."

The stranger looked up with a snarl on his lips. "I didn't ask for help."

"No, you didn't. But just the same, I know I can help you get your life back."

"Really? And how you gonna do that? Are you going to give me my leg back?"

"No, but there are prosthetics now like mine that are easy to adjust to. At least you could get around better."

"Not interested. I don't have a job, or a place to live. Hell, I don't have a life."

Harry was getting irritated at the guy's attitude. "Look, man, we all suffered from that war. You're not the only one with an injury. I lost my leg. It took me two years to overcome my wounds and a little PTSD. But you know a Marine never gives up. Do you remember that?"

The man looked at Harry in the eyes. "How did you know I was a Marine?"

"Don't worry about that. I just knew. Now here's my number. Call me. And here's some money for food. Don't waste your time drinking 'cause that's not going to get you anywhere. I can get you back to fighting shape if that's what you want. Or just get you to where you can work or do anything you want or need to do, in order to get your life back."

"Hard to believe that's even possible."

"If you'd seen me, you would not have believed I would have gone back to Iraq. And I haven't been home that long. You don't even see me limping."

The man shook his head in agreement. He looked at the card Harry gave him. "So you're Harry Downs?"

"Yep."

"I've heard of you. Cannot believe this. You're one of the best snipers in the Marines."

Harry was surprised but decided to keep that hidden. "I have worked my butt off to get back to fighting shape. You need to get a grip, man. Don't waste all that training just because you lost a leg."

"That's not the only thing I lost. My wife, my job, and many friends over there. Hell, I have nothing."

"Well, it's about time you started to build it back. Think about it. What's your name?"

"John Mason."

"John, nice to meet you. Call me soon. And if you know any other guys like you, give them my number. We're going to be doing work with wounded vets, and I want you to be there."

"I'll call you."

"And by the way, get rid of that sorry attitude. You will be in a room with guys who have no legs or arms. There will be no room for pity."

"I hear you."

"Good. See you soon."

Harry walked away with a purpose in his step. It made him excited to think about changing some of these men from moping giants to Marines. The fight was still in there with John Mason. It was just hidden in self-pity. He got into his truck and ruffled the fur on Hack's neck. "Okay, Buddy. We're headed to see Zach. You ready for some Christmas breakfast? 'Cause I'm starved."

Anna was in the kitchen fixing breakfast when Harry walked through the door. She came running to see him and he grabbed her and kissed her hard.

"Merry Christmas, Beautiful!"

"Hey, sweetheart. So good to see you after such a special evening."

"Tell me about it. I have to pinch myself to be convinced it's really happening."

"I told Zach. I asked him how he felt about it, and he just jumped up and yelled with excitement. I took that to mean that he was all in."

"I knew he would be."

"I don't think he cares what else he got for Christmas. He loves his dirt bike, and he is so excited about you being in our lives that he can hardly stand it."

"I'm pretty geeked myself. We don't waste any time, you and me. We just jump right in there."

"Well, we did wait at least ten years."

He laughed. "Yeah. About time. Good thing I didn't wait to call you when Zach turned eighteen. I would have missed most of his childhood."

Anna tiptoed and kissed his cheek. He grabbed her again and she laughed. He couldn't wait to get his hands on her. But timing was everything. They had a ton of planning to do and had to decide where they would live. He was hoping she'd choose the farm. He hadn't brought it up because it would have been too much too soon. But maybe in a day or two they could talk about all of that stuff.

Zach yelled out and Harry went over to him and slapped his hand.

"Good job, Zach. She never guessed that you knew."

Zach laughed and pointed to the bike. "Can you believe this thing? It is so cool."

"You do have some presents to open. You best get started. Looks like quite a pile under that tree."

"I have already gotten everything I need for Christmas."

"So have I, Zach. So have I."

Paper and ribbon were thrown everywhere as Zach tore into the packages. He got clothes for school and a new game for the Nintendo. Under the tree were a new ball and glove, and also a couple of books to read about the Marines. Harry got three nice looking shirts and Anna got a beautiful scarf, pretty pajamas, and Harry bought her season tickets to the local theatre. She was so excited.

"Harry, that's what I always wanted to do. I love to go to plays but haven't splurged on that. You remembered one of our conversations. I'm impressed."

"I knew you wanted to go, and I'm just thankful I was paying attention." He laughed.

"I'm learning more about you every day."

He sat down beside her and leaned back against the sofa. Zach was admiring his bike again.

"I have something to talk to you about. I've been struggling with what I wanted to do with myself if I don't return to Iraq. Well, I stopped on the way here to pick up a newspaper and there was a man standing against the side of the building. I walked over to him and shook his hand, and we talked for a moment. His name was John Mason. A Marine veteran who served in Iraq, like me. He was missing a leg, was homeless, and had nothing to eat. No family. He'd lost everything. So I talked to him, telling him I could help him get back on his feet. He wasn't having it at first. Bad attitude and no hope. But after we talked for a while and I shared how I lost my leg and worked out to rebuild my body and life, he listened. I think he might call me. I think that is the direction I want to go. I would like to have a place with Max where we train the men who have lost limbs and rebuild their bodies and minds. What do you think?"

"Wow! I mean, wow. That's the most I've heard you say since we started talking again. Look how excited you are about this!"

He grinned. "It feels good to be excited about something. And it won't pull me away from home."

"How will Max feel about this?"

"I think he'll get on board. We touched on it when we came back from our last mission."

"I'm so happy to see you this way. I was worried that you wouldn't be able to find anything that would fulfil that urge to serve. To go to battle. To have your life matter."

"I'll have to give it more thought and talk it over with Max. But it's a start. A great start."

"You get enough breakfast?"

He leaned over and kissed her. "I have you. That's all I need. I think I'm going outside and watch Zach ride that bear of a bike."

He tapped Zach on the shoulder and pointed outside. They both rolled the bike out the door and Zach hopped on it and rode down the street with Harry cheering him on. It was Christmas morning and everything was good.

CHAPTER FORTY-SEVEN

David had a knack for running into the right people at the right time. That was one trait that boosted his real estate sales over and over. He never thought about it working to his advantage while in France. But this one day, when the weather was just north of perfect, he was at a local market getting groceries and bread for dinner and ran into an old friend who had moved to France ten years ago. Phillip Jennings was one of those guys who could turn a dollar into a pot of gold. He woke up every morning with a rainbow in his bedroom. It was crazy sick and David never could figure out how the guy made so much money, but today of all days, there he was, alive and well. Flourishing, as usual. It took David a few moments to recognize him with his salt and pepper beard and glasses.

"Phillip? Phillip Jennings? Is that you?"

Phillip looked shocked that someone had called his name out. He turned David's direction and stared at him for a moment and then burst out laughing. His laugh was deep and rich. David walked over to him and they bear-hugged each other.

"David Downs. I can't believe it! What in the world are you do-ing in Paris?"

"We haven't seen each other in over ten years."

"You look the same damn way you did back then. Maybe a little less hair."

David laughed. "Well, I you have more hair on your face now than you do on your head."

They both laughed and slapped each other on the back. David pointed to two chairs over on the side of the market building and they walked over and sat down, pulling the chairs closer so that they could hear each other over the crowd that had accumulated outside the market.

"What in the world are you doing over here? Taking a break? Are you alone?"

"I'm here for a vacation during the holidays while the kids are out of school. I have two children now, Phillip."

"That's hard to believe. Where is your wife? I'd like to meet her."

"She's back at the hotel where we are staying."

"I'm working this afternoon but maybe we could all get togeth-er. Where are you staying?"

"At the Hotel Eiffel Seine."

"I may have something special for you, if you are going to be here for a few weeks. I know someone who rents out their villa at a very low price. You would love this place, David. Let me make a phone call and see what I can find out."

David sat back in the chair and shook his head. "You never cease to amaze me, Phillip. You are always making deals and know all the right people. How do you manage to do that?"

Phillip smiled but then looked serious. "I think I draw those people to me. I don't even try to do it. Does that make any sense?"

"I guess. I have never figured out how you are so successful, no matter what you try. I know you are a born salesman. I do okay for myself, but you always fly. I wish I could be more like that. I think I'm too introverted."

"Believe me, David, your type of personality is very believable. People would trust you immediately. Me, not so much. I am hyper and talk too much. Yeah, I make friends easily, but long term, it would better to have your quiet personality."

"Well, I've never chased money. I do need money to live, but it's not on my mind 24/7. I think it is with you. Am I right?"

"Actually, I'm not money driven. I'm a task-oriented person. I like to be the best. That may be the real reason. I like to win."

"I think you've hit the nail on the head. I envy you that. But I don't think I could ever be that way. It's not in my genes."

They laughed and shook hands. "Give me your business card and I'll call you in a day or two to let you know about the villa. I think your family would absolutely love being there. It's too good a deal to pass up."

"It sounds wonderful. Let me know. Taylor would really enjoy it, I'm sure."

"Be careful here, David. Things are a little unstable because of ISIS. Just keep your family close and keep your eyes open. You'll be fine. I'm sure you've noticed all the police around. It almost feels like war time."

"Good to see you, Phillip. I'll look forward to hearing from you in a day or two."

David watched Phillip walk away and scratched his head. *Go figure. I run into him and he's got a deal for me. It's insane how he does that.*

He finished his shopping and headed back to the hotel where Taylor and kids were. Clouds were forming and it looked like it might rain so he ran the last block to the hotel. When he got there he was out of breath and sweating. The kids were on the bed watching television and playing with their Nintendo DS. Taylor was redoing her nail polish, looking beautiful as ever.

"You'll never believe who I just ran into at the market."

She looked up for a second and blew on her the wet nail polish. "There's no point in my trying to guess."

"Phillip Jennings. Do you remember him? He and I were friends years ago in college. He moved to Paris over ten years ago, and as odd as it seems, I practically walked up on him."

"That's amazing. How's he doing?"

"He looked great. He's fast turning gray but it was becoming on him."

"I know you had fun catching up."

"The guy's a money magnet. He's absolutely amazing. He could sell a blind man a pair of glasses. But a great guy. I have always liked him."

"Sounds like you men are opposites. But I think you have made a good real estate agent. You do very well."

"I'll never be like Phillip. We discussed that. Even though he is a talker, you can't help but like him."

"I've known people like that."

"Besides, he told me that he has a connection with someone who owns a villa outside of Paris, and they rent it out for practically nothing. He will call us in a day or so to let us know if it is available."

"Is that where we need to be?"

"I think it's an opportunity of a lifetime to stay there. It's on a vineyard, I think. We'll see. He will call me soon to let me know."

"Would be nice to see the countryside and get out of the city. I love Paris, but there is more to France than this."

"I agree." He walked over to the window and looked out at the sky.

"It's fixing to pour. Good thing I made it back with the food because it may be raining too hard to go out for lunch. Is that okay with you?"

"That's fine with me. I have a blister on my foot from walking so much in my new shoes yesterday. And the kids are enjoying their

Nintendos, so they are fine. I hate those things but they sure do come in handy on a rainy day."

"He'll call us soon to let us know if it is available. I'm excited. It will be quite a change for us and I can't imagine staying in a villa."

Taylor moved over to the small sofa where David was sitting. "This whole vacation is wonderful, sweetheart. You have worked so hard to get us here, and I never dreamed we would take a vacation overseas until the kids were older or out of the house. It may not mean that much to them now, but you and I can enjoy all of this. The historical architecture is breathtaking. I could get lost just walking down a street. We don't have anything close to this at home."

David put his arms around her and pulled her close to him. "You know, when we spoke to my parents and Harry got on the phone, I suddenly realized how much I miss my brother. He sounded great on the phone. He has really been through it and I wasn't able to be there for him. When I get home, I need to spend more time with him."

"Did you just jump into the middle of a thought you were having?"

"I guess I did. I hear what you are saying. It was a chance of a lifetime and I thought I'd better do it while the opportunity was staring me in the face. If we wait on something like this, we never know what is going to come up."

"Right. I think I'm going to fix us lunch with the food we picked up at the deli, and then take a long hot bath. Maybe by then the sun will have broken through those dark clouds out there, or you will have heard from Phillip."

David kissed her and smiled. He was a lucky man to have such a beautiful wife. On top of that, she loved the children almost more than she loved him. She had the patience of Job. It was annoying sometimes and he often disagreed with her form of discipline. But the kids had been near perfect on this trip with absolutely zero whining, which was almost as rare as finding life on the Moon. Well, they weren't that bad, but Sara had the whining thing down to a T. And when she cried she could break glass. He was sure of it.

Taylor served lunch on the round table in the kitchen area of the suite and they agreed to allow the children to eat on their bed as long as they didn't spill anything. The rain had kicked up and the wind was blowing it against the window. It sounded like it was settled in for the afternoon but he was hoping he was wrong in his estimation of the weather. He kept checking his phone to see if Phillip had sent him a message. So far, nothing. So he fell into a deep sleep that lasted longer than he intended.

CHAPTER FORTY-EIGHT

Harry sat in his study listening to the rain. The pastures need-ed the water, and he'd put the horses in the barn. Hack lay at his feet, dozing but with one eye open in case Harry should de-cide to move. He dialed Max's number and rested his feet on the desk. He was leaning way too far back in the chair, but he was a dare devil at heart.

"Max, how's it going?"

"Hey, man. Been busy rehabbing and getting myself back in shape. I feel pretty good. How about you?"

"I feel good. Been a little lazy lately. And while I've been away from you, I proposed to Anna. So we will be getting married soon."

"Wow. That's huge. You ready for that?"

"More than. But that's not really what I wanted to talk to you about. I was out the other morning getting a paper and ran into a vet who was standing against the side of the building. He looked pretty rough. Probably homeless. I shook his hand and told him I'd like to help him get his life back. He was defensive but finally came around. I told him to call me. What do you think about us tackling the wounded warriors who feel like their lives have ended? We are proof that they don't end. But there is a lag between the VA and the wounded. I was hoping we could fill that gap somehow."

"That's a tall order, Harry. Have you talked without anyone yet?"

"No, I wanted to see if you were interested at all in doing this with me. You remember Murdock mentioned this to us a while back."

"Yes, I remember just fine. Don't think I'm going to let you get all the glory. Just let me know when and where and I'll show up."

"I don't have a clue what this will take and how many hoops we'll have to jump through to get it done but I'm going to pursue it as long as you are on board. It would be too much for me to do alone."

"I get that. You can count on me. Just let me know what you need me to do."

"Great. I'll make the phone calls and get it done."

Harry spent the next couple hours on the phone with several people trying to get an understanding of what it would take and how the military would help or facilitate the process. He knew he had to go by their guidelines, but first he had to find out who knew those guidelines. And maybe there weren't any, because nothing like this rehab facility had been set up yet as far as he knew. The wounded were kind of sent home on their own to figure it all out. And most of them didn't have the drive to push through the horror of losing a limb, not to mention the loss of their friends. The more he talked to people and the more he thought about it, the more excited and determined he got. What he didn't want to happen was get stuck in the red tape of the slug machine called the VA. He wanted to move fast with this so he could get to work and help the most people. He tried to relay that message to all the right people he was talking to, and tried to keep them from putting him off for weeks at a time.

While he was waiting on a call-back, Anna called.

"Would it be okay if Zach rode horses again? It is all he is talking about, now. I think you may have started something, on top of all the sports he is interested in."

Harry laughed. "Of course you can come. All of us will ride. I'll get the horses saddled up. It will do me good to get out of the house, as I've been on the phone the whole morning. It's been raining pretty hard, so let me check the pastures and I'll call you right back."

"We don't want to be in the way, Harry."

"In the way? Are you joking? It will do me good to see the both of you."

"We'll be right there. I'll wait for your call."

Harry hung up the phone, motioned to Hack, and walked out the back door to the barn. The rain had stopped but it was still cloudy and cold. Not the best riding weather. The road to the house had big puddles but the pastures seemed okay. He checked the weather forecast and it looked like the rain might be over for Memphis. He called Anna back quickly and began to saddle the horses. She would be there in about ten minutes.

He grabbed three horses, pulled down the saddles one at a time, and got the horses ready to go. Hack sensed something and was excited when he saw the horses coming out of the barn, saddled and ready to ride. Two minutes later, Anna pulled up and Zach nearly jumped out of the car before she had it in park. He ran to Harry and nearly knocked him over with his hug.

"Hi, Son! It's good to see you. You had a great idea, wanting to ride horses today. It's barely dried out enough to go into the pastures, but we'll see how it goes. You'll at least get a few minutes ride out of it. You guys ready?" He waved at Anna as she got out of the car.

"Whew. He was so ready to see you today. I told him it might be too wet. It poured at our house this morning."

"Here, too."

"What you been doing today, baby?" She hugged him and kissed his lips, which were hidden now by a full mustache.

"You like me with a beard?"

She backed away and saw the short growth on his face. "Mmmm. Not sure. You look good no matter what you do. I think I could get used to that tough guy look."

He laughed. "Just making a change. Hope it didn't turn you off. It's nice not to shave during the winter. And we've had some cold days lately."

"So what you been doing? You didn't answer me."

Harry motioned for Anna to mount her horse. "I've spent my morning on the phone with the VA and other departments in the military sharing my idea that I told you about the other night. What I am looking for is an opportunity to fix a broken system when it comes to the wounded men who have come back from war and have no way to rebuild their lives. There is a lag in taking care of the rehab for those men."

"I loved what you shared with me and I agree there is a great need. You would know much more than I do, because I've only seen it on television. And some of the fathers I deal with at school. Some of them were wounded and are struggling with what to do with themselves."

"I should hear something soon. It's exciting and Max is on board. I think I have him as pumped as I am, and it gives us a great purpose. You know I love a good challenge."

"Hey, Zach, I'll lead us into the left pasture away from the barn. I'm not sure how much water is still standing in the fields. We're lucky it's not pouring on us right this minute."

Hack stayed with Harry and ran alongside his horse, leading him into the pasture. The water had soaked in some but there were puddles. Harry knew this ride wouldn't be long, but it felt good to move around. He'd been sitting all day at his desk with the phone to his ear.

After about twenty minutes of working hard to avoid the puddles, Harry headed back to the barn. He could hear Zach fussing under his breath, and grinned. He loved that boy.

"Hey, Zach. I hear you. We'll ride another day. Old Hack needs to play with you. He's been bored stiff today. Let's get off here at the barn and I'll take the saddles off. You can help me."

Zach dismounted and walked his horse to the barn, where Harry lifted off the saddle and hung it over a saw horse with a red blanket draped over it. Anna followed behind Zach, and Harry let Zach try to lift the saddle off. It was a little heavy for him, but he grunted and groaned and threw it up on the blanketed wooden horse next to Harry's. He looked proud of himself.

"Way to go, Zach. You're going to get the hang of this thing fast. We will have a lot of work to do this summer. Maybe you'll be running this farm before I know it."

Zach was grinning ear to ear. "I know I can do it, Dad. It's heavy, but not that bad. I need to work out so I can get stronger. Do you think you'll come to my baseball games in the spring?"

"Of course I willther. I can't wait to see you play. We need to practice pitching and doing some batting practice so you'll be ready when spring comes. You can't just sit through the winter and expect to be on top of your game when spring season comes."

"Yes, Dad. I'd love to practice with you."

Harry still wasn't used to the "Dad" thing, but he loved it.

After they walked into the house, Zach took the dog into the hearth room and played. Harry took advantage of some alone time with Anna. "Come here, Anna. Sit with me on the sofa. I really have missed you."

Anna leaned against him and propped her feet on the rough-hewn coffee table. "This feels good. I missed you too, Honey."

"I've been thinking. Well, I've been thinking way too much lately. But about you and me, and when we might get married. I'm getting tired of us living in two places. What about you?"

She laughed. "Oh Harry, it's been so long. I don't know how we've stood it."

"Okay. I deserve that remark. But once I went with this relationship and found Zach, it makes me feel lonely when I go home and you and Zach are at your house. So what are we going to do about that? Which house can you be happy living in?"

"Oh, let's see. We could live in your house for the summer and move into mine for the school year, since it's so close to the school."

"Hmmm. Surely there is a better solution than that. I do like your house. But the farm gives us so much room. We can even add to the house if we needed to. In case you wanted another child."

Anna almost choked. "What? Another baby?" Oh, I don't know about that, Harry. We didn't talk about having kids. Are you serious?"

Harry was laughing so hard he had to get up and grab a glass of water. "You need something to drink?"

"Yes. But talk to me. Are you really thinking we will have more children?"

"Well, I was leaving a little room for that discussion."

"I don't know how strongly you are leaning in that direction, but I sort of thought I was done. Now that's not set in stone, mind you. But it is a scary thought."

"I was halfway kidding, but the point I was making was that we could make this house anything you wanted it to be. It isn't that large now. But we have so much land around the house that we could add on to the kitchen and make it larger. And the master bedroom could be larger. I know Joe could do that for me."

"What were you thinking about?

"I was asking you."

"I think we need to relax. This feels so good that I hate to ruin the mood."

Harry shook his head. "We're going to address this soon. I want us to get things taken care of so that you don't have to go home anymore. You will already be home with me. And Hack."

She looked into his eyes, and he could tell she was close to tears. "I'm still pinching myself to see if this is real. That you are real."

He kissed her mouth and held her close. "I know what you mean, Anna. It does seem like a nice dream. Until I look at Zach. Then I know it's reality in its best form. If this is a dream, then it's the mother of all dreams. And I sure don't want to ever wake up."

CHAPTER FORTY-NINE

Christmas in France had turned into a fairytale. David and Taylor pulled up at the villa that had suddenly been offered to them at the cost of a good hotel. When they drove up to the front door they stared at each other in wonderment. In the dead of winter, it was still beautiful. Rolling hills and trees, a huge vineyard which wasn't active in the winter, and a mansion that would hold two baseball teams. David was shocked at the favor of this owner. The children got out of the car and ran around screaming in delight. There was no one around to hear.

"Taylor, what did we do to deserve this gift?"

"I have no idea. You must have been really good friends with Sam for him to even mention this."

"He's just that kind of guy. Let's go inside. I think this is way above my pay grade."

"No joke."

David opened the door and the kids ran inside. The atrium was so large it echoed when the kids were talking loudly. A woman came walking out of the front hallway and nearly startled everyone to death.

"Good morning. I am Francois. Welcome to Palais Abbaye. We hope you enjoy your stay with us. Come. Let me show you to your rooms."

David grabbed Taylor's arm and they glanced at each other quickly and shrugged.

"Come on, kids, let's go see where we are sleeping."

The kids ran ahead, following Francois down the long mahogany-floored hallway. The ceilings were high and the walls were filled with massive oil paintings of different locations in France. Everything seemed oversized. Francois took them up the winding staircase where there were rooms on either side another long hallway.

"These are your rooms. You actually have the floor to yourselves. There is a fully stocked kitchen here and three bathrooms. Each of you can have your own room, if you like. The beds are down feather mattresses so they are very comfortable. There is a bell in each room in case you need anything. You have a full staff of servants at your beck and call. And they are waiting to meet your needs, so feel free to ask for anything. There is a menu by your bed so that you can choose your meals. This is all included in your stay here. So please feel free to go anywhere in the estate and eat whatever you like. It is your time to relax and enjoy yourselves."

With that, Francois walked out of the room and back downstairs. Taylor glanced around and decided to take a tour of each of the rooms so she could choose one for her and David. The kids had already claimed their room. They picked the one that had two full beds so that they could be in the same room. They dove on top of the beds and jumped up and down, laughing.

"Okay, guys. I know you're excited but we need to show some respect here. This isn't our home. And your mother never allows you to jump on the beds, anyway."

They answered in unison. "Okay, Dad."

Taylor grinned and pulled David into their bedroom. The four poster king-sized bed had posts that nearly reached the ceiling, which was so high you would get vertigo trying to change the light-bulbs in the chandelier. She sat on the edge of the bed and fell into the feather mattress. David lay down beside her and they laughed at how far they sank into the mattress. It was going to be an interesting night.

"I've never slept on a feather mattress. I wonder why they chose this type of mattress."

"Maybe it's popular in France. Who knows? But I bet we sleep well. It's a little chilly in the house and we have a fireplace in the bedroom. I love that."

"So do I. Let's tour the estate and then take the kids for a drive and find a neat café for lunch."

"That sounds wonderful. I'll get the kids and we can take a short tour of the grounds."

They walked downstairs and Francois appeared again. "Can I help you?"

"We just wanted to take a short tour of the grounds before we head out to shop and eat at a sidewalk café."

"I will show you were to go. One can get lost easily in this mansion."

They all followed her through the hallways and out the back of the mansion. It was a sight to behold. Hills covered in tall trees, looking down into the vineyard, which was massive. Even in the winter it was beautiful. They walked through the rest of the house and grand kitchen, and then out to the car. The kids were getting restless, so David drove to town and they parked, bundled up in their winter coats and gloves, and walked through the narrow streets looking for a café. David asked a store owner where the best lunch spot was and was directed down the street about half a block. It was a good walk and their appetites were growing as they approached the Café Normandie. Fortunately, some of the help spoke broken English, so they were able to order without too much of a problem.

"Isn't this fun? Look how quaint this café is." Taylor smiled at David.

"I still cannot believe the meeting with Phillip. It does feel like we are in a dream. This is going to make our trip. We would have never been able to afford such a luxury."

"Our friends will never believe you make this kind of money selling real estate. They're gonna think you are dealing in drugs or something."

He laughed. It felt good to laugh. "Let them think what they will. I was not going to turn this down."

"I'm glad you didn't. Let's eat."

The kids were already eating their sandwiches and drinking a milk shake. It was poured into a quaint glass with a glass polka-dotted straw. The place was crowded at lunch time and all the people around them were speaking French. It was the first time since they arrived in Paris where David felt like a genuine tourist.

"After lunch, let's take a walk down some of these narrow streets. I'll take some photos so we can show the folks how wonderful France is. I wish Harry and Anna could have met us here. It's times like this when his being in the military can get in the way of life. I just hope he makes it home this time."

"Oh, that would have been wonderful, David. I would have loved to have seen Anna again, and I know the kids would have loved to play with Zach. He's such a nice boy."

"Harry is a lucky man. I know it had to have been a shock to discover he had a son. But Anna has done a supreme job of raising Zach by herself. They seem very close. Zach is so respectful. He grabbed hold of Harry like nothing I've ever seen. They are kindred spirits, for sure."

"It's a beautiful thing. Let's get together with them when we get back home, if Harry's back. We'll be hearing wedding bells soon, I bet."

David nodded and waved at the kids who had gotten out of their seats and were staring out the window at the park across the street. They headed out the door and took a long walk down several narrow streets lined with tall buildings. The streets were brick and the buildings were built right next to the road. It almost felt like the buildings were closing in on David. He took photos of the kids running ahead. The sun between the buildings was casting shadows on everything in its way. It was one of the best afternoons on the whole trip. Although cold, the wind had died down so it was bearable. Enjoyable. David held Taylor's hand as they walked back to the car.

"Had I known we were going to walk so much I'd have worn my tennis shoes. I'm getting another blister."

"You want me to carry you back to the car?" David asked, being sarcastic.

"Watch out, Buddy. I may take you up on that offer."

"I bet I could still carry you. You haven't gained that much weight since we married." He laughed loudly and threw his head back.

"Okay, pick me up. Let's see how far you can carry me."

Jack was listening and squealed with delight. "Come on, Dad. Pick her up."

Sara Jane skipped alongside David, watching him struggle to carry Taylor.

"Well, maybe I was wrong. You feel heavier."

Taylor stepped down and laughed, as she punched David in the side. "You've gotten weaker. That's the problem. I'm the same size I was when we married."

David shrugged and smiled. "I give. It was fun, anyway. We're almost there. Are you guys ready to go back to the villa or do you want to drive back to the park and play for a while?"

"Let's go play. We've been inside too much. It's not that cold today." Jack sounded determined to play outside.

"Okay. Let's go to the park. Remember to stay close to us. We're in a foreign country. If someone grabbed you, we would never be able to find you."

Taylor grabbed his arm. "Don't scare them. I'll keep an eye on them."

"I just want them to realize we are not home. Things are different here. We would not even know where to look for them. Things happen, Taylor. We're not in the same world we grew up in."

"I know. I just hate to scare them. We're on vacation."

"We still have to be a little more careful while we're here. I don't want them to run off."

Two hours later, worn out and cold, they returned to the villa and climbed the stairs to their floor.

"I'm going to take my shoes off and rest my poor feet. You want to take a nap or what?" Taylor asked, rubbing her toes.

"I think I'll sit in the main parlor and read a little. The view from here is breathtaking, Taylor. Sit with me and just enjoy the view. I'm sure the kids will entertain themselves."

Taylor sat down beside him and propped her feet on the coffee table in front of the large overstuffed sofa. She leaned her head back and dozed off, occasionally snoring softly, to David's delight.

David grabbed an interesting book off the bookshelf about old Paris and propped his feet on the same table. He looked over at Taylor. She was beautiful in her sleep, even with the light snore. He had been so fortunate to find her. To be able to love her and have a family with her. She'd stayed by him when he was struggling in the beginning. She had never doubted him. And when Jack was born, she handled him with such ease. He was the perfect child. No complaining, but then again, Taylor seemed to know him so well. And when Sara Jane came, even though she was a handful,

Taylor amazed him at how she took to being a mother so quickly once again. It made his job easier because he didn't have to worry about what was happening at home while he was at work. She was the rock that held them all together. She was his sounding board. She always shared a bit of wisdom or shed light on the subject he was dying to talk with her about. She had never finished college, but her IQ was way over his head. She looked like the typical stay-at-home wife, but she was brilliant. He knew better and really strove not to take that for granted. He actually counted on her opinion, even if he never said it out loud.

He stared at her for the next few moments, wondering what her dreams were. He wondered if she was happy in this marriage and felt fulfilled. He wondered what the rest of their life would be like. But most of all, he was thankful to have walked this far with her.

For a moment, there was an unsettling feeling that came and went like a slight breeze that comes up before a rain. It left him feeling a bit uneasy, so he opened the book and got lost in the pages of old architecture and bridges. In the background, in the back of his mind, he was aware of the children laughing and playing. He wanted to grab that moment and hold on to it. He had gotten caught up in the remembering of their beginning, so much so, that he didn't pay attention to that feeling of dread.

Night came and dinner was served in the main parlor at a small table. It was dark outside but through all the glass windows that surrounded the room, they could see a lit up city with tall buildings and dark figures walking the streets.

"What a beautiful day we've had, David." Taylor had her mouth full of roast, carrots, and potatoes. It was a comfort meal after such a lovely day.

"It's been perfect, Honey." He patted her hand and suddenly a chill came over him. He grabbed her hand and kissed it.

"What's wrong, baby? Are you okay? You look white as a sheet."

He cleared his throat and took a sip of strong coffee. "No, I think I just got a chill. I'm fine."

But inside David was troubled. He didn't know why. He couldn't put his finger on it. So he shrugged it off and made himself enjoy the night.

As he lay down that night next to the most beautiful woman in the world, he felt like he had had an omen of what was to come. Did that really happen to people? He turned her face to him and kissed her and made love to her passionately. As they lay there about to sleep, he spoke to her in a low voice.

"I love you more than anything in the world, Taylor. Do you understand that?"

She smiled shyly. "Of course I do, baby. You've told me that a million times."

"I know, but this time I want you to hear it. Clearly. You're everything to me. I couldn't live without you."

"I hope you never have to, David. I feel that same way. If we go, we go together."

"I wasn't going to say that, but I was thinking it. We've had such a great day together with the children. We are blessed."

She snuggled underneath his arm and kissed his warm mouth. "We'll be all right, David, as long as we're together." She closed her eyes and was soon asleep.

But David lay there for hours, trying to let go of the dread he felt inside. He'd never felt that way before, but before he fell into a deep sleep he rationalized that it was because they were in a foreign country in a place he was so unfamiliar with. After turning over several times and struggling with getting comfortable in a bed that sank so deeply in the middle, he fell fast asleep with his arm over Taylor. In his dreams, he was trying to save her all night long.

CHAPTER FIFTY

S ometimes, not often enough, things line up in the universe. Harry had put all his marbles into one basket and that basket was the military. It was known for not moving quickly when it came to wounded warriors and their recovery. But somehow, Harry's request got into the hands of the right people, and when he least expected it, he got a phone call that blew his mind.

He'd just spoken to Max and answered question after question concerning the how and why of setting up a system to improve the lives of so many men who were struggling with their injuries. He hadn't had all the answers but he'd faked it so that Max would not lose his momentum in backing Harry in this endeavor. Impossible as it seemed, he and Max just might have a chance. because the next phone call Harry received was from the VA, and they were very excited about Harry's proposal.

Harry quickly set up a meeting and met with the program director currently in place that oversaw the rehab for all wounded vets. He admitted the current program was weak and was ready to listen to everything Harry had to say. So Harry took advantage of the moment and talked the director into allowing him and Max to take over, and even have other recovered wounded vets help in the rehabilitation of those currently wounded. It was a huge endeavor but not too much for Harry. He was a fighter and wasn't going to let this pass without giving it all he had.

The brass were impressed with Harry's energy and his own super-human recovery. Max and Harry were heroes among the wounded. Everyone knew who they were. So their reputation helped to get the ball rolling. The muscle needed to make this work would come basically from the two most powerful snipers in the military. But they were Marines first. Tough as nails. They had used that training and carried it into the recovery of their own bodies. Now they were willing to show other men how to get their lives back.

Harry was so excited he could hardly talk to Max. He hadn't believed it would be so easy. Although it had taken time to get to this place, now it was up to them to make it happen. And they had the backing of the military to get it done. Monies had been allotted to improve the gym and they were able to purchase all new equipment.

The first day open was the most nerve-racking day he'd experienced since his own recovery. He and Max were going to stand in front of men who were hurting, and struggling. These men weren't sure if they were going to ever walk again, much less serve their country in any valuable way. Outside the room Harry and Max sat at a small table and discussed the game plan again.

"Harry, when we go in there in front of these men, we go with strength. They have to feel the energy in us and the power. We know where they are inside and it's not a good place. They feel they've lost everything. They are rotting inside. I'm not sure how, but we have to turn that around."

"Take a deep breath, Max. We've already walked down this road. It's difficult, but they can do it. Our first action will be to give them hope. The reaction to what we tell them will work like a domino effect with their emotions. Let's go. We've wanted this opportunity and now it's here."

As they walked into the room, Harry stood still, scanning the group of men in front of him. He took a deep breath and started talking. He had no idea what he was saying, but it just came pouring out.

"It's so good to see all of you this morning. I know what it took to come here, and I admire all of you for making the effort. As you can see, we both wore shorts this morning for a reason. We wanted you to see our injuries and that we are just like you are. This room is full of wounded warriors and we are proud to be a part of that. But we have something to share with you, and I want to get started right now so that we don't waste any of your time."

Harry walked out in the middle of the men and stood there for a moment. "I'm Harry Downs, a Marine, and I know exactly where you guys are in your head. I remember it and I don't think I'll ever forget those feelings. You spent years training and honing your skills, only to get wounded and stopped in the middle of your careers. You feel less of a man, you feel overwhelmed at the thought of recovery, and you have no idea what you will do with your lives even if you did walk again. Max, my friend and fellow Marine, lost his leg and arm. But what we both did, without even talking to each other, was to push ourselves to the limit every single day as though we were driven to survive. To overcome. We allowed ourselves to have hope. And that is what I want you to leave today with. Hope. We are here to tell you that we are going to change your lives. It will be tough and sometimes you will want to quit. But dig deep, men, and remember your training. This will take every ounce of will-power you have. Every single thought you have must be focused on your recovery. You don't have time to sit and have a pity party. No more negative thoughts. This is your time to recover from injuries you incurred fighting for your country. I want you to understand there is a good chance that you can return to active duty. If you haven't thought of that, I want you to keep that in the forefront of your mind, if you are even remotely interested in doing that. It's a goal that is achievable and we are prime examples of that."

Harry paused and took a good look at their faces. Max stepped forward and smiled at the men, whose faces showed a mixture of relief and pain. "I'm Max McIntyre, and as Harry said, I was also injured in Afghanistan. It nearly took the life out of me. I was scared and felt hopeless. I know you guys have experienced that and I want to encourage you this morning because you are capable of more than you think, even at this stage of your recovery. You just need hope. And we are here to share that hope with you. New prosthetics have come into play in the military, made especially for men who want to return to active duty. As you can see, we both walk without a limp. We can do anything a man can do with two legs and two arms. But that took a lot of hard work and belief in the result. Once you begin this program there is no turning back. It's going to be every bit as hard as the training you got as a Marine. But you are experienced soldiers. Suffering and pushing yourselves won't be anything you haven't already done before. It will all be familiar, but you just have a few handicaps to overcome. And you will. We worked out for two years solid. We pushed ourselves without much help from the military or each other. You will have both of us guiding you, answering questions, and pushing you farther than you really wanted to go. It's an exciting time right now in your life. Listen to us and give it all you've got. I know you want to change or you wouldn't be here. So let's get started with some of the basics and then move forward as you progress."

The men all clapped and everyone could feel the excitement in room. Harry and Max spent the next few hours showing the men

the exercises they would be doing to strengthen their upper bodies and to prepare for the new prosthetics they would receive soon.
It was going to be a long painful journey but one that had to be
made in order for them to get back to living the life they deserved
and wanted.

At the end of the day, Harry and Max were worn out but elated
at the progress they'd made with the twenty men who had come
to the class. Tomorrow there would be another group to talk to.
So Harry and Max would split up and each take a group of men to
work with. They had pulled in some other active duty men who had
been wounded so that there would be enough assistants to help
the wounded to recover completely and get plenty of direction.

Harry sat down at the same table they sat at when their day
began. He was worn slap out. "I had no idea how tiring this would
be. And we've only just begun."

Max laughed. "No kidding. But you have to admit it makes you
feel productive in a different way. We get these men ready to go
back into active duty and think of how they will feel. They want
to fight just like we did. It's in their blood now. No one tells you
how difficult it will be to fit back into normal society after going
to war. Sure, there's help. But it's not enough most of the time. Not
only do these men deal with memories of watching their friends
get blown to pieces but they also have a military-instilled drive to
survive in the worst of circumstances."

Harry agreed. "Well, I would say they have arrived at the worst
case scenario short of death, and now we will see that change, that
metamorphosis, take place in front of our eyes. We are lucky men,
Max. No one watched ours. But somehow we were able to achieve
what appeared to be the impossible."

CHAPTER FIFTY-ONE

Anna and Zach were making dinner when Harry walked through the door. He could smell the chicken in the oven and his mouth watered as he walked into the kitchen. Every single time he saw Anna, it took his breath away. But he controlled his emotions only because Zach was standing there with a big grin on his face.

"Man, does that smell good. What are we having tonight?"

"I wasn't dead sure you would get here in time. One of your favorites. Chicken, rice and gravy, and fresh green beans. Zach made you some brownies for dessert. And yes, we have vanilla ice cream."

Harry laughed and he felt the stress fall off his back and onto the shiny hardwood floor. "This is just what I needed after a long day at work."

"That has a good ring to it. Did you enjoy your first day?"

"Oh, it was an eye opener, Anna."

"In what way, Honey?"

"All the faces of those men staring at me when I walked in with Max. It hit me like a ton of bricks. I knew it would be tough, but I didn't realize how I would feel seeing them sitting with no legs and in wheelchairs, some of them with no arms. But as they listened, a little hope showed up on their faces. And that is when I knew we were doing the right thing."

Anna walked over and kissed him. "There isn't a doubt in my mind that you are doing the right thing. You have gone to bat for those wounded warriors, the real heroes of the military. Now they will be given a real chance to recover. I am so proud of you."

"Anna, I don't ever want any medals for what I am doing. It's what these men need, and Max and I can do it. We saw the need. The way the military was dealing with the wounded was a catastrophe. Now they have a real chance. But we have a lot of work to do. This won't be a simple fix."

Zach was listening. And Harry was aware of it. He walked over to Zach and put his arm around him.

"Son, I want you to learn from this. If you learn anything at all from me, as a Marine, learn that you have to take care of the wounded. Those men gave it their all to fight. They need a chance to rise back up. Do you understand that, Zach?"

Zach was quiet for a moment. "Did anyone help you, Dad?"

"No. I did it on my own. But not everyone has that inside them. We are going to put it there. The drive to get better."

Zach nodded and grabbed Hack and went to his room to do his homework. Anna walked over and sat down on the sofa next to Harry, carrying two glasses of wine.

"I think you deserve a small glass of wine before dinner. I know you don't usually drink, but what a day to celebrate."

"Anna, you have no idea the suffering these men have experienced. The struggle to survive after coming home wounded. Even though they had tired faces and you could see a light come into their eyes."

"I know, baby. I know."

He sat his wine down and held her close and kissed her forehead.

"Do you know what you mean to me? How did we go so long without each other? I can't wait to come over here at the end of the day. I want to hear about your day and see what Zach is doing."

"We do need to discuss a wedding, I guess." She touched his leg.

"There is no reason for us to wait."

"Well, let's set a time, Harry. We're just floating along right now. I'm not trying to push you, and we haven't really settled on where we will live."

"I want you at the farm if you're okay with that. Can you see yourself there? Zach would have so much room to play and grow up. He loves the horses. We can sit outside on the porch and I'll get a fire pit for us, and we can roast marshmallows. Oh come on, Anna. It will be a good life."

She thought for a moment as she looked around her house. "It's just a house. A home will be where you are. I have worked so hard for this place. It was what Zach and I called home. But now that there are three of us, and I know you want us to have our house, a special place we call our home, I guess I can see myself on the farm."

"You don't sound too convinced!"

She grabbed him and kissed him. "I know I will love it. When are you thinking?"

"I was hoping for next week. I know that's fast, and we may have a lot to do to prepare. But we agreed to keep it very simple. Just family. What about your parents?"

"I doubt they will come, but I can text Mother and see if she is interested. You know I have not been a part of their lives since I got pregnant with Zach. She has never answered my calls. I finally got tired of leaving messages."

"It's hard to believe they have not changed their view of things. They have a grandchild."

"We need to tell your parents. Let's go see them tomorrow night. We'll share our news, and we could call David. I know they would want to know."

"I hate that they are going to miss the wedding, but unless something unforeseen arises, I think we are good with next week. Zach will be thrilled."

"In my mind, we are doing this for him, anyway. You and I wouldn't have to rush things. But for his sake, I think sooner is better."

Anna walked into the kitchen and took dinner out of the oven. She served the plates and called Zach down from his room.

"Harry, you get the tea glasses and I think we are ready. Zach is coming down the stairs right now with Hack."

They all sat down to eat and it was obvious that Harry was starving.

"This tastes so good. Did you finish your homework, Zach?"

Zach nodded and kept on eating.

"We have something to talk to you about. We've been discussing when to get married, and we were thinking about next week. How do you feel about that?"

Zach looked up and grinned with a mouth full of food. "Are you for real? Mom, are you really going to get married next week?"

Anna laughed and nodded. "Chew your food, please. And yes, that's what we're thinking. How do you feel about it?"

"I feel great. Does that mean we'll be moving to the farm?"

"That's exactly what it means." Anna glanced at Harry and winked.

"I was hoping you would give in, Mom. I know this has been our house, but what kid doesn't want to live on a farm with horses? It's rad. So cool. I can't wait."

Harry smiled and kept on eating. The kid was definitely his. It was a great ending to a productive day.

<hr />

Dinner finished and the dishes done, Harry and Anna were back on the sofa and Zach was upstairs taking a bath. Hack was curled up by the low fire across the room. It was quiet and Harry was feeling the tiredness from such a powerful day. He looked at Anna and it hit him that he was about to have a wife. He scooted closer to her and touched her face. She looked at him, quietly.

"Anna, this isn't how I wanted it to be. I know I already asked you to marry me. You have a ring. And we've told everyone that we are going to marry. But it has moved so fast that I haven't been able to be gentle with you. Slow. Letting you know how much you mean to me. We have worked, both of us, so hard that we haven't focused enough on each other. But tonight when we were talking about the wedding and where we live, it sounds so factual. I want this to be special for us. I want you to feel special. With Zach involved, both our focuses are on him for the most part. But this is about us."

He took his hands and placed them on her face and kissed her sweetly.

"Oh, Harry. You are so handsome to me. I'm so in love with you. I finally have allowed myself to say that after all these years."

"I'm in love with you, too." Harry smiled but something caught his eye near the staircase. Zach was peeking through the bannister at them, sitting on a step, smiling.

"Don't look now, but our son is enjoying our secret conversation."

Anna laughed quietly. "I know he's so excited and you have to remember he has never seen his mother in love, or with a man like this. It's all new to him. He seems to be getting a kick out of it. And he is so taken with you. I imagine he's the happiest kid in the world right now."

"I'm going to put him to bed. Then I need to get out of here. Tomorrow is going to be another long day with a new set of men."

Harry went up the stairs and walked Zach to his room. Zach climbed under the covers and grabbed Harry's huge hand. "I love having you as my dad."

"It's going to happen fast, Zach. Like maybe next week. But I want you to know that you are special to me, too. We're going to have a great family. Now you get some sleep so that you can do well in school tomorrow. I think I recall you have a math test?"

He rolled his eyes. "Yeah. But that's no sweat. I'm good in math."

"I'll see you tomorrow night. Love you, Son."

"Love you, Dad."

━≼┼≽━

After kissing Anna goodbye, Harry took off in his truck with Hack. It wouldn't be too long before everyone would be under the same roof. He was ready. But he wanted his brother around for the wedding. It just didn't look like that was going to happen with the timing of everything. The proverbial ball was rolling, and it even though he wanted this life that was about to unfold, he also was aware that his days of being a bachelor were about over. He reached over and touched Hack on the head.

"It's not going to be just you and me anymore, boy. We're going to be two lucky guys."

CHAPTER FIFTY-TWO

Day two of rehab started with a surprise. Max took the new group and Harry met with the same men he had seen yesterday. Harry had gotten up early and worked out in his home gym before showering. He was ready to supervise the men and take it to the next level. The weather was bad, rain all day in the forecast.

As Harry walked into the room the men started clapping. He was overwhelmed. One of the men spoke up as Harry took center stage to start the day's program.

"Major Downs, we all just want you to know we realize who you are and what you've overcome. You are known for your strength and endurance. You're a bear of a Marine. Your reputation preceded you, and we are so thankful for what you are trying to do with us and for us. We talked this morning before you came in, and we are all ready to do the work, if you are willing to sacrifice your time to help us discover what we are capable of."

Harry was caught off guard with this speech. But it confirmed that he was doing the right thing. "Men, we all are good Marines. We give it our all. We are trained to do that and it's obvious by looking at all of you that this is what you did. You gave it all you had. Now I am asking you again to do just that. All the things you will have to go through here will be an extension of your training as a Marine. But it will be harder because of the handicaps you have. It's another chance for you to overcome. And I think as Marines, we learn how to overcome. That's number one when you are battling the enemy. Right now your handicap is the enemy. But we have answers for that. There is nothing in this room that cannot be handled. And we are going to do that together."

Harry took a swallow of water and stepped up to the plate.

"Today, each one of you will be fitted for a prosthesis. I know it is scary and maybe you've waited so long for this that you've given up. But we have doctors here that work with injuries like yours all day long. The scheduling for wounded warriors has been sluggish, to say the least. But that's why we are getting this done now, so that you can go on with your lives. So I want you to come forward and fill out some forms, and get in line. Your name will be called and you will be taken into an examination room. They already have your medical records so the doctors pretty much know what you will need."

Harry could feel the tension and excitement in the room. He helped some of the men get in line for the forms, shaking their hands and slapping them on the back. Everyone was in good spirits even if they were scared to death. Harry knew that fear of the prosthetic. He had been worried that he would not be able to walk, or that he would limp the rest of his life. But he'd found out differently.

⥤⟊⥢

As the men were fitted for their prosthetics, they came out into the main room, where physical therapists worked with them one on one, taking their time, dealing with their hesitations and fears.

Harry walked around encouraging each one of the men, choking up as the scene brought back memories of his first few months of recovery. In spite of the awkwardness the men felt, underneath that cloak of fear was an immense power and strength that resonated off the walls of the gym. These men were still Marines to the bone, and they just weren't going to give up. Or give in. It would take time working through the problems of fitting the prosthesis and also learning how to walk with it or use their arms. But after a long day, Harry left the center feeling very positive about what was accomplished today.

Max walked out the front door at the same time Harry was about to climb into his truck.

"Hey, Harry! Wait up."

Harry stepped out of the truck and waved. "Hey, Buddy. How'd your day go?"

Max ran up to the truck and slapped Harry's hand. "It was a great day. Cannot tell you how pumped these guys are."

"Oh, I know. It was a different day for me, too, today. I was greeted with a wonderful speech from one of the men who was representing the whole group. Blew me away. Their eagerness to improve is what is going to make this life changing for them."

"Harry, this is exactly what these men were waiting for. To have us there, because we've been through what they are going through now, really shows them that it can be done. They can walk again or use their arms, and they don't have to be afraid."

"It's exciting to let them know they can be just as active in the military as they were before they were injured. I'm positive they had given that thought up, written it off as hopeless. I didn't because I was determined to get back to the battle ground. But these men have had no encouragement, or very little, from the military."

"Get some rest. Tomorrow will be a workhorse of a day. You done good, Harry Downs. This was one of your best ideas yet."

"Glad you're on board, Max. I wouldn't have been able to do this alone. We make a great team."

"Always have."

⟞⟝⟞

Harry rushed home to shower and called Anna to make sure they were still going to his parents' house. He was tired, but they needed to make some fast plans about getting married, if that was still okay with her.

"Hey, Sweetie. I'm headed home to shower and then pick you up. Is Zach home? Is he going, too?"

"You sound like you're on speed. You have to be worn out. Do you want to wait and go another night?"

"No, I'll be okay once I've showered. We didn't talk about what we're doing for dinner. I know mother will have something for us to nibble on, but I'm starving. Let's stop on the way and get a bite somewhere. Is that okay with you?"

"Perfect. We'll be ready when you pull into the driveway."

"Okay, Honey. See you in about thirty minutes tops."

He loved that woman. He wished the wedding was over and they were at the farm, all together. Zach was so geeked about living there and he knew it was the right place for them. He felt bad hurrying through the wedding, but both of them were ready to get this done so they could live together. He never thought his first wedding would be like this, crammed into a week like it was a chore that had to be done. This wedding was going to turn their lives upside down but in a good way. Anna had raised Zach all by herself, and even though he had to respect all the work she'd already done, it was going to be enriching to be able to influence Zach and show him how to be a good man. He already showed great promise and learned fast. Anna had done a fabulous job with the boy.

Harry showered fast and changed into jeans and a shirt, grabbed his coffee mug, and drove to Anna's house to pick them up. He tooted the horn and they came out running. Zach had a big smile on his face. They drove through the drive-through at McDonalds and grabbed some burgers, fries, and Cokes.

"Hey, Dad. We gonna tell Grandpa and Grandma that you and Mom are going to get married soon?" His mouth was full of fries.

Harry punched Anna and shrugged. "Yeah, I think it's the right thing to do. You excited about it?"

"I can't wait. I want to live at the farm with you, Dad."

"I want you there, Zach." Harry winked at Anna.

"I don't have any idea about the details of this thing, Anna. Did you try to talk to your parents?"

"I texted mother and also left another message on their phone. I haven't heard a word. They have my number, so if they want to talk to me, they just have to pick up the phone. I was hoping they would answer and we could have a decent conversation. I would think by now that they would want that with me."

"It's sad that they are holding out this long. Life is going by and you can't get it back."

"Tell me about it. I almost feel like I don't have parents or that I don't know them anymore."

"I can't imagine. My mother didn't want me to enlist, but she didn't cut me off. Parents just don't do that."

"Well, mine did, and they're pretty much sticking to it, it appears."

"We just wanted family at the wedding. It looks like it's just going to be Mom and Dad and us. Which is fine with me. I do wish David and Taylor could be there with the kids. Zach would love that, too."

"It's too bad that they're overseas. Why don't you call them real quick before we go in to see your parents?"

"I think I'll wait until we talk to them. We agree that we'll have the wedding at the farm? And just have family?"

"That's fine. Maybe ask Sam to come. He would be happy for us."

"I was thinking of that same thing."

"Okay, let's go in. They'll wonder why we're sitting in their driveway."

"Give me a kiss first, Beautiful. Zach, close your eyes."

Anna looked at Zach and smiled as he opened the door and grabbed Hack's leash and walked to the front door.

Harry held her in his arms and kissed her softly. "You're going to be the prettiest bride in the world. And I get to have you for life."

Anna laughed between kisses. "Well, don't be so cocky. Life is a long time."

"It goes fast when you're having fun. It won't be that long before we're sitting on the porch in our rockers."

"Oh, Lord."

CHAPTER FIFTY-THREE

David sat outside on the balcony looking out over the vine-yards, noticing a few scattered lights in the distance. He was enjoying this little piece of heaven that he didn't know existed un-til now. Taylor was showering and the kids were playing with their Nintendos. He hated to think that their visit was slowly coming to a close, although this break from routine had really lifted his spirits and given him the desire to work hard and move up the proverbial ladder. He'd gotten tired, a little burned out, because the real es-tate market had gotten saturated with realtors and it was dog-eat-dog out there. Brutal.

The moon was shining through the trees and it was just about the perfect night to be watching for shooting stars. Taylor walked out, wrapped in her white robe. She nailed him in two seconds. If that long.

"You feeling a little melancholy, baby?"

"No pun, I'm sure."

"I know when you're a little down. What's going through your mind?"

"Just amazed at how fast this vacation is going by, and I was trying to figure out how to slow it down. Isn't it beautiful out here? All those stars. And the quiet is deafening."

Taylor sat down and wrapped the robe tighter around her. "It is lovely here, Honey. We really were so fortunate to have been able to stay in this palace. Have you texted your friend Phillip to let him know how much we have enjoyed it?"

"I'll do that tonight. I was thinking that tomorrow you and I need to get away from here and take off alone. The kids can stay with the sitter here and I'm sure they will find things to do. We don't have to be gone long. Just a little time alone in this romantic place."

Taylor grinned. "You are such a romantic. How did I get so lucky? Of course, I would love to spend some time with you alone. It would be wonderful, and we better grab it now because when we arrive home we'll have no alone time."

"Things do seem to get in the way, especially with two kids."

"We have good kids, Honey. Trust me. They are so much better behaved than most I'm around."

"Oh, I know they're good. But having children diminishes our time together. All parents go through that. I just happen to not like the interference. We have to make a date to see each other now."

She laughed her golden laugh. She almost had a halo around her head, from the soft light of the moon.

"As they grow older, our time will return. We just have to hold on and enjoy the ride."

He closed his eyes and listened to her warm, soft voice. It had deepened just a little, but had such a lilt. He reached over and touched her, turning his head to see whose face was peeping out of the French doors. As usual, Sara Jane was watching with a mischievous grin.

He touched her hair and whistled. "You are gorgeous, do you know that?"

She blushed. He loved that. "I've lost so much of my looks having children, since you brought it up. But I don't care anymore. I just want to be a mother."

"That you are, baby. And you do it so well. But you are still very pretty to me."

She brushed his hair away from his eyes and kissed him softly, even though there were little eyes watching.

"Speaking of children, are we done with that? Or do you want another child to add to the mix?"

"I think we're done. How do you feel about it?"

"Mixed feelings. It's hard to say that I'm done birthing children. Sara Jane is seven. I haven't forgotten how wonderful it felt to hold her in my arms. A woman always wants another baby to hold. But the reality of raising another baby sets in and then I get a little squirrely about it."

He laughed. "Tell me about it. And the cost of raising a child comes into play. But if you were set on it, I would agree."

"I think we can say we're done. But if it happens on its own, I know we'll both love the child just like it was planned."

He pulled her to his lap and she leaned back on the chaise lounge against his shoulder. "Wow, look at the sky. It is absolutely breathtaking. I will miss this. Thank you so much for giving us such a lovely vacation. The kids really have enjoyed it, too."

He held her close. "You smell heavenly."

"Take it easy, we have eyes on us."

"I know. I'm ignoring that fact."

"When do you think we will need to head home?"

"I think the day after tomorrow. Which is Friday. That will give us the weekend to recover from the time change."

"That seems so soon."

"I know, Honey. But this has been such a retreat for us. We will make the most of tomorrow and then drive to the airport on Friday. Our tickets will be there waiting for us."

—≪┼≫—

The kids were unhappy about leaving. "Dad, do we have to leave so soon? We haven't seen everything yet."

"Actually, there's probably no way to see it all. We've driven through the town. You've eaten at almost every restaurant from here to town and back. I've thrown the Frisbee every day with you guys and you've watched so many movies it's not funny."

"Why don't we move here? We could go to school in town. Wouldn't that be cool, Dad?"

"It would be cool, Jack. But I have no job here."

David was walking to the bathroom when his cell phone rang. It was Harry. And he sounded excited.

CHAPTER FIFTY-FOUR

Once inside the house, everything broke loose. Zach couldn't keep a secret to save his soul.

"Grandpa, Mom and Dad are getting married next week. Isn't that the greatest?"

Joseph walked into the living room with his hands in his pockets, staring at Harry and Anna.

"I guess it is, Son. Is that true, Harry? You guys going to tie the knot?"

Harry walked over to his father and slapped him on the back. "I was going to tell you as soon as we got in the door, but Zach beat me to it. Yes, we have decided to get married next week. It will be a small wedding with just this family."

Martha came running into the room. "I heard that! What great news."

"Hey, Mother. Good to see you." Harry hugged her and kissed her cheek.

Anna walked over to Martha and kissed her. "We're so happy and relieved to have been able to make this decision, as it has been on both our minds for a while, now."

"I can imagine. Where will you have the wedding?"

Harry jumped in. "At the farm. It's the perfect place. Hey, Mother. I'm going to call David while I am here, so that you can speak to him, too."

Harry walked into the kitchen and picked up the house phone and called David's cell. He answered on the second ring.

"Harry? What a nice surprise. How the heck are you guys?"

"We're doing great. How's the vacation going?"

"Well, we're headed home Friday. Seems like these weeks have flown by. But Harry, it's been so refreshing. I feel like I have a new lease on life."

Harry grinned. "I'm so glad, David. Maybe Anna and I will take a trip like that someday. We've been busy here. I have so much to talk to you about. A lot is going on with the wounded warriors that I know you would like to hear about. Let's get together when you get back."

"Harry, I plan to spend a lot more time with you guys when we get back. We're not getting any younger and I already have missed some years with you. Tell me you are not going back overseas anytime soon."

"No, I think I'm done with that at this point. Marrying Anna will settle me about that dilemma. I'll always be a Marine, but not in the way I've been in the past."

"I admire you, Harry. You have such energy that I don't have. Pretty impressive."

"I'm glad to hear you guys have had a good visit there and I want to see the photos when you get home. Anna and I are getting married next week. It looks like you're going to be here for the wedding. For some reason I thought you were staying one more week."

"Well, we could have stayed a few more days, but I think I'm ready to head home. Staying at this villa has been fabulous, but I'm anxious to get back to work. If we stayed much longer, we would have to move to another location, as the kids are getting a little bored here. You and Anna would love it."

"I know we would! Our wedding will be simple. Just the family. Not even sure if Anna's parents will show up or not. She left a message with them but so far they've not responded."

"That is sad. They won't be able to capture this time again. It will be gone. So sorry, Harry."

"Anna has lived this way for ten years, ever since Zach was born. So she has adjusted. We were just hoping this wedding might be the catapult that would bring them all together. You never know. It could still happen."

"I'm so happy for you. I'll tell Taylor. She'll be over-the-top excited, as she really likes Anna."

Harry nodded. "It's good to hear your voice. You guys be careful on the return trip and we can't wait to see you."

"You too, Harry. Talk to you soon."

⚒

"Great news! David and Taylor will be at the wedding! I thought they were going to miss it, but it looks like they are headed home Friday. I'm so happy about the change of plans."

Anna clapped her hands. "Oh, that's wonderful news! It will make up for my parents not being here."

Martha smiled. "This trip has been so good for David and Taylor. I know the kids had fun, but really, David needed a break from work."

Joseph nodded. "The boy works too hard. But I'll feel better when they are home again, safe and sound."

"Don't sound so ominous, Joe. This trip cost David a pretty penny, and he deserved it. I wish we would make a trip overseas sometime, before we're too old."

"Not for me, Martha. You know that. I'll go anywhere in the States but I have no desire to fly overseas. Too much going on for me to be comfortable with that."

Martha rolled her eyes. "Oh, gosh. Well, we'll take a camper and travel the U.S.A., then."

Zach heard her and chimed in. "I'd love that, Grandma."

Everyone laughed. "Does anyone want some cake and ice cream?"

"Whoa. We just had dinner on our way over here." Anna rubbed her stomach.

"I'll have some. It isn't often a guy gets offered cake and ice cream. It would be stupid of me to pass that up." Harry punched Anna in the arm.

"Good. I'll get the cake, and Joe, you serve up the ice cream. Come on, let's go in the kitchen and get out some plates."

Harry walked over to Anna and wrapped his arms around her. "See? It's going to be the perfect wedding. You better be thinking about what you want to wear. Next week will come pretty fast."

Anna shook her head. "You trying to make me nervous?"

"No, I just know how women are about what they want to wear."

"I need to work on that. I'll wear a short white dress and you can wear a black suit. Maybe a tux. I've never seen you in that and I bet you look killer in a black tuxedo."

Harry grimaced but acquiesced. "I'll wear whatever you want me to wear. I just want to get this wedding over with so we can live in the same house. Taylor can be your bridesmaid and David can be my best man. How does that sound?"

"Sounds perfect to me. Now it really feels real. We are really going to do this!"

Zach spoke up. "Of course you're going to get married. What else would you do? I'm your son, Dad. You have to marry Mom."

"It looks that way, doesn't it, Son?"

Martha came out with two plates of cake and ice cream and Zach dove onto the floor and set his plate on the coffee table. Hack sat right next to him, hoping to get some crumbs.

"This is going to work out perfectly, Harry. You'll have your brother here, and our family will be altogether. It really warms my heart to think that we'll all be family at last." She looked at Zach and smiled.

"Did you know we're living at the farm when they get married?" Zach walked over to Martha and put his arm around her neck.

"Really? Is that okay with you, Anna?"

"It wasn't at first, but I've come around. Zach wants to be near the horses and help Harry on the farm. It really doesn't matter to me as long as we are all together. I will sell my house and move into the farmhouse with Harry. He even said we could add on to make the kitchen and master bedroom larger."

"Oh, you guys have really been giving this some thought." Joe took a huge bite of cake.

"Yeah, Dad. We want to cover our bases so there are no surprises. But even as I say that, I know there are always surprises."

"How's your work coming, Harry? How are the men reacting to your program?"

"Dad, it's an honor to work with them. They are developing the greatest attitude about the whole thing. I don't think we're going to see a pity party anymore. They are all in."

"Tough program for those guys. They have a lot to overcome."

"It will happen, Dad. What I am excited about right now is that I'll have my family with me at the farm in a few days. That's going to be one of the highlights of my life. Never thought it would happen. Never thought I would find Anna and sure as heck didn't think I had a son out there. It's been quite a year so far, and it's going to end with a bang."

"I'm happy for you, Son. If anyone deserves to be happy, you do."

"Thanks, Dad. Cannot wait to see David and Taylor. It's going to be a great day."

CHAPTER FIFTY-FIVE

The morning started with a glorious sunrise coming up over the hills of vineyards, whispering warm rays of sunshine across winter hills. Taylor was up early, excited about a day with David. She didn't remember the last time they planned a day just for themselves. She put on a light gray pair of pants and light pink sweater, gray boots and wore her hair down for extra warmth. David was already dressed and ready, talking to the kids, preparing them for a day of fun that was going to be a surprise from Francois. Taylor grabbed some snacks to keep in her purse in case they got hungry on one of their jaunts, and after she put her jacket on she squatted down to hug Sara Jane and Jack.

"Listen, baby. We won't be gone all day. We just want some time together and Francois has planned an exciting day for you. I have my phone so you can call me whenever you want. It's pretty outside, even though it's cold, so make sure you put your coat on and tell Jack he will get punished if he doesn't wear a jacket. I don't need you two getting sick because we'll be leaving tomorrow. Now be on your best behavior, okay?"

"Okay, Mommy. But I wish we were going with you and Daddy."

Taylor suddenly felt guilty. "I do too, Honey. But we don't ever do this, and sometimes it's good for Mommy and Daddy to do things alone. Thank you for being such a good girl."

Jack walked up and sighed. "Do you guys have to be gone all day?"

Sara Jane interrupted. "No, dummy. She said they would be back soon."

"Do we have to go with Francois? It's hard to understand her." Jack was frowning bigtime.

"Yes. She was nice enough to find some wonderful things for you both to do today. You won't be disappointed."

He didn't look convinced but nodded slowly. It was obvious that he knew he didn't have a choice.

David walked up and hugged the kids. "You guys behave. And have a good day. We'll be back before you know it. Now mind Francois. I don't want her to regret volunteering to take care of you today."

The two children stood watching as Taylor and David walked down the stairs and out the door.

Taylor looked back and waved. Her heart skipped a beat because they were leaving Sara and Jack with a stranger, although she seemed nice enough. She just wasn't used to walking away from her kids in a foreign country.

"You sure they'll be okay, David?' She asked as she got into their car.

"They'll be fine. Now let's get out of here before we change our minds."

David took off and drove down the mountain to the town where they were going to have a breakfast overlooking a beautiful river.

It was probably too cold to be sitting outside, and they could move inside if they felt too cold. But since this was a chance of a lifetime, he asked her if she'd be willing to try the outdoor table.

The restaurant was prepared for everything. They even brought out two warmed blankets so that Taylor could wrap herself up and keep warm. They were served soft scrambled eggs, bacon, toast on French bread, sausage, fresh strawberries that had been flown in, and fresh whipped cream. Everything was delicately made. It went down like a feather into their stomachs.

Even though she was chilled, Taylor was overwhelmed with the food and the way it was made. "Can you believe how good this is? It's just scrambled eggs but something is different about them. I'm not going to want to stop eating this."

"It is luscious. I could eat this every single morning. It's so light. Is that what you are feeling?"

"Yes. It is going down like nothing I've ever eaten before. I wonder if whipped cream is in the eggs."

"Not sure, but we could ask."

"Is that polite to ask how they made these eggs? Will that come across rude?"

"Who cares? We won't be here tomorrow."

"You're right. I'll ask when the waiter comes out."

They sat there enjoying the meal, taking their time. The sun was beginning to warm up the air so they weren't shivering anymore. The warm coffee went down into their stomachs and warmed everything up. It was perfect.

Taylor smiled as she watched David trying to drag out breakfast because the experience was so special. He took photos of them sitting at the table and posted them on Facebook. He took photos of the view and the waiter. And he took photographs of the food. He was having a ball.

Taylor watched as he played with the camera on his phone. She was so thankful that she had such a good relationship with him.

He was easy to be around. So giving and attentive. He loved the kids and never seemed to tire of them climbing all over him. And he was a romantic to the bone. This breakfast was so him.

"You ready to go, Honey?" He asked her with a smile. She could have swallowed him whole.

"Yes. Thank you for this wonderful meal. If we did nothing else today, it was worth getting away to share this meal with you."

He reached over and squeezed her hand. "I agree. It was perfect. But let's go see what the rest of the day holds. We've got several hours before we have to return to the kids. I'm going to enjoy every single moment with you."

She laughed and they walked to the car and got in, taking the blankets that the waiter had given to them. They would be something that would remind her of that delicious breakfast. David took off down through winding streets of the town, and Taylor held his hand, talking about how quaint the town was.

The sun was glaring into the windshield and it made it difficult to see. Taylor grabbed her sunglasses and hunted for David's.

"I can hardly stand to look out the windshield, Taylor. This is terrible. And the little bit of water on the windshield is making it worse. I am going to slow down so that I don't get into trouble, because I'm not familiar with these roads."

"That's a great idea, Dave. You need to go slow. I am looking for your glasses now."

"Traffic has picked up. I guess we weren't the only ones who wanted to get on the road today. This two-lane road sure is dangerous. And do you notice how fast everyone is going? I guess they're very familiar with the roads. I'm not feeling very safe right now. People are passing on this road like it's a six-lane highway. And there are so many turns and twists that who knows what's coming around the bend."

Taylor felt the uneasiness in his voice. "Honey, take your time. Don't pay any attention to what they're doing. Just keep your eyes on the road."

"I would if I could see the road. The sun is so bright it's killing my eyes. Did you locate my sunglasses yet?"

"Still looking. Give me a minute."

"Taylor, make sure you are buckled in. This is getting out of control. People are passing on the curve. I'm going to pull off at the next turn because I just don't feel safe on this road at all."

"You do what you have—"

━━┼┼━━

Suddenly David was hit head-on by a small car passing on a hill. He didn't know what hit him, and he lost control of the car. It went headlong off the side of the road and came crashing down the hillside. Taylor heard him screaming but he seemed far away. She grabbed the handle on her side of the car and held on for dear life. As they came crashing against the hill, David's head jerked against the window and broke it into a million pieces. His legs were crushed by the collision but everything happened so quickly that Taylor didn't notice. As they rolled she hit her head against the side window and blacked out.

She came to when the car had settled at the bottom of the valley, though her eyes would barely open. She felt like she was moving in slow motion and couldn't wake up. She looked over at David and his head was turned towards her. She tried to move her arms but they were broken. Tears were streaming down her face. She tried hard to speak but her throat was dry. David managed to make a sound.

"I'm sorry . . . Taylor . . . baby. I love you."

Taylor was crying uncontrollably and whispered her last words to David. "I love you . . ."

Inside the car, there was no movement. No breath taken. They were gone. The car was hidden by the brush-covered hillside, making it impossible to spot the wrecked vehicle from the top of the hill. A driver who had witnessed the crash placed an emergency call. Within twenty minutes sirens were screaming into the air, and soon medical personnel were on the scene trying to locate the vehicle. Equipment had to be lowered down to remove David and Taylor from the vehicle, which was totally demolished.

Both people were dead upon arrival. After searching the phone that was in David's pocket, a phone call was made to the last number dialed, which was his parents' home phone. After searching Taylor's purse, the medical team found a brochure from the villa and called Francois.

There was no good way to tell the people on the other end of the phone across a vast ocean. It was the last thing they would have ever wanted to hear. And Francois collapsed on the floor before she could gather enough strength to decide how to take care of the children. It wasn't long before she received another call from David's brother. But she weakened again as she listened to a grown man crying. It had been a glorious morning that had turned into one of the darkest days ever.

CHAPTER FIFTY-SIX

Joseph had left work early and was sitting at the kitchen table with a cup of coffee, waiting on Martha to come home from work. The house was quiet. It felt good to decompress alone sometimes. He was excited about the new drug possibilities that were being developed at Glassco, and was pleased with how everything was running. He stared out the window, feeling a little melancholy with winter still in full swing. It was a new year. That was a plus. But he hated the time between New Year's and spring. It seemed to take forever before the trees started to bud. He was wondering what they would eat for dinner when Martha came through the door.

"Hello, Honey."

"Hi. You got me a cup of that coffee? It's been a tough day."

"Sure. Sit down and take a load off. I've just been sitting here gazing out the window. Feels good to be home."

"It does. I haven't taken anything out for dinner. We may have to go out. Is that okay with you?"

Joseph rolled his eyes. "Whatever you like, dear."

"Well, it's not like we eat out that often. I know you get tired of the menu offerings around here."

"I just like your cooking. I realize in saying that that I sound like a male chauvinist. But you are a good cook."

The phone rang. Martha walked over to the kitchen phone and answered it.

"Yes, this is Martha Downs. Who is this?"

Joseph stood up and walked over to Martha.

"What do you mean there's been an accident? What kind of accident?"

She screamed and fainted.

Joseph caught her and grabbed the phone as she slipped to the floor. "What's going on? This is Joseph Downs. Now what is wrong? My wife has fainted."

"Mr. Downs, we are calling to inform you that your son David, and his wife, have been involved in a terrible car accident on the outskirts of Paris. They both were killed in a head-on collision. I am sorry to have to give you this terrible news."

Joseph sat down at the table and put his head in his hands. He started sweating profusely. He felt nauseous. "What kind of accident? You said head-on collision. How did it happen? Where did you find them?"

"They were travelling on a two-lane highway, a very winding dangerous road. I am sure they were unfamiliar with the twists and turns of the road. It is in a very hilly region. When they were hit head-on the car then careened down the side of a hill, rolled over several times, and came to rest at the bottom of a valley covered in brush and trees. The car was demolished. There was no way that they could have survived even though they both had their seat belts on."

"Oh, my God! I can't believe this. What do I do? Where are they?"

"Their bodies were flown to Hŏpital Cochin in Paris."

"We will need them flown to the U.S., of course. Is that possible?"

"Of course. We just need to make arrangements to have that done. You need to give me the address of the funeral home so that we can connect with them about transfer of the bodies."

Joseph gave them the name of a funeral home near their residence. "I'm in shock. I don't know what to do. What about the children? Where are they?"

"At this moment they are still at the villa in Normandy where your son and his wife were staying. They are being taken care of by a woman named 'Francois.' I do not have her last name, but we have spoken with her and she was in charge of the children for the day. I can give you her number."

"Yes, thank you. We will want to get them here as soon as possible."

"I will leave you my number in case you have any questions. I am very sorry to have had to give you this terrible news. I am certain you are in shock. I wish there was more that we could do to help."

"You have been very kind. I need to take care of my wife, and also make preparations to fly to Normandy to pick up the children. I can't believe this has happened. We just spoke to them not a day or so ago."

"Again, my condolences to you and your family."

⟜⊹⊹⟞

Martha was rousing and Joseph helped her to her feet and over to the sofa. She was crying uncontrollably.

"Martha dear, please calm down. I'll get you something to drink. Something strong. I need to call Harry and talk with him about getting the children."

He brought Martha a glass of wine and a few crackers to settle her stomach. She was white as a sheet and couldn't talk. She kept shaking her head in disbelief. Joseph phoned Harry. He had a difficult time with how to relay what had taken place, he was so shaken.

When he answered the phone, Joe could tell he was still at the rehab center.

"Harry? This is your father. There's been a terrible accident. I need you to come home so that we can discuss the whole situation."

"What's happened, Dad?"

"David and his wife have been killed in a terrible car accident outside of Normandy. Their bodies will be flown to the Davis Funeral Home around the corner from our house. Please come as soon as you can. We need to talk about getting those poor children home. Your mother is beside herself. It will do her good just to see you."

"I'll be right there, Dad. Tell her I'm coming."

Joseph put the phone down and sat by Martha, holding her in his arms.

"It's going to be all right, Martha, dear. Harry is on his way here. He'll take care of everything. It will all be okay."

Martha rocked back and forth, moaning words he did not understand. This was her oldest child. Their son. And he was just gone. Just like that. How could it have happened? David was an excellent driver. They were having such a great vacation. What in the world happened?

Joseph took a swallow of wine out of Martha's glass and leaned back against the sofa with her in his arms. When Harry came in, that is how he found them. Almost in a stupor.

⊷⊱⊰⊶

Harry came rushing through their front door out of breath. His face was flushed but he had an energy that they needed to feel. He walked over to the sofa and sat down near his father and mother. Martha started crying hard and had to be comforted.

"Mother, I love you. It's going to be all right. Dad, has she got anything she could take to calm her down?"

Joseph nodded. "I think by her bed there might be something. I'll go check."

Harry sat with his mother and held her close. He couldn't yet grasp that David was gone. It just didn't make any sense. He hadn't driven the roads near Normandy but many of those roads were very narrow and dangerous in the wine country.

Joseph returned with some Valium and gave Martha a small pill. She swallowed it with water and closed her eyes. "I just want this to be over. Surely it's not true. Both of them gone. What will the children do?" She sat up quickly.

"Will we take them in, Joseph?"

"Of course we will, Martha. Until we decide what else to do, they can live with us."

Harry nodded. "We'll figure it all out, Dad. I promise you. I'm shaking inside at this news. Cannot believe David is gone. I was so excited that they were coming home tomorrow. That he would be at my wedding. Just can't believe this has happened."

"We're all in shock, Harry. I have the number for you to call the villa where they were staying. A lady named Francois has charge of the children. Can you fly over and get those kids? Can you leave your job like that?"

"That's the last worry I have, Dad. Of course I can go get Sara Jane and Jack. They must be beside themselves. Do they know about this accident yet?"

"I'm not sure what they've been told. You need to call Francois and find out the details."

"I'll take care of it. You just get Mother to bed and let her rest. There's nothing she can do for now. But we'll need her to help with the children, so she needs to pull herself together."

Harry blew out a big sigh and walked to the telephone in the kitchen and dialed the number for the villa. Francois answered and started speaking in French. Harry had to slow her down so that he could understand her.

"Francois, I do not speak fluent French. Please speak in English. This is Harry Downs. David was my brother. I understand you have the children there with you?"

"Yes, I do. I am so sorry about the loss of your brother and his wife. I am in shock about it all."

"Do the children know?"

"I only told them that their parents have been in a terrible accident."

"Okay. I'm going to catch a flight to Paris and grab a car to drive to Normandy. When I arrive I will call you for directions. Is that understood?"

"Yes, we will be waiting for you. You must plan to stay overnight to rest. The children will be fine until you arrive. I don't know how you will tell them that their parents are gone. I just don't know how you will do that."

"I don't know, either. I pray I find the words."

CHAPTER FIFTY-SEVEN

The nightmare continued. Harry left his parents' home and climbed into his old pickup, with only one thing on his mind. He had to talk to Anna. His mind was going in ten different directions, trying to sort out the information he'd been told about his brother and the horrific accident and how to deal with the children.

When he pulled up in the driveway, Anna wasn't home, so he let himself into the house and sat on the sofa looking out towards the backyard. It was a sunny day, but he didn't notice. His brother was dead. Taylor was gone. He would never talk to David again. For a moment, he allowed himself to be human. He allowed the tears that were nearly choking him to come out, and he even allowed a guttural scream to come out of his throat. He was so thankful to be alone for a few moments, or however long he would have before Anna would come through the door. No one needed to see him like this. He wanted to scream David's name. He wanted so badly for this not to be true. But in his military mind, he knew it wasn't going to go away. He had to deal with it now so that he could handle everything for his parents and for the two children who were going to be left without parents. He was trained to handle any situation. To think on his feet. To shove back any emotions so that he could appear strong and capable. But for this few minutes, he let it all out. It felt good actually to feel the tears flowing. He hadn't cried in years. Even for himself when his leg was blown off. This was different. This ripped his guts out.

In about an hour the front door opened and Anna was home. He saw her walking into the living room and stood up to greet her. A smile was pasted on his face, and the tears were wiped off his cheeks. But she must have sensed something ominous because she sat down without a word.

"Sorry I just busted into your living room. I needed a place to just sit and be alone."

"You know that isn't a problem. That's why I gave you a key."

He put his hand on hers. "I needed to come here because I needed you."

She raised an eyebrow. "What's wrong, Harry. Why aren't you at work? Has something happened?"

"Yes, you could say that. Something terrible has taken place and I am trying to compartmentalize it so I can deal with the overflow."

"Talk to me, if you're ready."

"I got a call at work from Dad. He had just received a call from the police in Normandy. David and Taylor have been in a fatal car accident. They were hit head-on and their car careened off the side of the road and down a steep incline. They were both killed."

Anna started crying and Harry put his arm around her. But she got control quickly and wiped her eyes.

"I'm sorry. I'm in shock. I know you can't believe this has happened. What can I do?"

"Anna, I'll make it. My parents are beside themselves. I hated to leave them alone. It's just too much to comprehend and when it really sinks in, it isn't going to be a pretty picture."

"Where are the children?"

"They're in Normandy at the villa where they were staying. A woman named Francois is taking care of them until I can get there. I'm going to book a flight after we talk and hopefully get there tomorrow sometime."

"I wish I could go with you. What will you tell Sara Jane and Jack?"

Hearing their names brought tears to his eyes.

"I'll tell them the truth. They have to hear it and there's no pretty way to tell them that their parents are in heaven with God. Jack is a little older, but not much. I have to make them feel like everything is going to be okay but it will just take time. We will all take care of them. I don't want them to feel alone."

"Of course you don't. Are you sure I can't go with you?"

"I really need you here with Mom and Dad. They're going to be crazy dealing with this. If you and Zach are around, it will keep them a little distracted. I think Zach will be good for Dad. He loves that boy so much. We have to make it through this, even though it seems so surreal at this point."

Anna sat back on the sofa and wiped more tears from her face. "I'm so sorry for David and Taylor. The terror they faced in that accident. I hope they passed out when they were hit."

"We'll never know. I'm sure their bodies took a hit when the car rolled down that hillside. I don't think they suffered long." Harry got up and walked to the window. "I guess I need to make my flight arrangements. Those kids don't need to be left in the dark any longer than necessary. I need to be strong for them. They're too small to be without parents."

He turned and smiled. It was faint but she saw it. He asked, "What about our wedding? What will we do about that?"

"Oh, Honey, we can still get married. But we have to wait until after the funeral and things have settled down a little. Don't you agree?"

"I wish we'd taken Zach and eloped. I wish we were already married."

"I feel the same way, Harry. You are the kindest man I've ever known. But we will take care of that as soon as we can."

He pulled her up to him and held her a long time. "What time is Zach coming home?"

"He had ball practice. I'll have to pick him up in an hour."

"Let me make the plane reservations and then I want to spend this hour with you, alone."

She smiled. "You do whatever you have to do. I have no plans except for having to pick Zach up at the school."

—≺+ +≻—

Harry made reservations for tomorrow morning at eight. He would arrive in Paris around 11:00 P.M. and rent a car to drive to the villa. Anna was waiting for him on the sofa and had made a glass of iced tea and a couple of sandwiches for them both.

"Please eat this. I know you have so many things on your mind, but let's use this short time we have to relax and try to calm down. That is a long flight, Harry. I would give anything to make that with you."

He took his hands and placed them on her face. "Right now I'm not sure I can breathe without you. I love you so much. Do you see how this has played out, Anna? I hate to even speak these words. But it's almost like we were supposed to meet, find our love again, and marry so that things would be in place for us to take in these two children. Can you forgive me for saying that?"

Anna leaned into his shoulder and kissed his face. He wasn't sure if she'd thought about that option. But he felt comfortable enough with her to lay it before her as something to think about.

"Oh, Harry, I didn't even think about where they would go. I guess I was thinking they would go with your parents. But of course, the best place is with us and with Zach. They love each other. It's just like you to want to take them in. I've never known such a loving man."

"It's not in stone. But let that thought soak into your brain. Because there will come a time in the near future when we're faced with that decision. And it would be nice if we'd already come to that conclusion."

Anna nodded and snuggled into him. He just sat there feeling her strength and understanding. But the weight of what was ahead of him began to chip away at the mood in the room. It was going to be a grave conversation with those two little children. They were going to hear what no children would ever want to hear. Their worst nightmare. That their parents had been taken from them without a word. They couldn't even tell them goodbye.

Anna looked at her watch. "It's about time for me to head to the school, Harry. Do you want to go?"

"I better go home and pack a small bag and get my mind right about this trip."

"Do you want me to check on your parents?"

"You can feel free to go see them anytime you like. They will definitely need your comfort and the distraction."

"I'll take care of that. I will have to explain to Zach what has happened, and I don't look forward to that. He's older than they are, but it will still be a huge shock to him."

"I know, Anna. I'm so sorry that all of us are even having this conversation. You take care of Zach, and I will call you before I go to bed. Thank you for allowing me to crash here for a few hours. It has really helped."

He stood up and hugged her and walked to the door. When he looked back, she was crying.

"Harry, you come home to me, you hear? I just couldn't take it if you didn't."

He nodded and walked out without a word. Not because he didn't have anything to say. But because he was physically unable to speak anything at all.

CHAPTER FIFTY-EIGHT

Driving home in his truck with the window down, Harry got his mind right. He had squarely faced the situation and knew what he had to do. The cool wind felt good to his face and cleared his head. Now it was time for the Marine in him to take over. He called Max to discuss the situation at the rehab center and just hearing his friend's voice jacked his mood up a notch or two.

"Hey, stranger. I've been dying to call but didn't want to interfere."

Harry smiled. A real smile. "Nah. You wouldn't ever interfere. A lot going on, Buddy. I want to fill you in. But first, tell me how your day went."

"We had a fantastic day at the center. Your group spent all the time learning how to deal with the prosthetics and getting so much encouragement. They were smiling even if they were frustrated. My group is a day behind, so they got fitted today. I think we are heading in the right direction, Harry. I love what we're doing for these men."

"I couldn't be happier about what you're telling me. This is something you and I can do for however long we choose and still feel productive."

"Right. Enough about that. What's going on with you?"

"If I had called you earlier I wouldn't have been able to talk about it, but I've got a grip on things now. My brother David and his wife Taylor were in a terrible car accident and were killed. I don't know if I told you but they were vacationing in Paris for Christmas and were practically given a villa to vacation in for a week in Normandy. Supposedly it is a massive estate and wine vineyard. Anyway, they took a day to themselves to enjoy the countryside and now they are gone. I am headed overseas in the morning at 8:00 to see the children and bring them back to the States."

"I'm speechless. How in the world are you handling this? As I ask that, I know how. We're trained to deal with things like this. But it's different when it's your own family."

"Yes, it is. I had no idea how I would ever react to something like this, but now I know. It's gut-wrenching. I think I've got a handle on my emotions now but when I see those two kids, well, I could crumble."

"Harry, I've never seen you crumble and you've had plenty of opportunities, watching your buddies get blown to smithereens. I think you will handle this like the professional you are."

"I know I'm allowed to have emotions. But I can't fall apart. My parents are beside themselves, and I don't even want to think about how the kids will react. They're young, which is a good thing. I know kids are resilient. But this is asking too much of them."

"Do they know anything?"

"No. But Jack isn't stupid. His parents have been gone all night long. He knows something has happened. There really won't be a way for me to soften the blow. But I can reassure them that they will be okay. That we will take care of them."

"Where will they end up?"

"With my parents, for the time being. But I mentioned to Anna that I think we should take them in after we marry. Zach is already a good friend to them. They're cousins. So I think that would be the best scenario since my parents aren't getting any younger and they both work full time."

"You've got your hands full. I don't want you to worry about anything. We have plenty of volunteers showing up to work with the men. They miss you, of course. They were asking about you today. You're sort of a hero to them. Now a mentor. So I hope you can get back here fast. I need your help."

"Thanks, Max. I'll be back to work in a few days. Just want to get these kids settled for now. I have my phone with me all the time. Let me know how things are going. I'm sure we'll be talking during the next few days, anyway."

"Safe trip, Harry. Look forward to hearing how it all goes. I'm not a religious person per se, but I'm shooting a prayer up for those kids. They have too much on their plate."

"Talk to you soon, Max."

Hack was waiting on him when he walked in the door. After wrestling with him for a few minutes and letting him outside, Harry texted Anna to let her know he was going to be dropping Hack by her house on his way to the airport. He started packing a light bag and grabbed a bite of dinner for himself and Hack. He was a little nervous about dealing with the two kids, but he knew what had to be done. He pulled the covers back on his bed and Hack jumped up and made himself comfortable at the foot of the bed, facing the door. Harry leaned back against the headboard and called his parents. He didn't really want to talk to anyone at the moment, but he knew they probably needed to talk to him.

"Dad? You guys holding up okay?"

"I think we're going to make it, but your mother is still in shock. Well, so am I, if I'm honest. This has been a friggin' nightmare, Harry. I never thought I'd have to bury a son. It's settling in that he isn't going to come back. And I won't hear his voice again." His voice was shaky.

Harry sighed. "I know, Dad. We all are dealing with that. It sucks and there's no easy way to cope with it. These next few months we'll have to put one foot in front of the other and move forward. Even if we don't feel like it. Because that's the only way to survive an event like this."

"I hear you. But I don't like it."

"Is there anything I can do before I leave tomorrow morning?"

"Let me see if your mother wants to talk to you."

Harry waited, listening to the voices in the background. His parents were not old by any stretch, but they sure weren't prepared to handle the death of their oldest son along with having to care for two young children. Finally his mother came to the phone.

"Mom? Are you going to be able to handle this?"

He could hear her sniffing. "Sure, Harry. I'll be fine. It's just a shock and adjusting to the facts isn't easy. I've handled court cases that were similar to this accident. But this is my son we are talking about. And the mother of our grandchildren. I hate it. I absolutely hate it."

"I know, Mother. But we have to push through those feelings because I'll be bringing those kids home and we have to be strong for them. We have to make things a little lighter for them, if possible. It will be good for all of us to have them to take care of. Don't you agree?"

"I'm sure it will. At the moment, I'm lost. But I'll find some strength before you get back. Please be careful. If anything happened to you, they would have to put me down."

"I'll be back in a couple days. There's no point in us remaining in Normandy any longer than we have to."

"Thanks for calling, Harry. You always know what to do. I don't know how you stay so strong."

He winced. "It's a cover, Mom. Inside I have crumbled. But you know how I was trained. I'll do my best to take care of Sara and Jack. You and Dad find a way to deal with your pain so that when you see the kids you don't fall apart."

"I'll be strong, I promise."

Harry hung up and slipped down under the covers. He was worn out mentally and emotionally. But his strength was there waiting. He knew he would pull off the trip and get the kids safely home. David and Taylor had done a great job raising them and he knew it would be tough to fill their shoes. He wouldn't even try. What he would do was teach those kids what great parents they had. And how much they were loved.

He crashed, finally. But in his dreams he was saving David all night long.

CHAPTER FIFTY-NINE

O n the tenth of January, when the rain was coming down like sheets of broken stars, David and Taylor were laid to rest in the local cemetery. Everyone dressed in black except Harry. He wore his military uniform, and standing beside him was his best friend Max.

The children were silent, their tears falling on the already soaked ground. But as soon as the last words were spoken by the Methodist pastor, rays from the sun came poking through the huge thunderheads lining the horizon. It was both with relief and horrendous sadness that the family pulled away from the gravesite and headed home. The limousine was dead silent and the only sound was from the windshield wipers as they created a mournful rhythm, swinging back and forth across the glass. It was a day they wanted to forget but would remember as long as they lived. The story of their death would be passed down through the genera-tions. But the sun was going to rise again.

Two weeks later the estate went through probate and Harry received a call from David's attorney. He was nervous as he walked through the mahogany double doors and went three flights up. He wasn't sure what he was going to hear, but just in case, he had tucked his emotions into a file somewhere inside his Marine-trained heart.

The secretary was an older woman named Marie, who looked at him over her glasses. He sat down in a seat near the door and two minutes later, his name was called by Miss Marie in her deep raspy voice. He went through another pair of heavy wooden doors and took a seat in front of the desk of Harold Rothsberger, attorney. The office was paneled with shelves filled to the ceiling with heavy leather-covered law books.

Very impressive and could have been intimidating. Except Harold was one of the nicest men you'd ever want to meet. He seemed to snatch the tension right out of the air with his amiable demeanor and wonderful smile. He stood and greeted Harry and waved for him to have a seat in the red leather chairs on the other side of his desk. He didn't wait for Harry to speak. He jumped right in.

"Harry, I've called you in because I've opened your brother's will, and I wanted to inform you that he has asked you to take custody of his children if anything happened to him and his wife. I know this is a shock to you but I want you to think about this and take your time. Do you have any questions?"

Harry sat there looking at the floor. His throat felt like it was swollen shut for a moment. This whole thing seemed strange to him. The course of events just seemed to line up, and that was basically impossible. Life didn't do that. It never lined up. He rubbed his face with his hands and leaned back in his seat. His mind was moving quickly, thinking about everything that had happened to him up to this point. It was mind boggling. It took every bit as much muscle to hold in what he was thinking as it did to physically stop a freight train running on a track with no brakes. But he managed to look at Harold Rothsberger and force a smile that somehow made it across his face. He wanted to cry. He wanted to go berserk right there in the perfectly groomed office but he didn't. He held it in. And the conversation that followed appeared to be perfectly normal.

"Do you have any questions, Harry? There will be a hearing in the judge's chambers two weeks from today at 9:00 A.M., where you will appear before Judge Wilkins. It is then that you will receive custody of the two children unless you are unable or unwilling to do so."

Harry sat there still in shock. "I'll be there. At 9:00 two weeks from today."

"I will be there because I represent the estate of your brother and his wife."

Harry stood up and stuck out his hand. "Thank you, Mr. Rothsberger, for your help in this matter. It has been very difficult for my family. It was so sudden. We are all, including the children, trying to adjust to the fact that they will never come home again."

Harold Rothsberger pulled his large frame out of the well-worn leather chair he was sitting in and shook Harry's hand. "It won't be easy, but I know it was what your brother wanted."

Harry nodded and walked out of the office, ran to his truck, and sat there with tears running down his face. *Is there going to be a day when this doesn't rip my guts out?* Harry wiped his eyes with his sleeve and pulled out of the parking lot. It had started raining again and it was cold outside. And he had no idea where he was going. He blew out a deep breath and cranked up the volume on the radio. Anything to get his mind off David and Taylor. He was anxious to get back to work but he had a few things he needed to take care of before diving back into the rehab center.

First on his list was getting married. That word didn't have the rosy feeling it did a few weeks ago because of all that had happened. But he still wanted to do it. The deepest part of him wanted to be with Anna.

Without knowing it, he had turned down Walnut Grove Road and was heading towards her home. Almost like she was calling him home. His mother had always said things would work out the way they were supposed to. He had never believed her. Not once. But now, as things kept unfolding, he was beginning to wonder if she was right. He liked his world to be balanced. Logical. This was nothing like that.

When he pulled up to Anna's house, she was just coming home from school. He got out of his truck and followed her into the house, hugging Zach and slapping him on the back.

"How's it going, Buddy?"

"Great, Dad. I made an A on my science test today."

"That's my boy. Sounds like you've been studying."

"I told you I wanted to be like you."

That caught Harry's breath. "Yes, you did. But do it for you. It will help you later in life."

Zach shook his head and grinned. "Where's Hack?"

"He's home. I just stopped by to see how you guys are doing."

Anna walked in behind him and Zach ran up the stairs to put his books on his desk and get his homework done.

"How was your day, Harry? I was surprised to see you here at this time of day."

Harry pulled her close to him. "I needed you, Anna. Can we talk?"

"Of course we can. Give me a second and I'll fix us some coffee. It's still chilly out there."

Harry sat down on the sofa and looked out the window. There were birds eating seed out of the feeder he'd put up for Zach earlier in the winter. His mind was still. He didn't have one single thought running through it. He was worn out mentally but still wanted to talk to Anna. She finally sat down beside him with the coffee, putting it down on the coffee table. It was steaming and smelled great. He blew on the coffee and took a small sip. It burned all the way down.

"You have something on your mind, Harry."

He leaned back against the sofa and looked at her. "Anna, you wouldn't believe what happened today at David's attorney's office. I'm still in shock, I think."

She leaned back and sipped the coffee. "What happened?"

"This Harold Rothsberger guy proceeds to tell me that David and Taylor have designated me to have custody of their children if they both died. Do you see the irony in all of this?"

"It's mind boggling. Were you not expecting that?"

"I wasn't expecting any of this. Including you and me, and Zach. This whole year has been mind boggling. But it almost seems like I am walking a road that has been laid out before me, and I see it all coming to pass like it all was meant to be. I feel so weird about it all."

"Honey, no one expected David and Taylor to die in a car crash. It has rocked your world. Nothing could prepare all of you for that. I'm not surprised that he left his children to your care in the will. Who else would he have left them with?"

"I know you're right. I guess I just didn't like hearing it out loud. Everything has happened so quickly and I haven't had a chance to process it. They were killed, they were buried, and now I'm going to get the kids. It's almost too much. I can't imagine how the children feel."

"I'm sure they're in shock. They're so young to have to deal with all of this."

"I'll do my best to make this as easy on them as possible. That's naïve of me to even think I can protect them from the pain of losing their parents. But you and I can create a loving environment for them so that it nurtures them while they're healing inside."

Anna smiled. "Why, Harry, you sound like a parent. I'm kinda liking this."

He laughed. It felt so good to laugh. "I guess I do sound like a parent. And to tell you the truth, it feels pretty darn good. Anna, I've got to get back to work. It's time. Max can't handle all of those men alone. But we need to marry. We need to prepare ourselves for this big family we're going to have. We've never been married, either of us, and suddenly we have three children to raise. Are you ready for this? Are we?"

She leaned over and kissed him. "I wanted more time with you alone. Zach is old enough where most nights we wouldn't even know he was in the house. He has gotten that way since you came along. I think he felt like he had to be the man of the house. But now, he can relax and enjoy his world."

"I want time with you. But it looks like we're going to be surrounded with children right off the bat. It won't take long for the court to approve my getting custody. It's a formality, really. So let's just plan on getting married this weekend. I know it's a rush and you have no dress. But the longer we wait, the more complicated things get."

He held her face in his hands and kissed her. "I wanted to romance you. I needed that, too. But now it feels like we're being pushed. I didn't want that for us. I love you, and I want you for my wife. I'm almost annoyed that we won't have that much time alone. I know my parents will watch the kids if we want a weekend or a night alone. Let's not forget to do that often, so that we keep the "us" part of this thing working. Do you know when I saw your face on Facebook I could hardly believe my eyes?"

"What do you mean, Harry?"

"You looked so beautiful. You hadn't changed that much. It had been ten years since we'd seen each other, and I still got butterflies looking at you."

"Why, Harry!"

He stood up and held her close and slow danced to the music he hummed softly in her ear. She was on her tiptoes, and he put his arm around her waist and lifted her off the floor. He swung her around and she leaned her head back and laughed. It was that golden laughter and the light in her eyes when she looked at him that made him know, without a doubt, that they would make this work. And it would be a beautiful thing.

CHAPTER SIXTY

I t couldn't have been a prettier evening. Way too cold, but lovely just the same. Harry was in a rented tux and Anna wore a long sleeve off-white dress with a pale gray sash and shawl. Her hair was down, which Harry requested. Sara Jane was the flower girl and Jack carried the ring. It was Zach that gave Anna away, and Max stood strong as Harry's best man. The sun was not yet setting in the January sky, and there was little wind blowing. Martha had lit fifty candles along the walkway in the backyard and music was playing in the background. It was a quiet wedding, but maybe one of the prettiest ones that Martha and Joseph had ever seen. Harry was as strong as ever. He had written his own vows, unbeknownst to Anna, and when he read the words, tears were flowing from every face.

"Anna, we were separated by war and nearly lost each other. But our son brought us together again and I want you to know I will love you the rest of my life. I will take care of you and treasure every moment we share together. I will raise these children with you in a way that will make them grow strong and able to become what they were created to be. And we will walk hand in hand in this marriage, so help me God."

Anna wiped her eyes and spoke the vows she had written.

"Harry, I waited what seemed a lifetime for you. I thought you were gone. I am so grateful to become your wife and raise our son together. We now have two other children whom we already love, and I promise you that I will walk by your side, hoping that our lives count for something. That what we do from this day forward matters in the lives of others, until grace calls us home."

Joseph's chin was quivering and he reached for Martha's hand. Harry saw this movement out of the corner of his eye, and a tear ran down his face. But he was so happy, he grabbed Anna and they turned and walked back towards the house. The children were running after them, laughing and happy. It was a glorious day, even though everyone was freezing. As the sun set in the sky they all ate wedding cake and drank fruit punch until it was time for Harry and Anna to leave for a quick honeymoon.

As they climbed into the car, they waved at all three children standing by Martha and Joseph.

"That's our family, Harry. They are so adorable. I can't believe how well Sara and Jack are doing. Do you think they're really doing okay?"

"I imagine it hasn't sunk in totally that their parents aren't coming back. I still have an issue with that myself. But they're strong kids and I know they will make it. Zach is great with them. I'm very proud of him. Did you see the smile on his face after we said, 'I do,'?"

"I saw that. He's so happy. He has waited for this day since you appeared in our lives. I think he was determined that we would get married."

Harry laughed and pulled her towards him. "I'm so glad that this old truck has a bench seat, so that you can sit very close to me. Kids nowadays don't know what this feels like."

She leaned her head on his shoulder. "Yes, but I don't have a seatbelt on. Good thing we're not going far."

"We're going to the farm, and I'm going to start a fire in the fireplace and fix us a drink. Sound good?"

"This will be our first night staying in this house together. I love it."

"It is going to be your home, baby. Our home. I hate that Monday morning things have to go back to normal and that means work and school. We don't have much time to adjust to things."

"We'll figure it out, Honey."

Harry pulled into the driveway and parked the car under his tree. He walked around the truck and opened the door for his "wife."

Anna slid across the seat and put one foot on the ground, and before she knew it he had picked her up and carried her up the stairs and into the quiet house. He sat her down on the sofa and walked over to light the fire.

"Harry, I'm going to get my bag out of the truck so I can get into something more comfortable."

"You sit right there and I'll get it for you."

She grinned. "I could get used to this."

"Don't even go there."

"Oh, you know you love waiting on me."

He raised an eyebrow and ran to the truck to get her small overnight bag. When he came in, he unzipped her dress and kissed her neck. She smiled, kissed him, and walked to the bathroom to change. He went into the kitchen and poured them a glass of good wine and sat it on the coffee table near the fireplace. After turning on some music, he walked into the bedroom and changed into his favorite jeans and white shirt and caught her coming out the bathroom.

"Harry, I love you. You have to be the kindest man in the world."

"Wait until you live with me a while. Your assessment of me might change."

She smiled. He held her close and danced with her again, whispering sweet things in her ear.

"We haven't been alone like this for a long time. Let's sit down and enjoy the fire, and get warm. This house is a little chilly."

She sat next to him on the sofa and wrapped a blanket around them. The phone rang.

"Hello?"

"Dad, it's Zach. We were wondering if we could come home. I know it's your honeymoon and all, but we really just want to come home and be with you and Mom."

"Does Grandma know you're calling me?"

"No. Please, Dad. Can we come?"

Harry covered the phone with his giant hand. "Anna, the kids want to come home. What do you think? It looks like we're not going to have a night alone."

Anna laughed. "You're not used to having children around. Our days of being alone are very limited now, Honey. But one day we will have no one but each other."

"Is that a yes?"

She nodded.

"Okay, Zach. I'll be over to pick you guys up in about twenty minutes."

Harry smiled at Anna and nodded towards the bedroom. "This may be the quickest honeymoon in the history of mankind, but let's get in the bed and make the most of the twenty minutes before I have to go get the kids."

She laughed and dove under the covers. Harry pulled her to him and they kissed. "I'm the luckiest man in the world."

"Your assessment of me may change after you live with me awhile," Anna whispered, echoing his own words earlier.

Harry realized how short twenty minutes was for a honeymoon. But they laughed and dressed and drove to pick up the kids. When they arrived at Harry's parents, the three kids were looking out the window waiting for them.

When they got to the house they all ran upstairs to pick their bedrooms, hollering and laughing all the way up. Harry just stood at the bottom of the stairs and listened. He had totally forgotten what childhood sounded like. And now it was going on in his home. And he had Anna with him. Sweet Anna.

Hack wandered into the living room and sat at Harry's feet. He had moved to the sofa with Anna, watching the fire blazing in the fireplace. It seemed Hack was lost now that the other kids had taken Zach over to themselves. Harry reached down and patted his head.

"Looks like old Hack has lost his buddy to play with."

"Only for one night. They'll get used to having each other around and soon they'll be fighting instead of laughing. Zach loves that dog. I bet tonight he will come and get him to lie in his bed."

Hack raised his head almost like he knew what she was saying.

"I'm really enjoying this, Anna. This feels so right. Tomorrow we hit our workday and I'll be sad that this is over. But I guess that is a wrong assumption. It won't be over for a long time. Until they leave home. Do you realize we finally did it? We finally got married after all those years of separation?"

"Do I realize it? Oh, my gosh, Harry! I dreamed of this for a while until I had to let it go. It was killing me. We had talked about getting married our senior year. I thought it was a done deal until you went and signed up to be a Marine. I don't think you realized the impact that would have on your life."

"I was a kid. But I did know I was supposed to be a Marine. I just wish I could have slowed it all down."

"Nothing slows time down, unless you are in a dental office or in a dreaded history or math class. Remember those days? Lord, it felt like the day would never end."

He laughed hard and kissed her. "I hated school, but I loved sports and you. So it has its good memories."

"I do believe our classmates thought we would marry right out of high school."

"Probably. But we have now, and we're going to make the best of it."

"Harry, no one would believe our story. We have such a neat family now. A tragedy has taken place but somehow we all are working through it. We can't let Sara Jane and Jack ever forget their parents. We need photos in their rooms. We need to play those home movies that David was always taking when some time has passed and there's enough space between the death of their parents and the time they see the films. It's their family memories and I want them to love it and cherish the time they had."

"They had good parents. I hope we can live up to at least half of what they did for those kids."

Anna was quiet for a moment and then she asked him something he wished she hadn't asked. This was a repeat performance from the past.

"Do you think you would ever take the call if the military came after you for a mission?"

Harry sucked in air and walked over to the fireplace, leaning into the heat that was pouring out of the flames. That question hit him in the pit of his stomach. He hadn't even thought about ever going back to war. Until she opened her mouth and spoke those words.

"Anna, let's not even approach the subject right now. We have a lot of living to do. I'm going to focus on those men at the rehab and us building our family."

He walked over and kissed her. But he knew that she knew the answer to that question even before she asked it. It almost felt like a window had opened and a cold chill ran through the room. He sat down beside her and huddled under the blanket watching the flames lap over the huge logs he'd cut for a fire. In the background the children were laughing and playing and soon it got quiet upstairs. They were finally asleep. Hack curled up near the fireplace and Anna and Harry walked into their bedroom and climbed under the warm covers. The fire had burned down to where there were only red embers, and the night slowly slipped into dawn.

CHAPTER SIXTY-ONE

As the years passed, Harry watched his son grow taller and more like him. It was uncanny how they walked in step when they were together. Zach was almost as tall and was built like a brick wall. He was lifting weights and working out with Harry every single day. Anna was pleased but she was also aware of the consequences of the two men getting so close. Harry could feel her wariness. But another thing was taking place in the household that was ripping Harry apart. Hack was aging and going down fast. He no longer climbed the stairs to sleep with Zach, and his eyesight was failing.

The biggest surprise was how Sara and Jack had bloomed in their new family. They still asked questions occasionally about their parents, but they had accepted somehow that they were going to be okay. Harry and Anna both felt like they'd gotten the children at a perfect time in their lives. They were young enough to accept things and bounce back easier. Anna and Sara had bonded and Jack adored Zach. They shared a room until Zach started dating, and soon Harry built a bedroom over the barn so he could have his own room. At night, Harry would sit on the porch and watch Zach through the large window above the barn door, pouring over his homework or talking on the phone to Courtney. It was so weird even thinking he was old enough to have a girl. It happened to quickly. Like most things in life.

This night Harry was sitting on the porch with a cup of coffee, with one arm hanging down touching Hack's fur. Anna saw this from behind and walked up to Harry and put her arm on his shoulder.

"Honey, do you think it's time to put Hack down?"

Harry shivered. "How can I do that?"

"I know it is hard. I hate it myself. But he's suffering. He can barely walk and his eyesight is going. What does Sam say?"

"I haven't asked Sam. I know what he'll say. Of course, it's up to me, but he doesn't like to see animals suffering unnecessarily."

"There's no good time to do this. Zach will collapse. Maybe we should get a puppy before you put him down."

"I can hardly talk about it; much less get excited about buying a puppy to replace this dog. He and I have grown together. He knows everything about me. It's almost like I knew him when I picked him up. What a heart this dog has."

"I agree, and I've seen the closeness you have with him. It's uncanny. I've loved watching you two together all these years. But baby, I think it's getting close to the time for him to go."

Harry got on the floor and lay beside the dog. Hack raised his head for a moment and licked his face. "How can I let you go, Hack?"

Hack's tail wagged on the floor. But he didn't lift his head anymore. He was tired. Harry knew that the dog was ready. But he couldn't for the life of him bear to make that trip to the vet.

"Today we'll go look at some German shepherd puppies. In fact, I will ask Sam about a good place to buy one. Or rescue one. This is killing me, Anna."

"It will be a tough thing for all of us to handle. Even Sara Jane has taken to the dog and she doesn't even like dogs. He sometimes sleeps with Jack if he falls asleep on the sofa at night. I think when he no longer could sleep with Zach, he got depressed. And I took over his spot in your bed. Don't think he didn't notice that."

"I wondered about that. But I thought he was so happy being with Zach that he didn't care."

"Nothing gets by this dog."

"I know. He is amazing."

"Make that call to Sam. Let's get a puppy around here that we all can get attached to, and then it will be time to take Hack to the vet."

"I'll call tomorrow. Let's not say anything to the children until we're sure we are going to follow through with it. They're going to cry and I don't want to upset them until it's a sure thing. The puppy will help cushion the blow. But for me, no dog will ever replace Hack."

Zach came downstairs and Harry walked outside. "What you doing, Zach?"

"Not much. Just reading online about the Marines."

"Don't let your mother see you doing that. One Marine in the family is enough for her."

"Well, she better get used to the idea, Dad. It's going to happen."

"You got a lot of school ahead of you, Boy. Don't rush into things. I don't want you to rush your youth; you're young for such a short time. And adulthood has its drawbacks."

Zach laughed. "It's okay, Dad. I know what I'm doing. Mom will be okay. She'll adjust to it sooner or later. A guy has to make up his own mind about what he wants to do with his life. And I want to be like you."

"That's not exactly the highest goal to be aiming at, Zach. It's flattering that you want to be like me, but I want you to get a good education."

"I will. But I want to be a Marine just like you. And a sniper. When I'm out of school in a few months, I'm going to train. I want you to be ruthless and train me like you would anybody else. Just like you train those wounded warriors who want to go back into battle. I've seen you work with them, and you don't mince words."

"Those men are used to training. You aren't. It takes years to get like them, even with the injuries they've suffered."

"I'll get there, because that's what I want to do. Determination has to count for something."

"It does, Zach. It's huge. But you won't believe the work required to be a good Marine and sniper. Really anything you want to do in the military takes massive work."

"I guess I'll just have to find that out, Dad."

Harry nodded and hugged Zach. "How's your girl doing?"

"She was crying because she doesn't want me to join the Marines after we graduate."

"Sounds like a pretty smart lady, if you ask me."

"I've really gotten attached to her, Dad. But I know we won't last through basic training. You and Mom didn't last. So I'm trying to tell her that maybe when I get back, we'll get together. She knows your story. I don't think she wants a life like that."

"Your mother didn't, either."

Zach grinned. "But it turned out well in the end, Dad."

CHAPTER SIXTY-TWO

Martha and Joseph were getting up in years. They denied that they were old, but Harry could see a change in both of them. No zip in their step. His father still went in to work every day and was very excited about new drugs that were being developed. But after he got home, Martha had shared with Harry that he sat too much. His appetite wasn't very good and he was losing weight fast. David's death had taken a toll on both of them but tonight was going to be a great time to laugh and forget all that pain that lay beneath the surface like a sleeping dragon. The fire that it breathed was probably taking out the heart of his father. But tonight they would laugh and enjoy the kids.

Harry had purchased an Acura crossover so that the whole family could fit when they went somewhere altogether. It wasn't as cool as the old pickup, which drastically needed a paint job at the moment. But the kids loved it and Anna had gotten tired of riding everywhere in the truck. They pulled up in the driveway and all the doors swung open. Nothing in the car but teenagers now. No more babies. Sara had matured in the last couple of years and was making straight As in high school. Jack was on the honor roll and was excellent in track and baseball. But he was a reader and wanted to study and go to college. He already had a school in his line of sight.

Everyone filed into the house and Martha greeted them with a smile. But Harry saw the new lines on her face from weary sorrow.

"Oh, what a joy to see all of you! Just what the doctor ordered. Joseph? They are here. I swear the kids have grown a foot."

Sara rolled her eyes and slinked past her grandfather to the sofa, where she promptly plopped down and hit her iPad for the latest news on Instagram. Jack followed close behind. Joseph noticed that Hack wasn't with them.

"Where's the dog? Didn't he come with you?"

Zach stepped in fast. "No, Grandpa. He's not feeling too well lately."

"Oh, no. What's wrong with Hack?"

"Getting old, Dad." Harry walked up to Joseph and whispered in his ear.

"Don't tell me you're going to put him down."

"I'm not just yet. But the time is fast approaching."

Anna walked up and hugged Joseph. "Good to see you, Dad."

"Ya'll come in. Martha's got supper on the table. Your favorite. Hamburgers."

⋙⊹⋘

The kids were talking all at once, which is what Joseph loved. Harry watched as they all talked about their day and what their plans were after they graduated. It was hard to believe that they had all grown up and were thinking about college. It seemed like yesterday that he and Anna were talking about marrying. He glanced over at her while everyone was talking. She still looked beautiful to him. He saw the gray hairs mixed in with the brown. He saw the lines forming on her forehead and between her eyebrows. But when she laughed, time stopped. Nothing mattered except seeing her laugh. She was so kind, so loving to the children. And if he were honest, she had raised them to be wonderful human beings. He just held on for life while all this was happening before his eyes. He did his share around the house, but she was the one who led them and listened to their stories. She drove them anywhere they wanted to go. The house was full of friends all the time, but she never tired of the crowd.

"Harry, tell us how your work is going with the wounded warriors. I haven't heard you talk about it in a while." Martha took the last bite of her hamburger.

Harry shook his head. "Mom, these men are amazing. You talk about heroes; I have a room full of them. And so does Max. What we are seeing is that all they needed was to have the chance to work out and be able to be mobile. They are nearly ready to return to active duty. I am so happy with this program and how the men have responded."

"So most of them will go back into battle?"

"They have the opportunity to do whatever they want to do. That is the great thing about this program and the military. They will be considered as able as any man with all his limbs. There will be no difference in what is expected of them when they serve in the military." Joseph got up and walked into the living room.

Harry walked behind him and sat across from him in a leather chair. "Dad, you have no idea how proud I am of these men. They have worked so hard and earned every bit of the glory they will receive. It makes me want to work even harder."

"Does that mean you might go back into it, Harry?"

Harry looked over to see if Anna heard the question. She seemed to be busy talking with the kids. He turned back to his father and spoke quietly.

"Dad, this is a very touchy topic with Anna and me. We really try not to talk about it. But yes, I would go if I got the call. They know I'm working with these men, but I am still under active duty status. If they need me, I have to go."

"Son, when will it be enough? I just could not stand losing you after your brother's accident."

"I know, Dad. But as long as I am active duty status, I will have to respond to the call."

"I guess I need to prepare your mother then?"

"I wouldn't say anything to her. She's been through enough, Dad. And so have you. It may never happen, but if it does, you know now that I have to respond."

Joseph shook his head and walked over to the window, gazing out into the night with his hands in his pockets. He seemed to have shrunk to Harry; he seemed so small.

Just as Harry was going to say something to him, Anna walked up and said that the kids needed to go so that they could do their homework. It was a school night and they didn't need to stay out too late. He nodded and walked over to his mother. She was obviously enjoying talking and laughing with the kids. He almost hated to interrupt the evening.

"Mom, it's time for us to go. The kids have homework. Anna has drawn the line and you know how tough she is."

Martha laughed. "Oh, I bet she's a tough teacher."

Anna smiled. "Just trying to take care of these guys. They would stay up all night if I allowed it."

They piled back into the car and Harry drove the crew back home. The kids were silent in the back seat, lost in their own iPad world. Anna reached over and grabbed his hand and smiled. Sometimes, when she looked like that, it gave him pause. He only hoped he would be around to grow old with her. This woman that he so loved.

CHAPTER SIXTY-THREE

When Zach walked into the house he screamed. Without even getting through the back door, Harry knew what had happened. He grabbed Anna's hand and they ran into the kitchen. Lying on the floor, Hack was lifeless. Zach leaned over him crying. Harry got down on his hands and knees and tried to find a pulse. There just wasn't one to be found. The dog was still and not breathing. Hack was gone.

The scene in the house was one of great sadness. Harry found that his chest was tight and he felt like he couldn't breathe. He wrapped Hack in a soft blanket and carried his body outside towards the barn. Zach, Sara, and Jack followed close behind, crying and talking to each other in disbelief. He laid the dog down on the ground and went to the barn to get a shovel. He commenced to dig a deep hole to bury the dog and finally after reaching the depth of four feet, he picked up Hack's body wrapped in the blanket and laid it in the hole.

"Zach, you want to help me put the dirt back in the hole?"

All the kids moved towards Harry and got on their knees to scrape the dirt back in the hole. No one was talking. Finally Anna spoke in a soft voice.

"I know it's difficult to see this, but we knew he was getting old. His eyesight was failing. Let's be thankful for all the years we had with him. He was such a good friend to us all."

Everyone hugged each other and walked back into the house. Harry remained outside to cover the grave with the sod he had scraped off before he dug the hole. He pulled out his phone and called Sam. It was late, but Sam answered on the second ring.

"Hey, Harry. How's it going?"

"Hey, Sam. Not too great tonight. Just wanted you to know that we lost Hack tonight."

Silence. "You're joking. I know he was getting up there in age. And the last time I saw him his eyesight wasn't great. But I didn't think he was that close."

"We didn't, either. But we came home from my parents' house tonight and he was gone."

"I'm so sorry, brother. Is there anything I can do?"

"This sounds strange, but keep your eyes out for another German shepherd. Maybe two or three years old. I think it would be a good idea to get another dog in the house as soon as possible."

"I think that's a great idea. I will check around and let you know what I find."

"Thanks, Sam. I can always count on you."

≕⊹⊹≕

Harry walked inside and the kids were already upstairs. Anna was sitting on the couch waiting for him with a glass of wine poured. She shook her head slowly. She understood.

"I know what you are going through inside. "

334

Harry sat down and leaned back against the sofa. It had become their talking place.

"Yeah, it's a bummer. I just didn't think he was that close to dying."

"It's better that he went this way, in the house, rather than for you to have to take him to the vet and put him to sleep."

"I know you're right. That would have been miserable. I went through that as a child and never forgot it. But Hack, he was my man. We were so close. I should have known he was near death. I would have stayed with him."

Anna wrapped her arms around him. "Honey, that is the sweetest thing. I love your heart. I know he was your dog. He loved Zach, but he was your dog. We'll get another one soon. Would that help or can you even think about that now?"

"I already told Sam to keep his eyes open for another dog. An older one that's already house-trained."

"Good. I think that's a great idea. The kids took it better than I thought they would. It's not an easy thing to see. And it's awful to have to bury a pet."

Harry put his feet on the coffee table and picked up his glass of wine. He raised it in the air and Anna raised hers.

"To Hack."

"Yes, to Hack."

CHAPTER SIXTY-FOUR

Harry and Max were deep into training the men, preparing them for active duty if that's what they wanted and they were pretty sure most of them did. It was exciting to see how they'd changed since the first day they showed up at rehab. They were hopeless the first day, but now they were eager to push themselves beyond what they ever believed they could do. It was especially important that this group of men realized that they had to be the best of the best, because they did have a handicap that at some point could play into their ability to survive. So with that in mind, Harry was ruthless on them, just like he'd been on himself.

"You men deserve this. You deserve to fight again. You've already shown you have what it takes, even though you got injured. You will be some of the best in the military when we get done with this training. Max and I have seen you come from the ground to the mountain. You've done things you didn't know you could do. I am so proud of you."

One of the men who was near Harry asked a question. "How soon will we be ready to get back to the action?"

336

"Do you feel ready? I think you will know when you feel strong enough. I want you to the place where you don't even think about your disability anymore. I want you to feel whole."

"I almost feel that way. It isn't often now that I actually feel the prosthetic. My leg feels strong. I don't limp anymore. I am amazed at what I can do."

"That's the point of this training, Michael. To get your mind ready. Your body will follow."

Max walked up to Harry.

"You got a second?"

"Sure. Let's go outside."

Harry followed Max outside and they sat down on a bench on the side of the building.

"What's up?"

"I have had a few conversations casually with our commander. Don't be surprised if you get a call pretty soon. Are you ready to go again?"

"I just told Anna that if I got a call that I would respond. I know no other way. How about you?"

"I'm not married with three kids. I'm always ready."

Harry put his face in his hands. "It's not an easy decision. I know my kids wouldn't want me to go. And Anna won't talk about it. Really, I've avoided it myself. Because I knew it was inevitable. You have just confirmed that."

"Sorry, Harry. But we are good together. I've sort of missed it." Max slapped him on the arm.

"Me, too. We are preparing these men to go, and I want to go with them."

"That just may happen sooner than you think."

"Well, then, we better get these men ready to fight. Because if they get half a chance, they're going to take it. I've never seen such heart. I guess they are like us, in a way. The military gets in the blood and there's no getting rid of it." Harry smiled.

"It's like the plague, I think."

Harry laughed. They both got up and walked back inside. This time they hit the floor and did the work with all the men. This time they were preparing themselves to go back into battle. The call was going to come. They just didn't know when.

$$\blacktriangleright\!\!\!-\!\!\!\blacktriangleleft$$

At the end of the day, Harry drove home in his pickup with the radio blaring and the window down. It was warm out and a muggy evening. He felt excitement building inside, even though he dreaded the call. Anna wasn't going to handle it well, and Sara and Jack were going to be scared that he wouldn't come back. They still had memories of their parents dying.

The whole thing made Harry nervous about what was to come. He wasn't worried about making it back home, but he hated to upset the whole family. Zach would be the only one who would understand. He was fast heading in the same direction, and nothing or no one was going to stop him.

Harry loved this in his son, but he almost felt like Anna had been dealt a bad hand. Two men in her life that she loved were addicted to the military. And he knew she feared losing them both. He almost felt helpless as he neared the house. Because he knew the call was coming soon, and he also knew he and Max were going to be gone. It might very well be the last mission he participated in, and he was excited to think that it might include some of the men he just trained. They just possibly could be the toughest team he'd served with because of what they'd overcome.

Anna was home waiting for him. She'd made a meal he loved: meatloaf, potatoes, and green beans, with yeast rolls and peach cobbler that filled the house with an enticing aroma. . She greeted him with a hug and kiss. He wasn't going to do anything to dampen her mood.

"Hey, handsome. How was your day?"

"It was terrific. Maybe one of my best at the rehab. Those men are absolutely mind blowing. Their courage and strength just confirm what the human body is capable of overcoming."

"Wow. That sounds amazing. I wish I could see them train. It certainly impressed Zach the day you took him to work with you. He was younger then, but whatever he saw sure stayed with him. He still talks about it."

"I think at first he was scared to see the men with all their limbs missing. But soon, after he saw them working out, he realized that they were just people overcoming a disability. The men soon found out what they were capable of and it caused them to push even harder. I remember feeling that way."

"You've done a marvelous job, Harry. This is epic, what you've done for these men. You and Max will always be remembered for what has taken place in that rehab center."

"I hope it never stops. Even after we're gone, I hope that rehab center only grows larger so that more men can be helped."

Anna stretched out on the sofa and Harry rubbed her feet. She closed her eyes, tired from the long day, and Harry watched her, thinking about how to tell her that he was going to get a call soon. He decided not to bring it up right then. She was relaxed and it had been a long day for both of them. And who knew how long it would be before he got a call from his commander? He was going to let that sleeping dog lie for one more night.

CHAPTER SIXTY-FIVE

On the same day that Zach enrolled in the naval academy, Harry received a call from his commanding officer. It couldn't have come at a worse time, because Anna was already having to deal with Zach leaving home. She sat at the kitchen table and stared out the window, feeling hopeless and filled with a sense that her life was out of control. Harry walked in and sat down with her, and put his arm around her shoulders.

"Honey, talk to me. I know you're feeling overwhelmed. We both knew Zach was going to enroll. Tell me what you're feeling right now."

She turned to look at Harry, and the look on her face was unbearable to see. "I am afraid I have lost my son and my husband. The military has taken both of them away from me."

"Anna, I know you feel that way, but we both love you and don't want you to feel so afraid for our lives."

"Zach is on the path you were on years ago. He wants to be just like you. That is an admirable thing to do and I am so proud of him. He is showing great strength and courage and I know he'll receive a wonderful education at the academy. Most parents would be so happy for their son."

"We're happy for Zach. I think you're panicked because you know I've had a call from my commander and I'm going to be leaving again. Does this really have anything to do with Zach?"

She managed a smile. "Harry, I adore you. I don't want to live without you. Is that a problem? Am I being too weak or controlling?"

"No, baby. I feel the same way. I'm sure I won't be gone long. I don't know what the mission is, yet, but I'll find out soon. I just want you to trust me that everything is going to be okay."

"What you're saying without actually saying the words is that you want me to be okay no matter what. If you go to war or if you stay home. If Zach goes to war or if he remains in the area. I lived so long without you. I thought being separated from you because of the military was over."

"I guess it's never over, really. Because of what I do and what I'm good at, there will always be some form of a threat on my life. I don't like it any more than you do, but it goes with the territory. Are you saying that isn't what you signed up for when we married?"

She shook her head. "That isn't what I'm saying, but damn, this is pushing me to the brink. If you go and you're killed, what am I supposed to do? How will I make it without you?"

Harry winced at her words. He wasn't immune to her feelings. He was just trained not to go there. "You are a strong woman, Anna. You made it without me before and did a wonderful job. I have no doubt that you can live without me. But I don't want to die. I'll do all I can to return safely to you. You're the love of my life. I don't want to live without you, either. But here we are at that crossroads again, where I have decided to return to battle and you are left hanging. You don't know how much I despise this situation. I wouldn't hurt you for the world. I just don't know how to avoid it, because of what I have chosen to do in life."

Anna blew out a deep sigh and wiped her eyes. It sounded like resignation. She had no more tears left inside.

"I have good news, Harry. While you were in the shower this morning, Sam called and has a dog for us. He wants us to come to the office and see if it feels right to us. He is a purebred German shepherd that was turned in to Sam because the owner died and the rest of the family could not take the dog. It's a male."

Harry grinned. She knew this would make him happy. She hadn't told Zach because he was going to be gone for a while. Sara and Jack were elated that a dog was found so quickly.

"Let's get the kids and go check this dog out. Zach is going to be so happy when he finds out."

"Okay, I'll pull myself together and you tell them to head to the car. It will take Sara Jane forever to get ready."

As soon as they walked into the veterinary office, a beautiful dog came running towards them. Harry knelt down and hugged the dog, who was frantically yelping and licking his face. Sam walked out of one of his exam rooms and grinned.

"Looks like you've met our new dog. Isn't he grand?"

"Does he have a name?"

"The owner called him Dog. So you can name him whatever you like. I just knew it would be a good fit."

Harry stood up and looked at the dog as the kids were petting him.

"He is a beautiful dog. Do you guys agree that we should take him home?"

Anna stayed back, watching Harry and the kids with the dog. "I think we should name him 'Hack.' He looks like Hack. Don't you think, Harry?"

"You're right, Anna. He does favor Hack. It's okay with me if the kids are okay with it."

Sara and Jack were so excited about having a dog again that they weren't paying any attention to Harry.

"'Hack' it is. I guess he's had all his shots? You've checked him over good?"

"He's in perfect health. Just needs a family to love him."

"I think you can tell he'll get plenty of attention at our house."

Harry pulled Sam aside. "I've received a call from my commander today. Which means I'll be going out on another mission, Sam."

"Oh, no. I thought you were home for good this time."

"So did Anna. I wasn't really planning on it, but I am still active duty. Will you watch over things at the farm, Sam? Check in with Anna from time to time?"

"Of course I will, Harry. More than happy to. Do you know how long you'll be away?"

"I have no idea. Probably won't know until I get over there. I really appreciate this. You have no idea how bad I feel leaving Anna again. But with you poking your head in from time to time, I will feel much better. I want her safe."

"Where is Zach? I didn't see him come in with you guys."

"He enrolled in the naval academy today. We're so proud of him."

"So Anna has two of her men in the military. I understand now why she seems so quiet. She's not her usual bubbly self."

"No, this hasn't been good day for her. What do I owe you, Sam?"

"Nothing. Just make him a good home. He'll guard your home for you while you're away."

"He will be loved, I promise you that."

Harry grabbed the leash and the others followed him out to the car.

Anna hung back and spoke to Sam quietly.

"Sam, thank you for finding this dog for us. We felt quite empty around the house without Hack. Now, in a small way, he's back with us. And now that Harry's leaving again soon, I'll feel safer with this dog in the house."

Sam put his arm around her. "Anna, I'll be by from time to time to check on things. If you need anything, and I mean anything, please call me. You have my cell number. Use it."

She blushed and smiled. "Thank you so much. You've always been such a good friend to us."

"I'm here 24/7 for you. Just do not hesitate if you need me."

Anna walked out of the vet's office and climbed into the car. Harry looked at her and she nodded.

"Everything is going to be okay. I'm going to be positive and just be planning all kinds of wonderful things for when you come back home."

"That's my girl."

CHAPTER SIXTY-SIX

Harry sat on the plane next to Max, thinking about his conversation with Zach. He'd told him how proud he was of him, and that he was the man of the family, along with Jack, until his dad came back home.

Max was in high spirits, but Harry was remembering telling Anna goodbye. It was an awful moment, sweet, but heart-wrenching. He loved her so much and watching her reaction made him wonder if he had made a huge mistake in deciding to remain in active duty status. He felt his heart was in the right place, but seeing the look in her eyes when he turned to leave, he realized that being married and expecting your spouse to accept that you may be heading into a deadly situation and be perfectly okay with it was asinine.

Finally Max couldn't maintain silence any longer and spoke up. "Harry, I've sat here and watched you torment yourself for the last hour. Would you stop it, already? Anna knew you were a Marine when she married you. Whether she admitted it to herself or not, she also knew that unless you were retired from the military, there was always the chance that you would be called out again. I know there is a limit to what you can expect from your wife, but you made the decision to accept the call. Now you've got to get your mind ready for this mission or something bad will happen to us both. We're counting on each other, and I want your mind settled and ready for what we're going to have to face."

Harry sat back and looked at Max. "You have no idea how hard it was to leave her. She's my life. But as far as what you just said to me; have you ever known me not to be ready? At one hundred percent all the time we are working?"

Max grinned. "I wanted to get you fired up and I succeeded. Now we're ready."

Harry shook his head. There was no winning an argument with this guy.

━╬╌╫╪━

Nine hours later they landed on the outskirts of Helmand Province at the operating base, where they ate dinner, crashed for eight hours, and ate a huge breakfast. It was time to load into a Blackhawk and head towards Helmand, where there were troops on the ground receiving incoming fire. It was an explosive situation and high risk. There were two Blackhawks travelling together.

Harry and Max were planning their moves as they approached drop-off point. The chopper was just about to land when an incoming missile was shot into the chopper and exploded into pieces. The noise was deafening. The Blackhawk went down fast. The secondary chopper laid down suppressing fire and landed to check for survivors. The Hawk was totally engulfed in flames. It was obvious that no one survived the explosion.

News travelled quickly back to the States where their commander was informed of their deaths. Mike Murdock sat in his chair with his head in his hands. War was full of death. But the loss of these men hit him hard.

⟫⟪

Anna was home from school pouring over tests that her class had taken when she heard a knock on the door. She thought it was some friends waiting for Sara and Jack, but when she opened the door she nearly fainted. There standing in front of her were two Marines in full uniform. They didn't have to say a word. She knew what had happened. Harry was gone. After expressing their condolences to Anna, they hugged her and shared how much they had loved Harry and Max. How much they had sacrificed for their country. She somehow held up until they left and then she went to the floor. She lay there lifeless until Sara and Jack came downstairs from doing their homework.

"Mom! Mom! What's wrong? Are you sick? What's happened?" Jack knelt down and lifted her head. She was crying uncontrollably. "Sara, help me get her to the sofa. I think we need to call Grandpa and Grandma. They will know what to do."

They laid Anna on the sofa and called Joseph and Martha. It wasn't a good phone call.

"Grandpa, we came downstairs and found Mom on the floor crying. I think you need to come over now."

"Take it easy, Son. We'll be right there."

⟫⟪

In fifteen minutes Joseph and Martha were at Anna's side, soothing her. Finally she was able to sit up and asked for a glass of wine. Joe poured it and handed it to her, while Martha sat with the kids.

"Anna, tell us what has happened."

Anna took a long sip of wine and leaned her head back on the pillow. "Oh, Dad! I don't know if I can say it."

"Has something happened to Harry?"

She nodded. "He's gone, Dad. He's gone."

Martha screamed and ran for Joseph. They both cried, which sent the two teenagers into tears.

"Mom, you mean Dad is dead? What happened?" Jack's face was in a painful grimace.

"His chopper was shot down in Afghanistan. They didn't have a chance. There were no survivors. Which means Max is gone, too."

The family clung to each other, crying and trying to make sense of it all. Suddenly the front door opened and Zach walked in and ran to his mother.

"Oh, Zach! How in the world did you get here so quickly?" Anna was pale and weak.

"They told me at school I could go home. That my father had died in battle."

Anna grabbed him and sobbed. It seemed like a horrific nightmare and no one was able to make any sense of it. It was what she had dreaded would happen. But for now, her mind couldn't wrap itself around the fact that Harry would not ever be coming home.

━╬╬━

Joe and Martha stayed all night with Anna and the kids, trying to soothe them and keep each other from falling apart. There was nothing that could be said that would make anything right. The bottom had dropped out of their world and nobody had the pieces to put it all back together. It was the worst night any of them had experienced except for the accident that had taken David and Taylor away from them. Harry was such a large figure in all their lives. It was impossible to think of living without him.

Zach was stricken with grief because he had lived so much of his young life without knowing Harry. But when he found him it was the best thing that could have happened. He ran to his room

348

and stayed there for hours, going over in his head the last conversation he'd had with his dad.

Harry had told Zach that he was to be the man in the family while he was away. That it would be his job to hold things together. He hadn't been through all the training yet that would make him tough as nails. But he was solid in his commitment to his father that he would fill his shoes while he was away at war. Now there would be no taking those shoes off. He would be the man of the family now, and he knew he had better get his act together or the whole family would fall apart.

Somehow, somewhere within Zach, a part of Harry came shining through. He managed to gather himself up and walked downstairs to his mother, who was still on the sofa, not eating, staring into space. The other two kids had fallen asleep on the other sofa, and Joe and Martha were in the guest room trying to rest. Zach sat down by his mother and held her close. All the things he learned from watching his father were whispered in her ears.

Anna felt the change in Zach and opened her eyes. For a moment she thought she was looking at Harry. But in a second she realized that Zach had just become a man.

EPILOGUE

In the days that followed, Anna learned to put one foot in front of the other and managed to finish raising the half-grown children that were in her sole care. Sam came by numerous times to help with things on the farm and check the horses. There were many mornings when he sat and had coffee with Anna, and they reminisced about the wonderful times they'd had with Harry. But when e was alone, lying in bed, it was difficult to believe that one day wouldn't come walking through the door.

e military funeral Harry and Max were given was breathtak- ut what really touched the whole family was seeing all the ing. led warriors surrounding the flag-covered caskets. Those had worshiped the ground he and Max walked on. Harry had ed a vision of all those wounded men going back to battle as le men. Every single one of them laid a rose on the casket and pt because inside they knew there lay the remains of a fallen hero who had changed their lives.

Zach finished his education and became a Marine, just like Harry. It was remarked over and over in the ranks as he moved forward that he resembled Harry Downs in more ways than just looks. Somehow Zach had developed into the same kind of man Harry was, even when most of his life was spent without his father by his side. It was in the blood and the bones. And truth be known, Zach loved every single moment of it.

On a day when the sky was gray and Zach had the afternoon off, he went to the graveside of his father and stood there in full dress with his dog Hack beside him. It was quiet in the graveyard and a slight mist was falling on Zach's shoulders. But he no longer was of this world anymore. For the moments when he came to stand at the base of the grave, staring at his father's name engraved on the tombstone, Zach spoke in a low tone, words that only his father could hear.

"I know you're in a good place, Dad. I just had to stop by and talk to you again. Things have been tough since you left us. And this is my safe place to come when I feel the need to be near you. I have Hack with me, Dad. I want you to rest in peace knowing that I have done what you asked me to do. The family is doing fine, and Mom has finally let go of the horrific pain that was always written on her face. I actually heard her laugh last night.

"We need her to come around, Dad. I'm sure you've noticed that she hasn't been by to see you. But it's hard living without you. I make a good show of it, but I'll never get over losing you. Just rest in peace knowing I'll take care of things and I won't ever let you down."

Zach leaned over and touched the tombstone and then grabbed the leash and pulled Hack away from the grave. He wiped the tears away quickly as this was the only time he allowed himself to cry.

⟞⟝⟞⟝

One day, weeks later, when he was walking towards the gravesite, he saw a figure standing at the foot of the grave. Her hair was blowing in the wind. A thin figure, she knelt down slowly and laid herself across the grave. He knew then that it was his mother who had finally come to grieve the loss of the love of her life. He stood for a moment watching and then suddenly felt like he needed to let her be alone. He whispered "goodbye" to his father and walked the rest of the way home.

Sometimes we are not totally
Aware of the gravity
Of our decisions.
We simply leap blindly
Into our
Destiny.

 We only have one life to live, and in the years I have lived so far, I have discovered that we never stop growing and changing. In my younger years, I had no idea what my capabilities were. Nor have I reached my limit even now. It is a wonderful thing to wake up excited about what the day will bring. I am thankful for the opportunity to write, both in words and music. I can only say to those who have read my books or listened to my music; don't sit and let your life go by. For it will. Step out and do those things you have dreamed of, and even some you haven't dared to dream. We all need what you have to give.

Nancy lives in Sandestin, Florida with her husband Richard. They have ten grandchildren and two great grandchildren. She is a watercolor artist, pianist, and author. She has owned Magnolia House, a gift shop in Grand Boulevard, for twenty five years. In her spare time, rare as it is, she might find her way to the edge of the sea to watch the waves roll in. And it is there she might find the next thing that could change her life and those who stand near.

She has written nine novels, five inspirational books, and released ten piano CDs. She has written over one hundred songs that have touched many lives in hospitals, cancer centers, and schools. She received the Key to the City of Memphis for her humanitarian efforts for mankind. Her work can be found on ITunes, YouTube, Amazon and Magnoliahouse.com. And no, she isn't done yet. And neither are you.

Made in the USA
Lexington, KY
05 January 2019